EARTH TO ALIS

LEX CARLOW

For Mom, Dad, Jaclyn, and Linds.
You guys are the reason I have always known love (and can
write books about it, too).

CONTENT WARNINGS

EARTH TO ALIS contains heavy subject matter. While this is ultimately a hopeful story that advocates for recovery, it is nonetheless told by an unreliable narrator affected by mental illness and doesn't shy away from depicting difficult experiences. Readers are encouraged to be aware of the following content warnings and read safely and responsibly:

- Self-harm
- Physical and emotional child abuse and neglect
- Bullying, including brief incidents of homophobia and off-page racism
- Panic attacks
- Dissociation (derealization/depersonalization)
- Disordered eating
- A scene depicting manual strangulation
- A scene depicting an epileptic seizure; discussions of epilepsy

- Blood, vomiting, and brief injury/medical detail
- Mentions of past suicidal ideation
- Mention of hypothetical violence against animals; references to off-page animal death
- Mention of past illness and death of a parent
- Underage drinking and smoking; references to off-page marijuana use
- Profanity and sexual references

PART I

PARIS

1

I'm in the middle of fixing my nails when the turbulence starts, sending a jet-black smudge onto the side of my finger. I curse as the plane shakes hard enough to rattle my teeth, but just manage to swipe up the bottle of nail polish before it spills all over the tray table.

It's possible there'd been an announcement about this, but I wouldn't have heard it. My headphones are top-notch noise cancellation, and most of the music I listen to involves crashing drums and shrieking electric guitars. Now, as we're all knocked around in our seats, I drag them off my head so I can hear if anybody's screaming.

There's the muted wailing of a baby a few rows back and the tumble of luggage in the compartments overhead, but only when the plane gives a particularly violent lurch does someone—hopefully one of my classmates—full-on squeal in terror. I snort, glancing next to me to see if Mr. Kepler is also losing his shit, but if it weren't for the muscle jumping in his jaw and his white-knuckled grip on the armrests, I'd think he was asleep.

I wonder what he'd do if I held his hand. The thought is funny enough to distract me from the anxious little voice at the back of my mind telling me this might actually be the end, until I make the mistake of glancing out the window. The wing is flashing red, white, red, white against the brightening blue of the horizon, and it's shuddering like it's hanging on for dear life, like it's about to come unstuck and spin into the ether.

I decide to look up at the ceiling instead, and my mind helpfully supplies me with the image of an oxygen mask tumbling down over my head and the pilot over the PA shouting "Brace! Brace!" as we plunge into the Atlantic.

My hands start to sweat against my will. I shut my eyes, clutching the nail polish tight in my fist. I'm pretty sure the colour is called *Emo for Life*. I'm thinking about how ironic it would be to be a dead body wearing *Emo for Life*.

Is that irony? Or is that just tragedy?

Just when my heart starts squeezing with panic, things begin to calm down as quickly as they started. The plane gives one last tremor, like a death rattle. When I open my eyes, Kepler's spindly hands are relaxing on his armrests. Eventually I hear a few sighs of relief and some scattered laughs in the spirit of *Wow, we sure overreacted!*

I don't think I overreacted, though. I think I did a fairly good job of keeping my shit together. And hey, at least I've just gotten confirmation that I'm not suicidal anymore, so that's a win.

I curl my fingers in to check them. Except for that one

botched nail, the paint is unblemished, but half of my right hand is still chipped to hell. I unscrew the bottle and splay my fingers out on the tray table again.

"There's more coming," Mr. Kepler says, his voice tinny. "You may want to put that away now."

I scrape a stray fleck of paint from around my thumbnail. "What are you, psychic?"

I knew I'd end up saddled next to a teacher, but I was really hoping it'd be Mrs. Lachlan. At least she understands the art of self-expression, whereas Kepler once asked me "Is there a reason you do this?" while gesturing to my entire person. He'd been wearing a white polo with yellow stains at the armpits tucked into a pair of ill-fitting khakis. I'd been wearing a lot of eyeliner, multiple articles of shredded clothing, and the very same spike-studded combat boots that I'm wearing right now.

"I'm not sure you should be doing that on an airplane in the first place, Alistair."

I glare up at him around the curtain of my hair. He's got a permanent sneer and these creepy ice-chip eyes, the kind that feel like they're trying to pierce past your clothing, past skin and muscle and bone, right down into your soul.

"Show me the law against it and I'll stop," I say. "I'm not looking to get arrested."

Kepler scoffs and turns back to the black screen in front of him, the smirk lingering on his face. I know from experience this means he's resigning from the conversation. I suppose he can't really threaten to send me to the principal's office when we're forty thousand feet above the ground. Or maybe he's just in a milder mood because we're on our way to Europe, because who doesn't love a vacation? I'm not even being paid to be here, and I'm among (almost) everyone in the world that I hate, but even I've managed to cultivate a good mood for myself.

Granted, there are a few dimensions to this good mood, and not all of them have to do with Europe. For one, I don't have a shred of studying to do for a week, and I can't remember the last time I had that long of a respite. For another, my mother won't be in Europe. My father *may* be in Europe—he's always on business trips abroad, and I never have any idea where he is at any given time—but that's inconsequential given he usually pretends I don't exist when we're in public.

But mostly, it's because I'll be far away from Jordan.

Not that this wasn't already the case, considering we'd both been doing a good job of avoiding each other like the plague for the past month, but still—in that school, that suburb, I see her everywhere even when she isn't there, like walking around the world's bleakest museum.

I've never been to Europe with her, though. I've never been to Europe, period. So for the next week, I'll be free not only of her, but of our entire doomed friendship haunting me around every corner. And if I'm free of that, then I'm free of the other thing: the night of her party, when it all came crashing down. The night that exhausts me every day because I have to keep running from it. There were a few close calls this last month when I could feel it swiping at the air just behind me, and I thought it might grab hold. But I kept running.

And now I can slow down a bit because it can't catch me on the other side of the ocean. I'm going to be so well and truly culture shocked, I won't be able to spare a moment to think about her. Or *that*.

As I blow on my nails, I look at the screen embedded into the seat in front of me. There's an animation of a plane flying over the globe, hovering halfway over the Atlantic Ocean with a dashed line trailing from its departure point in Toronto. The timer in the corner tells me we've got another four and a half hours to go, which makes me groan loudly.

"Alistair," Mr. Kepler says. His creepy eyes are closed again, which is just as well. "You may want to try and be considerate toward those of us who are trying to sleep."

I roll my eyes. It may be two in the morning, but there are plenty of other people on this plane making noise. The baby is still screaming its throat dry five rows back. He just likes to pick fights with me because I wear eye makeup and dress funny to him. I suspect this is the same reason he refuses to call me Alis—it's always *Alistair* in that admonishing hiss or *Mr. Woodson* like I'm fifty years old.

I glare at the side of his smug face for a long time, but this doesn't seem to scare him the way it has recently started scaring most of my classmates. That's one of the perks of being rumoured to be a vengeful arsonist: the people who used to think you were just a skinny gay weakling now think you're going to burn their house down if they look at you funny.

Eventually I find I no longer have the energy for him because, well, it *is* two in the morning, and I haven't slept a wink since we left home. So I opt for putting my head-phones back on to drown out the crying baby, then curl my legs up under me and lean my head against the window, my hair falling like night over my face.

Four and a half hours.

Four and a half hours, and I might actually be free.

"Stay with a partner! We're going straight to Arrivals. Follow me, Mr. Kepler, and Mr. Bilodeau, and do *not* get lost," Mrs. Lachlan announces as she makes her way to the front of the plane.

My classmates are all in various stages of disembark-ing, some half-standing in their seats, others reaching for their bags from the cabin compartment. It's one in the afternoon in Paris, but back home, it's still only seven in the morning, so most of them are bleary-eyed and looking around themselves like they've just been teleported from their beds.

I've been standing since the moment the plane came to a stop, gripping the tops of the seats, my bones buzzing. Luckily for me, I've been graced with a short stature, so the angle isn't all that uncomfortable. Mr. Kepler, on the other hand, has to hunch like Quasimodo as he waits for the woman in the aisle seat to get a move on.

By the time I'm out of that airplane, I'm practically flying down the jet bridge. I tail Lachlan, who's walking even faster than I am despite the giant purple backpack that extends from the top of her half-shaved head all the way to her thighs. Swinging in her hand is the ubiquitous Rainbow Tablet: an iPad in a striped rainbow case that she once told us contains her "class notes." I suspect it's actually an extensive database of information on everyone at our school, like their best and worst subjects, their friends and enemies, their moral alignment, their tells, their personality disorders, and so on. I don't even want to imagine what it says about me.

At the mouth of the jet bridge, Lachlan turns around so suddenly I nearly run into her ample stomach.

"Oy!" she barks. "Is everyone still with me?"

There's some muttering imbued with varying levels of enthusiasm.

"Good. *Àndale*," Lachlan says before marching on.

I look at my feet, staring at the seam where the jet bridge meets the airport floor. I'm going to savour this. If I appreciate this moment hard enough, maybe I'll be transported to a parallel universe where every bad thing in my life is undone, every horrible memory erased.

I let someone pass me. Then another.

Then something slams into my shoulder, and I trip forward, right over the line.

I snap my head up to glare at whoever it was, but I already know. Eric Tulson is walking backward in front of me, splaying his arms and pursing his lips in the universal gesture for *What can you do?*

The irritation that runs through me is like an electric current. Eric is a stocky brute who exclusively wears sports memorabilia and smells of cold-cut meats under a thick veil of Axe cologne, and his sole mission in life is to piss me off. I'm about to shoot him the finger, but then Connor, Eric's curly-haired lackey, jostles me as he passes—nothing he ever does is original—and Eric cracks up. Connor runs up to pinch his ass, laughing and ducking as Eric rounds on him, his fist poised for a punch that never lands.

I let a few more people drift past me, forming a barrier between us, before I hike up my backpack and start following.

As I walk, I notice that Paris Charles de Gaulle Airport isn't much different than Toronto Pearson. About the only hint I have that we're in France is the signage; here the French is written above the English instead of below it.

I hope that Paris starts to look like Paris in a minute because, so far, this is all very anticlimactic.

At the Arrivals terminal, Mrs. Lachlan stops in front of a coffee vending machine with Mr. Kepler, waiting for everyone else to circle round. Not including the teachers, there's about twenty of us, which is only two-thirds of my graduating class. The other third either weren't allowed, couldn't afford it, or recently suffered a house fire and had to take back their deposit.

I shrug off my backpack as I wait, spotting Theo—Eric and Connor's lord and saviour—sauntering down the terminal with Maya at his side.

Theo Grant is one of those people who is handsome enough to just look plain. If you went into a frat house and looked at all the photos on the wall commemorating generations of Pi Beta Alpha Optimus Prime, you'd be able to spot him ten times over in each photo. Except he'd probably be the leader of the frat, the one who preaches that fraternity is not all about partying but *brotherhood* and *connections*. And instead of flip-flops and Hawaiian shirts, he'd be wearing knits, loafers, and that godawful leather bracelet with the gold *J* charm that makes my stomach turn every time I see it.

He's the head of what I call the Halfwits—him, Eric, Connor, and Maya. Admittedly, I could've been more creative, but I was fourteen when they were christened. They've continued to make my life a misery since then, so the name just stuck.

Maya Papadakis, who has refreshed her fake tan for the trip and is dressed in a travel-chic combo of leggings under an oversized sweater, appears to be talking Theo's ear off about something while his thumb flies over his phone screen. She's being so blatantly ignored that I might even feel bad for her if she didn't have a raisin for a soul.

When everyone's gathered in a semi-circle, Lachlan flips open her Rainbow Tablet. "Faster you all shut up, faster we can get a move on."

Kepler translates: "We're going to take attendance if you could all quiet down."

"You already took attendance, Lachlan," someone calls from somewhere behind me. Probably Craig.

"Thank you, Craig"—Bingo!—"but since we've just travelled across the ocean, we're going to do it again."

"Ma'am, I think we would've noticed if someone jumped out of the plane," he says, gaining a few snickers.

"Depends who jumped," Eric mutters. I roll my eyes.

"Eric, watch it. That's enough now." Lachlan holds up

her hand in a pinching gesture and looks down at her tablet. "Jordan Abbott?"

The silence that falls after that is almost comical. Almost.

"Oh, nope," she says, swiping a finger over her screen. "Sorry."

She moves on, but the damage is already done. The Halfwits are burrowing into me with their eyes. Half the class is doing that furtive whisper/side-eye combo I've long become immune to, and the other half either didn't register what just happened or don't want to incur my wrath in case I decide to burn their houses down, too.

2

I'm sitting with Mr. Bilodeau on the coach to the hostel.
He's got to be at least a hundred years old, with a silver
cloud of hair and dark skin freckled and liver-spotted with
age. I hope we don't accidentally leave him behind somewhere because I do like him, despite his annoying
penchant for speaking in French no matter how hard you
try to get him to switch.

He's telling me about all the landmarks I should look
for when I'm up on the Eiffel Tower tomorrow, arranging
his shaky hands into the shapes of buildings. I like
watching them and thinking about all the places they've
been and the work they've done and the people they've
touched.

I've never been able to see myself getting old. Every
time I try, it's like there's this white space in the middle of
my brain, a void where there should be some semblance of
a future. It doesn't make sense, considering I can't

remember a time when my parents weren't drilling into me how important it is that I think about my future. Every decision I make should be informed only by the future, never the past, and *certainly* not the whims of the present.

They were right, I guess. Every time I settled in for an all-nighter to study for my next test or read and re-read my essays until my eyes blurred, I kept reminding myself that this one assignment, this one grade, could be the thing that tanks my GPA and has me homeless after graduation, and that kept me going. There were only three majors and three schools my parents were willing to pay for, and if I didn't get into at least one of them, they promised to cut me off.

"And trust me, Alistair, you're as good as dead if that happens," my mom said, pointing at the chart she pulled up on her computer. She's a lawyer so she's all about having evidence to back up her claims, and she loves showing me charts of the astronomical rent prices across Canada. That was four years ago, but I checked just last week and it's worse now. Even if my parents let me get a job, I can't imagine how I would ever make enough.

But I did the work, and I got into all three schools. Now I just had to choose one, something my parents left entirely up to me, which was really kind of them. *Alistair, would you rather kill yourself for a law degree, an engineering degree, or a medical degree? Just know that whatever you choose, we'll be hounding you every step of the way!*

"I have a feeling you're not listening to me anymore," Bilodeau says in French.

"Hm?" I glance back at him. "No. Hôtel des Invalides, east side, gold dome. Got it."

A crease forms between his rheumy eyes. "You're not excited to be in Paris?"

Au contraire, I am very excited to be in Paris, where I should *not* be thinking about school for once in my life.

At least, I think this is what excitement feels like, but there must be something on my face that makes him say this to me, so I just frown and shake my head like I have no idea what he's talking about before turning back to the window. We're stopped in traffic and there's rain streaking the window, so I'm looking at the bright smudge of orange pylons surrounding what looks like a sinkhole on the side of the road.

God, *where* is the culture shock? Any kind of shock, really, is ideal. For the past month, I've been walking around in this sort of fog that never lifts, which at first I was okay with because it meant I didn't have to feel any of the looks shot my way or the dread that came with wondering what they're actually whispering about. I would be somewhere, and then I would blink and I would be somewhere else, and then I'd blink and I'd be home and ready for bed.

But now that I'm far away from home—and far away from Jordan—I want to wake up and remember that there is actually a point to my existence. I want to be so far removed from the things I know that I might start to feel something that I've never felt before, like maybe my neurons are able to fire in ways that make me feel good, but I just haven't been in the right conditions for it.

We pull up to our hostel, and I'm disappointed to find we're not staying in one of those haunted Renaissance tenement buildings we'd been passing on the way here. I like being in places knowing hundreds of generations of people have stood where I'm standing; it's a comforting reminder that me and my problems are insignificant when held up to the whole of human history, and soon I'll just be dust in an old building like everyone else.

Instead, the lobby we file into is excruciatingly ordinary, a rustic concrete affair with colourful abstract paintings on the walls and a front desk decorated like a theatre marquee. As Lachlan's passing out our keycards, I'm practically vibrating with the need to go out and explore the *real* Paris, rain be damned. But she informs us that we're going to head to a fondue restaurant in an hour for what will essentially be our breakfast at three in the afternoon, and that we shouldn't go far in the meantime.

When my classmates disperse, I stride up to her. "Can I skip it?"

She levels me with a disapproving look. "No, you can't *skip it*. It's fondue."

"What if I don't care about fondue?"

She sighs and crosses her arms over her Rainbow Tablet. "Is this how it's going to be for the next week? You trying to sneak off and avoid everyone?"

"I don't *avoid* people," I say, scowling. They avoid me. And I mean that literally—since that fire, I've been enjoying an especially wide berth in the hallways.

"Alis, you know," she starts, and I follow as she heads toward the bank of elevators. "You don't have to do everything by yourself. I promise you're not an alien and will hit it off with at least one of the nineteen human beings here if you try."

I ignore this because it's been four years with these people, and I think that ship has long sailed. "Is that a category on your rainbow thing?"

She presses the button for the elevator and gives me a look that is at once amused and bemused. "What?"

"Alien versus human."

She narrows her eyes. "I don't *categorize* my students."

"Do you categorize teachers? Pretty sure you should mark Kepler down as alien."

She shushes me, but I can see her trying to hide her smile.

I ride the elevator up with her and get off at the fourth floor. I search for my room, praying to anyone who will listen that I'm not rooming with the Halfwits. I'd like to think Lachlan is perceptive enough not to make me sleep in a room with someone like Eric, but I'm pretty sure the room assignments are random, and the Halfwits are rather subtle anyway. None of them have ever roughed me up besides some head whacks and shoving; they prefer things like quietly cutting off a piece of my hair at the back of the class or starting rumours about my being a necrophiliac who worships Jeffrey Dahmer and takes bath salts.

That is, until a Monday morning last month when I was greeted at school by a punch to the face. I ended up on the pavement with Theo's yelling in my ears about how he *knew it was me* and *her cat was in there* and I was a *fucking lunatic*, et cetera. I was confused by this—not just because my head was ringing from the punch and he was screaming about cats, but because, normally, Theo had a lot of fun giving me shit for whatever he could come up with, and he was livid then. He risked getting expelled to hit me, and I had no idea why, except that it was about his girlfriend. About Jordan. Because somehow, those two things had become one and the same.

It turned out he thought I burnt her house down over the weekend, and by the end of the day, so did everyone else. So naturally, the first thing I hear when I open the door to my hostel room is the tail end of what I think was: "Dibs on not bunking with the Unabomber."

The boy who'd spoken looks over his shoulder at me in the doorway from where he's dumping his bag out on one of the bunk beds. He widens his big Bambi eyes at me and quickly turns away.

Interesting how I've gone from burning someone's house down to mailing out shrapnel bombs.

"This is cozy!" Craig says on another bottom bunk, pushing his feet up into the underside of the bed above him.

Craig Miltenberg is that one guy who thinks he's a comedian and never shuts up. I'm not sure if he's athletic —he's not part of any sports teams, and he's on the heavier side—but he's one of those perpetual blushers who always looks like he's just run laps around the gym. Combine that with the fact that he acts like a child on a sugar high, and I get exhausted just looking at him.

As I scan the rest of the room, I see that someone is in

the middle of claiming the bunk above Bambi Eyes while two other boys have taken another.

The good news is: no Halfwits. The bad news is that the last bed is the one Craig is currently trying to deadlift with his feet.

I walk over to him, crossing my arms. "I'm gonna need you to stop doing that."

It appears he didn't notice I came in because he drops his legs and darts up on his elbows so fast he almost smacks his head on the underside of the bunk. He adjusts his yellow beanie and visibly gulps.

"You... you're"—he points at the bed above him—"up there?"

I bug my eyes out at him, gesturing at the room around us. "Do I have another choice?"

Christ, he's looking at me like I'm holding him at gunpoint. Maybe he thinks I'm going to burn his hat in the night. He literally never takes it off. I bet if I peaked at Lachlan's Rainbow Tablet, there'd be an entry next to his name that says *Weakness: Hat.*

"Sorry, no," Craig says, his voice pitched an octave higher than usual. "You're good. Welcome aboard."

I roll my eyes and climb halfway up the ladder to toss my bag on the bed. Then I grab my toiletry bag out of it so I can go re-do my eyeliner because if I'm going to be forced to sit through *fondue* with these people, I at least need to look like I have my shit together.

As I hop back down from the ladder, I notice there's a smell in here suddenly—something waxy and greasy and all too familiar. It makes my skin prickle and my stomach turn because that smell is *not* supposed to be here.

This is Europe, and she's not here.

I turn to see Bambi Eyes sitting on the side of his bed, rubbing his hands together. The spiked buckle of my boot tinkles as I step toward him, and he pauses, his eyes flicking up to me under his lashes.

"What is that?" I ask.

His eyes grow wider. "Um, hand cream?"

"Don't use that shit around me."

"I need it for—"

"Use another fucking *brand* then."

"Right, okay," he stammers, holding up his shiny hands on either side of him. I turn my back on him, feeling everyone else's eyes on me as I leave the room.

As I get into the hallway and that smell is shut behind the door, I feel a twinge of guilt for taking that out on him. But already my head is swimming, jogging the memory of the first time I ever encountered that smell, standing in line outside homeroom on the first day of second grade.

It was wafting in from somewhere behind me, and I turned to see a girl I'd never seen before, her large ears sticking out from the straight silky hair that sat flat against the sides of her head. I had a hard time deciding if it was blonde or red. Then I noticed the skin around her lips was chapped and raw in a way that looked painful, and she was rubbing cream on her elbow.

"What is that?" I asked.

"It's my special cream," she said. "I have to use it

because I have eczema. Which, by the way, is not spelled with an X."

I'd always been good at spelling. I was the best speller in the second grade, and I told her as much. She stopped rubbing her elbow and squinted at me in challenge. "Okay, spell it."

I did, and then I waited for her approval. She pursed her lips, still squinting at me. Then she broke into a grin. "Yeah, that's actually right."

I beamed at her, and she started challenging me to spell a whole bunch of things until I got her last name wrong and swore. Jordan gasped, putting her hand over her mouth, and her eyes were so wide it made me laugh.

"What?" I said, but she kept staring at me, and my laughing turned a bit nervous. "What's wrong?"

She dropped her hand and whispered, "My parents would be so mad if I said that."

I frowned. "My mom says it all the time."

"She lets you say it?"

"She didn't say I couldn't."

"That's crazy," she said, her voice filled with awe. "But cool."

I felt a zinging sensation through my whole body, and a warm feeling settled in my stomach. I'd never been called cool before.

For the rest of that day, I couldn't focus on a word our teacher said, because Jordan had her desk next to mine and she seemed to be radiating heat like a furnace. I still had fireworks going off inside of me from the memory of her calling me cool, and how she smiled at me in a way nobody my age had ever smiled at me. I had this gnawing fear that she stumbled into the wrong school and I would never see her again.

But then she was told to introduce herself to the class because she'd just moved from Saskatchewan, and the teacher asked for a volunteer to show her around the schoolyard at recess.

I'd never raised my hand so fast in my life.

3

The restaurant we're filing into, Le Refuge des Fondus, is nightmarishly small. It's composed of a single room, its walls and ceiling covered in colourful scribbles as if we're meant to sign our names when we leave. There are only two long tables extending from the front of the restaurant to the back, with no way around them, and I'm watching as a punk-looking waitress guides one of my classmates onto a chair, then *over* the table and onto the bench on the other side. The girl, who I'm at least seventy percent sure is named Kristen, is looking very pleased with this unconventional restaurant seating, until she sees that I'm next in the aisle. I watch her face go slack as she realizes what this means.

I walk over to the waitress, ignore her helping hand, climb onto a chair—"Wait," says Kristen, her round eyes filling with panic—and step over the table. I plop down next to her, the chains on the sides of my pants jangling as they hit the bench.

Kristen tucks her elbows in like a T-Rex to avoid touching me. I don't know much about her, except that she has a hot stepbrother in the year below us, so everyone assumes she has a sordid crush on him despite having no evidence except for the fact that he's objectively good-looking. I'm pretty sure there's a logical fallacy in there somewhere. I'd bet even if Kristen came out as lesbian, these people would still find some way to insist she has a crush on her stepbrother.

Just like how when Jordan's house fire was ruled an accident three days after it happened, that was of no consequence. Because that was three days in which the rumour was spreading, and not only spreading, but mutating into wilder shit, like how someone had seen me at the Esso station earlier that day funnelling gas into a canister, or how Sir Elton John (Jordan's cat) had supposedly been mutilated before he burned. So, even with the police, fire investigators, and local news confirming it was an accident, it was too late—Theo had told everyone I was this vengeful, cat-murdering arsonist, the rumour was spreading like wildfire, and I was basking in it.

It was the greatest gift Theo could have ever given me. Before that Monday morning when he punched me, I'd spent a whole weekend feeling the most powerful dread I'd ever felt at the thought of going back to school. Jordan's party had happened the Friday before, and I'd spent every second after it sat in the darkness of my bedroom, thinking vividly about all the ways I could end it. I weighed the pros and cons of doing that against facing everyone; the thought of anyone looking at me, let alone talking about what happened, had me gripping my bedside table and trying not to vomit into the garbage pail I'd placed on the floor.

But all that worrying had been for nothing thanks to Theo. No one was talking about the party—they were talking about the fire. The looks thrown my way were ones of apprehension or hatred and nothing worse than that. I could've shaken his hand for what he'd done for me if the thought of touching him didn't make my skin crawl.

Despite both of us being at the centre of the rumour mill, I think I can safely say Kristen feels no kinship with me, given that she's still frozen in her seat like a lemur. It's so ridiculous that, by the time we get our drinks (which, weirdly, come in baby bottles), I make no secret of staring at the side of her face. I think she believes I can't see the big *help me* eyes that she's making to her friend across the table. I watch as the other girl subtly shakes her head, smirking.

The waiters bring out several platters of amuse-bouche, which consist of little chunks of cheese, boiled potatoes on toothpicks, pickles, cured meats, and two types of olives. The platter is put right in front of me, and Kristen side-eyes it as if debating if I'm going to bite her when she reaches out for something.

I decide to make her more comfortable by taking out the lighter I keep in my back pocket and holding it in my fist on the table. Then I start flicking it, over and over. If the boy on my other side cares, he doesn't show it. He's got his earbuds in, which is a fantastic idea that I didn't think of when I left my headphones in the hostel.

Kristen looks toward the lighter, swallows visibly, then leans in on her T-Rex arms to call to a girl a couple seats down. "Wanna swap?"

"Uh." The other girl's eyes dart toward me, then to the lighter in my hand, then to my face. I raise my eyebrows at her, daring. She swallows and shakes her head. "No. Sorry."

"Can you ask Noor?" says Kristen, and I have to roll my eyes. She really is going to make her way down the whole goddamn table to try and get away from me.

I put the lighter away, cross my arms, and stare at the ceiling instead. I try and pick out names from the scribbles while the chattering of my classmates overlaps into nonsense.

Soon, we're all served with vats of oil and fondue cheese, along with wicker baskets full of soft bread cubes, beef chunks, and potatoes. The narrow table shakes like an earthquake when people fidget in their seats, which helps me understand why the drinks are in baby bottles. Mr. Bilodeau stands up to explain, in French, how we're supposed to stick the meat skewers in the boiling oil to cook before dipping it in the fondue. I opt to dip some bread in the melted cheese, and when I put it in my mouth, it's gooey, tasteless, and hard to chew. And I know that's just me because most things I eat are gooey, tasteless, or hard to chew. Meanwhile, several people are rolling their eyes into the back of their heads and moaning like this is the best meal they've had in their lives.

When we're on desserts, I realize I've made it through this entire dinner without anyone speaking to me. Everyone's in their own little worlds, telling stories and laughing too loud and feeding each other fondue. Kristen has finally seemed to forget I exist and is deep in conversation with her friend across the table. Further down, Noor is throwing olives into Craig's open mouth, and people are cheering with every successful catch.

Then Maya stands from her place among the Halfwits and lifts her phone in the air, scanning it over our heads.

"Isn't it cute?" she squees. "And look—"

She grabs her baby bottle and sticks the nipple in her mouth, then holds her phone up as if to take a selfie with it. That's when I catch a glimpse of her screen and see a flash of strawberry blonde hair and a smiling mouth. There's the barest tinkle of a familiar laugh above the noise of the restaurant.

Jordan.

I feel a fist closing around my heart, squeezing. Maya drops back on the bench, her and her FaceTime call once again obscured by the rest of my classmates. I grit my teeth against the pain in my chest as I look down at the untouched chocolate cake on my plate, then pick up my fork and start slicing it up, just to have something to do.

Then, when the cake is thoroughly mangled and I'm left staring intently at the fork in my hand, something starts to happen to me. It's happened many times before, but I never get used to it.

One moment, everything will be normal, and the next, things will start to look bizarre and incomprehensible.

Like now, I'm looking at this fork, and it's turned impossibly flat, almost two-dimensional, and the tines are wider than I feel they should be. I don't remember forks ever looking like this, and I don't know when someone could have replaced it. It disturbs me enough that I drop it on my plate and look up, but there's this fuzzy, anemic tinge to the lighting that's making everything look washed out and far away.

I drop my gaze to my hands on the blood-red table-cloth, and it's like I've never seen my fingers before. They're long and rubbery, and the nails are like black holes, making me queasy. And worse, I suddenly have no control over them. It's like the world's been yanked out from under me and put on a TV screen, and I'm simply watching.

I'm clutched suddenly with this cold terror at the thought of being stuck like this forever, paralyzed in anti-space with this screen in front of me, unable to get back inside it. The terror grows and grows until time blips to the end of dinner, and my body is getting up with everyone else's. All around me, people move in this creepy, glitching way, like they're all cartoons. I'm travelling through them, but I'm not the one steering my own legs. I feel like screaming, but I don't even know if a scream would come out of me if I tried.

Then I come back to myself, and I'm looking at the bright red neon sign of the Moulin Rouge, and Bilodeau is attempting to usher everyone into a group photo in front of it. A chill of unease runs through me when I see that the sky behind the windmill on its roof is turning violet.

It was only late afternoon when we entered the restaurant, and now suddenly it's evening.

That's the thing about the dream state—it's terrifying in the moment, but when it ends, I can barely remember what it felt like while it was happening. I can barely remember what happened at all.

4

By the time night falls over Paris and everyone has long settled in their beds, there's this squirming, acid-coated thing writhing around inside me, burning holes in my stomach lining. I don't know exactly what it is, but it's been there for as long as I can remember, wreaking havoc on my insides. Now, as I shut myself in a stall in the hostel's communal washroom, I can feel myself shaking with the need to get rid of it.

I asked my dad, a long time ago, if he sometimes felt like he was in a dream, too. He was watching golf—during the rare times he was home, he was usually watching golf—and I watched the images of sloping green grass and warped faces flashing in the reflection on his glasses. He turned his face toward me but took another few seconds to drag his eyes to mine. "What?"

"Sometimes I feel like I'm in a dream," I said. "And I don't know if that's normal."

He snorted. "I feel like I'm in a dream at work all the time."

I tried to explain myself better. "I mean, in a dream, like... nothing is real, and everything is weird."

"Hey, kid," he said, looking back at the TV. "Why don't you go over to that Jordan girl's house?"

I remember feeling in that moment that the dream state couldn't be all that important, so I never brought it up again. It's a good thing, in retrospect, because I'm pretty sure my parents would disown me if they knew I was losing my mind. They might even go to more extreme measures to disassociate themselves from me. Stage an accident, maybe, or send me so far away that no one could ever trace me back to them.

And then there's this: me, pulling my pants and underwear down to expose the side of my thigh, pulling my lighter out and tipping it so the flame coats the metal top. They don't know about this either.

Once I've counted the seconds—I know how long it takes now for it to get hot enough—I flick the lighter off.

I stop breathing, and then I plunge it into my thigh.

For that first split second, there's a cold flush that runs from my head all the way down to my toes. I imagine it's washing me clean, like maybe my insanity is just a layer of grime on my skin, easily sloughed off.

Then the pain comes, and it's like flying directly into the sun. It's blinding and disorienting and shuts off every other thought in my mind until there's only the white-hot blister screaming on my thigh.

And that's what this is all about. Because when I do this, there's nothing else but this.

As the metal cools against my thigh, my muscles are trembling, and I'm blinking away these little white sparks, but that squirming thing in my stomach has slowed, as if I've shocked it into submission.

When I remove the lighter, there's a little swatch of skin that looks textured where it used to be smooth. It's going to blister, then it's going to scab, and then it will leave a subtle scar; a pale, misshapen square, joining the ones around it.

As I walk back down the deserted hallway, I hold my hair up in a nest on my head so the air cools the sweat on the back of my neck. When I come to my room, I slip inside and shut the door gingerly behind me. I start padding toward my bunk, and that's when I hear something that makes me stop cold. Something that makes me want to immediately turn around and leave again.

I look at the shape of Craig Miltenberg in the bottom bunk, and my first impression is that he is actually masturbating in a room with five other guys. I don't know why that's where my head goes—it just seems like something he would do, and it's the first explanation I have for his quick breaths and why he's making those little whimpering noises.

But as my eyes adjust and give way to the orange city light seeping through the gauzy curtain, I see that his eyes are closed, and his hands aren't where they would be if he was doing that. They're fisting the sheets on either side of his body, wrenching at them like they're the only things keeping him from being dragged away. His face is snapped to the side, away from me, but I can see sweat shining in the column of his throat.

A nightmare, then.

I'm staring at him, frozen with what I realize is, actually, fascination. I feel how I imagine marine biologists must have felt when they discovered that octopuses could do puzzles. I've been going through high school under the impression that none of the people I'm surrounded by every day have more depth than a kiddie pool, and Craig especially has always struck me as this happy idiot whose only problem is deciding what colour sweatpants he's going to put on in the morning.

Can a happy idiot have nightmares? It doesn't seem likely. It's like my mom says: *only stupid people are happy.* So, if Craig's not that happy, maybe he's not that stupid either.

His head turns, and I flinch, thinking he's caught me watching him. But he's still locked in whatever is going on inside his head, his face drawn into this miserable grimace that is such a sharp contrast to his usual grin that it makes me feel a little off balance. Not to mention, he's not wearing his hat, which is a bit like seeing a turtle without its shell.

I creep toward the ladder leading to the bed above him, feeling a slight twinge of guilt that I think is what encourages me to make a lot of noise as I flop onto the mattress and kick under the covers. Then I pull the sheet up to my chin and stare at the ceiling, listening.

He's no longer making those pitiful noises. I hear him take a deep breath, slow and heavy and shaking a bit on the way out. Awake.

It's possible his nightmare could have *also* been about sweatpants. Or maybe he was standing under a meteor shower of olives and trying to catch them all in his mouth before they hit the ground and exploded.

But as funny as I find that, the look on his face is singed into my mind now, and I can't really believe it.

5

I've got my fingers wrapped around the fence that lines the Eiffel Tower's observation deck, sticking as much of my face as I can through one of the squares so I can smell the air.

From up here, Paris is a mottled sea of bone-white buildings and smoke-grey roofs. They stretch all the way out to the horizon, cutting winding patterns through the verdant trees, dotted here and there with the jagged points of cathedrals. The silver sash of the River Seine bisects it all, the boats cutting slow, rippling trails over its surface.

To my right, the gold-capped dome of the Hôtel des Invalides rises over everything like a beacon, just like Mr. Bilodeau said it would. I start walking along the platform, winding between people. It's not so busy up here that you can't move, but busy enough that everyone's conversations are overlapping into a rumble.

I come to a stop next to one of the telescopes, where a

very tall woman is bending to see through the eyehole, and that's when I hear Eric's obnoxious voice rising above everything else.

"I didn't know there were toilets up here. Can't believe I just took a shit on the Eiffel Tower!"

What an absolute moron. I don't dare look for him, but a hand claps me on the shoulder anyway, and I flinch in spite of myself. I figure it's Eric, but turn my head to see Theo instead. His dishwater hair is sculpted into that same boring swoop it always is, and his neat clothes are the pastel colours someone might use to decorate a baby's bedroom. He's peering out at the city with this mock-pensive look on his face that tells me he's about to say something atrocious to me.

"You should do it," he says. Then he looks at me, and despite that thoughtful face he's putting on, he can't hide the smoldering hatred in his eyes. "If you're thinking about jumping, you should do it."

From behind me, Eric bursts into incredulous laughter, as if this is the first time Theo has ever implied I should kill myself. It really doesn't take much to impress him.

I get this sudden vision of biting down on Theo's hand where it curls around my shoulder, of ripping his finger from his body and the sounds of his screaming as I spit it through the fence, spattering red on those beautiful white buildings below. The vision is so strong I can feel my teeth grinding in anticipation.

Before I can decide if I'm willing to bear the taste of it, Theo gives me one more bone-crushing squeeze and drifts off into the crowd of tourists, Eric still laughing on his tail.

The woman who'd been crouching at the telescope straightens, her head turning to follow Theo and Eric as they disappear. Then she looks back at me, her lips moving, sound coming out—

I turn away immediately, burying myself into the crowd. I suppose there's a possibility she was just going to comment on the weird shape of a building in the distance and I'd just imagined the pity in her eyes, but I wasn't going to risk it.

I pull my headphones up from around my neck and set my music to shuffle, cranking up the volume on a wall of noise until my skull rattles. When I find another spot, I stare out at the endless blue of the sky until it wraps around my peripheral and swallows me.

I'm half-hoping that when Lachlan's voice sounds over the deck announcing it's time to go, I don't hear her, and they leave me here and never notice I'm gone. I could forget graduation and just stay in Paris on my own. I'm second best in the class in French, so I already have that going for me. It'd probably be a while before my parents would think to cut off my credit card. I could get a bed in a hostel, which should give me enough time to find a data entry job where I can just listen to music and speak to no one all day. But could I do that without a visa? How would I—

There's a hand waving next to my face. I turn to see Craig Miltenberg standing next to me, leaning a shoulder against the fence. He's wearing a green plaid overshirt rolled up to the elbows, and it's a good choice for his skin tone. His hair curls out from under his yellow hat, and the colour reminds me, weirdly, of braised ribs. I can feel my stomach growl and have no idea how loud it is, given the music still assaulting my eardrums.

He raises his eyebrows and makes a motion like he's taking off a pair of invisible headphones.

Most of me is irritated at the interruption, but there's just enough curiosity that I pull my headphones down. Given how he acted around me at the hostel, this is shockingly brave behaviour from him. Still, I'm hoping the glare I'm giving him will be enough to convey that I will push him off the Eiffel Tower if he doesn't make this worth my time.

He looks down at the toe of his sneaker where it's grinding in the crease between the floor and the wall. "So, I was looking for a light, and I thought *hey*," he says, lifting his eyes to mine. "I know the perfect person to ask."

Is that it? Is that his joke? I was on the verge of manifesting my new life, and he interrupted me for *that*?

I narrow my eyes further and say nothing, hoping to strike the fear of God into him. But he just raises his eyebrows again, reaching up to tug a cigarette from behind his ear.

"I am happy to share," he says.

I glance at it, then back at his face, waiting for some other punchline. Then I look around myself, searching for the eager faces of my classmates dotted among the tourists. I see a few, but they're either concentrated on the views or one another.

Craig is still the picture of patience. He's also smiling,

but he's always smiling, so that doesn't really sway me one way or another as to whether he's trying to set me up.

It's possible that he just wants to light this cigarette. I've never seen him in the smoker's pit at school, but I've also never heard him make an Alis-related—or even an Alis-adjacent—joke. I can't imagine why he'd want to start now without an audience.

I keep my eyes on him while I pull the lighter out of my back pocket and extend it to him. I have this fleeting thought about how I just used that to melt my flesh yesterday, and now he's going to use it to light a cigarette without knowing that.

But Craig doesn't take the lighter. Instead, he wraps his fingers around the fence and uses that to pull himself a step closer to me. Then he sticks the cigarette between his lips and juts his chin out expectantly, eyes glinting like amber.

I roll my eyes and light it for him. He scans my face, and whatever he finds there makes his lips quirk around the cigarette, which has my teeth grinding. I quickly stow the lighter and look back out at Paris. He offers the cigarette to me before he's even dragged on it, and I shake my head.

"You're not a smoker, but you carry a lighter."

It's not a question, but he lets it hang there between us anyway, and I'm not in the mood. I turn away from the fence. "Goodbye, Craig."

"Sorry! Sorry," he says, waving his hand. "You were here first, I'll go."

I pause, still half-turned to leave. He hasn't gone yet because he's puffing on the cigarette he's sticking out of one of the squares in the fence. I watch as his face pinches, and he erupts into the most dramatic coughing fit I've ever seen. He buries his face in his arm, stomping his foot, and there are heads turning all around us. Then he recovers with a ragged gasp, his eyes red and watering.

"That was very cool," I tell him.

His voice is tight when he speaks. "I'm out of practice. I'm what they call a *social* smoker."

"Yet you're standing over here with me."

He frowns, letting out one last cough. "Are you not sociable?"

I glare at him and say nothing, but somehow, I've ended up back in my spot, and I let him stand there next to me. Our tentative silence lasts all of ten seconds.

"I don't actually smoke either," he says. "But we're in *Paris*."

I take back all doubts I had last night. He's an idiot, and his nightmare was definitely about olives.

But unfortunately, now I'm thinking about last night, when he wasn't wearing that hat and he looked like a different person with his face all twisted like that. I'm not thinking about it, because it's weird and invasive and, more importantly, I don't care.

"What were you listening to?" he asks. Clearly, he has a pathological aversion to silence. He wouldn't survive a second in my parents' house.

I pull out my phone and show him. As he looks down at it, I notice he's got these tan freckles spattered over his nose, disappearing into his ruddy cheeks.

"A Place to Bury Strangers," he reads. His eyes flick up to mine. "That's unsettling."

I shrug, putting my phone back in my pocket. He turns his face toward the sky. "A Place to Bury Strangers," he says again, frowning like he's doing mental math.

"Don't hurt yourself," I say.

This appears to fly right over his head. He scratches at his cheek with his non-cigarette hand. "I was just trying to think if they were on this goth mixtape my pen pal sent me. Unless you're more into screamo? That could be a screamo band name. Or maybe grunge."

While he's saying this, Lachlan materializes out of the crowd, coming toward us. She's sweating, the swath of hair on the unshaved side of her head is frizzing, and her face is extremely unimpressed. I decide not to tell him because I want to see what happens.

She sidles up next to Craig and taps him on the shoulder. His eyes widen, and he quickly drops his cigarette hand down beside his thigh.

"Just in case you haven't been paying attention in French class for the last twelve years: these signs around us? *Interdiction de fumer*? They have an English translation right under them."

He grimaces at me as if to say *yikes*. "Yes, ma'am. Putting it out."

She rolls her eyes and mutters something about her nerves before stomping off to continue her rounds.

Craig sniffs as he watches her go. "I like that she knows

how to be authoritative while still remaining cool, you know? I think that's a rare skill that—oh, crap."

This last part is directed down at the hand that was once holding a cigarette but is now empty.

"You dropped a lit cigarette off the Eiffel Tower," I say, glancing up at him. "Probably onto someone's head."

"Maybe," he says, wincing at the ground a thousand feet below. When he looks back at me, his eyes turn suddenly mischievous. "Why? Is that something you'd be interested in seeing?"

Ah. There it is.

I feel something inside of me deflate. His attempt was lame, and I'm not even surprised, but maybe I'm a bit disappointed. There was a moment there when I thought he was just existing next to me, without any ulterior motive besides needing a lighter. Really, he was just finding the right moment, the best comedic timing.

I turn back to Paris. "Good one."

"I'm not trying to bully," he says, but I don't look at him because I don't want to see the stupid, teasing smile I know is on his face. "I was just hoping you'd tell me yourself if you're this raging pyromaniac like everyone says."

"Didn't know you knew what that word meant," I mutter.

He's silent for long enough that I look sidelong at him to see how that hit. But he *is* smiling at me, and he's doing it like I'm a child that just tried to swear. "You're not very good at this."

I wrench back from the fence. "At making people feel like shit? I should work on that then."

His face falls. "No. No, I meant—"

I don't let him finish. I feel small and stupid, like I've been set up just so he could catch me off guard. I want to scream at Lachlan: *this* is what you get when you talk to these people, when you assume they aren't out to get you. You get belittled, deservedly, because you're naive.

I tap into that starving anger still roiling in me, the kind that made me want to bite Theo's finger off. "You know, it'd be great if you could stop whimpering and moaning all night so I can get at least one good night's sleep on this trip."

As soon as I say it, the squirming thing rears up in my stomach. I hold my ground, hoping he'll get angry, tell me to fuck off, maybe hit me.

Instead, his head does this jolting thing like someone's just snapped in his face. He gives me a wounded little smile.

"Jeez," he says, and it sounds like a broken laugh.

So I'm the one that storms off, feeling like an asshole. There must be something exceptionally inhuman about me, that people can say shit like that to me all the time and keep coming back to do it again without any remorse. All I feel is like I've pushed a baby bird out of a nest and watched it break its neck against the ground.

Maybe I'm less like a baby bird and more like a wasp. Everyone wants to kill a wasp. They're not easy to kill, but once they're dead, you feel better knowing they're not out there flying around, ready to sting you or burn your house down.

As Lachlan finally announces that we're done with this

claustrophobic tower, I at least feel better knowing that Craig probably isn't going to attempt whatever that was again.

One more month. Just one more month, and I'll be graduated. I may not be going anywhere better, but at least I can become someone else, and whatever these people think about me will be none of my concern anymore.

6

We're given the rest of the day to roam around on our own before we meet in Montmartre at sunset. Kepler tells everyone that they're to buddy up during free time and not leave each other's side, and I swear during this speech, Lachlan is squinting knowingly at me. Because I know she's watching, I float along with a couple of my less skittish classmates, pretending to follow them until I'm clear of her prying eyes.

After wandering aimlessly for a while, I end up walking up the white gravel pathway toward Luxembourg Palace, marvelling about how there are palm trees in Paris. No one told me that, and I didn't expect it.

I start to wonder if this is, finally, culture shock.

But I find I get over the palm trees rather quickly, so I suppose they're not shocking enough.

As I walk around searching for various landmarks, I get harassed by three different guys trying to sell me roses ("For your girlfriend!" one yells, shaking it at me like it's burning his fingers), and by an American woman with a large camera who tells me she loves my look and how it "juxtaposes with the weather." I flash her a polite smile and speed walk away before she can ask me for a photoshoot, and all the while, I'm just imagining Jordan in hysterics. Her favourite kind of person to make fun of is a pretentious art snob who tries to squeeze a big word into every sentence. When I first found this out about her, I was so concerned that *I* was an art snob that I ended up asking her one day while I was drawing on her arm.

"Obviously *you're* not," she said, frowning down at the design coming to life above her wrist. She wanted a human heart being torn down the middle, in honour of her freshly divorced parents. "Tattooing is for real tortured artists, not the fake ones."

I never classified myself as a *tortured artist* so much as a person who doodles sometimes, but she had this way of saying everything like it was a fact, and I took every word she said as gospel since the day I met her.

Until, you know, she lost her mind and started having sleepovers with Halfwits, the people who tormented us for three years. Then I had to seriously re-evaluate everything she ever said to me.

Still, as if she's controlling my strings from across the ocean, this fleeting memory of her has me stopping at the first tattoo parlour I come across. The buzzing neon letters in the window spell out PIERCING and TATTOO, and in the shop beyond, I can see a woman with fire-engine red hair working on a guy's calf. The walls around them are covered in framed designs of all styles—traditional pieces bursting with colour, puzzle-like tribal patterns, gothic blackwork and spiky cybersigilism.

That last is one of my favourites. I'd practice drawing those scythe-like patterns in the margins of my notebooks during my more boring classes, in awe of how one design could look at once like a raptor's spine and a lash line, or a butterfly's wing and a wall of flame, depending on how you were feeling when you looked at it. My mom once used those drawings as evidence during a diatribe she was on about how maybe I wouldn't be skating by with a 78 in calculus if I didn't spend classes doodling. I remember my dad chiming in from FaceTime with "Gotta smarten up, kid," because that was generally how he filled his parenting quota for the week or the month. Neither of them is ever the good cop, but I think I prefer my mom's ranting and screaming over my dad's detached remarks broadcasting in from another country. At least she disciplines with passion.

I still draw sometimes, especially in Mr. Kepler's class, but I'm more careful now to destroy the evidence. Sometimes, I wonder what it would be like to do that every day, and on real *people*. I've always liked the idea that you could put yourself through pain like that and have something beautiful to show for it on the other side. Or, you know, maybe not always beautiful—I've seen *Ink Master*—but at least something that means a lot to you. Something permanent, but not in a bad way.

I've got a lot to show for the pain I put myself through, and none of it is beautiful or meaningful, and all of it is permanent in a bad way.

I decide to head off to the Louvre, figuring that's bound to shock me, because it's the *Louvre*. As I'm standing outside that giant glass pyramid in the museum's courtyard, I say to myself: *You've seen this so many times in pictures, and now you're standing in front of it. This is crazy.*

And then I wait for it to actually feel crazy, and it never does.

I think *surely* the Mona Lisa is going to be it, and I wait in a massive line-up for what feels like hours until finally, I'm in among a sea of people, and there she is: the Mona Lisa, raised up behind a pane of glass against an otherwise bare wall.

Cameras flash all around me. I stare at this painting and wait for the awe to strike.

But isn't this painting kind of average? And also *small*. Since when was it this small?

Then I roll my eyes and leave, because of course I'd come to Paris and shit on the Mona Lisa. It's like I'm allergic to enjoying things.

———

I hate eating in the morning, and I only had a croissant for lunch, so I find I'm actually hungry by the time I get to Montmartre. Luckily, dinner wasn't included in our trip fees tonight, so I can do that alone, too.

I'm really craving ribs for some reason, and I find this pub that gives me a whole rack and a big glass of white wine. Then I eat it like an animal outside on the patio.

I'm watching this guy across the cobblestoned street

playing a whimsical French song on an accordion. He has a dreamy smile on his weathered face, and his eyes don't open, ever. I'm just thinking about how I want to body swap with him, just for a minute to see how it feels, when my ears perk at a familiar voice.

"...literally no point to a phone if you don't answer it!"

It's Craig, standing a little ways down the street. He hangs up his phone and shoves it in his pocket before looking around like a lost child, swinging his fists at his sides. My pulse spikes the moment his eyes meet mine, and I look quickly down at my half-eaten ribs, because *no, thank you.* Not after what I said to him.

But I can see him coming in my peripheral, so I wipe a giant cloth napkin over my barbecue sauce-covered face and begin chugging the last of my wine before his shadow falls over me.

"Hey," he says, tapping his fingers on the edge of my table. "Sorry, but have you seen Noor?"

"Hm?" I say into my giant wine glass, then realize it's empty and put it down. "No."

He clutches the back of his neck and squints down the street, the sun shattering behind him. "We were going into the shops, and I started to get tired, but she wanted to go into this one last place, so I told her I'd wait outside. But she was taking forever, so I went back in to get her, and she wasn't in there. She straight up disappeared, and now she's not answering her phone."

His voice wavers a bit at the end, which makes me shift uncomfortably in my seat. "Oh. I'm sure she's fine, though."

"I keep having these visions of her being kidnapped by a mime," he says, and it's very jarring how he makes jokes all the time but can also make something that is clearly funny sound so *not* funny.

I clear my throat. "Should you maybe go back to where you last saw her?"

"I—yes." Craig nods. "I will. Sorry, didn't mean to interrupt."

He starts to go. I stare at his wide back and the way his one hand is pulling at the hair curling out from under his hat and the other is clenched at his side.

"I'll go with you," I blurt out.

Maybe I feel a bit warm and daring because I really did *chug* that wine just now, and I'm not a big person. But I also still feel that lingering guilt from this morning and figure I owe him.

Also, I'm not a monster. Like, if I could choose one of my classmates to go missing, it wouldn't be Noor Amini. She looks like a sugar glider.

Craig turns around as I get up, throwing my napkin over my unfinished ribs. I can see him better now that he's not blotting out the sun, and his freckled face looks drawn with anxiety. I swear I've seen more expressions on Craig Miltenberg's face in the last twenty-four hours than I've seen in the last four years.

"Oh," he says, swallowing visibly. "I mean, you don't have to."

I shrug. He still doesn't move, so I gesture in the direction from which he came, trying not to be irritable about it. "This way?"

"Yes. Uh, yes," he pivots, leading us down the sidewalk. He pulls out his phone and calls Noor again before making a frustrated noise. "If it doesn't ring, does that mean it's dead?"

"Probably. Did she say it was dying?"

"No, but her battery is messed up. I told her to get a new one. Like fifty times I told her."

His voice breaks, and he doesn't say anything else. I find myself chewing on my cheek because I'm not about to *comfort* him, but also if I don't comfort him, is he going to cry? Because then I might step in front of the first moving vehicle I see to escape this situation.

I decide on: "Just because her phone's dead doesn't mean she's dead."

That definitely wasn't the right answer judging by the speed at which Craig's head whips around toward me. "I *know* that."

"Sorry, I've been drinking."

He's pulled his phone back out and is trying to call her again. I decide it's probably better if I keep my mouth shut and let him keep beating the dead horse.

We walk for three more minutes, Craig seeming to vibrate at a faster speed as time goes by. We've been going uphill, and on the precipice between a vintage store and a bakery, someone says his name.

We both spin. It's Noor, standing there with the same frizzy wolf cut and unimpressed look on her face that she's had since the ninth grade. She slides her eyes between us, sucking her fingers like she just finished eating something sticky. "This is why you ditched me, then."

For a second, I think Craig's collapsing next to me, and I flinch like I have to catch him or something, but no—he's just sagging forward, putting his hands on his knees.

"Oh my God," he wheezes.

Noor's brow furrows. "You're the one who said you'd wait, and then you didn't."

"I went to look for you!" Craig exclaims, flinging an arm toward one of the shops. "You weren't in there!"

Noor removes her thumb noisily from her mouth. "The place has a downstairs. I'm guessing you didn't check the downstairs."

Craig drops his arm. He's silent in a way that tells me he didn't check the downstairs. Then he ducks and scoops Noor up into a hug that lifts her off her feet.

"I thought you were kidnapped by a mime," he says, his voice muffled in her hair.

"Oh, not the mime, Craig," Noor says, patting his back. "There were no mimes."

As I watch this happening, there's a pang in my stomach so strong and so surprising that I almost put my hand on it. When Craig puts her down and wipes a hand over his eye, I have to physically restrain myself from circling around to look at him dead-on, because is he actually crying? I was partly joking when I considered that as a possibility. He's crying because she was lost for ten minutes?

That pang in my stomach has settled into this stretching ache, opening up like a chasm, and I need it to stop. I clear my throat, hoping this reunion wraps up soon.

Noor turns to me, giving me a once-over. "Search party, then."

"Yes." I give her a once-over right back. "You should probably fix your battery."

Craig gestures wildly to me in agreement, but Noor just says, "Hm," and fixes her eyes back on Craig. She has to look up much higher for him than she does for me. "I just had a very large donut, and I need to sit down. I'll meet you at the Sacré-Coeur."

Craig tenses. "Wait, what? No, we're—"

"I won't get kidnapped on a five-minute walk, Craig. Sunset's not for another hour, and you guys should go into that pink shop down there if you'd like to experience a sugar-induced orgasm."

Noor turns and leaves us standing there with the word *orgasm* hanging over us. She kicks a pebble as she goes, and it skips over the cobblestones and disappears into one of the cracks.

"I don't like sugar," I say, just as Craig says something else.

I glance at him. He doesn't *look* like he was crying, so maybe he just had an itch.

"Sorry, what?" he asks.

"Nothing. I'm gonna go now."

I start walking back down the hill.

"Okay, but—" his arm comes out in front of me as if to block me. I stop just before I bump into it, raising my eyebrows at him, and he snatches it back. "Sorry. Just— thank you. For coming to help even though I feel stupid now and I'm kind of wishing she *was* kidnapped by a mime."

Why is he thanking me for walking down the street with him even though earlier that day, I said some really uncool shit to him? That's incredibly annoying. It's insufferable, actually.

I decide to clear the air myself if he's not going to do it.

"It was the worst thing I could come up with at the time," I say. He frowns in confusion, and I notice how thick his eyebrows are when they're all bunched together like that. I swallow, waving my hand helplessly. "What I said to you on the Eiffel Tower."

"Oh." He cocks his head, his frown turning curious. "I don't think that's an apology *or* an explanation."

"I'm telling you I didn't mean it," I snap.

"Well, thanks. I mean, I might never sleep again, but I accept your... that you didn't mean it," he says, and why is he always on the verge of laughing? Doesn't it get tiring?

I roll my eyes and start walking again. Craig's shoes scuff against the cobblestones as he starts after me. "Wait, what about the sugar orgasm, though? You didn't finish your ribs."

"I don't like sugar."

"I actually refuse to believe that," he says, falling into step next to me. "Listen, if you think Noor ditched us because of you, that wasn't it."

"I actually wasn't thinking that, nor do I care."

"I think she ditched us because I was crying a little, and she gets weird about people being vulnerable. Like, she even hates the word. I swear, bring up the word *vulner-*

able with her, and she'll cringe so hard; she thinks it's disgusting. Which is weird because once you get to know her, she's actually really open about all kinds of deep stuff. And don't tell her I told you, but I was having a bad day a couple weeks ago, and she actually started *petting my hair*—"

"Craig," I say firmly, swinging a hand out like I'm about to karate chop him. Because now that I've said my piece, and we're square, I just don't understand why he's still here. It can't be for any good reason. "Why are you speaking to me right now?"

He falters in his steps. "What do you mean?"

"Don't act stupid."

He sighs, and his shoulders sag as his head rolls back on his neck. "Come *on*, dude. They said that fire was an accident. I don't get why you let people believe you did it, but that's your business, I guess."

I cross my arms, ignoring the heat in my cheeks. "You have *never* spoken to me."

"You've never spoken to *me*."

Neither of these statements is entirely true. I'm pretty sure I asked him for an eraser once in tenth grade, and last month, when Craig, Noor, and I were in the same group project and Craig was out sick for half the week, he came back to school and told our group, "Someone's gonna have to catch me up on this," and I'm pretty sure he looked directly at me when he said it despite the seven other people there.

In fact, that's how I know Craig and Noor weren't at Jordan's party, because they spent a good five minutes arguing about how Craig made Noor miss "the rager" to bring him saltines and ginger ale instead, and she was pissed because she didn't get the chance to switch the alcohol out for non-alcoholic and see if people still acted drunk. That was shortly before I excused myself to the washroom for some quality time with my lighter.

"So, you're talking to me because you think I *didn't* start a fire," I say flatly.

Craig blows his lips like a horse. "I don't know. Why do I need a reason to talk to someone? I like talking. Sometimes, things just happen, and it leads to talking. Which, by the way, is what I was trying to say on the Eiffel Tower. That you're not very good *at talking.*"

Just because he wasn't *at* the party doesn't mean he doesn't know what happened there, right? But if he did, wouldn't he have brought it up already? Like that first Monday after, when Dakota Mitchell came up to me in the hallway fidgeting with her fingers, and her face was full of pity, and she said, "Hey, um. I just wanted to say, if you want to talk about what happened—"

And I said, "Who the fuck are you? Leave me alone," and she flinched as I pushed passed her.

He would've done that already, right? If he knew? Either that, or he wouldn't be talking to me at all. There's no world in between that.

"You are like, *really* thinking about this," Craig says, sounding almost impressed. "I can leave you alone if you want."

"Oy!" someone yells. Craig and I both turn to see Lachlan coming out of a shop, the door chiming behind her. She has a takeaway box under her arm and a pink nightmare of a macaron in her hand. When she steps out of the shade of the shop's awning, the shaved side of her head sparkles in the golden sun.

"That looks yummy," Craig says as she crosses over to us.

She ignores him, jerking her chin at me instead. "Who'd you hang out with today?"

"Is that your business?" I ask.

She looks to Craig. "Was he with you?"

I roll my eyes strongly enough that my arms slap down against my sides. "For fuck's sake. I don't need a babysitter."

"Everyone needs a babysitter, that's my point," she says, cupping her hand under her mouth to catch some crumbs. "Buddy system. Do you understand how it works?"

"I'm *eighteen*."

"So?" She laughs. "You think your parents won't kick my ass if I let you get lost in Paris?"

Kick her ass? No. Shake her hand? Probably.

"Do you have more macarons in there?" Craig asks her, wiggling his fingers toward her box. She guards it from him just a moment before conceding, handing the box to him.

"Don't touch the chocolate ones."

As he opens it and begins what sounds like is going to be a very long-winded story about his mother and French confections, I skirt behind him and start slipping down the street, hoping neither of them will notice.

"Hold on," Lachlan says, cutting Craig off. She calls

after me. "I don't want you going off on your own anymore during free time, Alis!"

I turn around, spreading my arms out. "Well, maybe you should stop calling it *free* time, then!"

Craig snorts, and Lachlan swats him on the arm. When I glance at him, his eyes are twinkling, and he's got his arm over his mouth like he's trying not to spit out his cookie, and I notice there's something going on inside of me. A wriggling sense of pride for having made him laugh.

Which is actually so humiliating that I really do leave this time and don't turn back.

7

The morning we're supposed to leave for Interlaken, I'm thinking about the night before and the way the sunset looked when it was setting over Montmartre.

We'd all been scattered over the hill that slopes down-ward from the foot of the Sacré-Coeur—a gleaming white basilica like something out of a dream—looking out at those tooth-like buildings that stretched all the way out to the horizon. The sky was patching up with scrappy peach clouds, and as the sun sunk lower, I watched it turn pink.

I'd seen bits of pink sky before, but I never saw a *fully* pink sky, like a rose-tinted dome had been placed over Paris. It made Sacré-Coeur look like a sandcastle. It made all the people hazy and dream-like in a way that didn't scare me. And while I was watching this, hugging my knees to my chest, I had this frightening, unprecedented thought:

Maybe pink isn't so bad.

And that was my culture shock.

Obviously not because a pink sky is somehow exclusive to Parisian culture, but because it gave me that feeling I was looking for: an awe strong enough that, for a minute, I forgot who I was and everything about my life and just sat in a world without stories and memories and bad feelings and took it all in, thoughtlessly.

It was amazing. And everyone left me alone—Craig included. I think I was sat far enough away that my presence wasn't offensive to anyone, nor was it inviting as it for some reason was to him. When we got back to the hostel, I had the longest shower of my life and didn't once feel the need to turn the water temperature to either extremity.

As I stand on the platform at Paris Gare de Lyon, that's what I'm still thinking about when something taps me on the shoulder. I jump, swirling around to face what I'm sure is Theo winding up another punch or Eric dangling something nasty in my face. Instead, I see Lachlan blinking rapidly, as if I just kicked up dirt into her eyes.

My heart falls back into place. "Why do people *do* that? Why can't they just go up to your *face* where your *eyes* are and say 'Hi, I'm trying to get your attention!'"

Lachlan purses her lips, hugging a box to her chest. "That is a valid point, and I'll remember that for next time."

I don't know what to say when someone says something reasonable in response to what was, in retrospect, probably an unreasonable outburst. I stand there with my teeth gritted for a few seconds more before I flick my eyes down to the box she's holding. "What is that?"

"Okay, so," she starts, her eyes glittering excitedly as

she holds it out to me. On its front is a painting of a farm under a giant, low-hanging sun with the words *The Settlers of Catan* written within it. "I think we could kill at least half of this seven-and-a-half-hour journey with this."

Seven and a half hours? Good lord. I knew she said we'd be travelling all day, but somehow *all day* sounded better than *seven and a half hours* inside a silver bullet with these assholes.

I bug my eyes out at her box. "I don't know what that is."

"It's the best board game you'll ever play in your life."

"So it involves other people?" I start turning away from her. "I think I'll pass."

"We need one more person, Alis. Come on." She's in front of me again, shaking the box from side to side with this ridiculous grin that makes all the bones and tendons in her neck stand out. "I'll give you extra credit?"

I fight a smile at the look on her face. "I have a 97 in your class."

"98 if you play Catan. Don't tell the others."

I don't know what comes over me. Maybe it's that stupid look on her face, or the lingering lightness from the pink sky. Maybe it's *seven and a half hours* still pulsing like a headache behind my eyes. But I sigh and ask, "Who's playing?"

I've been listening to Lachlan and Craig talk over each other for the past twenty minutes trying to explain this game to me, and I'm so confused that I'd rather they just keep talking if it means I won't have to play.

"—and *these* ones are your main bargaining chips—"

"—but you can also exchange for development cards, which would get you, like—"

"—knight cards, points cards, and other tricky cards that let you steal resources—"

"But you keep those hidden so that no one else knows your game plan, yes? You look confused. Which part are you confused about?"

"I would suggest, at this point, that we just start playing and see if he catches on," Noor says, her elbows on the table and her hands sliding up into her hair. She's staring at the hexagonal board set up between us with a faraway expression in her dark eyes, like she's been hypnotized by the sounds of their voices.

"I think my little brain can handle it," I say, glaring at her. I immediately regret my overconfidence though because I still have no idea what's going on.

At least this train has compartments, so for the next seven hours, it's Craig across from me, Noor next to him, and Lachlan next to me, and we're separated from the rest of the world by a sliding pane of plexiglass.

When I glance at Craig, he's grinning straight at me.

I feel a stir of apprehension. "What?"

"Nothing. I've just never met someone grumpier than Noor."

"I'm not *grumpy*."

"Yes, you are," Lachlan says. She finally shakes the dice and tosses them onto the table.

As the game begins, I find that everyone takes their turn very seriously, which is to say they take fucking forever. They frown at their cards in consideration, bartering them like it's a business transaction, and study the board as if there are secret messages transcribed across its surface. Meanwhile, I do as little as I can get away with, until I roll a seven.

"Ah, *merde*," Lachlan says. She puts a bunch of her resource cards back, and I have no idea why.

"Way to keep your swearing educational, boss," says Craig, and he does the same thing.

They all look at me. My mouth goes dry. Should I ask what I'm supposed to be doing? Or should I pretend to do something constructive and just move on? I put my cold hand on the back of my neck, under my hair. It feels like a furnace back there.

"Are you going to get mad at me if I tell you what you're supposed to do right now?" Noor asks, and I find I have to mentally add in the question mark given the remarkable flatness of her voice.

"No, I'm not going to get *mad* at you," I say. They all stare at me like they're wondering if I can hear how mad I sound. I slouch back in my seat and say, in the way of explanation, "It's fucking hot in here."

Noor picks up the little grey man from the centre of the board. "You have to move the robber from the middle and put it on top of the resource tile for whoever you want to screw over. But try not to screw over yourself in the meantime."

I take the grey man from her and do as she says,

choosing to screw over Lachlan because she made me play this game.

As it goes on, I think I'm getting the hang of it because I start pissing people off with the moves I make, and that makes me feel good. It also means they start screwing me over, too, instead of treating me like a baby, which also feels good.

Craig takes the longest to take his turns. At some point, he pulls off his hoodie, and I notice there are freckles sprinkled over his arms, too, which are way more refined than I remember them ever being. In fact, I don't think I've ever thought about Craig Miltenberg's arms, but he's massaging the back of his neck so that the muscles in his forearm flex, and—

"Alis."

I startle, my eyes snapping to his, and all the blood rushes to my cheeks. "What?"

He puts his arm down, and a grin spreads slowly over his face. "I was asking if you had any sheep you wanted to trade."

Right. I glance down at my cards, then glare at him under my lashes. "I do have sheep, but I'm not giving them to you."

"Fair play," he says. He's still smiling as he rearranges his cards because he definitely knows I was ogling his arm, and I don't know if I want to slap him or myself more.

Later, Lachlan does something foul and builds her settlement right at the end of my road, cutting me off.

I stare down at it, then look up at everyone else. "Is that allowed?"

Craig giggles mischievously. Noor says, "Pretty sure it's allowed."

"Give me the rule book."

"Oh, come on," Lachlan laughs, rolling her head back against the seat. I snatch up the book myself and start scanning it.

"While he's doing that, I'm going to take my turn," Noor says.

I hold up my hand. "Nobody moves."

Lachlan is still laughing at me, and Craig is making a show of banging his forehead rhythmically against the table, but I don't let them break me. The rules are there for a reason.

I don't find what I'm looking for in the book. I throw it down, pull my boot up under me, and wave my arm. "Proceed."

Craig is cracking up with his head on the table. When he pulls back up, he looks almost drunk with that perpetual flush in his cheeks and the way the laugh lingers in his eyes even when it's done. Somehow, when he looks at me, it doesn't go away.

PART II

SWITZERLAND

8

The ground is wet in Interlaken, and everything smells like rain. It's like we're walking through a toy town nestled in the middle of a fantasy world; the lawns we pass are manicured, the houses sleek and undecorated, the hedges trimmed, the trees evenly sized and placed at regular intervals. Yet, rising above nearly every gabled roof is the slope of a hulking blue mountain, its peaks grizzled with snow. I can't stop staring up at them, at their impossible scale and majesty. I feel oddly comforted by them, like something is watching over me, and I'm wondering if this is what it must feel like to believe in God.

As we walk deeper into town, the houses grow into rustic chalets in pastels and rich brown woods, and mountains become textured with fog and towering pines until I feel like I'm standing in a Swiss postcard. We pull up to a honey-coloured lodge with red-shuttered windows, the gravel driveway crunching under our feet.

"Okay! This is it," Lachlan booms over the group. She

leads us to the back of the lodge, where a red canopy stretches out from the back of the building, sheltering picnic benches and a long buffet table. While she and Bilodeau go to check us in, the rest of us sit, and I find a table as far away from my chattering classmates as I can manage. As I swing my bag off, I look up to see Craig and Noor settling down on the bench across from me.

After Lachlan eventually claimed her victory in Catan and Craig swore his revenge on her, she ended up leaving the compartment to check that nothing was on fire. When the door slid shut behind her, Noor said to me, "I doubt anything is on fire, since you're not there."

I stared at her. She stared back at me.

"Was that a joke?" I asked eventually.

"Yes," she said.

Then Craig told us we were fascinating to watch and launched into a story about how he discovered these things called binturongs at the zoo and found they always looked mad at each other, even when they were cuddling.

Later, when we lapsed into a comfortable silence, Noor took out a book of crosswords—I even helped her fill in some of the clues when she asked—and Craig had his arms crossed and his eyes closed, his head swaying with the motion of the train. In passing, I noticed that the slope of his nose was pretty much perfect.

There was this sudden, tingling warmth spreading through my body as I watched them just sitting there, existing in my presence like it didn't bother them at all. I couldn't remember the last time I was in a situation that involved other people where everyone, including me, felt comfortable.

And now, they're here again, willingly sitting with me.

"I am just...starving," Craig says miserably, putting his head down on his crossed arms. I get this intense urge to reach out and pull that yellow eyesore of a beanie off his head, but I manage to control myself.

"She said dinner was pizza," Noor says.

"Yes but *when*," he moans. "*Where.*"

Noor pats his shoulder. "There, there."

He might be starving; meanwhile, I'm sweltering. The post-rain humidity has my hair clinging to every inch of skin it can find, and Noor's hair is frizzier than I've ever seen it. I'm almost considering pulling off my sweater and just chancing it with the long-sleeved shirt I'm wearing underneath, but I always feel uncomfortably exposed with just that thin layer over my arms, like people can see the texture of the scars through the fabric.

I decide to pull my hair out from where it's trapped beneath my headphones and start gathering it up. But as I'm twisting it into a bun, looking at the wood grain of the table, I get this niggling feeling.

I glance up just in time to see Craig look very quickly away from me and start randomly patting Noor's hand on the table. Then he looks back at me and smiles politely like he hadn't already been looking at me.

I feel a prickle of self-consciousness, wondering if the humidity has also ruined my eyeliner. I start rolling a hair tie out of my sleeve, but now I'm off my game, and I pull too hard, and it snaps. It flies, and Craig ducks just in time.

I freeze up. I watch him pull himself back up, his eyes wide and his mouth hanging open.

"I just saw my life flash before my eyes," he says. He looks around himself, then reaches down and picks up the broken elastic from the ground, holding it up for us to see.

"Good thing you still have your eyes," Noor says. Then she pulls a hair tie off her own wrist and holds it out to me.

I stare down at it. A bird trills loudly overhead.

"I don't have lice," Noor says. "Or cooties."

My brain unfreezes, and I take it quickly from her. "No—yes. Thank you."

She squints at me as I finish tying my hair. I look like a jackass now, but it's just that it's been a long time since someone offered me something.

Well, except for the rose guys in Paris, but I don't think Noor wants my money.

Then I remember how I almost blinded Craig, and I sink a little on the bench as I look at him. "Sorry."

"No, it's cool," he says, smiling. "I liked the adrenaline rush."

Lachlan and Bilodeau come back then, and they give us all our keycards and tell us where to find dinner. As we get up from our picnic tables and start filing into the hostel, I notice that Craig is still rolling that broken elastic between his fingers.

My room on the top floor of the lodge reminds me a bit of the sauna my dad had built in our pool house and never used: slanted roof, wood panels on all sides and smelling overwhelmingly of cedar. Except, unlike the sauna, this room also contains Eric Tulson, who appears to be trying and failing to open the skylight embedded in the middle of the roof.

"Oh, it's my favourite boy!" he exclaims when he sees me. He frowns, dropping his arms. "Girl? Boy? Sorry, I get confused because of the…everything."

Honestly, this kind of shit stopped bothering me a long time ago, when I realized I didn't really care whether I looked like a boy or a girl or both or neither. But I am in a decently good mood for once, and I'm pissed that he's trying to ruin it, so I say: "Maybe it's your feelings that are confused. I'd offer to make out with you to find out, but I think I'd just puke in your mouth."

The fake cheer vanishes from his voice, and he jerks his chin at me. "Try something with me, and I'll knock your head off your toothpick neck."

I don't think he quite understood my insult, but that's not surprising, given the inside of his head probably looks a lot like a sauna as well: bare wood walls and a whole lot of vapour.

As I make my way to a bunk against the other wall, I think I hear him start to say something else, but the door opens, and I turn to see Connor coming in with two other boys—neither of which is Theo.

I feel a bit of the tension in my shoulders release.

Three weeks ago, I would've been far more concerned about sharing a room with Eric than Theo, but that was before that day in front of Jordan's burnt-down house.

It had been over a week since the party, since the fire that followed it, and I figured I'd go take a look at the damage I'd supposedly wrought in case anyone got the courage to ask me about it.

It was harder than I thought it would be. For most of my life, that house had been more of a home to me than my parents' house, and though I knew I never would have set foot in it again after that party, I still wished it had been mine that caught fire instead. My house is this huge, high-ceilinged void with white and grey walls and fluorescent lights. The decorations are minimal and tasteful, the cupboards full of chemicals and suitcases, and it only ever smells like air conditioning or floor cleaner or both. And *everything* echoes. Everything.

But Jordan's house was always full to the brim with decades of stuff. If you needed something, they would have it. Every room had a hand-knitted blanket, and even though they smelt like cigarettes, I didn't really mind. The ceilings were low, so nothing echoed, and the bulbs in the lamps were yellow and buttery. The volume was always up on the TV or the stereo, there was craft stuff strewn over the dinner table, and you were constantly stepping over piles of photo albums or boxes of old clothes and toys.

When I visited that day, all that was left of the house was a husk—the blackened outline of a window here, the charred bones of a wall there, the rest of it just a landfill of pulp and wood and curling black paper.

This is the last time you'll ever see this house, I thought. I stood there until that thought stopped hurting so much, and I was just ready to go when I heard a car door slam.

I looked over my shoulder at the Mercedes Benz parked on the other side of the street. Theo was walking out of it toward me, because of course he was. I felt this sense of hysteria building like a laugh in my chest. I really had to start clueing into the fact that I was a very unlucky person.

"Funny," Theo said. "I didn't know you lived around here."

He stopped on the sidewalk next to me and looked up at the house. It was spitting rain, and the drops clung to the wool of his peacoat like dew.

"Funny," I said. "I thought it was a free country."

His hands slid into his pockets as he looked at me, his expression carefully neutral. "Just going for a stroll, then."

"No, I came to look at the house. You?"

He jerked his chin toward the memorial on the chainlink fence dedicated to Sir Elton John. I had been trying very hard not to look at it. "Taking it down. Jordan couldn't stomach it."

"Right," I said. "Well, good luck."

I turned to leave, but his hand caught me by the forearm, and though it was firm enough to stop me, it wasn't very hard either. When he spoke, his voice was light and curious. "Why do you never deny it?"

I tried to wrench my arm out of his grip, and that was when it tightened. He yanked me toward him, embarrassingly easily, so that I was pulling my arm in against my chest and he wasn't moving an inch.

"No, really," he said, and a piece of damp hair fell over

his forehead, shaking a little. "Does it get you off or something? Being a big bad arsonist?"

"Would you fucking let go of me?" I was trying very hard not to sound as scared as I was, but there was just something about him in that moment that struck me as deeply wrong in a way that not even Eric could touch. I watched him look down at his hand where it was wrapped around my arm, and when he glanced up from under his lashes, it was like someone had thrown a dark veil over his eyes.

"Jordan told me that you look like you've been through a paper shredder," he said. "Is that true?"

Sometimes, when I would cut myself, there would be a slash so quick and vicious that, for a second, I couldn't feel it. There'd be a white line on the skin, barely perceptible, and I'd stare at it and wonder if I'd pressed hard enough.

Then, all at once, there'd be this fierce, prickling burning and the blood would fill the line with red, growing thicker and thicker.

That was how I felt—like a machete had swiped down from my sternum, so sharp and efficient that, at first, it was like the stroke of a butterfly's wings. And then the pain came, and it nearly knocked my legs out from under me.

Theo cocked his head, his eyes darting across my face. "From your reaction just now, I'm going to say yes."

All I could think was, of course she told him that. Of course she did. The thing about Jordan was that I could never figure out if I did something to make her hate me or if I just didn't do enough to make her love me. Either way, I didn't know why I continued to be surprised when she hurt me. It was all she did lately.

I was so rocked by this that Theo managed to put his other hand on my arm and start pushing my sleeve up, and only then did I slam back to earth with a cold, lurching terror. I wrenched away from him, stumbling back with the momentum as he let go of me. I could see from the smirk sliding onto his face that he got exactly what he wanted.

My whole body was ice cold as I started walking away as fast as I could without running. I had at some point entered that strange and terrifying dream state, and I don't remember now what happened in it, except for Theo's voice from far away: "Don't *fucking* come back here!"

I knew I wouldn't. Someone could hold a gun to my head, and still, I wouldn't go back there again.

9

When I get outside, the sky is turning a soft periwinkle, and the humidity has been wiped away by a breeze. Some of my classmates are filing out of the tiny pizzeria next to the hostel with boxes of pizza, bringing them over to the picnic tables at the back of the lodge.

Unfortunately for my growling stomach, food is going to have to wait. I checked my pockets for my lighter earlier—not to use it, but just to know it was there—and came up empty. I have no idea where it ended up, but I can't do anything else before I find a replacement.

I'm standing outside the front door of the lodge, looking up nearby stores, when I hear a light scuffling. A pair of shoes enters my frame of vision: dirty white canvas sneakers with a pen drawing on the toe of two stick figures in a sword fight.

"Hi. I'm trying to get your attention."

I look up to see Noor standing before me with her hair

in a vestigial ponytail, most of it still falling in layers around her face. In response to my frown, she says: "Yes, I saw that whole exchange at the train station."

"Oh. Well, thank you for not tapping me on the shoulder."

"I also hate people touching me without my permission. Only Craig and my parents get to touch me."

"Noted." I'm trying to stop frowning at her, but she still hasn't told me why she wants my attention.

Her eyes flick down to my phone. "Are you googling grocery stores because you don't like pizza?"

"Yes," I lie.

"Well, I don't like cheese, and they don't have any without, so I'll come with you."

"Where's Craig?"

"He already ate an entire pizza."

"No, I mean..." I wave my hand as if to indicate his absence.

Her eyes narrow. "I have been known to survive without him."

"That's not what I meant." I think that is what I meant, except I was wondering more about how Craig is surviving without *her*.

She gestures toward the road. "Lead the way, then."

So, I guess this is happening. I choose the nearest store that I think should have what I'm looking for and start following the blue dotted line on my phone. At least if Lachlan tries to chew me out for wandering off, I can throw the buddy system in her face.

The walk is quiet but surprisingly not uncomfortable. I

think we're both admiring the way those hulking mountains are turning dark and shadowy and how there's barely any sound except for the birds, the occasional passing car, and the dripping of raindrops from overhanging eaves.

When we come upon the glowing yellow sign for a place called Lidl—which is actually not little at all, but a large supermarket—Noor says, "By the way: 'Golf legend Sam.'"

"Snead," I say automatically.

She pulls the crossword book out of her back pocket, opens it up to the dog ear, and pencils it in. "Weird that you know that."

I kick a pebble across the parking lot. "My dad's annoying about golf."

In fact, I think him trying to get me into golf when I was little was his last-ditch effort to bond with his evidently queer child, and when I didn't take to it, he gave up.

"You're telling me you have a golf dad," Noor says.

"Yes."

"Like wears polos and visors and hangs out with twats."

"Yes."

"So, a big influence on you, then."

This makes me snort a laugh, which is so shocking to me that I stop walking. She grabs one of the carts by the front door and looks at me over her shoulder, waiting. She's probably thinking about how weird I was with the hair tie, too, and she's rethinking her decision to be alone with me.

I clear my throat and keep walking, falling into step

beside her. We enter the automatic sliding doors into Lidl, which has that familiar fresh grocery store smell and is playing Matchbox Twenty overhead. I almost feel like I've been transported back home.

"What do... your parents?" I wave my arm as if that will help me form proper words. "Like, what do they do?"

Noor puts her foot on the back of her cart and kicks off, riding it down the produce aisle. "My mom is a secretary, and my dad works at that nursing home just down from the school."

"Oh, I did my volunteer hours there," I say.

I enjoyed it there, actually. I liked it when the old people would mistake me for someone they love. At first I would correct them because it felt wrong to pretend somehow, like I was deceiving them, but I didn't like how that made their eyes dim. They just looked so happy to see me, so I started to let them kiss me on the cheek and call me Richie or Taylor or "my baby." Not that I would ever tell anyone this, ever, but there was once this tiny old woman that kept telling me her dead daughter had hair just like mine, and one shift, I sat in front of her and let her run her fingers through it over and over until I almost fell asleep.

Noor says, "Yes, I remember my dad asking me if I know that '*Addam's Family*-looking kid' from school."

I snort. "Are you fucking with me?"

"No. He's the head nurse—big, balding Iranian guy. His name's Shakir." She takes an apple off the shelf next to her, looks at it, then puts it back. "In case you didn't hear the many tired Shakira jokes Eric was making for months after he found that out."

I feel a jolt of surprise, both at her random honesty and the fact that Eric went after her at all. "I didn't know he messed with you."

She gives me a flat look. "He messes with everyone."

For a moment, I actually feel comforted in this knowledge, before I realize how gross that is and the acidic, leech-like thing in my stomach starts squirming around again.

Which reminds me, I'm supposed to be looking for lighters.

When Noor rides her cart into an aisle muttering about ramen, I tell her I'll be right back, and I go looking. Everywhere. And all I find are barbecue lighters, which I know from experience don't work the same way.

I feel my hands getting clammy. Noor's going to know I'm doing something sketchy if I tell her we have to go somewhere else, and it's getting late. I don't think the shops are going to be open for much longer.

I think I'm on the verge of full-blown panic in the craft aisle when I finally see it: a folding utility knife. It comes with a case and extra blades.

I stare at it for a long time.

I haven't done it like that in a while, and the thought of it makes me a bit queasy.

But it's just in case. I don't need to use it. I just need to know I have it.

"I found ramen." My head whips toward Noor at the end of the aisle. Her eyes slide from me to the shelves I'm looking at. "Unless you're planning on guzzling crazy glue."

I shake my head. "No. I'm looking for... I was looking for an adapter."

I grab one off the wall and hold it up. It's definitely not for a North American plug type, but hopefully she doesn't notice.

"Well, I got a lot." Her four cups of ramen in that giant cart look ridiculous. I think she just took it so she could ride it around. "We should go before Craig starts thinking I got kidnapped by a lumberjack."

I nod and hope I don't look as guilty as I feel. I end up following her to the self-checkout and only realize after she's paid that she bought ramen for me, which brings on a fresh pang of guilt. I've been too distracted waiting for my opportunity to say: "I forgot something. I'll meet you outside?"

I'm already backing up, but she's narrowing her eyes at me, so I add: "Do you want anything else?"

"No, just—hurry up," she says, her gaze lingering before she moves toward the door. I go back to get the folding knife and grab some granola bars so if she asks me what I forgot, I have something to show her. I double-bag all of it before meeting her back outside.

As we walk back to the hostel, she doesn't ask me what's in the bag. We talk more than we had on the walk there, and I find myself laughing more than once at the wry humour that I never in a million years thought she possessed. Eventually, I stop thinking about the knife and instead think about how, in some parallel universe, maybe she and I could have been friends.

10

"You missed a time last night," Craig says, sitting down across from me at a picnic table with the most overloaded plate of breakfast I have ever seen. He brings his fists down on either side of it, fingers curled around cutlery.

"Did I?" I hold up a hand against the morning sun bouncing off his butter knife and hitting me in the eye. "That's a bummer."

We were informed last night that the hostel has its own private club in an old bomb shelter just behind the lodge, and our teachers rented it out for us for a few hours so we could blast music and hang out. When Craig started begging me to come for some reason, I told him I would rather drink gasoline.

"But you like music and darkness, though," he said.

"I like my own music and the darkness of the back of my eyelids," I corrected him.

I wasn't about to tell him the whole truth, which was

that I could never attend anything that remotely feels like a party, ever again. Especially with those people.

Craig notices he's blinding me and lowers his butter knife with a little *oh.* He clears his throat and starts cutting into a mini croissant. "Do you know how drunk Eric got? My Uncle Perry fell asleep in the middle of the dance floor at my Bar Mitzvah because he was so drunk, and I think Eric was drunker than that."

Actually, I do know how drunk Eric got because I was woken up at two in the morning to Connor and Mr. Kepler helping him into our room, where he rolled facedown onto his bed and fell asleep. Connor, who was pissing himself laughing, was telling the rest of the room that Eric told Bilodeau that he had "acute colonitis" and had to go to the bathroom every five minutes. So he would go to the bathroom, chug something from his stash, and come back drunker every time.

"I'm really happy for Eric," I say. Really, I'm very happy that he was so far gone that he didn't draw a penis on my face or try to smother me with a pillow last night. Let's hope he does the same tonight.

"He is in deep doo-doo. Lachlan took the night off, but when she finds out..." He shakes his head, tutting disapprovingly.

Did he just say *doo-doo*? Also, is he putting jam and cheese on the same fucking croissant?

"You're coming tonight, yes?" he asks before taking a large bite of it.

I'm about to say the gasoline thing again before I remember I already used that one. I pluck a cheese cube from his plate and show it to him. "I'd rather choke on this."

He swallows his food. "Can you actually put that in your mouth, though? I swear you don't eat."

Thankfully, I don't have to dignify this with a response because the smell of vanilla perfume hits my nose, and Noor slumps down on the seat next to me with a bowl of yogurt.

Craig brandishes his fork at her. "Noor, tell Alis he missed a time last night."

She squints thoughtfully at her breakfast before looking at me. "I'd say that's accurate. Not a good time, not a bad time. Just a time."

"*Noor*. How could you—"

He's cut off by Lachlan's voice booming over us from where she's standing near the back door of the lodge with the other teachers.

"So, this morning," she begins, and then raises her Rainbow Tablet in the air and waits for the chatter to die down. "This morning, those of you who have opted for paragliding will come with me. Those who want to go up to the Schynige Platte, you'll be with Mr. Bilodeau. Then whoever wants to climb Harder Kulm will go with Mr. Kepler."

Craig raises his hand but doesn't wait to be called on. "Can I do Easier Kulm, please? I've got a bad knee."

Noor snorts. Someone boos his lame joke, and there are a few giggles among my classmates. Craig grins as he leans back in his chair, looking proud of himself.

Mr. Kepler, however, is not amused. He pierces him

with his ice-chip eyes. "You're wasting our time, Mr. Miltenberg."

Craig bows his head, holding up a hand in apology. I stick my tongue in my cheek to hide the stubborn smile on my lips; not because of his dumb joke, but just because it's nice to see someone else getting on Kepler's nerves.

When the teachers finish their spieling, Lachlan comes over to our table. She's wearing a gold fanny pack that sparkles violently in the sun, blinding me for the second time today.

"Craig, a moment, please?" I'm too busy shielding my eyes to look up at her face, but she doesn't sound particularly mad. She also doesn't sound particularly happy.

Craig makes his yikes face at me, then gets up to follow her down the gravel driveway. I look at Noor to see if she's smirking or something, but she's squinting suspiciously after them.

"So, you don't know what that's about?" I ask.

She shakes her head. She starts shovelling yogurt into her mouth, staring over my shoulder at the spot where Craig disappeared. I swear they have codependency issues.

When he returns a few minutes later, to my absolute shock, he is no longer wearing his hat. Instead, it's in his hands, and when he slumps back down in his seat, he starts fidgeting with it on the table. His hair is ridiculously thick, and the morning light is bringing out the red in it. It's like a genuine auburn, which I didn't think was possible outside of a box, but I doubt he dyes it considering he hides it under that abominable beanie all day long. It's all sad and misshapen, and the urge to reach out and fix it has me clenching the side of the table.

"What was that?" Noor asks.

When he looks up, he gives us what appears to be a forced smile. It's something I've never seen on him before, and it's just as surreal to look at as his nightmare had been. "That was nothing."

I squint at him. "So, she just brought you over there, said nothing, then brought you back."

"Sus," Noor agrees.

His eyes flick between us. The forced smile almost looks angry now, making his nostrils flare a bit. "Okay, fine. She told me I was getting too cheeky with authority. She actually used that word. Who says that?"

I don't buy that for one second, not only because Craig has never been too cheeky for Lachlan, but also because he is apparently a terrible liar. I have my mouth open to call him on it when I glance at Noor. She's looking at him with concern until he meets her eyes, and her face smooths out as if she's come to an understanding. She glances at me very quickly, then occupies herself with her yogurt.

That's when I know they have some kind of secret, and I'm not supposed to know it. I become painfully aware that I've been hanging around them for barely three days while they've known each other for years. It's not like I blame them for wanting to keep stuff from me. But I do feel a wall come up, and with it, a searing embarrassment for having gotten so carried away.

Still. At least now I know what Craig looks like when he lies.

<h1 style="text-align:center">11</h1>

I spent most of the excursion to Harder Kulm hanging over the viewpoint railing, trying to force a pink sky moment.

It was a bust.

I didn't really understand why—the whole hike up, I was catching tantalizing flashes of cerulean river and smokey blue mountain range through the trees, and I thought for sure the view at the top was going to snap me out of the fog that was swallowing me.

Instead, as I squinted at the hazy peaks of the Alps and the roofs of Interlaken spattered over the valley below, I thought about how twisted and wrecked my body would be if I fell from that height. I thought maybe I could wake myself up by leaning over as far as I could, looking down the lengths of my hair at the brush of trees along the cliff face, but my stomach didn't even do that rollercoaster swooping thing it should do. Then Kepler started giving me shit ("Do those look like monkey bars, Alistair?"), and I was corralled into a panoramic restaurant with the handful of classmates I was stuck with, where I spent another lunch in silence.

Now it's nearing evening, and I'm back at the lodge in the little rec room off the lobby. Bambi Eyes had been playing a nice song on the console piano until I arrived, at which point the music cut off with a discordant key smash, and he scurried out of the room as I flopped down on one of the couches.

I decide to put my headphones on and try my brain-numbing ritual, which is when I listen to a song as loud as I can on repeat until my ears are humming and my head feels like mush. I choose *40 Days* by Slowdive and think about how satisfying it would be if I could listen to it forty times over without interruption.

I'm only on the tenth listen when fingers start wiggling over my eyes, obstructing the gun-shaped water stain I'd been staring at on the ceiling. I follow them to see Craig standing over me, holding a grocery bag.

Noor told me on our walk back from Lidl that she and Craig had opted to go paragliding today, and I'm glad to see he didn't plunge to his death.

Then I feel a little twinge of anxiety when I notice he's alone.

"Where's Noor?" I ask, sliding my headphones down.

He furrows his eyebrows at me. "Hello to you, too."

"Did she fall?"

"She didn't *fall*. She's gathering reinforcements. We're taking over this room because Eric ruined bomb shelter privileges for all of us, so thank you, Eric!"

He shouts this last part toward the open door. Then he sits down on the floor in front of me and starts sorting through the plastic bag in his lap. "It's too bad you didn't come. You would've had fun flying around in your spiky boots."

I barely hear what he says to me—I'm noticing how close his face is to mine; I can almost count the eyelashes fanning over his freckled cheeks, fluttering as he reads the labels on his food, and I feel a little thrill in my stomach.

Then he meets my eyes, holding a sandwich on either side of his face, and I feel the heat rushing up my neck like I've been caught. "I hope you're not a vegetarian because they only had *pouletschnitzel* and *thunfischsalat*."

I blink. See, I don't speak German, but to my ears, that sounded like perfect German. "They only had what and what?"

He brings his face a millimetre closer to mine, raising his eyebrows. "You pronounce it correctly, or you don't pronounce it at all."

I must be really starved for human connection after not speaking a word to anyone since breakfast because I find all of this—his proximity, his lowered voice, the German, the way he seems to be in a bit of a bad mood—to be incredibly alluring. Then I hallucinate his eyes darting to my lips and back up again, and I know my mind is taking me to dangerous places, so I sit up.

"Finally," Craig says, moving to stand. "I thought you were going to make me sit down there forever."

"There's a whole other couch over there."

He ignores this and sits next to me, tossing a sandwich in my lap. I mumble a thanks, even though I have no idea why he's brought me food when I didn't ask for anything.

He starts unwrapping his own sandwich and is about to take a bite when he notices me and stops.

"Why are you making that face?"

I didn't mean to make a face, but my nose must have wrinkled automatically. "I can never understand people who eat mustard. It tastes how body odour smells."

Craig stares at me for three seconds before he cracks up. I think it's just going to be a snort, but it splits into a laugh. Like one of those high-pitched, eye-crinkling laughs that you can't fake.

"Why do I—" he cuts off, hiccuping. "Like, I get what you're saying, so now I don't get why I *like* it."

"Because you're disgusting." This sets him off again, and I continue through his laughter, "You were putting cheese and jam on the same croissant this morning."

He drops his sandwich in his lap and puts his face in his hands, his shoulders shaking.

"Oh, man," he says once he's recovered. "It's not even that funny, but your *delivery*. God—" He puts his thumb and index finger together in approval, then shakes his head and tears into his sandwich, still giggling around his mouthful.

Apparently, he's not in as much of a bad mood as I thought, though I'm still thinking about that fake smile he gave us at breakfast this morning and wondering what that was all about.

Just as I think about asking him, Noor enters the room,

and every good feeling I'd had a second ago goes *splat* when I see who she's brought with her.

They come to a stop in front of us.

"Alis, Dakota. Dakota, Alis," Noor says, as if we haven't shared a school for the past four years.

I do notice Dakota Mitchell's done something different to her hair since that day in the hallway. Before, she was straightening it, but now it's a neat little afro with purple barrettes at the sides, and she looks different enough that I think maybe I can pretend she's another person until she smiles politely at me and says, "Hi, Alis."

Then I'm back in the hallway, and she's coming up to me with her fidgeting fingers. *I just wanted to say, if you want to talk about what happened—*

Who the fuck are you? Leave me alone.

"Hi," I say, my mouth as dry as a desert. I can't look at her anymore, so I flick my eyes to the other Mitchell twin standing just behind her, and Noor introduces us, too.

I don't know much about Drew Mitchell except that he constantly looks like an Urban Outfitters threw up on him. He's wearing an oversized purple t-shirt over slime green pants, and there are four necklaces of varying sizes dripping down his front. Though I will admit that the swirling design shaved into the undercut on either side of his head is very cool.

Drew jerks his chin toward my chest. "Is your jacket Vanson?"

I narrow my eyes, feeling both surprised that he would know that and apprehensive that he would bring it up. "Yes."

He pushes out his lip in approval. "Nice."

And that's it. A very awkward silence falls where maybe I'm supposed to say thank you, but I'm still not convinced that what just happened actually happened in the way that it looked like it happened.

Thankfully, Craig breaks the silence, and soon everyone is scattered around the room with their dinner—Noor and Drew on the opposite couch, Dakota on the piano bench. I've started nibbling at the sandwich Craig gave me, and it's not as gooey and tasteless as I'm used to.

"Since we're all getting to know each other," Drew says, "I think we should play Never Have I Ever."

"Uh, we don't have drinks," Dakota says.

"We'll just do the finger version."

I don't know what this game is, but the *finger version* sounds unappealing.

"I think it's a fantastic idea," Craig says, then looks at me. "Are you in?"

"I don't know what it is," I say.

Drew frowns. "Do you live under a rock?"

I shoot him a glare just as Craig starts explaining the game to me as enthusiastically as he did with Settlers of Catan. "So basically, when it's your turn, you say something you've never done, and then if other people in the circle *have* done it, they put a finger down, like this. As a peaceful example, I could say: never have I ever gone to Switzerland with my twin. And then Dakota and Drew would both put their fingers down because they are twins in Switzerland together."

"We're not twins," Dakota says, her frown mirroring

Drew's. And I must be mirroring the confused look on Craig's face because they've been the Mitchell twins in my head for the last four years. I swear there was one time in ninth grade when it was *their* birthday.

"What do you mean you're not twins?" Craig asks.

"He's a year older than me. He just failed kindergarten."

"Screw you, I didn't *fail* kindergarten," Drew says. "They held me back because I was born—"

"Born in December, yes. Keep telling yourself that."

Craig is still frowning like someone told him Santa Claus doesn't exist. I raise my eyebrows at Drew. "You know that everyone calls you the Mitchell twins, right?"

It's Dakota who answers despite me steadfastly avoiding her eyes. "I mean, okay. But we're not."

I watch as they both pop potato chips into their mouths and start chewing in tandem. I have to wonder if their parents are lying to them.

Noor raises her hand. "I knew they weren't twins."

I know I should probably drop it, but it's bugging me for some reason. "Did anyone even ask you guys? Or do they just assume?"

Drew makes a thoughtful face. "I think I've heard a few people say it, but I just didn't bother to say anything."

"Why?"

"I don't know. You don't deny starting that fire, even though that's obviously not true."

My heart drops to my stomach, and I feel my hands go clammy.

"That's actually the perfect place to start," Craig says. He clears his throat and sits up straighter, putting up all ten of his fingers. "Never have I ever burnt someone's house down."

The rest of them all look at me and hold up their hands.

I swallow, hoping I sound way more nonchalant than I feel when I say, "This is extremely stupid."

"Nope," says Craig, shaking his head. "No, it's not. It's your chance to clear your name once and for all."

"Can I just say?" Drew cuts in, tilting his thumb between him and his sister. "We don't think you did it. Mostly because there's no way you did it and they wrote it off as an accident. It's actually a really hard thing to make arson look like an accident. Fire investigators train for like—"

"Drew, this is one of those subjects you know too much about, so you should stop before you make people uncomfortable," Dakota says.

He makes a face and shoots her the finger. Dakota ignores him, looking at me. "It's true you haven't denied it, though. And Kristy said you were being weird with a lighter at the fondue restaurant."

I make a frustrated noise. "Who cares? Theo believes it, so everyone else does, too."

"So you didn't do it."

"Dude, if you didn't do it—"

"*No*, okay? I didn't start any fucking fires. Are you happy now?"

I direct this last part at Craig, and he at least has the

grace to keep the smile off his face. "Depends. Do you feel better?"

I don't feel better—I feel like I've been ambushed. There's a cold prickling under my skin as I look at the Mitchells, and I'm certain everything's about to change. Now that the fire has gone out and they're no longer afraid of me, they're going to see me flayed down to the bone, and all I'll be is that pitiful excuse for a person that Jordan turned me into at that party.

But before I can answer, Noor says, "To be clear, you would not, at this point, put a finger down."

And Drew adds, "Also, it's your turn."

My pulse is thumping heavily in my neck as I slide my eyes toward Dakota. She's digging through her bag and pulling out a sack of baby carrots like nothing at all happened. She takes a bite of one and looks at me expectantly, raising her free hand.

Finally, I clear my throat and hold up my own hands. "Fine. Never have I ever killed anyone's cat."

Dakota tips her head to the side in consideration. "I mean, that's good, but you do actually have to say things that someone might have done."

"What, is he the only one capable of being a cold-blooded cat killer?" asks Craig, hooking a thumb toward me and looking genuinely offended. "Bit rude, Dakota."

Dakota makes a sound of protest around a bite of carrot, furrowing her brow defensively.

"I've killed a goldfish," Noor chimes in. "By accident, but still my fault."

"I think that counts," Craig says. "Goldfish are the cats of the fish world."

"Pretty sure that'd be catfish, bro," says Drew.

As the game goes on, it doesn't get any less ridiculous, but there are no further uncomfortable questions. No one looks at me sideways, and nothing blows up, and it's as if these weights that have been hanging off my shoulders are being slowly cut off, one by one, until I feel like I could float away.

I'm back up in that slanted wood room, sitting on my bed with Craig's forest green hoodie in my lap. He left it on the back of the couch in the rec room, so I took it up with the intention of giving it back to him tomorrow. Now I'm staring down at it and feeling like an utter creep for how badly I want to smell it. I keep trying to justify it, and none of my justifications are making me feel any less creepy.

There was a point tonight when Craig was monologuing about the difference between latkes and potato pancakes, and I looked at everyone watching him with their eyes sparkling and their mouths beaming and wondered what it must feel like to have people look at you like that. I thought if I stepped into Craig's shoes, they'd eject me so fast and so hard, I'd end up a splatter on the side of the moon.

At some point, he may come to his senses about hanging around me, seeing how he's spoilt for choice. I could wake up tomorrow and give this sweater back to him, and he could never speak to me again after that. I will have missed my chance to know what a person like that smells like.

Only when my heart starts hammering like I'm about to commit a bank robbery do I finally roll my eyes at myself and shove my face into the sweater.

Mingled with the musky smell of boy and sweat is cut grass—maybe from a day in the mountains—and an older, deeper smell, like it's been in a cedar chest among piles of old quilts. I close my eyes, and I'm seeing warm lamp light and overflowing saucepans and shelves crowded with knick-knacks and picture frames. I'm seeing the flash of a laughing smile and squeezing arms and a smattering of freckles. All the while, there's this clanging in my heart, and it hurts like mourning.

Sometimes, when I left Jordan's house, I would steal a shirt or sweater of hers from her bedroom and take it home with me. My parents didn't mind me going over there once in a while, so long as all of my schoolwork was done and up to Woodson standards. If I was at Jordan's, it meant they didn't have to deal with the sound of my voice, and they've always been huge fans of silence. My mom never watches TV but sits at the kitchen table working on case files or typing miles a minute on her laptop, the clacking seemingly the only sound she can tolerate. If my dad is home, he's either reading in the armchair or watching the TV on mute so as to not bug my mom.

Jordan and I learned pretty early on in our friendship that hangouts at my house would never work—not when we had to be quiet as church mice, and we could never make a mess, and there was this constant tension in that godawful silence, like it could shatter at any moment. I could tell by her face that being there made her uncomfortable, and it embarrassed me enough that I started to insist, always, that we go to hers.

When her house became my favourite place in the world, that's when I started to get this anxiety every time I left, like I might never be back. Under my parents' roof, if I lied about not having homework, or talked back, or did whatever I did that my mom decided she could no longer tolerate, I'd be on house arrest. Depending on the severity of the crime, this could last for weeks, and their fancy surveillance cameras all throughout the house meant I could never escape it. The one time I did sneak away to Jordan's when I was twelve, I tried to lie to my mom by telling her I'd actually been in one of the washrooms—the only places without cameras—for five hours straight. She slapped me so hard across the face that I was blinking away stars, and then she took away my phone, and my freedom, for a month.

So because I knew there might come a time when I'd only ever be able to see her at school, I started stealing pieces of Jordan's clothing from her room, always smuggling a new one when the smell faded from the others. I felt a bit bad when she accused her mom of throwing away her stuff, but whenever I thought about coming clean, the thing in my stomach would start splashing acid everywhere. Plus, the thought of having to stop, of not having something to bury my face in on the really bad nights when I just needed to be somewhere else, was unbearable.

And now the squirming thing is seeing me with my nose in Craig's sweater, and it's beginning to wake up again. I can't blame it—this is beyond pathetic—but, *God,* it smells good. I kind of want to put it on, but he's going to smell me on it if I do, and I don't think my smell is as nice as this.

Instead, I drape it over the railing at the foot of the bed before putting my headphones on blast. And if in the middle of the night, when I feel more daring, I decide to take it up again, I'll only allow myself to smell it in little doses.

12

In the morning, I find Craig stretched out on that same couch in the rec room with his ankles crossed, playing Sudoku on his phone. This is so attractive to me for some reason that I want to take a picture of it. But then I notice he's wearing green sweats that are the same colour as the sweater I'm holding, which makes me think it might be part of a set, and maybe he's been looking for it.

I feel very nervous suddenly, so I look to the opposite couch, where Drew jerks his chin at me in greeting before returning to his phone, and Lachlan perches on the arm next to him, tapping on her Rainbow Tablet. Last night, she told us to meet down here at 5:30 a.m. if we wanted to see a lake in Unterseen, and I sure as hell didn't come to Europe to sleep. I also had high hopes that most of my classmates would opt to stay in bed, and judging by this poor turnout, my dreams are coming true.

"Morning," Lachlan says, glancing up at me. "We're

waiting a couple more minutes, then we're gonna head out. Do you want a breakfast bar?"

I shake my head. Craig hangs his head back over the arm of the couch to look upside down at me. Then his face twitches into a frown, and he sits up. "Is that my sweater?"

"Hm?" I say, though I heard him perfectly well. I look down at the bundle in my arm, then extend it to him. "Oh. Yes. You left it—yesterday. On the thing."

That was really eloquently said. Craig is giving me this slow smile that makes me think he's thinking the same thing.

"Thanks," he says, taking the sweater from me. "I was looking for it."

Just as I'm seriously considering going back to bed, I hear familiar laughter behind me that makes me feel like my skin is on all wrong. I spin around, praying it's not her, that it's just a giant grey parrot imitating her voice.

But no, there she is. It's Maya. I didn't think she had non-Halfwit friends, but soon-to-be valedictorian Bianca Fellini is standing at her side, and it looks like she's there of her own free will.

The worst thing about Maya is that she doesn't even have to say anything to me—it's all in her eyes. They're always swimming with this unsettling cocktail of amusement and scorn when they look at me so that I find myself suppressing the urge to glance down at myself to make sure my clothes haven't fallen off. When she meets my gaze now, she does it like she has every shameful thing about me on the tip of her tongue and is just waiting for the right moment to let them fly.

"You guys know it's like ten degrees out, right?" Drew says, looking pointedly at the wispy kaftan Bianca is wearing over her bikini, then at Maya's bare legs and flip flops.

"So?" Maya says. "We're going polar dipping."

"It's very good for you," Bianca adds. "And it's a natural high."

"I'll stick to getting *un*naturally high, thanks," Drew says, to which Lachlan tells him to at least pretend to care that she's an authority figure.

Only one other kid shows up after that, and Drew greets him with one of those bro handshakes that all bros seem to know by heart. Then we start heading out, and I ask Craig, "Is Noor not coming?"

He widens his eyes at me. "God, no. She's homicidal this early in the morning."

I'm surprised at how bummed I am about this. But it doesn't last for long because as soon as we step out the door, I know I'm going to have a good day.

It rained last night, and the smell of wet wood and wildflowers is so sharp it clears the fog right out of my head. The sky is a dusky blue except for the spot between the two mountains bordering the hostel, where I can see an orange burn at the horizon. There is no sound but birds and gravel crunching underfoot.

It feels even colder than ten degrees despite my jacket, and Craig shrugs on his sweater next to me. He doesn't zip it up, which is good because that would make him look like a giant cucumber.

"You know what this reminds me of?" Craig says,

shoving his hands into the pockets as we start following Lachlan down the drive. "Algonquin Park. You ever been?"

I shake my head. "I've always wanted to."

"What about just camping in general?"

I shake my head again, and he widens his eyes at me. "Seriously? Okay, there is *nothing* better than waking up at five in the morning while you're camping because no one is up at five, and everything still smells like last night's bonfire, which is the best smell in the world. So it's just you and the birds and—actually, I once saw a momma moose and a baby moose come out of the woods right in front of me, and I swear she looked me right in the eyes to make sure I wasn't going to murder her kid. Then she actually *nodded* at me before walking past me down toward the lake. Did you know they can swim? Really fast. I followed them, and their antlers were already halfway to the island."

I actually believe that a moose would nod at Craig. I don't say anything, though, because it feels like he wants to keep talking, and I want him to keep talking.

"But the best thing is the coffee." He squares his hands in front of us like he's framing an image of it, and he's bent down enough that his shoulder brushes my shoulder. "Camping coffee just hits different. It takes ten years to make a cup of coffee on a crappy portable stove, so then when it's ready, you don't even care that the mug you left out last night has dead bugs in it. You're so desperate for coffee that you just pour it in and drink it while it's way too hot, and it's the best thing you've ever tasted. Even if you don't drink coffee, which I don't think you do? But still, I want this for you."

That same feeling from last night, when I was smelling his sweater and longing for something, overcomes me. I think I would give anything to drink a shit cup of coffee in Algonquin Park with him at five in the morning, and it feels so absurd that I can't help how sad it makes me.

"Yes, that... sounds nice," I say, and he's quiet for a long moment after that. I don't look at him because I don't want to know if I failed to keep the sadness out of my voice and ruined the mood. But he doesn't say anything about it—he switches effortlessly to the subject of Switzerland and how they have three official languages, and none of them are called Swiss.

We get on a public bus, and we're the only people on it. Lachlan immediately starts up a friendly conversation with the bus driver. I grab onto a pole further down the bus, and Craig sits in front of me while Drew and his friend head toward the back. Maya and Bianca sit in the seats on the raised platform just next to me, only a pane of plexiglass between me and Maya's tanned, sandalled foot.

When the bus starts moving, it does so suddenly and violently, and I nearly go flying. I stumble, my grip tightening on the pole, just as Craig's hand shoots out to grab me round the wrist. My body acts of its own volition, recoiling against his fingers, and my arm snatches back from him, pressing into my stomach.

I didn't mean to do it, but it doesn't matter. The bus evens out, and I can see the hurt flash in his eyes as plain as day, though he's quick to hide it behind a very weak, very forced version of his yikes face.

"Sorry," he says, his ears blazing red. "I have that—I have that thing that moms have, you know, in the car when they step on the brake too hard, and their arm comes flying out to keep you from going out the windshield? I have that."

I can't say my mom has ever tried to keep me from flying out the windshield. In fact, I think if she were here right now, that would've just planted a nice idea in her head.

"Craig, you know, if you saved me from going out a bus window, I would've just said thank you instead of spazzing out," Maya says lightly, wrapping her arms over the edge of the plexiglass and resting her chin on them.

I don't know why every nerve seems to be concentrated in my wrist right now, heat blazing where his fingers were. He didn't even grab me hard. And now, not only do I look like some kind of startled stray animal, but I hurt his feelings. So when I look at Maya, I feel like spitting venom. "What are you, flirting with him? Good luck."

She raises her eyebrows. "And that's supposed to mean...?"

"It means you're an asshole, and you'd be better off sticking with your own kind. Maybe try your luck with Eric since Theo's off the market."

This doesn't phase her, and when I see the way her eyes brighten with realization as they flick between me and Craig, my blood runs cold with dread.

"Oh my God, wait," she says, her voice full of wonder. "Wait, do you *like* him?"

My hand turns sweaty where it's wrapped around the pole. I roll my eyes, hoping that might stop the heat rushing to my face as I turn my gaze to the window above Craig's head. "Grow up, Maya."

"You're *blushing*. You actually do, don't you?" She's leaning over her arms in my peripheral, like she's trying to get a better look at me. "No, that's actually so cute. Kind of sad, though. Craig, did you know? That must be so awkward for you."

The last thing I need to do right now is look at Craig, but I can feel myself doing it as if in slow motion. He's got one hand tangled in the hair at the back of his neck, the other in a fist on his knee. His eyes are round and morti-fied. As I watch, they move from Maya to me, his Adam's apple bobbing. Then he opens his mouth, and I cannot, will not, hear what he's about to say.

I whip my head back toward Maya. "You know, on second thought, I don't think Eric would go for you, considering your fake tan makes you look like a fucking Oompa-Loompa."

I can see the arrow hit in the way her eyes sort of dim, but she just scoffs, slumping back in her seat. I wait for triumph, but all I feel is that horrible burning thing in my stomach throwing a fit.

She just drives me insane. I don't understand why she's always there, always opening her mouth when she doesn't have to. I'm so fucking sick of it.

"Okay, I think that was pretty unnecessary," Bianca says, frowning at me.

"Really?" I say, scoffing. "You want to talk about unnecessary?"

"Hey, can we just stop?" Craig says. He has his hands in prayer position over his mouth, his eyes closed as if asking God to grant him the patience. "Like, please, can we stop?"

And because no one seems to want to disappoint Craig Miltenberg, we stop. We fall into an uneasy silence, me with my white-knuckled grip on the pole, Maya with her head down, staring at the place where Bianca is holding her hand in her lap. She's rubbing her thumb over Maya's knuckles like she's supporting her through a cancer diagnosis, and I roll my eyes and look away from them.

For the rest of the ride, I watch the neighbourhoods of Interlaken rolling by, blending into Unterseen: half-timbered frame houses with Swiss flags fluttering on poles and red-shuttered windows lined with flowering geraniums. I look at the neutral faces of the people walking down the sidewalks and passing us on their bicycles and wonder, why aren't you smiling? Why aren't you just beaming all the time about living in a place like this and not being in high school and not having some kind of mental affliction that makes you freak out when a nice boy tries to save you from falling?

13

Lachlan leads us off the bus on the outskirts of a campground, where we walk along motorhomes, glamping pods, and tents scattered about until we reach a gravel path leading into some woods. Most of us aren't speaking, and those who do are doing so very quietly, as if the woods are sacred.

On the other side, we're spit out on to a secret, deserted beach, surrounded by woods on one end and a soft purple mountain range on the other. The lake is so still, it looks like a mirror reflecting the peach sky, tendrils of fog creeping over its surface.

"No way," Craig breathes.

Lachlan looks pleased with herself. "I told you it'd be worth it."

Drew's friend is the first one to start down toward the lake, his earbuds blaring a tinny rap song. He puts his hands on his hips in the centre of the beach, staring out at the water. Drew follows, kicking up sand behind him. He stops just at the edge of the water, tips his head back and screams: "This is *sick!*"

His voice reverbs off the mountains, birds taking flight from the woods all around us. Bianca chuckles; Lachlan curses under her breath.

I don't waste any time—I march down the beach, chucking my phone and jacket into the sand as I go. When the sand starts darkening and cracking under my feet, I stop and unlace my boots.

Drew stands from where he'd been gingerly putting his pinkie in the water, shaking out his hand. "Nah, don't put your feet in there. That shit is *freezing.*"

My heart is thumping heavily in anticipation as I kick off my boots and peel my socks off. I'm standing barefoot in my jeans and my long dark sweater, and the sand is freezing under my feet. But it's not enough.

I walk into the water, and my chest locks up. I bite down on a gasp. I keep going, not breathing, and every lap of the water seeping into the fabric at my calves sends a shockwave through me.

It's perfect. After how I acted on the bus, I need it.

The water gets deep fast, and I'm only about ten feet from the beach when it reaches my stomach. I breathe hard through my nose and try to stop myself from sucking in.

"*Bro,*" Drew calls. I turn to see him with his hands on the back of his head, grimacing at me.

Craig is loping down the beach, tossing his shoes down next to Drew. He looks at me with his hands on his hips and a crinkle between his eyes. "You really just... you just went in there, huh?"

"You should try it," I say, trying to keep my voice from hitching as the water catches a dry spot on my shirt.

Then I notice Lachlan stalking over to us, looking pissed.

"Uh oh," I say.

She sticks her arms out at her sides. "Alis, what the hell?"

"What?" I say, my teeth chattering. I gesture to Maya and Bianca, who are up to their knees in the water, holding each other's hands and squealing. "They're doing it."

"Yes, *they* brought bathing suits and towels."

I bug my eyes out at her. "Okay? Sorry."

She points a firm finger at me. "If you get hypothermia and die on the way back, that's not on me."

I think that probably would be on her since she's technically my guardian on this trip. But I *am* eighteen, so maybe she wouldn't be liable.

Lachlan stalks away, shaking her head, just as Craig lets out a yelp so loud I almost jump out of my skin.

"*Shit,* that is cold!" he says, hopping back from the water and shaking out his hands at his sides. Then he puts a hand over his mouth and widens his eyes. "Don't tell my mom I said that."

Have I not heard him swear? It's such a natural part of my world, you'd think I would've noticed its absence.

But no, I don't think I've heard him swear. I also heard him say *doo-doo* yesterday. I can't tell if that's irritating or endearing.

"It's nice now," I say. Technically, I'm not lying. It's still cold as all hell, and I can't feel my bottom half, but at least my mind is clear.

Craig grimaces at the water again, considering. "I will put my *legs* in the water. For you."

"You don't have to if you're scared."

He shoots me a challenging look. Then he pulls his pants down.

My virgin heart takes off like a rocket, but he's wearing swim shorts under them. Still, his legs are just as nice as his arms and have that same reddish-brown hair covering them. I quickly look back at his face, though, because I've learned my lesson from ogling his forearm on the train.

"Always come prepared," he says, grinning at me. He folds his sweatpants up and pats them as he sets them on the sand. Then he strips his sweater off and starts walking into the water in his t-shirt and shorts.

"You guys have fun with that," Drew says. "I'm gonna go see if Bianca needs someone to keep her warm."

He swaggers off down the beach, and I wait another decade for Craig to wade over to me. He makes noises that wake up every animal within a mile radius.

"Okay," he pants. "Stay here 'cause I'm not getting my shirt wet."

I sink lower, dunking my arms in and letting the water rise to my chest. I blow out a long, steadying breath as it seeps into my own shirt. The water is actually painful, but it's not the sort of pain I'm used to. Instead of that burning, focal pain that wrenches my mind away to a single point on my body, this is an all-encompassing pain, like every nerve-ending is standing at attention. It somehow makes my head feel fuzzy and sharp all at once.

Craig shudders as he watches me. "Are you actually enjoying that?"

I'm not sure if *enjoying* is the right word, but I don't know what else I would call it. "Yes."

He puts his hands under his armpits, which makes all the right muscles in his arms stand out. "I think my nipples could cause injury right now."

I let out a jittery, breathless laugh.

Craig's eyes sparkle as he grins. "I knew I'd get you at some point."

This makes my cheeks heat fiercely despite the cold. There's this feeling of elation coming over me, which I think is a mix of the *natural high* and the way the sun has peaked out over the mountain range, shattering orange over the water. Craig's eyes are the colour of maple syrup, and the bit of hair curling out from his hat looks like it's burning.

But then his face sobers, and he swallows hard and says, "You know, that stuff on the bus—"

"I know," I say quickly. I don't need to be admonished by him. "She just drives me fucking crazy."

"You could just ignore her."

"Solid advice, Craig, I didn't think of that."

"You say that sarcastically, but have you actually tried it? I mean, I used to get fat jokes, and those just sort of went away when I didn't react to them."

"She's not going away," I say, and it's true. I've got a high-definition film reel of every shitty thing that's ever happened to me shelved at the back of my mind, and the Halfwits star in a great deal of them. I don't have any control over what's playing at any given time, so even after graduation, they're all coming with me.

But that's as far as I'm willing to take this conversation, so I decide to dunk myself all the way into the water.

My ears fill with warbling, and the shock of the cold closing over my head overwhelms any other feeling. I keep my eyes squeezed shut and hold my breath until my lungs burn. Then I come back up, gasping.

I drag the water off my face and open my eyes to see Craig half-wincing, half-smiling at me. "Lachlan's gonna kill you."

The wet knot of my hair is pulling painfully, so I take it out and rough my hand through it. "She's gonna kill me for getting hypothermia and dying?"

"I won't let you get hypothermia," he says as another shiver rolls through him. "I'm like a furnace. Except for my legs, currently."

"What are you gonna do, cuddle me?"

"If I have to, yes."

I snort, looking back to the beach because I'm not sure what my face is doing. "That'd be one way to ruin your social life."

Craig is silent for long enough that I glance back at him. When I do, he has his hands out in front of him, looking down at them with a frown. He clenches and unclenches them. I look at them, too, but I don't see anything wrong with them. They're quite nice, actually.

He squeezes his eyes shut tight and opens them again.

I'm about to ask him what's wrong when he says, very seriously, "I'm gonna get out."

His face looks almost pained. I can't help the nervous little laugh that escapes me. "Okay."

He starts going, and I start following him. He's moving just a little ways before me, and the water reaches his calves. Then he stops dead.

I get this bad, weightless feeling in my stomach.

"Craig," I say, but all of a sudden he's falling.

My heart swoops, and I lurch forward and catch him under the arms, but he is way too heavy, and I collapse under him, falling onto my ass in the shallow water. I catch myself on my hand behind me, my wrist smarting on impact. Craig's head slams back against my collarbone, and I frantically try to pull myself up higher.

Someone shouts, but I can't look at them because his whole body has started jerking rhythmically in my arms, and I really don't think he's joking around.

Lachlan splashes into the water next to me. "Get him out, get him—"

She moves in on him, but I think the adrenaline finally kicks in because I'm able to drag both him and myself over to the sand with little help from her. Craig's head is snapped to the side, his eyes have rolled back in his head, and he's making these horrible little noises in the back of his throat. I feel numb with fear at how stiff he is in my arms. Lachlan scrabbles around on her knees and grabs his sweater from where he left it on the beach, balling it up on the sand. She presses up next to me to help pull Craig off, then rests his head on the sweater and kneels behind him, resting a hand on his chest.

"What should I—should I do something—" I say, but Lachlan is shaking her head, looking down at the watch on her wrist.

"He's okay," she says. I look down at Craig's legs, which are spasming the same as his arms, so I look back at his face, but that's worse—there's a line of drool seeping out of his mouth and down over his jaw, and I feel like all the blood has left my body.

"He doesn't fucking look *okay*," I say, my voice a few octaves too high.

Her eyebrows are at her hairline when she looks at me. "Alis, he needs you to be calm, all right?"

He needs it? Can he even hear us? He looks so gone, he doesn't look like he can hear a thing. But Lachlan starts talking to him gently, telling him he's okay, her hand smoothing the hair from his forehead. So what do I know? I don't know what the hell is—

"What's happening?" Drew's voice sounds from somewhere, and I look up and see all four of my classmates standing around, their expressions various combinations of fear, alarm, and confusion.

"He's fine, just—give us some space, yeah, guys?" Lachlan says, looking at her watch again.

Drew leads my classmates further up the beach like a sheepherder. I ask Lachlan, "How long until he's not fine?"

"Five minutes."

"How long has it been?"

Before she can answer, Craig's whole body shudders,

differently than before. He makes a choking, wheezing noise, and I dig my hands into the sides of my cold thighs and swallow against the heartbeat in my throat.

Then, all of a sudden, he seems to be relaxing, the jerking of his muscles becoming fewer and farther between. He sounds less like he's hyperventilating and more like he's panting.

"There you go, Craig," Lachlan says softly. "You're okay."

She starts turning him onto his side, and I try to help. I don't think my helping is actually helping, but Lachlan appears to be happy to let me think it is. She gently turns his head, shoving the sweater over, too, so his face doesn't land in the sand. His eyes are closed, and he may as well be dead for the way his limbs flop over. My insides are twisting themselves into knots.

I put my hand on his arm where it's folded over his stomach. It's all grainy with sand, and when I try to brush it off, I notice my hand is shaking.

Lachlan rubs circles on Craig's back, then lowers her head and starts speaking to him in this remarkably light voice, telling him where he is and that he's okay and that he's had a seizure, like nothing at all is wrong.

I sort of figured that's what was happening, but the word strikes fear into my heart anyway. I wonder if Lachlan is calm because this is some kind of condition he has, and she has it logged away on her Rainbow Tablet somewhere, along with all of the right things to do. I watch as she wipes the drool from his face with his balled-up sweater and grit my teeth to keep from asking all of the stupid questions spinning around in my head.

Eventually, Craig starts blinking heavily, and I'm flooded with relief until his gaze lands on me. I'm gripped by this sudden fear that he's not going to recognize me and that the Craig I knew was somehow destroyed by all those terrible things his body was just doing.

He blinks sluggishly at me. "What..."

That's all he says. I wiggle on my knees in the sand, shooting Lachlan a desperate look.

She squeezes his shoulder and says to him again, "You've had a seizure, Craig."

He closes his eyes, looking exhausted. I don't think I've ever seen anything that looks so tiring in my life, so I can't say I'm surprised, but I am selfishly hoping he bounces back in a second. Otherwise...

Otherwise, I don't know. I don't know what I'm going to do. And that—this helpless feeling like I'm one of those cartoons wheeling uselessly in the air seconds before falling—feels different than anything I've ever felt before.

14

Craig is finally able to pull himself into a seated position, where he stays with his eyes closed for a full minute, swaying a little. When he meets my eyes again, he gives me this feeble little smile.

"You look sick," he says, and his eyes fall closed again.

I blink at him. "I—me? I look—what?"

His smile widens and then flickers and fades again, and it's like my heart is soaring and plunging in time with it. I look at Lachlan, who's still rubbing his back. She sticks out her bottom lip and shakes her head, which I take to mean that I shouldn't listen to him.

"That feels nice," Craig says sleepily.

Lachlan smiles. "That's good, kiddo. I'll keep doing it until you wanna get up."

At some point, Bianca came back down the beach, and she stands nearby with her eyes round and her arms wrapped around her stomach.

"Are you okay, Craig?" she asks, and she actually does

sound concerned. But if Craig hears her, he doesn't answer.

"He's good," Lachlan says. "Tell the others to get their stuff together, please?"

She nods and goes. Craig is soon able to stand with Lachlan's help, and I scramble up after him. He is literally covered in that grating wet sand, and I don't know what comes over me, but I say: "You have... sand. Can I...?"

I don't think he understands me, but he nods. I snatch up his sweater from the ground and start wiping him down as Lachlan holds him steady.

When most of the sand has fallen away, I step back, clutching the sweater to my stomach and feeling very stupid. "Okay."

"Thank you," he says, smiling dreamily at me. His blinks are still heavy, but he appears to be able to keep his eyes open now, and I feel some of the tension leaving me.

We make our way—very slowly on account of Craig moving like a geriatric—back to the bus. When the adrenaline wears off, I learn the hard way that the cold of walking into a freezing lake is not remotely the same thing as the cold of wet clothes clinging to me in breezy ten-degree weather. And also that I messed up my wrist when I fell on it and I'm trying to ignore it because who cares about my stupid wrist right now?

On the bus, Lachlan and I sit on either side of Craig, except I leave a seat between us so I don't graze him with my freezing wet clothes. When the bus starts moving, he puts his elbows on his knees and his forehead in his palms, his fingers curled like claws. My heart is still beating heavily with that suspended feeling of uselessness, like it's begging me to kick into action and do something.

I slide over so I'm only half on the seat next to him and ask through my shivering, "Is it your head?"

He nods into his hands.

"Can I do something?" I whisper, hating how pathetic I sound but feeling like I might explode.

"It's okay," he whispers back.

Okay. He says it's okay, so it's okay.

My teeth are chattering. I try to shrink myself deeper into my shirt as if I can peel the fabric from my skin, and that doesn't work at all. My knee bounces uncontrollably. I look around the bus, and there are other people mixed in with my classmates now, and I wish they would all disappear. I don't know why. They're not even doing anything—they're all being very civil, not looking at the sandy boy with his head in his hands or the wet rat-looking one with his vibrating knee.

Then something so shockingly warm lands on my leg that it seems to enhance the cold, and a violent tremor runs through me. I look down at one of Craig's hands on my knee, holding it still.

"Sorry," I say.

He shakes his head in his hand but says nothing. He keeps his other hand on my leg until we get off the bus, and all I can think about is how it must be freezing now because of me.

We say goodbye to the Swiss lodge and head off to the train platform a couple hours later. I don't run into Craig again until we're all huddled on the gravel outside the hostel with our bags. He's changed into grey sweats and this horribly bright yellow hoodie that clashes with the mustard yellow of his hat. I re-did my eyeliner—it's meant to be waterproof, but it was pretty messed up after my swim—and changed into a thousand layers. This seemed like the right call when I was freezing my ass off, but I am now regretting it as the morning sun beams down on me.

Noor appears to be talking Craig's ear off about something, which feels uncharacteristic for her. He looks significantly better than he did before, but he also looks exhausted. He's sitting on top of Noor's rolling suitcase, holding himself like his bones are trying to drag him down. It's like I'd gotten so used to this constant vibration of energy from him that this is all the more jarring to me.

I decide to leave him alone, even though my mind is still reeling with questions. I trail at the back of the group as we walk, rolling my injured wrist. It stings like crazy when I move it, but at least it's not sprained. Pinched nerve, maybe. I keep rolling it.

But then on the train, Craig smiles softly at me as I come down the aisle, patting the seat next to him.

I hesitate. "What about Noor?"

"She's sitting with Drew," he says. I don't move, and he looks pointedly over my shoulder. "You're holding up traffic."

So, I guess I have no choice but to sit with Craig. I swing off my bag and put it in the overhead, feeling jittery as I take a seat next to him. I do want to talk to him, to find out what the hell just happened, but I don't know how to bring it up without sounding like a prying—

"I have epilepsy," Craig says.

I freeze, my blood spiking in my veins. Then I pull my eyes to his and the only thing that comes out of my mouth is, "Oh."

I have no idea what my face is doing, but his eyes are sliding all over it, and his lips are starting to quirk. "You look *terrified.*"

What do I say? Do I tell him that sucks? Do I say I'm sorry? Do I say—

"Ian Curtis had epilepsy."

I just barely suppress a wince because there is absolutely no way that would make him feel better. Why was *that* what I landed on?

His eyebrows knit. "Who?"

"Lead singer of Joy Division?" I say squeakily. "He would get seizures on stage."

His smile is wider now, and I hope my face doesn't look as hot as it feels. "That would definitely suck."

Yes, well, he did kill himself. Now I have to look away from him because I'm an idiot and I need to learn not to speak. I can only hope he doesn't start Googling after this conversation.

"Please relax," he says through a laugh. "I'm actually afraid for you right now."

I whip my head around. "Okay, you know? That was really scary, so fuck me for being a little on edge right now."

He sobers, but the outline of the laugh is still there in his face, like an after-image burned on your eyelids. "No, I know. Sorry. You're just..."

Whatever I am, he doesn't tell me. He leaves it hanging there for a moment before he moves his eyes to his lap, clearing his throat. "Anyway. Epilepsy sucks, but it's been manageable. I haven't had a seizure in almost a year until today. Right now, the part that sucks most about it is that my mom panicked and thought to go behind my back and retract her permission for me to go paragliding, and I spent all day yesterday watching *other* people have fun. So, in case you've never relished being eighteen, I'm telling you now: relish it. Relish it hard."

Oh. So Lachlan dragging him away at breakfast yesterday makes a lot more sense now.

The bitterness in his voice has something inside me standing at attention. "Is your mom really strict?"

The train gives off an electric hum as it starts to move. Craig pulls down his seat tray, then puts it back up again. Then he pulls his hat off and starts kneading it in his lap. "I mean, not at all, really. She's just overprotective some-times. She had a bad time when I was first diagnosed, and none of the treatments were helping me, and I barely had the chance to process it because she was doing all the worrying for me. She's always had these depressive episodes, and I guess my diagnosis just triggered a really bad one for her. For months, I swear all I was doing was trying to cheer her up. I was twelve and dumb and didn't understand what was happening."

You must hate her, I want to say. "That must've been hard."

"Nah, it wasn't like I was on my own. My dad was around then, before they split, and my big brother. It was a little weird, though, seeing her like that. Like, if you met her, you'd think she never got sad, never mind depressed. But I guess I just felt this responsibility to help her because she was always there for me, you know? Even though she told me I wouldn't have a social life if I kept hanging out with my mom after school."

He glances at me with a little side smile. I'm rolling my injured wrist in the aisle and hoping my own smile doesn't look like a grimace.

"But eventually, she got help," he continues, "and she's been a lot better. And to be honest... I know how messed up this sounds, but helping her is kind of what helped me, after the diagnosis. I stopped thinking about when I was going to have another seizure or whether my next one would be my last one because every day, it was like my *mission* to make her laugh at least once. I just really wanted her to get better."

He looks down at his hat, and I look at the perfect slope of his nose and the mess of all that hair he hides away all day, and I stop rolling my wrist.

Initially, there was something that plummeted and died inside of me when I realized he didn't hate his mom at all. Maybe I thought, if he did, he and I could have something in common, and I could tell him about my parents, and he'd believe me.

But I find myself much gladder to know that he doesn't.

I think the fact that we have nothing in common is one of the reasons I've hung around him this long in the first place. Also, I don't think he'd be the way he is if he hated his mom, and I like the way he is.

He pulls his hat back on and leans back in his seat, letting out a long breath. "But yeah, the overprotectiveness is still a pain. I want to shake her sometimes. Like, even if I did have a seizure six hundred feet in the air, it's not like I'd be up there without the instructor. I actually do like my life? So I'm not an idiot about this kind of stuff. Sometimes she acts like I'm about to go stare at a bunch of strobe lights."

He's gesturing in this petulant way that makes me feel like laughing, and when he crosses his arms and starts *pouting*, I have to bite down on my smile.

Apparently I'm not quick enough, because Craig furrows his brow at me. "Are you laughing at my pain?"

"No," I say. "I'm just wondering if you're a whiner."

I feel my eyes go wide as saucers and snap them to the seat in front of me.

Jesus *Christ*. Why did that sound so dirty? I did not mean for that to sound dirty, but even my *tone* sounded dirty and we both know it—I can feel him staring at the side of my face.

Then he snorts, chasing it up with a laugh that melts all the awkwardness away, and I could kiss him for saving me. But not really, because that would probably ruin my life, and right now I might actually have a life to ruin.

"God, your face is the best," he laughs, and if my cheeks weren't on fire before, they are burning now.

PART III

ROME

15

Our hostel in Rome is exactly the kind of old tenement building where I was hoping to stay in Paris, with orange stucco walls bleached to a pale apricot from hundreds of years in the sun. The cobblestoned alley outside is buttery with sunlight and crowded with parked motorcycles and Vespas. I thought it was a myth that everyone rides around Italy on the back of a Vespa, but the streets are so narrow at some points that I don't even think a car would be an option.

Lachlan informs us in the lobby that tonight's dinner is at this fancy place, and that we should make an effort to look nice or risk offending the locals. I'm pretty sure everything I've packed is going to offend the locals, but I head to the showers anyway. I've felt so helpless all day after what happened with Craig, I just want to be in control again; so I'm going to wash my hair, and then I'm going to dress like a nightmare.

In the shower, I'm trying not to ruin my mood by

thinking about how ugly my body is, but there's not much else to look at. I'm staring at my arms, crisscrossed from wrist to bicep with scars—some squares, mostly slashes; some thicker than others, some longer, some raised, some faded, but all made by me—and I'm thinking about how strange it is to know that no one else will ever see them. The next person that's going to look at these terrible arms is the guy who dresses me up for my funeral, if I even have one of those. I think my parents might just break out one of those fancy bottles of wine from the cellar they're always bragging to their friends about and then bask in the silence after I'm gone.

As I wash my hair, I stop thinking about my arms and start thinking about Craig's arms. At first, I'm wondering what it must be like to have really nice arms like that and to be able to wear t-shirts when it's hot. Then I'm just thinking about how they're really nice arms. Then I'm getting visions of the arms wrapping around me and squeezing really, really tight and lifting me up off my feet like they did with Noor. And maybe my nose is, like, right in his neck so I can smell that sweater smell again, except it'll be a hundred times stronger where the beautiful barbecue sauce hair curls up against it. He's also not wearing that hat, so I can reach my hand up in it and feel how thick and soft it is, and then maybe I pull on it, and he makes a noise like he was doing that night in Paris when he was all covered in sweat—

I crank the dial on the shower all the way to the cold end. I put both my hands against the tile and stand there under it as it gets colder and colder, gritting my teeth so I don't make any noise. It takes enough concentration that all of the thoughts dissipate, so I'm just watching the water running off the scars.

Afterwards, I put on these black cargo pants that are so wide they look more like a skirt, with silver chains on the sides. The long-sleeved shirt I'm wearing has thumb holes, which makes me feel protected from that imaginary scenario that's always lurking in the back of my mind, where I put my arm up, and the sleeve decides to loosen and fall down. Over top of that, I put on a t-shirt that is so full of sagging holes it may have been shredded by an animal. Then I put on rings—a lot of rings, so if I punch a person, they'll come out looking like the shirt.

After I've put kohl on my eyes, I put my hair into these low pigtails because I have Eric in my head going *Girl? Boy?* and Kepler with his *Is there a reason you do this?*, and I want to make them both sweat.

By the time I leave the washroom, I feel like I've donned my armour. I make my way to my room, hoping I haven't ended up with anyone too objectionable, and I'm about to stick my keycard in the door when I hear a voice behind it. It's irritated, and loud, and definitely Theo.

"Yes, I get it," he snaps. I wait for someone to respond, but there's just a pause. "Jesus, I'm sorry for caring."

I frown, listening through another beat of silence. Theo lowers his voice, and I move closer to the door. "Sorry. Sorry. I just *hate* that you're not here. And I told your mom like fifty times that we could help with the deposit—" He cuts off, sighing. "But it's not just that, babe.

I feel like I have to call you every five minutes, like I can't even relax."

I scrunch up my nose. Gross.

"Can you just promise me, please?" he continues. "Okay. Call me if you need me."

Call me if you need me, he says, like he wasn't just complaining about feeling like he had to call her every five minutes. What an asshole. I don't know how she can stand him.

Not that I care, at all, about what Jordan does with her life anymore.

Theo doesn't say anything else, so I run lightly back down the hallway until I hear the door click open, then start walking toward it again, casual-like.

As he comes out, it's hard not to notice that he looks like shit. He's not known for looking like shit (though his sliminess ensured that I never once felt attracted to him), but today he's got an *I don't care* vibe that doesn't suit him. He looks like he hasn't slept, and his hair is unflatteringly fluffy, like he didn't bother with any product.

I walk toward him, and he walks toward me, and when our eyes meet, he stops walking. I keep going, ignoring the swoop of my heart. I feel his eyes on me as I stick the keycard in the door.

"You're in there, then," he says flatly. "That's really good to know."

I ignore him, but there's this prickling down the back of my neck as I open the door and shut it behind me. The room is empty, so I sag against the door and breathe for a second. I have no idea what he meant by that, but I can't say I feel good about it; I almost would have rather run into Eric.

The thing about Eric is that his motives are clear: he gets joy out of making people feel like shit, and he doesn't really care who it is that he's making feel like shit. His actions are predictable, his jokes repetitive.

With Theo, though, I never know what to expect—whether he's going to ignore me, or say something horrible, or try to shove my sleeves up. All I know is that everything he does is personal. Something about me has always rubbed him the wrong way, and that's only amplified since he started dating Jordan and amplified again when her house burnt down. I just get this feeling, sometimes, like there's only so much more it can amplify before he does something about it.

The lobby is deserted when I get down there, except for Lachlan and Bilodeau talking by a ficus with little Italian flags sticking out of the soil. They both glance up at me where I've just come out of the stairwell door.

"You have to teach me how to do that," Bilodeau says, hovering his fingers over his eyes like he's applying eyeshadow. I have this very strong urge to hug him but settle for a smile.

Lachlan directs me to the hostel's courtyard, and among my classmates, I find Noor sitting on a couch up on a deck, her eyes closed and her sneakered feet out on the coffee table. She's wearing a glittery purple blouse over white skinny jeans, and I notice her wolf cut isn't as voluminous as it usually is.

"Are you napping?" I ask, stepping up to the deck.

She opens her eyes and rolls her head along the back of the couch. Her gaze slides over me, and then she actually *smiles*. It's not this big beaming thing like Craig's—it's a small uptick to the corner of her mouth, the barest lightening of her eyes—but somehow, it feels precious, and something flutters inside me. I smile back before plopping down next to her on the wicker couch.

"You look scary," she says.

"Thank you. Your hair looks nice."

She runs her fingers through it. "I used a straightener on it. Took me an hour. Never doing it again."

"Where's Craig?" I ask, and then cringe a little as I realize I keep asking her where Craig is.

"He's gone out to find wine. He's going to come back and tell you it's the finest wine in Italy, but I guarantee he spends ten euros max."

I snort. "Isn't he seventeen?"

"He's convinced no one will card him, even though he has baby cheeks."

He does have baby cheeks. But when you're built like a bear, maybe you just automatically get a pass.

"And I think he needed to be alone for a bit," she adds, "since Maya helpfully supplied him with the information that he fell on you when it happened. Just so you know not to bring that up."

"I wasn't going to," I say irritably. "She's such a fucking little—"

There's a thump on the deck. "You better watch the next word that comes out your mouth, princess."

I roll my eyes before turning to look at Eric, who's coming round our couch with Connor in tow. "Or what?"

He pulls out the coffee table so Noor's legs fall from it. Then he sits on the edge of it, right in front of me, and puts his hands between his legs like he's a parent about to have a serious talk. "Or I might do an *oopsie* tonight and cut off one of your little pigtails in your sleep."

Connor lets out a puff of air through his nose. I glance up to where he's standing just behind Eric with his arms crossed, a stupid grin on his face. I know he should piss me off far less than Eric does, but the way he's always standing around, laughing on command like the Halfwits' live studio audience, rubs me the wrong way.

I narrow my eyes at him. "Did you have any empty threats to add, jackal?"

"Ooh, *jackal*," says Eric, turning to raise his eyebrows at Connor. When he looks back at me, his eyes are glittering with amusement. "Man, with your hairdo and your makeup, throwing around insults like *that*? I'm shaking in my goddamn Nikes right now."

"Is there a reason you're here?" Noor interjects.

"Oh shit, I didn't notice you were there," Eric says lightly. He straightens up, giving her a once-over. "You know, you'd actually be kinda hot if you smiled more."

I feel a pulse of heat in my skull. "You'd be mildly less disgusting if you took a shower once in a while."

Eric rolls his head back to me, his smile morphing into a sneer. "Hey, you wanna know why I haven't fucked you up yet, princess?" He lowers his voice, leaning forward. "Because Jordan asks us not to, so Theo asks us not to. But the thing is, Theo's been a bit stressed lately, and since his bitch isn't around, well. Who knows what could happen by the end of the week?"

He reaches out toward my hair, and I press back into the couch. Then he stops because Noor's hand has shot out and wrapped around his wrist.

My whole body goes cold. He looks at her, a split second of surprise on his face before he lets out an incredulous laugh, his fist curling above her grip—

Connor hits Eric's shoulder with the back of his hand just before Lachlan's "Oy!" sounds over the courtyard.

Eric's gaze darts over my shoulder, and Noor snatches her hand back. I turn to see Lachlan approaching, her face severe. She looks at each of us in turn. "What is this?"

Eric stands up and stretches his arms over his head. "We were just playing."

"Right," Lachlan says. She looks between him and Connor, then jerks her head. "Get lost."

Eric gives her a salute and jumps off the deck, Connor following. When they're gone, Lachlan's eyes flick between me and Noor. "What was that?"

"It was actually nothing," I say.

She's quiet for a moment, narrowing her eyes at me. Then she points a hard finger at the pair of us. "You better tell me if it becomes something."

I nod, still feeling like I've just been doused in cold water. The moment she's out of earshot, I round on Noor.

"Are you stupid?" I snap. "Don't do that."

The light changes in her eyes, and the couch creaks as she leans away from me. "What?"

"Don't get *involved*, Noor. I'm serious. Don't do it again."

One second, I'm looking at Noor's dark eyes flicking across my face.

The next, there's an overlay where she used to be, and a phantom fourteen-year-old Jordan takes her place, sitting in a stained Toronto Blue Jays sweater, her eyes red-rimmed and her overgrown pixie cut matted and unkempt. I'm back in that day, that day she told me—

"I tried it."

I remember how the back of my neck prickled with unease, as if I already knew. "Tried what?"

Jordan lifted her sleeve and showed me her forearm. There were two lines there, one of them faint and pink like a scratch, the other shorter but the angrier red of a fresh scab. The marks told a story: of the first try, when she couldn't will herself to press deep enough to cut. Of the second try, when she managed but bailed halfway through.

"I wussed out," she said, pulling the sleeve back down. "It hurts, and I don't know how you do it."

I was so cold, the air was frozen in my chest. "Why would you—why—"

"Because you don't get how lucky you are!" she said, her teary eyes wild. "You have a way of dealing with stuff, and I just feel like I'm drowning all the time. I'm just so angry at how *ugly* I am. But then the scissors were too dull, and I was too scared, and it just made things worse."

"I didn't tell you because I thought you should *try it*, Jordan, I told you—"

I snapped my mouth shut before I could say what I meant: *I told you because I wanted you to tell me to stop.*

The splashing acid in my stomach was unbearable, and I shot up from Jordan's couch, my hands curling into fists.

"Don't do it again." I meant it to sound firm, but it shook all the way through. "Don't do it again, Jordan. It's not going to make you better."

Her brow furrowed. "Are you seriously mad at me right now?"

"I'm not mad, I'm telling you it doesn't work."

She shook her head, confused. "I know it doesn't work. That's what I just said."

The squirming thing was tearing a hole in my stomach lining, and I could barely hear her anymore. I needed to go deal with it. I told her I had to go, and she followed me to the door, asking me why I was being an asshole, and I couldn't answer. I knew I was, but I couldn't answer.

I had one of the worst nights of my life after that because I had to decide if I wanted to stop being friends with her to keep her safe or keep being friends with her knowing that I was terrible for her. At home, I shut myself in the washroom for long enough that my dad actually came to knock and say, "You okay in there?"

I wasn't at all—I made a cut that was so big I had to google how to take care of it without stitches—but I told him I was, and he went away.

As much as I weighed the options and knew what was

right, I also knew what I would choose. Still, in the weeks that followed, whenever Jordan and I got into fights, I would try to be as vicious as possible and hope that she didn't forgive me. But she always did, and I always let her. And it ate me alive to know I was so selfish.

I come back to the present still looking at Noor, and whatever she's searching for in my face, I don't think she likes it when she finds it. She blinks, then stands from the couch and stalks off, leaving me there without another word.

16

I'm still sitting on that couch ten minutes later when Craig bounds up to the deck, and my heart does a double take at the sight of him.

The hat is gone, and so are the sweats. He's wearing jeans and a dark green button-up t-shirt with little pine trees on it, and his hair has this beachy, devil-may-care quality to it like it's begging me to mess it up even further. He also seems like he's got most of his energy back, maybe because he slept the entire train ride here, completely unmoving, while I sat next to him and googled everything I could about epilepsy.

He rounds the couch, his eyes wide and glinting and stuck right to me.

"Holy sh—itake mushrooms," he says, sitting down next to me. "Can I touch your hair?"

Okay, so he's definitely been drinking already. I couldn't really tell by just his face because his cheeks are always flushed like that.

I nod, and he reaches out both hands and runs them down the lengths of the pigtails, just under where the hair ties are, and he watches himself doing it with those same glossy, awe-filled eyes. He does this for long enough that I start looking at his parted lips and wondering what they feel like.

A smile spreads on his face, and he meets my eyes. "Amazing. You're... why are you sad?"

My heart skips a beat, because how does he *know* that? I clear my throat and say, "I'm not. Noor said you had wine?"

He looks suspiciously at me for a moment, but his smile is already fighting its way back on to his face. "I do have wine, and it is, actually, the finest in *Roma*."

I smile back at him until he fails to produce the wine. "Where is it?"

"Noor has it in her purse thing. Shall we bounce?"

Right. Now I have to spend the whole night with Noor after being weird with her—again—*and* she's holding the wine hostage.

Then again, maybe it's better that she's mad at me, so she has no reason to defend me again.

Craig gets off the couch and holds out both his hands like he wants to pull me up.

Straight boys do that, right? Especially tipsy straight boys. Plus, it's two hands, not one, which is different.

I take his hands, and their warmth fills me all the way up so that I'm pretty sure I look like a tomato when I'm back on my feet. He smiles down at me, still holding them.

Then there's a shriek of laughter somewhere that

seems to remind him where he is, and he lets go of me a little too quickly. So, apparently, he does have a sense of self-preservation.

Later, as everyone is walking mob-like through the streets of Rome, I stop to "tie my boot" and ask Craig if he can go get the wine from Noor while I'm at it. She's been walking ahead with the Mitchells, which is just as well. He brings back a gigantic silver water bottle, and I twist it open and start chugging. Craig's eyebrows are rising higher the longer I go on.

I gasp as I pull away, my stomach burning deliciously. Then I hang on to it because I don't want it going back in Noor's purse.

There's a live band playing mandolins inside the restaurant, and their music follows us to the patio, where two long tables are set up under a gazebo lined with fairy lights. I sit at the end across from Craig, who's sitting next to Dakota and Drew. Noor sits next to me and says nothing as she looks at this dainty little menu with five items on it. Not that it's uncommon for her to say nothing, but this silence feels like a string pulled taut between us. There are two, three times when I open my mouth to say something, and then it's like a dark tide ebbs over my mind and washes the apologies away. So I stay silent, too.

"Do you think they take requests?" Craig asks when the band starts in on a new song, this one a bit slower and moodier. "Because I learned all the words to *On An Evening in Roma*."

Drew snorts. "Isn't that in Italian?"

"It's half in Italian, and I have an ear for languages."

"He has a 100 in French," Noor says, which makes me snap my head up from the menu I've been pretending to read.

"Wait, what? *You?*"

Silence falls over our corner of the table. Noor's face snaps to me in my peripheral, and Craig's eyebrows knit. Drew looks at his lap and mouths, "Ouch."

My mouth goes dry. I hadn't really meant to let Craig in on the fact that I thought he was an idiot for the past four years, especially since I've long figured out how wrong I was. "Sorry, I didn't mean like... I didn't mean like, *you* you. I just—I've been trying to figure out who's been beating me in French this whole year."

To my relief, Craig's face spreads into a grin. "*Beating* you?"

My relief bubbles into embarrassment. I sound like a fucking child.

I've got this split mind where I'm aware that school isn't a competition and that the difference between an A and an A+ doesn't really matter in the long run, but that part of me doesn't gel with what my parents have been teaching me my whole life—that if my grades aren't perfect, I'm not trying hard enough.

When I was little, they drilled this into me by not letting me eat until I got every question on my homework worksheets correct. My mom would say, *If you can read the textbook, you can get the answers right.* Sometimes, I'd go hungry for a long time because I just didn't get it no matter how many times I read the textbook, and that was never an answer they would accept. I would scream and cry and bang at my bedroom door, and if my dad was home, he'd poke his head in and ask, *Do you want your mother to come up here?* and I'd shake my head and fall quiet. I learned pretty quickly that the screaming and crying only ever made things worse.

If I came home with a bad grade, they would take away anything that brought me joy for an indefinite amount of time, including my after-school hangouts with Jordan. Since I've been in high school, this usually just meant taking away my credit card, so I'd be entirely reliant on them—and they aren't very reliable people.

Sometimes, I could get by with less than perfect if they knew I was top of the class because then at least I was the best relative to everyone else. But that's the bottom line: I'm a Woodson, so I have to be the best. And I'm not the best in French.

Craig's still wearing that teasing smile, so I busy myself with reaching for the wine at the foot of my chair and taking another long swig.

"Are we gonna have to carry you home tonight?" he asks.

I glare at him under my lashes as I screw the cap back on. "I'm fine. I'm like a tank."

Drew snorts. "Yeah, you're huge."

Dakota smacks him on the arm. "You're what, like half an inch taller?"

"Right, but I'm *stacked*," he says, flexing his arms inwards like a pro wrestler. My glare must get to him because he drops his arms. "No offence."

Craig leans back in his chair and fans himself with his

menu. "You know, I like my friends pocket-sized anyway. Easier to piggyback."

I think the wine is kicking in because I don't even care that he just called me *pocket-sized* or that he called me his friend, which I feel should shock me more deeply than it does.

The waiters come to take our orders, and I get the truffle ravioli because on those cooking shows I fall asleep to, they only make like three pieces of ravioli. I can handle three pieces of ravioli, even if they're gooey.

By the time the food arrives, I can feel my pulse in my cheeks and ears, and the sun has just disappeared. The fairy lights twinkle prettily in the blue light, and the music's a bit louder now as more people start crowding into the restaurant behind us. Someone puts ravioli down in front of me, but I'm distracted because the top three buttons of Craig's shirt are undone, and I'm looking at the way the knobs of his collarbones move as he breathes and talks.

It turns out there are way more than three pieces of ravioli served at this restaurant, but when I finally put one in my mouth, it's delicious. I don't even really know what a truffle is, but holy shit. I end up eating three-quarters of it before I'm so full, I feel like I might explode.

"Can I eat that?" Craig asks me when his pizza paddle only has crumbs left on it.

"Yes, please," I say. I don't know why I say *please*. My head feels very fuzzy, but not in a bad way. Not like the fondue restaurant. In fact, I feel like nothing bad could possibly happen to me right now.

He wiggles his fingers at my pasta bowl eagerly, and I push it toward him just as he starts pulling it, so his fingers brush over mine for an eternity. When he's secured my ravioli, he claps his hands together.

"Okay! Let's practice making friends in college." He clears his throat, turns to Dakota, and says in a valley girl accent, "So, like, what are you studying?"

Dakota grins at him and puts on her own accent. "I'm in psych at TMU. What about *you*?"

"Bachelor of Education at York, baby."

"Wait, actually?" Dakota says, dropping the accent. "I thought you were doing business?"

"I was, but then I met Lachlan and realized you could be cool *and* a teacher, and I was like, you know what? I could give some learning journeys a little bit of Craig flavour." He sprinkles something invisible over his ravioli.

"Well, I'm doing a fashion apprenticeship because Yeezys don't have shit on what I've got planned," says Drew.

Noor raises her hand. "Synthetic and Catalytic Chemistry at UofT."

"Cataclysmic chemistry?" Drew says. "I can *so* see that for you."

"What about *you*?" Craig puts his elbows on the table and his chin in his hands, blinking cartoonishly at me.

I know if I wasn't buzzing from the wine, I'd feel like I was sitting in a den of hyenas. But because I *am* buzzing from the wine and because the ambience is so nice, it's like the words just tumble out of me. "I have no fucking idea."

For some reason, this is really funny to me, and I snort

—like a big, sloppy snort that makes me cover my mouth on instinct. Craig drops his hands from his chin and his mouth falls open like he's just seen a comet, but he's looking at me. His eyes are doing this twinkling thing that makes me feel sort of self-conscious, so I take a sip of my ice water and try not to pig-laugh into it.

"Wait, are you not going to school?" Dakota asks me. "I mean, not that there's anything wrong with that. I just thought you were one of those really smart gifted kids."

"Mm, not smart," I say. "Very stupid, actually. I just get good grades."

"Oh, I get it." Drew gestures to me with his lemonade. "Book smart but not street smart."

"Not any kind of smart," I insist. I put my glass down and sit up straighter in my chair. "See, like, smart animals, if their foot is stuck in a bear trap, they'll gnaw off their own leg. Otherwise, they'll die there. But I haven't eaten my leg because I'm stupid, and I actually believe I'm going to survive this. I'm an idiot that studies very, very hard just to die in a fucking bear trap."

When I look at their faces, I know even through my haze that I've killed the mood. I can barely manage a full second looking at Craig because he's gone so serious, he looks like a different person. Dakota has her brow furrowed and her mouth open like she's weighing what to say, and I can feel Noor's eyes on the side of my face.

"That's... dark," Drew says. His expression is merely a mix of confusion and curiosity, so he's the easiest to look at. "I've been trying to figure that out, actually. Like if you really are *dark* or if that's just an aesthetic, but—"

"Drew, shut up for a second," Noor says. I feel her turn in her chair, and I meet her eyes, which are dark and heavy and boring into me. "What's the bear trap?"

I feel a lump form in my throat, and my voice comes out barely above a whisper. "I didn't think you were ever gonna talk to me again."

"I was waiting for you to say sorry. What's the bear trap?"

Why is she suddenly putting her own question marks at the end of her questions? She doesn't usually do that. I don't think I like it.

"I am sorry, though," I say.

"It's fine. Don't hug me."

"I wasn't gonna. But I'm sorry."

"I heard you. You're forgiven."

Drew says, "What is *happening* right now?"

"Binturongs," Craig says. He's smiling a bit as he looks between me and Noor, but it's not nearly the smile I'm used to, and I wonder if I ruined the whole night for good with my drunk, self-pitying nonsense.

But then Craig starts telling that same story about the grumpy binturongs at the zoo, and everyone moves on to discussing if a binturong is a rodent or a marsupial or neither. I have to concentrate very hard on getting rid of that painful shard in my throat before I'm able to join in.

17

When we get to the Piazza di Spagna, the sky is a dark violet, and Rome is lit up like a beacon. The Spanish Steps are crawling with tourists, and their rumbling voices fill the air over the sound of running water from the boat-shaped fountain in the centre of the square. At the top of the steps, there's a church cast in a ghostly white glow, and I start moving up toward it like a wine-addled moth to a flame.

"Wait!" Craig calls. When I turn, he's bounding up the steps toward me, biting his lip with excitement. "You need to come see this."

He takes my hand in his big, warm one and pulls me through the sea of tourists to the other side of the steps. Then he waits only semi-politely for a large family to get out of the way. I say semi-politely because he's practically breathing down the woman's neck waiting for her to take her kids and go, which feels like a step down from telling them to get lost, and I'm giggling.

151

The family finally drifts off, and Craig leaps on to the concrete ledge they'd been circled around, one of the many that trisects the steps.

"Do you know what this is?" he asks, his eyes gleaming.

"A ledge."

"This is *the* ledge where Audrey Hepburn ate her tiny ice cream in *Roman Holiday*."

I start giggling again. "That's a big deal."

"Shut up and take my picture. My mom is going to crap her pants."

He hands me his phone out of his back pocket, and I open up the camera as he poses with the backs of his hands under his chin like a debutante.

"The lighting is making you look like you're in a beer bottle," I say.

"Ooo, that sounds artsy."

"It's not, it looks—" I snort another laugh. "You look like a fucking headlight."

He makes a noise in the back of his throat and jumps off the ledge to come help me. He goes behind me and puts a hand on one of my shoulders while he reaches over the other one. I'm not paying any attention to what he's doing on the screen because I think his chin is grazing my head, and his fingers are overtop of my fingers on the back of the phone. I feel like this is all extremely unnecessary of him, but he probably doesn't even notice. He does this to everyone. He's a tactile person. If he knew my heart was doing somersaults in my throat, he'd probably be like, *Um, why?*

Then he's gone, but just as I'm mourning his presence,

his foot scuffs, and he's back again. He takes the phone from my hand. "Actually, you go."

I wrinkle my nose. "Your mom doesn't want a picture of *me* sitting on Audrey Hepburn."

"Yes, she does. Go before someone snags it."

I do as he says, frowning. "Your mom doesn't even *know* me."

He starts positioning his phone, grinning. "She basically does."

"What does that—"

I'm cut off as this asshole kid jumps onto the ledge and starts kicking her feet, screaming, "Mom, look! Mom, look where I am!" at the top of her lungs. I widen my eyes at Craig, and he takes the picture.

"That is perfect," he says, beaming.

Later, on our way to the Trevi Fountain, we pass shops with expensive Italian names and glowing windows full of jewellery and watches and menswear. We go down an alley between buildings that have arched doorways bordered with thick stones in the shape of old-fashioned vampire coffins, and I stop to stare at one of them. I smell Noor's vanilla perfume and feel coils of Dakota's hair against my neck as she leans close. "Whatcha looking at?"

I point up at the stones. "I want a vampire door."

"Maybe for your birthday," Noor says.

Once we get to the Trevi Fountain, I have another pink sky moment. There is no actual pink sky—night has fallen, and the clouds are a dark, electric yellow—but there are a lot of people crowded around the fountain, and I can understand why. It's huge, lit from beneath so the water is glowing aquamarine, and the marble figures at its head are impossible in their detail and their stature. They look like the real Roman Gods frozen in motion many millenniums ago, their winged horses still reared up for battle.

But as impressive as they are, it isn't them that does it; it's all the people at the edge of the basin who are curling their fists over coins and closing their eyes before throwing them over their shoulders into the water. So many of them, all doing the same thing—making their wishes, tossing the coins from behind. I'm wondering how this strange little ritual has passed on for years and years and how, no matter where these people come from, they're all here to do the same thing. Everyone's just bumbling around, wishing their lives were different, and I feel all at once this huge sorrow for everyone but also a deep sense of solidarity.

I find Mr. Bilodeau among the crowd with a little smile on his face, the blue of the fountain reflecting in his eyes. I go up to him and ask in French, "Do you have a coin?"

His eyebrows spring up, and he holds up a finger and digs around in his pocket. He takes out a Canadian quarter and plops it in my palm. I just love that old people always have coins, even in the wrong currency.

"Merci," I say, and he smiles and nods at me. I wade through the people until I'm at the edge of the basin next to an Indian couple in a saree and dhoti. They're doing one of those long, awkward kisses where they just hold their faces together while someone takes their photo, and I wonder if they just got married and my elbow and pigtail are going to be in their wedding photo.

I look down at the quarter in my hand and realize, in this pink sky moment, that I have no problems. I don't feel like a special person at all. I feel empty, and I feel full, and I feel ordinary. I look at all of those wavering coins at the bottom of the basin, and I close my hand over the quarter and wish that all of these other peoples' wishes come true. Then I turn around and toss it in.

The wine does eventually begin to wear off. Noor and Dakota keep checking on me and speaking to me in those delicate voices you use with drunk people and children until I finally say, "Okay, you guys can chill out now," and that seems to convince them that I'm not going to fall on my face.

We come into the Piazza della Rotonda, where more people are swarming the Pantheon, which I find out has been casually sitting there since *113 AD*. Its grand pillars are washed in this dim blue light that turns the cobblestones silver and slick. I'm up on the Pantheon's portico, weaving between the columns and feeling like I'm in a moon colony, when Craig finds me and asks me if I want gelato.

"Pistachio," I say.

He grimaces a bit and looks like he wants to say something before his face clears and he waves it away. "No, never mind. I'm not going to judge you even though that is objectively worse than mustard."

"You're the bigger person," I say distractedly, splaying

my hand out on one of the columns, like maybe I can feel the whole of its vast history through the stone.

As he heads off, I notice a couple in the middle of slowly vacating a sweet spot at the front of the Pantheon. I pull a Craig and hover impatiently behind them until they move, then sit down and stare ahead at yet another fountain, this one lit up in green so the ghoulish marble faces look like they're spewing poison into a cauldron.

I didn't know Rome would be so spooky.

I'm thinking about how many people have died where I'm sitting over the past couple of thousand years when Craig returns, sitting down next to me.

"You're nuts," he says.

I feel a stab of panic at this before I see he's holding out a tub of pale gelato, his eyes darting pointedly to the crumbled pistachio overtop. I roll my eyes, taking it from him, and he cackles.

I notice his own gelato is bright yellow, and I'm about to make my own joke about mustard when he puts his tub down and holds his hand out. "Can I put my number in your phone?"

I stare at him. "Okay."

He stares back at me before cracking up again. "Your face is like—it's like I just asked you if you want to see my Barbie doll collection."

"Okay, well." I bug my eyes out defensively. "It was just random."

I pull my phone out and unlock it for him, and he starts tapping around on it. "I'm really loving the fact that your wallpaper is just darkness. Wait, is this *outer space*?

No, that's—I thought there was a star, but it's just darkness."

He's giggling to himself as he puts his number in. I'm shaking my head as I eat my gelato, which *is* gooey but not in a bad way. I glance over at the screen and see he's putting his name in as Craig with a black heart next to it. Then he texts himself something, but I'm no longer looking because Noor has materialized in front of us, licking her own gelato out of a waffle cone.

"Now, if you get kidnapped by Mario, I may be able to find you in time," Craig says as he hands my phone back.

"Not Mario," Noor says, "but maybe Eric."

I groan and lean back against the two-thousand-year-old column. "Noor, *please* don't kill the vibe."

Craig's head whips toward me. "Is there a vibe?"

"So we're not going to talk about how he threatened to 'fuck you up'?" Noor says.

Craig's head whips back to her and then to me, and the smile on his face is dead. "He what? Like, as jokes?"

I close my eyes and sigh. "Yes, as jokes."

I can hear Noor's shoes scuffing as she sits down on the cobblestones. "If you're rooming with them, you need to ask for a swap."

"He *always* says stuff like that. There's no follow-through." I open my eyes to give her a pointed look. "Unless he finds out that I ran crying to Lachlan, *then* he's going to have some fun. So no."

"What exactly did he say?" Craig asks Noor, and she recites exactly what he said as if she has some kind of eidetic memory.

Craig pinches the bridge of his nose, then picks up his gelato and shovels a bunch into his mouth. "Okay, why do those guys hate you again? Don't say it's the house fire because I don't think they're that dumb."

I stab my spoon into my gelato and don't look at him. "It *is* the fire, and they are."

"But they didn't like you before that either, right?"

I shrug. "I'm pretty sure Theo's religious and thinks I eat babies at witching hour or something."

Neither of them say anything. I look up to see Craig squinting suspiciously at me and Noor giving me an even flatter look than usual. I don't know what they want me to say.

"You know," Noor starts. It sounds like she's about to tell a story for the first time, so I sit up from the column. "When I was in a group project with your old friend Jordan, and she was giving me shit for 'never moving my face' and 'always creepily staring,' I just asked to be switched out of her group. Then I aced my project because I didn't have an annoying person nattering in my ear about what she doesn't like about me. I feel like that's the obvious thing to do in a situation like that, and your reluctance to do it is weird to me."

Something inside of me is wilting. "Jordan was saying that?"

"Is that what you just got from—"

"No, no—sorry, I'm listening. But it doesn't matter if I move to a different room, okay? They'll be there in the morning if they really want to do something to me, but they won't risk it. They're not about to get expelled before graduation."

"I can swap rooms with you," Craig offers. "I'll say it's because of... uh, the lighting? So I asked you to switch with me, and you said yes."

"Yeah, they'll buy that."

"Okay, how about—"

I feel a spike of irritation and slam my gelato down next to me. "Jesus, can we move on? Like, do you guys *actually* care about this?"

There's a beat of silence as I'm looking between them, waiting, and then Craig looks down in his gelato, swirls it around, and says, "Well, I care about *you*, so yeah."

You'd think I'd just fallen through the floor and into the ocean. I'm suddenly enveloped in a prickling cold, hit with a wooziness so severe that I have to grip the step beneath me.

All night, he's been close to me, bracing himself on my shoulder, touching my fingers, touching me. And now, suddenly, he's too close. I can feel him there next to me like he's a lightning rod that's just been struck, crackling energy and heat, making my head buzz.

Noor says my name. I think she said something before that, and I didn't register it, but I can't answer her—I can't find my tongue.

I need to get away from them. Over Noor's head, I notice my classmates slowly starting to merge over to where Lachlan and Bilodeau are standing by the fountain. I get up and start moving toward them, becoming far too aware of my own legs, so aware that they become disconnected from me, and I forget how to use them. I look straight ahead, determined not to separate, trying to stay in control. But there's a sound like a billion radio channels overlapping, and it won't get any clearer. I'm seeing everything through a telescope. A yellow light crystallizing. A pockmarked cobblestone. A wrinkled elbow. A water droplet. A mouth moving. And all the while, I'm locked behind that door in my head, trying not to scream.

18

I'm standing on the stairs in the hostel stairwell, alone, and I don't remember how I got here. Trying to remember is making my head pound, so I drag my feet up the stairs, find my room, and don't turn on the lights. I unlace my boots and kick them off, then crawl up the ladder to my bed and let my eyes adjust to the fuzzy darkness, listening to the faint ringing in my ears.

I remember what Craig said—what he's probably said to a lot of people—then that feeling like someone dumped cold water on me and my brain imploding with the desire to get away from him. After that, there's this recollection of walking through the city that is so hazy, it's more like an idea than a memory.

I really hope there isn't anyone in this room with me, because I start laughing. I can't help it. I just had one of the best nights of my life, and then it ended like *that*, like my brain was luring me into a false sense of safety just so I would land harder when it pulled the rug out from under me.

I know there's something deeply wrong with me, but the last time I felt *this* crazy was that day almost two months ago now, when Jordan told me she needed a break from me.

It had been a few weeks since she and Theo became official, and after a blowout fight about it, I told her I was going to try to be happy for her, and we agreed to keep hanging out. The thing was, it was difficult to be happy for her when she was on the arm of the guy who made her cry on a weekly basis since the ninth grade. No matter what she said to convince me he'd changed, that he loved her, it never made any difference. The dissonance of it was splitting my brain apart.

She figured out pretty quickly that she couldn't bring up her Halfwit friends with me, and then we had less and less to talk about, because she spent more and more time with them.

The one thing I thought was sacred was our lunch period on that dusty ledge between the lockers in the art hall. It felt like an unspoken vow, from the day we found that ledge, that that was where we would always be at lunch. But that day, she didn't show up. I spent half the period there, staring down the hall, willing her to come around the corner.

I found her where I was afraid she would be: in the cafeteria, at the Halfwit table. It was Jordan and Theo, and Maya and Connor on the other side.

I ignored the hot knife in my heart and marched up to

her, tapping into that anger that was always simmering at the back of my skull. "What the fuck?"

Jordan scanned me with these bugged-out eyes that looked exactly like Maya's. "What, dude?"

"You couldn't have texted me? At least?"

Her brow furrowed. "I *did* text you."

Maya leaned forward on her elbows. "Hey, maybe your service is—"

"I'm not *talking* to you," I snapped. She held up her hands and slouched back in her seat, her eyes swimming with amusement.

Theo snaked an arm around Jordan's shoulders and raised his eyebrows at me. "Maybe you should relax, yeah?"

I put up a hand to block out his face and asked Jordan, "Are we still hanging out after school?"

"Yes, we're still hanging out. I just—I thought I texted you—"

"Oh my God," Theo groaned, rolling his neck. "Would you just put him out of his misery, please?"

She spun on him. "Theo—"

He ignored her, raising his eyebrows at me. "She doesn't *want* to hang out with you anymore."

"*Theo.*" She gripped his knee, hard, and he mouthed "what?" like he said nothing of consequence. Her eyes were wide when she whipped her head back to me. "That is not true, I never said that."

But I could see the way her neck was patching up with red like it did when she was stressed. I could see how many people were turned to stare at us, how Maya and Connor were exchanging smirks, and Theo was still arching his eyebrows at me expectantly, like I'd been dismissed.

I usually ignored that feeling I got when I knew Jordan was lying to me because the lies she told were so much easier than the truth. But I couldn't do that then, not when everyone else knew it, too.

I left the cafeteria without another word. I thought I heard her calling after me, but I was convinced I was making that up just to feel better. I felt numb all the way to the washroom until I looked at my pale reflection in the mirror and went cold with dread.

It was over. It was really over this time, and there was no one left.

My stomach roiled violently, and I spun around and burst into a stall, diving over the toilet. I heaved over it, and nothing came up. I heaved again, my chest spasming.

At some point, I felt someone kneel down next to me on the grimy floor of the boys' washroom, putting a hand on my back. I could see her shiny copper hair in the corner of my eye, the way it looked almost green under the fluorescent lights.

I thought for a second that things might be okay, but when I lifted my head, she was looking at me like I was losing my mind. Her eyes were wide and watery, and I could see her throat working as she swallowed.

"Alis, I'm always going to care about you," she said softly, tentatively, like walking on glass, "but I also care about them, and it feels like you can't accept that."

I tried to keep my voice steady. "Last year, when I asked you if you had a crush on anyone, do you remember what you said? You said there wasn't a chance in hell you'd date anyone at this school. And then you said—you said to me, *you are the only person I'm ever going to care about, ever.*"

She dipped her head, tucking her hair behind her ear. "Okay, I don't remember saying that. But if I did, then... I was being stupid. Obviously I have to care about other people. Do you not care about anyone else?"

I hated her for asking me that when she knew the answer already. I sat back against the wall of the stall and ran my hand down my face. "This is why I asked you if you really meant it, and you said you did."

She was looking at me helplessly, like I was speaking Spanish, and part of me began to wonder if I hallucinated that whole conversation.

"Jordan, like—" I cut myself off with a frustrated growl, fisting my hair. "Sometimes, I actually feel like my head is broken, so I just need you to tell me the truth. Do you not want me around anymore?"

She looked at her legs folded beneath her, and I saw a tear darken the fabric of her jeans. When she brought her eyes back up to mine, her chin was trembling.

"Maybe I just need a break," she whispered, and my chest caved in.

There was the truth. I was too much. I was too crazy, and I embarrassed her, and she didn't want me around. My head was spinning because I just didn't understand how that and the other thing she said, that she would always care about me, could co-exist. Because I knew for sure I cared about her—I loved her more than anything—and I wanted her around all the time. And I knew my parents didn't care about me, and they never wanted me around. I was questioning everything she ever said to me, feeling like I was falling through empty space.

She left after that, and that was it. We didn't speak again until weeks later, at the party I never should have gone to.

Now, lying in the dark, tracing the fissures in the ceiling with my eyes, I can feel the urge clawing at me. I want to get up, dig the folding knife out of my bag and shut myself in a stall, but I feel both too empty and too heavy, like all my insides have been scooped out and replaced with wet sand.

I'm woken up by my phone buzzing against my thigh. The time tells me I've only been asleep for twenty minutes, and when I see the notification beneath it, I'm wide awake again.

CRAIG ♥

New iMessage

A cold needle plunges into my heart.

What did I do tonight? What did I look like? What did he see? No one's ever told me what I look like in the dream state. Did I say anything? Did I start screaming even though I thought I couldn't?

I let the phone fall onto my chest and squeeze my eyes closed, pressing a fist to my forehead.

This is it—he's texting to tell me that he can't be around me anymore.

The phone buzzes again, and it nearly slips from the sweat on my palm when I turn it around.

CRAIG ♥

2 iMessages

I know I'm just stalling. It's not like I can ignore it. I'd rather confirm what I already know, see it written there so I can take it to the washroom and give myself one cut for every word.

I tap open the messages.

The first one I see is the one Craig sent to himself when he put his number in my phone:

Hello Craig it's the prince of darkness

Then:

Hey plz don't answer this if you're sleeping. But if you're not sleeping, just wanted to say that I'm sorry if I said or did something tonight that made you uncomfortable? I'm just a bit worried. But again plz don't answer if you're sleeping. Ok goodnight

But also you could just send a skull emoji or something to let me know you're good

Jesus, what did I do? What did I *do* tonight that he would send me this? *I'm just a bit worried.*

I get another notification, this one from a random number.

> hey alis it's noor. if you're awake can you send craig a message? he's being extremely annoying

Noor. Noor would've been there. She might even remember everything I said, every word, like she had with Eric. And hearing it from her, deadpan and matter-of-fact, that will be easier to swallow than Craig trying to break it to me nicely so he doesn't hurt my feelings.

I sit up and tap on her message, my heart hammering. I start typing:

> Where are you?

Her typing bubble comes up almost immediately.

> going up to 203

> Alone?

> yes

> Can I come?

She thumbs-ups my message, which I assume means yes. I nearly slip on the ladder on my rush down. I don't bother putting my boots back on, even though I know it makes me half an inch shorter, and I really don't have that much height to spare.

I book it down a level and follow the signage to 203. Once I get outside her door, I text her that I'm there because I don't want anyone else to answer when I knock. There's a dim light on the wall to the left of the door, and the bulb casing is full of dead bugs. I stare at that and take a deep breath, but my chest feels uncomfortably tight.

Noor slips out a moment later, having changed into sweats and an oversized Algonquin Park shirt. Her hair is still flat and shiny, but there are little flakes of mascara under her eyes. She moves to lean against the wall, which is striped this awful yellow and red like a circus tent.

"I need to ask you something," I say breathlessly.

She crosses her arms. "Okay."

"Did I—" I can't fucking catch my breath. I try again. "Tonight, did I—"

It feels like a brick wall is forming in my chest, stacking higher and higher. When I try to inhale, my breath halts against it and refuses to go any further.

Her gaze flicks over my face, and she drops her arms. The yellow and red stripes behind her are suddenly verging on green.

"Are you having a panic attack?" she asks. Little white sparks burst around the sides of my vision and swarm her.

When I try to take another breath and it doesn't come, I feel suddenly like I've been teleported to the top of a very tall building, and I'm way too close to the edge.

I wave my hand in front of my face, trying to tell her I

can't breathe. Her eyes dart to something over my shoulder, then back to me.

"Come here," she says, rolling off the wall and swiping her keycard through the reader. "There's no one in here."

I'm barely through the door before I'm bending over with my hands on my knees, sucking in nothing.

"No, hey," Noor says from somewhere. "Look at me. Look how I do it."

I lift my head, and she inhales deeply, her eyebrows rising to her hairline. I try to copy her, but I can't. I can't.

I'm rocked by a cold, lurching terror.

I'm going to die.

I'm about to fucking die—

"Alis, you can breathe. It's just in your head. There's nothing stopping you."

She's so calm. How can she be so calm? This isn't normal, this isn't—

But she's so calm. She's bringing her hand up on her inhale, then pushing it back down on the exhale, nodding encouragingly at me.

I try to do the same motion. My lungs feel ready to explode, and I know my hand is flailing, but she says, "Yes, like that. In and out."

Suddenly, I inhale. It's like a fist punching through that brick wall, but once the air is in, my chest locks, and I can't get it out again. My blood goes cold with fresh dread.

"It's okay," Noor says. "One more time."

I try it again, keeping my eyes on her as she does it, and it comes again—another gasp, another fist through the wall. This time the bricks crumble around it, and I fall onto my knees with relief, my lungs burning with the fresh air.

I drag myself, panting, over to the nearest bed so I can lean my shoulders against it, then put my trembling fists on my forehead.

"God, what the fuck," I breathe.

I feel Noor settle down on the floor next to me. "I get them, too."

"What?" I lift my head to look at her. "What was that?"

She frowns. "You've never had one."

"No, I get—"

I'm about to tell her about the dream state, but it's like something wraps itself around my tongue and yanks it silent. I rub my palms over my knees instead, my fingers trembling from the evaporating adrenaline.

Noor cocks her head. "To be honest, I thought that's what might have happened tonight."

My eyes widen. "I was doing *that*?"

"No, you were just... spaced out. At least, from what we saw of you. You stayed far away from us the rest of the night."

"I didn't mean to. I... What did I—did I do anything else?"

Her eyebrows twitch together. "I mean, no, but you're asking me like you can't remember."

I open my mouth, not knowing what I'm going to say, when the door makes a mechanical whirring noise. Maya starts inside, stopping when she notices us on the floor.

She frowns, pointing at me with the phone in her hand. "Are you lost?"

Noor looks at her over her shoulder. "Could you go outside for a second?"

"This is *our* room. How about *he* goes outside—"

"Just go and wait for two minutes, or I'll shred your clothes while you're sleeping."

Maya looks between us, her eyes widening under her furrowed brow. "You know what? Gladly. Fucking nightmare people."

She backs out the door and slams it.

Noor and I look at each other.

"*Nightmare people*," I parrot.

"I like it, too. We should start a band."

I breathe a laugh, grinning at her. Then I remember I feel like a wet paper bag that's been whipped around in the wind all day, and I put my forehead back on my hands.

"You'll probably sleep like the dead," she says. "They're the worst things in the world when they're happening, but I usually feel better afterwards."

I don't know if I'm feeling better. I'm feeling, I think, like my body is in revolt, and I need to see a doctor.

Then I remember what Noor said: *It's just in your head. There's nothing stopping you.*

So no doctor, then.

"Is that all you wanted to ask?" Noor prompts. I lift my head to see her sitting there so calmly after she just saved my life, after she told me that she, too, gets these panic attacks. Like it was nothing. So I don't know why conjuring up the question I now want to ask still feels like sticking my hand in a dark hole, not knowing what's on the other side.

Do you ever feel like you're in a dream?

I open my mouth, and what comes out is: "Yes. Thank you."

She's looking at me like she doesn't believe me, so I know it's time to go. I use the bed as leverage to pull myself to my feet, feeling rubbery and heavy. She follows me up, and now that it's over and we've fallen into silence, my skin feels tight and hot with embarrassment.

"Um," I start, "also, thank you for…"

She has the grace not to let me finish. "You're welcome. But also, please text Craig. I know he's staring at the ceiling right now, thinking you're never going to talk to him again."

Maybe that wouldn't be such a bad thing if talking to me means talking me down from *panic attacks* now, too.

As I head back to my room, my mother's voice is ringing in my head:

Sometimes you are way more trouble than you're worth, you know that?

And I do. I know that now more than ever.

19

Noor was right—I slept like the dead. I slept so deeply, in fact, that I didn't feel it when Eric wrote *cock* on one of my cheeks and *sucker* on the other.

It's so unoriginal that I can't even be offended, but I am annoyed as I stand at the washroom sink trying to scrub it off. I'm also fucking embarrassed because at least three people passed me in the hall and said nothing about it. At least none of them were my classmates.

Of course, as soon as I think that, Drew walks into the washroom. I only glance at him long enough to see the bright, mismatched chaos of his outfit before I'm shoving my face back in the sink.

"You're doing that way too aggressively," he says. "Slow circles, dude, not up and down."

I feel him stop at the sink next to me, so I decide to get it over with and straighten up, giving him a flat look in the mirror. The words are slightly smudged but still legible.

Whatever expression was on his face before slackens. "Oh."

I go back to scrubbing. I can feel Drew doing nothing next to me and wish he would get back to minding his own business. "What is it, Sharpie? Lemme google."

I spit water and soap. "It's fine."

"Already googling, bro. I'm assuming you don't have olive oil, or rubbing alcohol, or—*oh*." He knocks my arm with the back of his hand, and I look up to see him showing me his search results. "Nail polish remover."

He tips his head as if to say *you're welcome* as he puts his phone away.

I really don't think I should be putting nail polish remover on my face, but as I look in the mirror and see how hopeless my scrubbing is, I know I don't have a choice. I start digging around in my bag at my feet.

"Who was it? Eric?" Drew asks. "He's a dick. He once tried the finger-in-warm-water thing on me when we went on that tenth-grade overnight trip. Luckily, I've got a bladder of steel."

I pause, frowning up at him. "I didn't know he messed with you."

Drew starts putting toothpaste on his toothbrush. "He always thought I was gay because I have good hygiene and I like clothes." There's a beat, then his eyes widen at me in the mirror. "Not that there's anything wrong with being gay. I love the gays."

His panic makes me snort, which seems to help him relax because he grins and starts brushing his teeth. Once I find the nail polish remover, I soak some toilet paper with it. It takes a long time given it keeps disintegrating on my face, but it does the trick.

I throw my hair up in a knot because it has this ugly kink in it from the pigtails last night, then finish changing in a stall. Drew is still at the sink gelling his hair by the time I'm done, and I pause on my way out, clearing my throat.

"Thank you," I say. "And also, I'd appreciate it if you didn't tell anyone."

I really don't want to hear Noor and Craig's *I told you so.*

Drew crosses his hand over his chest. "To the grave, bro."

I feel a warm rush of gratitude for him, which is why I add: "Also, your hair is really cool."

He looks at me over his shoulder, and his dimples aren't as pronounced as his sister's, but his smile is just as contagious. He runs a hand over the swirling designs shaved into the side of his head. "Thanks. Let me know if you ever plan on shaving your hair off, 'cause I know a guy."

"Maybe like a side shave. Then I could tattoo my skull."

"Bro, that would be *sick*," he says, turning back to the mirror. I smile to myself before leaving him to his hair gelling.

I realize this is the second person, after Noor, to whom I've said *I didn't know Eric messed with you.* I'm starting to think I've had my head so far up my—and Jordan's—ass these last four years that I just didn't care to notice, and I'm wondering how different my life would have been if I had.

On my way to the courtyard, I catch sight of the Halfwits pushing through the front doors into the lobby. It's a free day today, so they could have been anywhere, but from the looks of it, they didn't have a very good time. Theo looks even more like shit than he had the day before, and Maya is walking with her arms wrapped around his arm, talking lowly in his ear. He keeps pushing his hand back through his hair and nodding, but I see the muscle ticking in his jaw.

There's definitely something wrong with him, and I'm wondering if maybe Jordan broke up with him after that gross phone call I heard between them.

Not that I care. At all.

Eric and Connor trail in behind them, and when Eric catches my eye, he gives me that shark-like grin before doing an obscene gesture involving his hand and his tongue in his cheek. Theo follows his gaze, and I watch his face go slack when he sees me.

I don't like the look on his face at all. I don't like it so much, in fact, that I can't even muster the dignity not to speed-walk when I head down the hallway toward the courtyard. I have that feeling I used to get as a kid whenever I had to come back upstairs from the wine cellar in the dark, like something was about to grab my leg and pull me back down.

But nothing grabs my leg, and my heart settles as I push through the door and spot Craig and Noor on the deck. They're pressed together on one of the wicker couches, looking at something on Craig's phone. He's wearing the hat again, along with a red plaid overshirt that clashes with his pink cheeks, but at least he's made one good decision in rolling the sleeves up to the elbows.

When I got back to my room last night, I decided to send him a skull emoji like he asked. Then he hearted the message, and I promptly passed out. So, I don't really know where we stand, and my stomach is fluttering with nervous butterflies as I approach them.

"Hey," Noor says to me, sounding grumpy, but no more than usual. "We went to the Colosseum without you."

My phone was dead when I woke up and is still charging upstairs, so I have no idea what time it is. Either they got up early, or I actually *slept in* for what feels like the first time in forever. My parents would be appalled.

Craig smacks Noor lightly on the arm. "You weren't supposed to tell him that."

She shrugs and says to me, "I'll go again if you want to."

"It's fine." I did want to see the Colosseum, but just the fact that they're acting like we're a package deal or something has my nervous butterflies transforming into giddy ones.

Craig gives me a slightly mischievous grin when I meet his eyes. "I have to show you something immediately."

He starts scooting over until Noor is crushed between him and the metal arm of the couch. It looks uncomfortable, but they're both looking at me expectantly, so I sit down next to Craig. It is immediately very, very squishy.

When Craig goes to show me his phone, the back of his hand hovers over my thigh, and I have to physically restrain myself from rolling my eyes when a flush of tingling heat rushes through me. I'm the biggest virgin on the planet.

I concentrate on what he's showing me and see it's a text conversation with MOTHER. There's a bear face emoji next to her name. He's sent her the photo of me sitting on that ledge last night, looking frightened as the little girl next to me screamed her head off. Under that, MOTHER wrote:

> He's giving early 1980s Iron Maiden

> First concert I ever saw and my ears rang for 4 days after!!!

I frown down at it. "Does that say 'he's giving'?"

"Yeah, she loves to learn the lingo." His voice rumbles against my entire arm, and I have to suppress a shiver when his breath tickles my ear.

I clear my throat and wave my hand at his phone. "Okay, look up 1980s Iron Maiden."

"I already did, but there are better comparisons to be made."

I whip my head up, which was a terrible idea because I almost clip his chin. Our faces are so close that my eyes dip automatically to his lips. I snap them back up just as quick, but my pulse has accelerated. "Like what?"

His ears are going red like his shirt. "No, I'm not telling you."

Noor sticks her head out from behind him. "He thinks you look like 2004 Gerard Way."

"For God's—you're actually a rat," he says. Now he's full-on blushing, I swear to God. Like, more than usual.

"I disagree, by the way," Noor adds.

I have no idea how to react to this conversation, but those butterflies are going crazy.

"What do the rest of the texts say?" I ask, unable to keep the smile off my face. I start grabbing for his phone, but he snatches it away, holding it up and out of my reach.

"She said that I should invite my *edgy* new friend for Friday night dinner. Noor comes sometimes when she feels like she can tolerate my mother's chronic extroversion."

My stomach swoops. Then I realize, "Friday night? We're in Venice."

He gives me that smile that I recognize from the Eiffel Tower when I tried to insult him about not knowing big words, and my cheeks heat. "No, like, Friday night dinner is every week. It's a Jewish thing. My brother comes home from college every Friday night, so we can have Shabbat."

"Miranda is a very good cook," says Noor.

Craig raises a finger. "True, but she's going to make you eat. Like eat, eat."

"I can eat." I realize I've basically just accepted his invitation, which fills me with something that I'm not sure is terror or excitement but has me fumbling to add, "But I'm only going if Noor is going."

"Noor can't protect you," Craig says, carefully putting his phone back in his pocket. "My mother already asked her all of the questions. It's going to be all about you next time."

Oh. On second thought, I'm going to tell him I'm sick and can't make it.

"You've scared him now," Noor says.

In a desperate attempt to change the subject, I say, "We should go get food."

"I thought you'd never ask," Craig says. He raises his eyebrows at me. "Literally, I thought you'd never say those words."

I roll my eyes and get up from the couch, half-relieved and half-mourning his body heat. "I have to go up and get my phone first."

Craig tells me he wants to change—thank God for that, I hope he burns that shirt—and heads upstairs with me. We pass Connor on a couch in the lobby, and it's weird seeing him alone. Even weirder, though, is how he glances up from his phone and gives me a look like I just caught him rifling through my underwear drawer. Then he ducks his head again so quickly, I convince myself I imagined it.

Craig slips into a room down the hall from mine, and when I get to my own door, I hesitate.

Theo and Eric could be in there.

And do I even need a phone? Who is texting me? The only two people in the world who would text me are going to be with me.

For a moment, I think I might roll with this and walk away, until I decide there is no way I'm going to let the mere *thought* of them drive me away from my own goddamn room. I'm not scared of Eric and his Sharpie or Theo and his psycho death stare.

Still, I stand there frozen for another ten seconds before I have this sorry little thought that maybe I should wait for Craig and have him come in with me. It's humiliating enough that I finally open the door.

I walk in to see Theo sitting on the edge of his bed, his forearms on his knees, apparently doing nothing but staring at the floor between his feet. I pause halfway into the room, feeling a prickle of unease when he doesn't lift his head, like he doesn't need to bother because he knows exactly who it is. Then I hear a scuff behind me and spin to see Eric stepping away from the wall. He'd been hiding behind the door.

That's all I need to know before my body kicks into flight mode. I lurch for the door, but Eric is already slipping out of it, pulling it shut just as I grab the handle.

When I pull down on it, it doesn't budge, and on the other side I hear him shout elatedly:

"Out of order, princess!"

20

Maybe he's not actually that strong. He can't be that strong, right?

But he is that strong, and the door handle won't move despite me practically hanging off of it.

Okay, I think, releasing it. *Okay.* I'm not gonna start panicking because that's what they want. This is a prank, and I can handle it. I always handle it.

I move into the room, curling my hands into fists because I can feel them shaking. I glare at Theo and try not to think about that day in front of Jordan's house.

"What?" I snap.

He finally lifts his head, and his eyes are flat and dark in a way that makes my hair stand on end. "I just got off the phone with Jordan."

I try very hard to keep my voice even. "Okay?"

"I think you should know that I know the fire was an accident." The bedsprings creak as he stands slowly to face me. "I didn't when I hit you, but I knew when the police confirmed it. Who can blame me though, right? Hell of a coincidence. The party, then the fire."

For one brief, head-spinning moment, I'm wondering if this is an apology. Or at least a really shitty warm-up to one. But then he says, "I kept up appearances, though, because I have a duty to my peers to keep them away from you."

It's good to know that I have enough self-preservation not to snort at *duty to my peers* as much as I want to. Or maybe it's not so much self-preservation as the cold stone of dread that just dropped down in my stomach, because if he knows I didn't start the fire, then *what* is his problem with me?

"Good for you," I say. "Can you get to the point?"

"Sure," he says, watching his feet as he steps closer to me. "You know that fucked up little habit of yours?"

She told me you look like you've been through a paper shredder.

I feel my lips go numb as the blood leaves my face.

"Did you know she's started doing it, too?" he says. "Because she's sitting around at her dad's place losing her mind, and that's all she can think to do."

There's an agonizing pang in my chest, but it's quickly swallowed by the white-hot anger that surges through me. I've spent enough time blaming myself for this that I know exactly what he's implying, but for some reason, hearing it from him pisses me off more than anything else. "So you went off to Europe instead of staying with your girlfriend, and that's somehow my fault?"

He raises a finger at me, and the *J* charm on his

bracelet glints maliciously. "It's *your fault* because you taught her how to do it."

"Taught her? I didn't—"

"*It works for Alis,*" he parrots, doing an impression of her voice that makes my skin crawl. "*I don't get why it doesn't work for me.*"

He takes another step closer, and I take a step back, vividly aware of the chest of lockers at my back and the lack of windows.

"I haven't touched you because, for some reason, she still gives a shit if you live or die. But I *know* that if you'd never been in her life, she wouldn't be so—" He points a finger at the side of his head and spins it around, bugging his eyes out.

My mind is splitting itself apart trying to reconcile what he's saying, because wasn't she always sad? Wasn't she always raiding her parents' liquor cabinets and smoking weed and doing stupid adrenaline junkie shit just to feel something? Wasn't she always breaking things and slamming doors and screaming? She was always like that.

But then, she didn't seem sad when I met her. And I was always around after that, and she only ever got worse. And then she cried as she told me she needed a break from me, like I was sucking the life out of her.

There's a second where I think I might just accept it and let him kick the shit out of me or whatever he's planning to do. But then I look at his face and see the curl of disgust to his lips and the way he says he *knows*. He *knows* she would've been better off without me, just like that first day back at school after the fire: *I know it was you*. And he didn't know shit. He thinks he knows everything, and I hate him for it, and I hate her for the things she's told him and the things she's made him think.

"Did you ever consider," I say, "that maybe she's just doing it for attention?"

There's a moment of suspension when he's looking into me, and it's like his eyes are sinking into dark pits.

Then he lunges, and my head smacks into the lockers behind me as his hands close around my throat.

He can't be serious?

He can't—

I can hear the wheezing sound I make when I try to breathe. There's no air, none at all. I look at his face, his lips curled back, the bottomless hatred in his eyes, and that's when I feel a jolt of panic like a rocket tearing through me.

I start pulling with all my strength where my hands have latched onto his, but they may as well be encased in cement, and he only squeezes harder.

There's a pressure building in my head as my ears fill with buzzing, and I think it's going to explode. My head's going to explode.

My lungs burn for air, and a fresh wave of terror has me digging my nails into his hands, his arms, trying to rip his flesh open. There's an orange tint to the world that wasn't there before, and through it, I see his face mutated by rage, the veins popping at his temples, red skin rippling with the force of crushing my throat.

He's going to kill me.

My vision is blotting at the edges, like black lace being pulled slowly over my eyes.

He's going to kill me.

I'm so lightheaded, and my hands start sliding uselessly against his. The panic begins to ebb, replaced with this crushing grief, knowing that this is the last thing I'm ever going to see. But I no longer feel afraid. It's like I've plunged beneath the surface of a lake, with nothing but the roar of water in my ears and the peaceful feeling of being far removed from the chaos above the surface. I seem to hover here for ages.

Then suddenly—drowning.

I'm choking on the breath I'm trying to suck in, and the world spins like I've just been slingshotted. The blood rushes too fast, too hard back to my head.

Someone is shouting, garbled by the roaring in my ears and the violent tearing of my own coughing. Each one explodes in my skull, sending stars prickling across my vision. Everything is happening at once—spatters of mucous and spittle on yellow tile, frantic speaking, the hot, grounding pressure of a hand on my upper back.

When the coughing subsides, I feel this crawling sensation up the back of my neck, and I heave myself up onto my ass so I can see where I am. Then I immediately start tipping over because my head feels like a bowling ball, and an arm braces me across the shoulders. I'm looking at a pair of legs in sweatpants folded next to mine.

"Get him out!"

This time, the words are bright and clear, and I feel

them vibrate in my shoulder. Somehow I know it's Craig, even though it sounds nothing like him. I keep trying to lift my head, and I see flashes of things: a bunk bed, Theo with his arms twisted behind his back, a backpack, Connor's stricken face, a shoe, Theo glassy-eyed and breathing heavy.

"Connor, are you deaf?" Craig snaps, his voice at a hysterical octave.

I hear shuffling feet, and a fresh spike of anxiety gives me the strength to keep my head up. Connor is leading Theo out like a jailer, which seems to bring him back to his senses. He wrenches himself out of Connor's grip, and Craig's arm tightens around me as he passes. He doesn't look at either of us as he flies out of the room, running a hand up into his hair as he goes. With one last wide-eyed glance over his shoulder, Connor disappears on his tail.

The moment they're gone, Craig whips around and puts his hand on the side of my face, guiding it up to his. His eyes are wide and terrified, all the flush gone from his cheeks.

"Are you okay?" he asks, a tremor in his voice. "Are you okay?"

The look of him makes the thing in my stomach rear up, because *I* did that. I made his face look like that, I made his voice sound like that. It doesn't matter if his hand against my face is the warmest, most solid thing in the world. It doesn't matter if I want to close my eyes and let it take all of my weight. I need to get up.

I start to tell him I'm fine, but it's like it's coming up through a straw in my throat, and the coughing starts up again. It's the most horrible thing I've ever felt, and it sounds like I'm hacking up a lung. When I surface from it, my head has tipped forward into Craig's chest, and my vision is pulsing red.

What is wrong with me? Get up. Get up. Get up—

"Okay, just don't—don't talk," Craig says. "I'm sure it's fine. I'm gonna call Lachlan."

The vibration of his voice in his chest is so soothing, I think I might fall asleep on him. But then he talks on the phone, and I hear how his voice is still wobbling over that warm, living rumbling under my ear, and I can barely believe how much of a selfish fucking baby I am.

I need to get up. I need to get up, but I'm just staring at the crook of his elbow. I'm trying to tune in to the sound of his heartbeat, to see if I can slow it down with my mind.

Get up get up get up get up—

His hand starts rubbing up and down my arm, and I close my eyes as that burning, writhing thing in my stomach nearly makes me puke.

21

Lachlan makes me see a doctor. I kind of figured she would—I don't think my being eighteen would allow her to get away with my death due to medical negligence. Still, she said she was calling an embassy or something, and it all sounded very complicated, and I could tell she was stressed. So now, as we sit in the back of a cab together, the squirming thing is lashing around inside of me at full force.

"Theo and Eric are going home," Lachlan says. "We don't know about Connor yet. Mr. Bilodeau is talking to him and Craig now."

I lean my elbow against the door and rub the flat of my hand against my forehead. I wish they would just leave Craig alone. He's supposed to be enjoying Rome with everyone else, and instead, he's getting interrogated for saving my life.

"Alis," she says, and I know she wants me to look at her even though I'd rather do anything else. But she's probably going to be spending a good chunk of her day with me, so I figure I owe her this much.

Her mouth is downturned at the corners, and her eyes are sad. "I'm very sorry that it got to this point. I know you didn't want to tell me what was happening, but I should have—"

No, I can't. I can't. I shake my head at her and look back out the window and hope she stops talking permanently, but it's too late. My insides feel like they're corroding, and suddenly I'm seven years old again, sitting in the passenger seat of my mom's car after she'd picked me up from the hospital.

I had decided to rearrange the furniture in the living room after school that day, but the couch was too heavy when I tried to lift it into place, and it came down on my foot. I didn't want to have to call an ambulance; the idea of it scared the living shit out of me. But I'd tried calling my mom so many times, and my dad, too, even though I knew it was late where he was, but neither of them answered, and the pain was unbearable.

So I did—I called the ambulance. On the way to the hospital, the paramedics asked me all kinds of questions about where my parents were and if I had a babysitter and if I was alone a lot, and I don't remember the things I said because I was numb with fear, and it hurt so bad. But judging from how long I had to stay in the hospital and how many people my mom had to talk to and how angry she looked in the car, the answers I gave them weren't the right ones.

"You do *not* involve other people in this family like that,

Alistair." It was dark out, and the red glow of the stoplight made her look even angrier than she sounded. "You just don't. You wait for me to get home, and we deal with it together, do you understand?"

I spoke as quietly as I could, looking down at the big astronaut boot they put my foot in. "It was hurting a lot."

"You could have gotten me into a lot of trouble, you know that? What would you do if they took you away, hm? Just because you couldn't wait five more minutes. You wouldn't get to live in a nice house like ours, I'll tell you that. How do you think you're going to cope—"

I sniffed, and her head whipped around. I held my breath and tried to stop, but it was too late; my throat was burning, and the tears were coming freely.

"Christ, *why* are you crying? Have you not done enough fucking crying?"

I shook my head, wiping my fist over my eye. I didn't know what to say. I wrapped my arms around the roiling guilt in my stomach, and my head pounded with how frustrated I was at myself for never getting anything right. But she started up again, her voice alternating between deadly soft and shockingly loud, her words needling into me over and over, and I was staring at the handle of the car door, thinking about undoing my seatbelt and rolling right out of it.

"Do I have to start hiring people to come watch you again?" she was saying. "Because I thought we agreed you were old enough—"

"*I am!*" I screamed. I just needed her to stop talking. I

felt like my head was going to burst, and my heart was pounding hard enough to make me feel faint.

To my surprise, my screaming worked—she was quiet the rest of the way home, except for the steering wheel creaking under her grip. But I couldn't relax. It felt like my skin was crawling over me, trying to slough itself off.

When she pulled into our driveway and shut the engine, I unbuckled my seatbelt as fast as I could and reached for the door.

Her hand was like a viper, striking out and latching around my wrist. I jumped in my seat, gasping as her fingers dug into the spaces between my bones. The fluorescent light shining above our garage door made her face look white like chalk.

She squeezed, pulling my arm toward her. "Next time you raise your voice to me like that, I'll give you something to really cry about. Do you understand?"

"Yes," I whispered, frozen with my back against the door, my free hand gripping the handle as I tried not to wince. I didn't realize she could be so strong, and I was scared she might grind my wrist to dust.

Then she released me. She hit a button, and I heard the rest of the doors unlock. I threw my door open and caught myself just a second before slamming it, shutting it quietly instead. I bolted into the house as fast as I could with my foot in a boot, then flopped facedown onto my bed and looked at my wrist through a blur of tears. There were red stripes where her fingers used to be, which throbbed in time with my pulse.

I closed my eyes and focused on those five little aches,

throbbing in harmony, until I stopped feeling anything else.

The good news is, I can talk. The bad news is, I need someone to babysit me for at least twenty-four hours to watch for worsening symptoms and signs of brain damage —doctor's orders.

In the cab back to the hostel, Lachlan starts with, "Look, I know you're not going to like this—"

"No," I say, my voice a bit thinner than normal.

"If you take a bed in my room tonight—"

"*No.* Seriously? No."

Even she knows how that would play with my class-mates, judging by her wince. Even if they *knew* that I was in there because of potential brain damage, they wouldn't let me live it down.

She looks hopelessly at me. "How am I going to know you're okay?"

"I'll ask someone else, and I'll text you every five minutes."

"'Someone else' as in a dumb teenager?"

"Yes. But I saw him playing Sudoku the other day, so he can't be that dumb."

She sighs. "Okay. *I* will ask Craig, because I need to know if he's actually up for it, and *you* will text me every hour. And I'm going to check on you in the middle of the night."

"Wonderful." Yes, I'm so glad this is happening to me. I

hope Theo and Eric get sucked out of their airplane over the Atlantic.

We get back to the hostel, and I'm standing in the lobby waiting for Lachlan to finish talking to the person at the front desk. I have a wicked headache brewing and want nothing more than to be asleep despite it being barely eight o'clock. And if it's bedtime for me, then I guess it's bedtime for Craig. Lucky him.

As if summoned by my thoughts, Craig and Noor come flying around a corner a moment later.

Well, Craig comes flying, and Noor walks calmly behind him with her arms crossed.

"You know you're *not* good at texting, Lachlan?" Craig says, storming up to her. She holds a hand up to him because she's still talking to the front desk person, so he rounds on me instead. "And *you* don't even bring your *phone!*"

Then his hands fly up to his mouth in prayer position, and his eyes go round. "Sorry, can you talk?"

"Let's pretend I can't." It sounds less hoarse every time I speak, but it still feels weird coming out, like my throat's a different shape than it used to be.

Craig folds over in that same way he did when he found Noor in Paris, and there's this terrifying, thrilling, heart-stopping moment when I think he's going to pick me up like he did to her. But he just murmurs to the floor, "Oh, thank God."

I look at Noor where she's hugging her ribs a little ways behind him and assume she knows everything, but I find I don't care if she does. Actually, I'm thinking I should've asked her to be my babysitter because I have a feeling Craig is going to be insufferable about it. But when Lachlan starts leading him away to give him the talk, I don't stop her.

When I look back at Noor, she's chewing on her cheek. "I'm assuming you're okay."

"Yes."

Her eyes flick down to my throat before she looks away, and I think I see her fingers digging into her sides. "Kepler took Theo and Eric out of here an hour ago."

I'm not even really relieved about it. I just feel tired. Like, good riddance, and thank you for leaving me with a headache and a mess. "My heart bleeds for them."

She gives me a little smile. "Me too."

We stand there in a silence that is not exactly comfortable, and I have to wonder if she's restraining herself from saying *I told you so.* She'd have every right, and just the thought of it has my face heating.

"Can I just say how honoured I am that you would want to put your life in my hands?"

I turn to glare at Craig where he and Lachlan are strolling back over to us. "Not *want.* Forced."

He frowns at me. "Forced to ask me specifically?"

"Craig, I'm going to fucking—"

"Okay, so here's the plan!" Lachlan barks. I snap my mouth shut, and we both turn to her.

The plan is that, now that Theo and Eric are gone, Craig and I get a room to ourselves. And I'm really, really trying not to freak out about that. I don't even know why I'm making a thing about it. I think I can admit to myself at this point that I feel a modicum of attraction toward him, but I think me dying from brain damage in the middle of the night is more likely than him wanting to fool around with me.

The front desk woman comes upstairs with us and unlocks that room that used to be mine, and I'm eternally grateful when Craig wordlessly follows her in to get my bag for me, because my heart is pounding and I feel uneasy at the thought of going back in there.

When he comes out, he has it slung over his back and doesn't give it to me. So I guess he's holding it for me.

She leads us to Craig's room, from which his three roommates were kicked out and moved into my old one, and we smile politely at her until she leaves. Then Craig turns to me. "I will say, I am kind of bummed your voice isn't like, a little bit huskier? You know, like sexy sick voice?"

I stare at him, because *why* is he bummed about that? But I think he misinterprets my stare because his face goes slack with horror. "Sorry. Sorry. That was—I don't mean to like, make jokes about it? That's just—that's how I deal with stress and sometimes I don't even realize I'm being insensitive—"

"I like your jokes."

His eyes go round with surprise, and his voice softens. "You do?"

"But I have a headache."

"Okay." His eyes widen. "Is that on the list? Lachlan said there was a list of stuff."

"No, that's just what happens when some asshole chokes you out."

He extends his hand. "Where's the list?"

I roll my eyes and pull it out of my pocket. He unfolds it, and his face starts going pale as he reads.

"Coughing up blood." He shows it to me, his eyes bulging. "It just casually says *coughing up blood*."

"Craig, I'm not going to cough up—"

"I think I'm going to kill him," he talks over me, and his voice has flattened. There's a distressed look on his face, and the paper is shaking a little in his hand. "I'm not normally homicidal, but when we got him off and you just *dropped*, I thought you were dead and that I was going to kill him."

A slideshow of horrible images starts playing at the back of my mind that I need to shut down immediately, so I say, "Do I need to ask someone else to do this? It's fine if—"

"No, I'm doing it. Go." He points to the door behind me, his face serious. I try to stop the smile creeping onto my face, but it's hard because him ordering me around is really funny. I think I manage to turn fast enough to hide it, just before I open the door to the room. To our room.

22

Craig puts his hands on his hips, frowning at the two bunk beds. "Hmm."

I sigh. "What?"

He gestures to one of the top beds. "Well, you can't take a top bunk because then I won't be able to see if there's something wrong with you—" he points to the bottom bed, "—but you can't take the bottom because there's no side rail. You'll just roll right off onto the floor, which is not good for someone with possible brain damage."

I narrow my eyes. "*Roll off*?"

He gnaws his lip in thought. Then he raises a finger in the air, his eyes lighting up. I watch him stride past me, grab the rail at the foot of the bunk bed and start pulling.

He drags the bed over to the other side of the room with what appears to be great difficulty, then jogs around to push it against the other bunk bed so the bottom beds are flush.

He grins at me, breathing heavily. "I'm a genius."

My stomach twists with embarrassment, and I glare at him under my lashes. "I'm *fine*, Craig."

"Unfortunately, for the next twenty-four hours, I'm not going to believe a word you say about your own health." He points at the makeshift double bed. "You go on the far side, so if you start rolling, you'll either run into me or the wall. And I'm very solid; you don't have to worry."

I don't know what to do about the heat under my skin. Is this something a straight boy would do? Maybe he's just that nice and that comfortable in his sexuality that this is nothing for him. But he's fucking seventeen, so that would be really annoying.

I notice his eyes are going a bit round as he looks at what he's done. He grips the back of his neck. "Sorry, is this weird? This is weird. I'm not, like—I'm not forcing you or anything. I'll just—"

"It's fine," I say shortly, because he's the one making it weird. I scoop up my bag from the floor and start heading back toward the door. "I'm going to shower."

I hear the slightest sound come out of Craig's mouth and spin on him, *"Don't* even."

Craig bites his lip, his eyes crinkling. "But what if you slip—"

I put my fingers in my ears, then use my elbow to push down the door handle. I stick my foot in the crack and wrench the door open with it, managing to escape without hearing whatever stupid excuse he was going to make for why he needs to follow me to the shower.

When I reach the washroom, I realize I didn't stop to get the folding knife. That thing in my stomach had been writhing around so hard in the cab and at the doctor's office, I thought for sure I needed to do something about it. And then I didn't.

And I still don't think I need to do it.

I swear it's the first time it's ever calmed itself on its own.

When I get back, I'm exhausted enough that I'm not even thinking about the sleeping arrangements. The shower was so warm and soothing on my muscles that I now feel like cooked spaghetti, except for the headache at my temples and the strange, tight ache around my throat. I tried to scrub at it, to get the feel of Theo's squeezing hands off of me, but it didn't work. Now it just feels raw in addition to the tightness.

Craig is lying on his bed with his ankles crossed, his phone held above his face. He's changed into a loose grey t-shirt and pyjama pants with anthropomorphized pizzas on them, and his hat is gone. There's this awkward intimacy to the whole thing that makes me avert my eyes when he props himself up on his elbows.

"Okay, no more showers," he says. "I had to lie to Lachlan when she texted me because I'm a terrible babysitter."

My throat hurts enough now that I don't want to speak

anymore, so I throw my backpack down by the radiator under the window and stand over him, waiting. He just sits there smiling up at me, until I have to bug my eyes out and swipe my arm in the universal gesture for *get the hell out of the way.*

"Oh!" He jumps up to his feet. "Sorry."

I start crawling across his bed, then roll on to mine. I exhale heavily and close my eyes, my wet hair soaking into the pillow.

I can still feel Craig hovering. When I open my eyes again, I see him wiping his palms down the sides of his pizza pants in my peripheral. He's probably regretting pushing his bed so close to mine and is trying to figure out how to tell me he's taking the top bunk instead.

"You need to either lie down or go away," I say hoarsely. "And turn the light off."

"Yes. Doing that." He jogs over to the light switch, and the room is plunged into darkness. I watch the shape of him moving back toward the bed, a solid silhouette against the hazy black.

He sits down on the side of the bed for a few seconds before swinging his legs onto it. I watch him tapping his fingers on his stomach in the corner of my eye.

"Do you care if I play on my phone?" he whispers.

I turn over, my back to him. "Mm-mm."

My eyelids are so heavy that they close right away, but I find that the only image I see in the dark is Theo's red, bloated face; the bead of spittle on his bottom lip, the fat vein in the centre of his forehead. I grit my teeth and open them again, willing the hammering of my heart to slow.

I watch the changing light patterns Craig's phone is casting on the wall and listen to the faint tapping of his fingertips until, eventually, the light disappears.

For a few moments, there's nothing but silence, as if he, too, is holding his breath. Then he whispers in the dark: "Are you okay?"

There's this desperation to it that makes me think he's been wanting to ask it for a long time, and my heart wrenches.

"Yes," I whisper back.

There's a very long pause. "Would you actually tell me if you weren't?"

I hate him. I fucking hate him for asking me that, and I don't know why.

"Just go to bed, Craig," I say. My heart hurts way more than anything else on my body right now.

I hear him shift as he gets under his covers. I don't bother with my own. I don't know how long it takes me to actually fall asleep, but at some point, I blink, and I'm looking at a different shape in the dark.

Craig is on his back beside me, his head turned away from me. The back of his hand is lying on the pillow, his fingers curled right next to my nose. His other hand twists in the fabric over his stomach, and I realize then what woke me: the sound of his breathing, quick and uneven, punctuated with those same little whimpers I'd heard back in Paris.

The moonlight seeping in around the curtains brightens as my eyes adjust, and I can see the way his face is pinched with anguish; his mouth twisted into a frown, his eyes screwed shut. The hand next to my nose curls into a fist, squeezing.

There's a pang in my chest. It's like there's this dark thing drowning all the lightness in him, and I have this uncontrollable need to banish it.

One of my hands curls over his fist, and the other reaches out to wrap around the far side of his face. His skin is hot and damp under my palm.

"Hey," I say, the pain of using my voice making me wince. I try again, louder. "Hey."

He takes these three quick inhales, the hollow of his throat sweaty and twitching like he can't get enough air. I slide my hand down to his wrist, squeezing, and then I pat his face. When that does nothing, I pat it a little harder until I'm basically hitting him.

Craig's chest spasms under my arm as he startles awake, gasping. My hand falls to his neck, where his pulse flutters against my thumb.

"Craig," I say.

His eyes land on me, wild and glinting in the moonlight, and for a split second, there's nothing behind them. Then he does a double-take, and it's like his soul drops back into his body.

"Jeez," he whispers. He lets out a soft, nervous laugh. "Sorry."

The laugh breaks through the concern I'd been feeling, and I'm suddenly vividly aware of every part of my body and the way I'm draped half over him, my hand on his neck, my nose grazing his shoulder, my knee pressing against his thigh. Craig is sat halfway up in the bed, looking down at me with glassy eyes and parted lips, his beautiful hair a mess. I watch his Adam's apple bob as he swallows.

"Sorry," he breathes again. This time, he says it like he's not sorry at all.

I let my hand drift further down from his neck, like maybe it's an accident when my fingers slide down over the ridge of his collarbone, and my palm stops on his chest. I feel the warm hammering of his heart under my hand.

"Alis," he whispers, and it's like someone lights a match in my lower belly. Any and all thoughts fly out the window until I'm nothing but the animal impulse that has me pulling myself up, smashing my lips against his.

Craig makes a small noise of surprise, the momentum tipping him back against the wall.

There's a terrifying moment of weightlessness when I'm expecting to crash into the ground.

Then he's pushing forward, his lips warm and alive on mine. His hand comes up in my hair, fingers blazing trails over my scalp. He's still breathing a bit heavy, and it's as if he's trying to inhale me as he starts hiking himself up further beneath me. I break away just long enough to grab his shoulders and swing my leg over his lap, straddling him, and he gasps. He looks up at me with his lips parted and his eyes dark and glittering like I've never seen them, then pulls me in again by the waist.

Our mouths crash back together, and I think I can feel him hard beneath me. I let one of my hands roam down his arm, making a very embarrassing noise as I wrap my hand around his bicep. My head fills with exclamation points at the feel of him, of his scorching skin and soft, warm mouth and hungry breaths. I'm pretty sure my inexperience is extremely obvious, but my mind doesn't have the bandwidth to think about anything except—

Except his hands creeping under the back of my shirt. His fingers burning on the bare skin of my lower back, climbing higher, the hem of my shirt rising, rising—

I yank away from him, snatching my hands back to my chest.

"Sorry," he says quickly, holding his hands up. "We don't have to..."

"No," I whisper, my blood still buzzing just beneath my skin. "I mean—I didn't mean to—but I can't do that."

His throat bobs as he swallows. He nods fervently, his eyes round and worried, all of the darkness gone. "Okay."

Feeling suddenly mortified to be sitting on his lap, I roll off him. I stare at the rail at the foot of my bed, my head floating.

Next to me, Craig pulls his legs up to his chest and curls over them, scratching at his forehead. Just as the silence gets unbearable, he says, "I'm gonna go get some water."

I don't reply. I look sidelong at him as he gets up and pads barefoot across the room, slipping out into the bright hallway. I don't know what he's going to put his water in; he left his water bottle on the windowsill.

When the door shuts, I fall back on the bed and sling an arm over my face, exhaling all the breath from my body. A moment later, I'm up again, scrambling for my headphones so I can drown out that singular, screaming thought that's going to keep me spiralling for the rest of the night.

What did you do?

I crank the volume on my phone all the way up.

What did you do?

23

The moment I open my eyes, I'm not thinking about anything but the pain.

It turns out being strangled hurts. A lot. My neck feels like it's made out of knots, and my throat is a column of fire in the middle of it, flaring to life when I swallow.

But then I flip over, and my arm falls through empty air and hits the crack between the two beds—mine, and the one pushed up right next to it.

"Fuck," I whisper. I scrunch up my face, not just because it physically hurts to speak, but because I want to curl up and die from humiliation.

The way I threw myself on him. The way I clung to him like a koala, trapping him against the bed.

I stick my face in the pillow and groan, and it hurts. So I keep doing it, louder, until it feels like there's an inferno in my throat.

Last night, after he told me he was getting water, he didn't come back for twenty minutes. The music was still blaring in my ears, but I closed my eyes as soon as I saw the door open. I could feel him hovering, like maybe he was checking if I was still breathing. Then I could feel when he was gone again, and I opened my eyes to stare at the empty darkness.

Shortly after that, Lachlan texted me:

> If you're sleeping, I'm going to come check on you now

I really did *not* want her to come in here and see our beds arranged like this, so I wrote back:

> I'm awake and I feel fine.

I don't know if Craig ever came back because, at some point, I fell asleep again. If I had to guess, he stayed far the hell away from me, brain damage be damned.

What the fuck was I thinking? As if he could possibly want me like that?

He was hard, though. I felt him—

But yes, of course, he was hard. It was dark, and he's a teenage boy. He'd probably get hard if he saw a cucumber and a peach sitting too close to each other.

He's going to come back in here and tell me all the reasons why that's a big *thanks but no thanks*, and he's going to do it in a gentle little voice so he doesn't hurt my feelings. I'm not going to have any choice but to flee the country because there's no way I'm going another three days—

The door clicks open. My heart trips into a gallop, and

I scramble up in bed, pressing my back against the wall as Craig slips into the room. He slowly closes the door, shutting it very softly, then he looks over his shoulder with a wince. I watch the tension melt from him as he sees me. "Oh, thank God. I promise I peed as fast as I could."

I pull my knees to my chest, my pounding heart making me dizzy. I feel like a very small animal cornered by something with very big teeth, waiting for it to lunge.

He comes across the room and pulls open the curtains. The room fills with bright morning light, stinging my retinas.

The best-case scenario would be that he doesn't mention last night and acts normally right now.

Actually, no—the best-case scenario would be if he somehow suffered amnesia overnight, but I don't think I'm going to get that lucky.

A flurry of dust motes dance around Craig as he turns to me. The hat is back, and he's no longer in his pizza pants but in a pair of grey sweats and a white t-shirt with The Clash's *London Calling* album on the front.

I watch his face fall as he looks at me, his arms going slack at his sides. "Jesus Christ."

My heart stops, thinking I'd somehow lost my sleeves overnight. But when I look down at myself, my chin connects with the bruises on my throat and reminds me. I reach up, my fingers grazing over it.

"It doesn't feel that bad," I say hoarsely.

Craig's eyes bug. "Okay, well, it *looks* like a nightmare."

The word *nightmare* drops like a penny in church, the sound of it seeming to echo around the room. In the loaded silence that follows, I see rapid snapshots of Craig's heaving chest, the sweaty column of his throat, my fingers curling over the side of his face.

And then, more—the slide of his lips on mine, the slopes of his arms, his hands in my hair—

Craig clears his throat. "Do you feel anything else?"

I pray my face isn't as flushed as it feels as I pick at a piece of fluff on my crossed legs. "Hm?"

"Like, from the list."

I glare at him from under my lashes. "You've fulfilled your guardian duties, Craig. You can lay off now."

"Actually, I haven't fulfilled my duties for another..." he looks at his bare wrist, seems to realize there's no watch there, then scans his eyes across the ceiling. "Eleven hours."

There are three soft knocks on the door. Craig looks toward it, then back at me. "I asked Noor to bring these pain pills she uses when she's on her period."

"The doctor gave me ibuprofen."

"These are different. Just—" he waves dismissively at me and goes to open the door.

Noor comes in with a purple pill box clutched in her hand. I brace myself for her to say something about the furniture arrangement, but she doesn't. She comes over and sits on the edge of Craig's bed, and I watch her eyes fall to my throat, then to the mattress. "That's completely insane what he did."

I shake my head. "I said some shit to him."

"*Um*," Craig says, loudly. He's standing on the other side of the room with his hands on his hips, outrage pinching his face. "What if it were Noor he attacked? Is that just no big deal because she *said some shit*?"

I feel a shock at the humourless look on his face and the way his voice has gone hard in a way I've never heard before.

"Of course not," I say. "I just—I knew he was pissed and I—"

"No. He's bigger than you, and he knows it, and he shouldn't have put his fucking hands on you. Can you —*stop* doing that?" His voice cracks at the end, and his hand is flung out toward my throat, his eyebrows raised to his hairline.

I realize I've been pushing, rhythmically, on the bruises. I snatch my hand back, my eyes widening. His own eyes are wide and wild like he's looking at a crazy person, and I feel so mortified I want to sink through the mattress and disappear forever.

"Craig, maybe you should go for a walk," Noor says over her shoulder.

"No, I'm—" he stops because his voice is still loud. He looks at her, then looks at me, and his face softens. "Sorry. Sorry, I'm not yelling at you. I'm just angry. At him. And I can't stop seeing—but I'm fine. And you're fine. So we're good."

He grabs the water bottle off the windowsill and comes to kneel on the floor by the bed. He doesn't look at me as he takes the pill box from Noor and fumbles it open, tapping two of them out on his palm.

"Uh, just one," Noor says.

He puts one back. Then he holds his hand out to me

and gives me the water bottle with the other, wordlessly. I accept both, feeling this weird urge to laugh even though nothing at all funny has happened.

"Those make me feel like someone's put numbing cream on my uterus," Noor says. Then, "Oh, wait."

I freeze with the pill halfway to my mouth.

"Does caffeine give you anxiety?" she asks.

I snort. I think I just *am* anxiety.

I take the pill with a swig of water. Craig is watching me, so I try not to wince when it feels like a giant marble going down my throat. I think I fail because a muscle jumps in his jaw just before he drops his head, rubbing his forehead with his fingers.

"Okay. I'm going now," Noor says. She takes her pills and makes her way to the door. As she opens it, she says to Craig, "You better stop swearing, or I'm telling Miranda."

Then she's gone. I look down at my fingers in my lap so I don't have to look at Craig.

The bed creaks with his weight, and my heart starts ramping up again.

I'm sorry if I gave you the wrong impression, he'll say. *I just want to be friends,* he'll say. Then he'll disappear from my life forever.

"I didn't mean to yell at you."

I look up to where he's taken Noor's spot. There's sunlight stretching over the bed from the window, making the hairs on his arms glitter and turning his eyelashes copper. His face is somber, and I think about how I might not ever see him smile at me again. I feel a sudden, overpowering grief at what I've ruined.

He swallows and continues, "I just have a really hard time understanding people like that."

He actually means it, too. I can see how confused he is, imagining that even someone as well-bred as Theodore Grant could be capable of something like this.

All my life, I've brought out the worst in people, and he's not even able to believe that the worst of people exists.

I reach up toward the bruises again but curl it into a fist on the way there, putting it back in my lap. I know I'm getting too close to revealing to him my *fucked up little habit.* But I suppose it doesn't matter now anyway. He's only still here because he promised Lachlan he would watch over me and because that's the kind of person he is.

So, eleven hours, then. Eleven hours before he breaks it off.

"Anyway," Craig says, sniffing. "I'll tell Lachlan you're a decent shade of purple, I guess. But it'll look worse tomorrow. And the next day."

That urge to laugh comes over me again. I think it's stemming from the fact that he's seventeen and wearing a beanie and giving me a prognosis. "Is that your professional medical opinion?"

When he looks up and sees my lips quirking, his own smile comes back, and I feel such relief I could cry. "You know I skateboard, right? I've seen things you wouldn't believe. Gnarly things."

"*Gnarly?* Of course you skateboard."

"Don't stereotype me," he says. He reaches for his backpack at the foot of the bed and slings it over his shoulder as he stands. "I skateboard, yes, but I also like boys. So."

My blood spikes, and I feel my eyes widen despite myself. The top bunk obscures his face until he's far enough away, by the door. He looks back at me with his eyebrows raised innocently. "You should get dressed, actually. We're gonna be late for *Firenze*."

He leaves the room, and I can see him smiling to himself as he shuts the door behind him.

PART IV

FLORENCE

24

I went to look in the mirror that morning, and I didn't think it looked as bad as Craig said it did. It wasn't a nightmare. There's a bit of mottled grey colouring around my throat, and a bit of the colouring is thumb-shaped, but it's not *purple*. I think in the right lighting, you might not even be able to see it. As I stared at it, though, it started to morph, and I began seeing little faces in it. Then, when I looked back at my eyes, it didn't look like me at all. So I was very, very late, and Craig had to come get me to tell me we were going to miss our train, and that's why we're all breathing heavily as we stand on the platform at Roma Termini.

Needless to say, I don't think I'll be looking at the bruises again.

At least I finally feel some relief for the first time since it happened, because when I look around, there are no more Halfwits. There is only half of the Halfwits. The Quarterwits, Maya and Connor, are standing together, despondent, not saying anything to each other. Maya hasn't put any makeup on, and Connor has shadows under his eyes. I'm thinking back to that guilty look he gave me yesterday before it happened, and I have a very strong urge to go over there and slap him.

"As you might've noticed," Lachlan announces to our huddle, "we're now down to two teachers. Mr. Kepler has escorted Theo and Eric back home. They are no longer with us for reasons that are, and I will say this once and *only* once: none of your concern. Anyone comes poking around, I'll make your last month of school exceptionally unpleasant. Understood?"

There is some muttering of assent and some confused murmuring, and some heads lifting and noses twitching like bloodhounds searching for a scent. My hair is down, and the sweater I'm wearing is high enough in the neck that it covers most of the bruises around my throat, but still I find myself shrinking into it a bit.

The train arrives, and Lachlan starts leading us down the platform. I'm walking with Craig when Connor comes up to us, picking his fingers nervously.

"Hey Alistair," he says, walking alongside me. "Are you... how are you doing?"

I bristle, but before I can do anything, Craig says, "Connor? Walk away."

"I'm just asking—"

"Don't ask. Don't speak."

Connor's face scrunches with indignation. "You know I tried to stop him—"

"Did you?" Craig says, astonishment colouring his

voice. "Well, thank you for the bare minimum. Do us a favour and stick with that since you're so good at it."

Connor stops walking, and we leave him behind.

I'm fighting a smile as I look up at Craig. "I didn't know you could be sarcastic."

Apparently, Craig is not in a smiley mood. He shakes his head, his jaw tight. "I came up to ask Eric what the hell he was doing because I had a bad feeling. I got the door open, and only after *I* went in there did Connor come help me out. And you know what he tells Bilodeau? *I didn't know what he was going to do. He just wanted to be alone with him.* Like, what did he think you guys were doing, Seven Minutes in Heaven? *Didn't know,* my ass."

At first I thought his seriousness about the whole thing was kind of funny, but even the word *ass* doesn't feel right coming out of his mouth. As I take in his obvious agitation, I feel the squirming thing start up again, and I'm wracking my brain for a way to get him to forget this ever happened. I don't know what I'm going to do if I've permanently messed up his face.

When we get on the train, he slides into a seat across from me, shakes out his arms, and makes a frustrated noise at the back of his throat. Then he takes a deep breath, and the smile breaks over his face like the sun slipping out from behind a cloud. "Better. Where is Noor?"

I stare at him. It's unbelievable to me that he can drop back into contentment so quickly. Is he faking it? He doesn't look like he's faking it. His eyes crinkle when Noor arrives. His cheeks are rosy. Maybe I was wrong, and he wasn't all that upset about it in the first place.

Noor kicks him out of his seat and makes him sit next to me because she and Drew want to watch *RuPaul's Drag Race* on his phone. Before they do, Noor dips under the table, and when she straightens up, she's holding out her white sneaker to me.

"Um," I say, leaning back in my seat.

"I want you to draw something on my shoe," she says. "Craig drew me and him sword fighting, Dakota did the squirrel, and Drew did the middle finger. You can put what you want."

"Um," I say again, and she reaches into her hair and pulls out a pen, because that's normal.

When I still don't take the shoe or the pen, she shakes them insistently at me. "I promise it doesn't stink."

"This is basically Noor asking for a hug, so you better not hurt her feelings," Craig says.

This makes me take the shoe. As the train gets moving, I stare at it with a stomach full of nerves and the pen motionless in my hand.

At first I'm thinking I should just do something purposefully bad because if I actually try and she hates it, that'll sting. But I could really use the distraction. If I try hard enough, I might even be able to make it last the whole ride to Florence, and I won't have to think about how I threw myself all over Craig last night.

Plus, I think I can risk defiling this shoe when Craig's drawing looks like *that*.

I decide to write out two words on the side in a gothic font. I use angular strokes like in Old English script but with snake-like tails on the serifs. I can feel Craig watching me, and it makes the back of my neck burn, but my self-consciousness falls away as I become absorbed in the task. It takes a while because it's pen on canvas, and the train is shaking beneath me, but I think it turns out semi-decent.

I turn the shoe to show Noor, and her eyes widen. She tugs the earphone from her ear, staring at the words.

Drew leans forward to squint at it. "*Nightmare People.* That's sick. Is that a band?"

Noor meets my eyes and says, very seriously, "I love it. I want it tattooed."

My heart leaps. I can't *believe* she just said that to me. I smile at her, trying to keep it from splitting into a shit-eating grin. I start handing her the shoe back, but Craig intercepts at the last second and pulls it close to his face, his jaw dropping as he runs his thumb over the inked canvas.

"On a *moving train*?" He turns to me, and I feel butterflies fluttering up to my head at the way he's looking at me, like *I'm* a pink sky moment. "You're actually amazing."

There is nothing I could possibly say to that, so I just bow my head to hide my burning, smiling face. When it's safe to glance up again, Craig is still admiring the shoe, Noor looks like she's chewing her cheek to stop that little smile from coming out, and Drew is staring at Craig like he's a puzzle he's seconds away from solving.

For the next half hour, I watch over Craig's shoulder as he plays Sudoku on his phone with my blood fizzing and my stomach, for once, warm and still.

As we line up outside Florence Cathedral, a sprawling white basilica patterned with pale green and soft peach marble, I stare up at its dark, serrated eaves and notice that the windows look like spiderwebs, and I think I'm falling in love with it.

That is, until we've waited for twenty minutes, then thirty, then forty. Then I think I hate it a little because the sun is beating down on me and I'm sweltering in my black layers. Everything is sticky and swampy, and I have to put my hair up and hope that no one looks too closely at my throat.

I'm expecting a crowded chaos when we get inside, but despite there being about a hundred people roaming the cathedral, the only sounds are low murmurings, slow foot-falls, and the occasional echoing squeak of a shoe. It's like everyone is in the thrall of this place, like we're all walking under the eye of a much older, much wiser ancestor.

I quietly slip away from the rest of my classmates, passing people lighting candles at votive stands, peering at plaques on the walls, and staring up at the stained-glass windows that are so bright they make your retinas ache. By the time I get to the far end, my skin is covered in goosebumps.

Above my head, the ceiling arcs into a dome, and I stare in wonder at The Last Judgement. It appears to be glowing from the inside. There are biblical characters perched on layers upon layers of clouds, and each layer splices the dome in misaligned strips from bottom to top, so it feels like I'm falling into a kaleidoscope. My eyes dart from winged devils to smiling cherubs to Jesus Christ himself, and the longer I look, the more detail I find. I think you could stare at it forever and still not see everything.

How does someone *do* this?

"Probably with a lot of patience and neck pain."

I startle, turning to look at Dakota, who has materialized next to me. "What?"

"Oh, sorry. I was just saying"—she points up at the fresco—"because you asked how someone could've done this. Patience and neck pain."

I did *not* realize I said that out loud or that anyone was standing next to me. Do I actually talk to myself, or was this a one-time thing? Was I walking around the Louvre muttering to myself about the Mona Lisa? Also, it's uncanny that she mentioned neck pain just now. I have this bizarre thought that maybe she's not Dakota but something sprung from the painting over my head— whether it's an angel or a demon remains to be seen.

"It's just so cool how humans have always been doing art, you know?" she continues, gazing wide-eyed at the fresco. "Like it's always been a thing, even when the Black Death was going around. Or like, cave drawings? We'd barely evolved, and we were spending our time drawing pictures. That's crazy, right?"

My heart skips a beat. *That's crazy.* She's doing what I do. She's looking for the awe.

She laughs nervously at me. "Are you staring at me because I'm making no sense?"

I decide that this is actually Dakota and not a divine manifestation. "No—no, I mean, I agree with you," I say quickly, and then, for some reason, my mouth keeps moving. "I actually didn't think I said that out loud, which is why I was... but your thoughts are exactly my thoughts."

Dakota gives me her dimpled, crinkly-eyed smile. My heart speeds up suddenly, and I feel this rushing sensation, like my next words are carried out of me on a wave. "I'm really sorry for what I said to you in the hallway."

The wave crashes back down, and I tense up, my eyes widening. I don't know why I would bring that up when she'd so gracefully forgotten it, and now I'm terrified she's going to say to me again what she said in the first place, and I'm going to snap at her, and the whole cycle is going to restart.

She looks confused for a moment, and it's like I can see the words running behind her eyes as she remembers. *Who the fuck are you? Leave me alone.*

"Oh," she mouths. Her eyebrows knit together as she shakes her head. "No, that's—it was bad timing. It's okay."

Another wave rises, and my stomach swoops like I've jumped off a cliff. "You're the only one. I want you to know that you're the only one who said anything to me after that night. So, thank you."

I'm standing there just long enough to see the way her eyes go round and her lips part, and then I leave her under the fresco with my pulse thundering in my ears.

There are people everywhere, but I slip behind a pillar, out of sight of the duomo. I put a hand over my mouth as if I can push the words I said back in, but it's too late; now, I'm standing on a precipice, waiting for the squirming thing to start screaming, for the acid to start spewing.

I fix my gaze on the votive stand in front of me, my eyes unfocusing so the flames of dozens upon dozens of tealights blur into a burning tree. I listen to the reverent hush of low voices and those slow, strolling footsteps, and instead of the squirming, I notice a new lightness to me, like I've had a layer of dust sucked off my soul.

All I'm thinking about is that wave that carried those words out of me and how it made me feel like I'd been scraped raw and put back together again. I stand there marvelling at this new feeling for so long that Lachlan has to come looking for me when we start to go.

It is, I think, the best pink sky moment I've had yet.

25

As much as I liked the cathedral, the thought of waiting in another line for the Uffizi Gallery has me audibly groaning on our walk over, and Craig ends up asking me if I want to go get food instead.

"It's barely eleven o'clock," I say.

"Okay, well." He hugs his stomach defensively. "I didn't go down for breakfast earlier because I didn't want you to die while I was shoving my face."

I can't tell if he's full of shit or if he genuinely thinks I might keel over from brain damage, but I agree to skip out on the *Birth of Venus* and go to lunch with him. We end up at Il Fratellini, which appears to be the world's tiniest sandwich shop—like, literally just a counter in a hole cut out of the side of a building, behind which are shelves packed with wine bottles and two men stuffing paninis.

Craig stops at one of the menus on the wall and squints at it with his hands clasped behind his back like an old man. He looks over his shoulder at me. "You're getting a sandwich."

I wrinkle my nose at him. "Never said I wasn't."

He squints suspiciously at me before turning back to the menu. I don't know why he's acting like I don't eat. There's a difference between actively not eating and just not being hungry, and I barely get hungry because of that thing in my stomach. Plus, things just don't taste good. But since the squirming thing didn't show up after I vomited my feelings all over Dakota, I think I can handle a sandwich.

I move in close to him so our arms are touching, and I try to focus on the menu. Under the Italian sandwich names are English descriptions, so I point at the one that has the word *truffle* in it. "That one."

Craig grins. "No, say it."

"No! You say it." I really want him to say it.

"I'll order it for you." He moves into the line, and when we get to the front, he says the sandwich names like he's been speaking Italian since he left the womb. I could listen to an Italian audiobook narrated by him, not under-standing a word and enjoying every second.

I start pulling my credit card out of the fold in my back pocket. Craig doesn't look at me as he puts his hand out on my hands and taps his own card on the machine.

This is a date.

I stand there, stunned at this ridiculous thought that just entered my head. Because what the fuck? No, it's not. You'd think if he wanted to take me on a date, he would've brought up last night by now. But he hasn't because it was embarrassing.

He's just a very nice boy who likes to show off his linguistic skills and pay for his friends. He also happens to like boys, but that's fine; I can deal with that. It's not like it can happen again anyway because I can't think of anything he could offer me that would make me take my shirt off, and I think anyone would find that weird enough to run far, far away, no matter how nice they are.

"Earth to Alis," Craig says.

I'm seeing a wrapped sandwich held out in front of me.

I glance up at him. His freckled cheeks are flushed a beautiful pink in the heat, and his lips—which I know now are very soft—quirk into this smile that if I didn't know any better, I would say looked almost *fond*, and I just can't stand it. I decide that looking at him is no longer a good idea, and direct my eyes back to the sandwich, taking it from him. "Thank you."

We continue down the alley, and Craig spins to avoid a family doing photoshoots with their wine glasses before walking backward beside me. "I really would kill to know what you're thinking about when you do that."

My blood goes cold. "Do what?"

"You like... go really quiet," he says, waving his hand to speed up swallowing the giant bite of sandwich he's just taken. "And you start looking at nothing? You do it a lot."

So not only do I speak my thoughts out loud without realizing it, but I also have a space-out face, and I *do it a lot*. The blood that's already sitting in my face pulses with fresh heat, and I look down at my boots, feeling seconds away from melting into a puddle.

I feel Craig stop walking, but I keep going. His shoes scuff on the cobblestones as he catches back up to me. "Not that—I meant you're just very deep and mysterious, is all I meant."

Right, and the deep mystery was whether this boy was taking me on a date despite not *asking* me on a date. A real conundrum.

There's acid corroding my stomach lining, and suddenly I remember the sandwich in my hand, and feel this tumbling dread thinking about how I'm possibly going to eat it, even though I know I have to now because he bought it for me, and I said I would—

"Whereas me, I'm not deep or mysterious at all. Not even my nightmares are deep."

I feel my eyes widen because I thought for sure that was verboten. There's silence as we're spit out into the parking lot of the Museo Galileo, at the end of which is a redbrick embankment stretching along the River Arno. It reminds me that I, too, am acting like a brick wall, so I clear my throat and ask, "What are they about?"

He smiles mischievously at me. "Guess."

"What? How am I supposed to guess?"

He takes another bite and puts his fist over his mouth like that's going to help the fact that he's talking with his mouth full. "I'm just really curious what you would think they're about."

There's a pause in which I am struck by a memory, and I try and fail to stop my lips quirking.

Craig swallows his food, his eyes widening. "What is *that?* Why are you smiling right now?"

I shake my head, still smirking.

"No, tell me immediately," he says.

"No, fuck you." We reach the embankment, and I stuff my sandwich in the pocket of my sweater before crossing my arms over the bricks. I lean over, trying to catch some spray from a boat so I might no longer feel like I'm sitting in an oven, but there's only a lone red canoe cutting through the murky green water. I look down the river, and there I can see—

Craig's hand, because he's blocking my view with it.

"You don't get to see Ponte Vecchio until you tell me why you're smiling." He leans his hip against the embankment, crumpling his sandwich wrapper into a ball with his other hand.

I glare up at him, but he only raises his bushy eyebrows in challenge, which is actually a very attractive look on him and sends lava gushing into my lower belly. I hate him for making me want to kiss him so bad.

"I thought your nightmares were about olives," I say.

Craig drops his hand, blinking rapidly. "I'm sorry, what?"

"I thought your nightmares were about you trying to catch a meteor shower of olives in your mouth."

His brow smoothes out. "Were you watching me catch olives in Paris?"

"No, I just happened to see it because you're not the most subtle person in the world."

His eyes are very, very intense on my face. "But you were thinking about it afterwards."

Yeah, I really shouldn't have told him about the olive thing. Also, I don't know if he's putting some kind of spell on me with those maple syrup eyes, but my hairline has started prickling, and I feel very lightheaded suddenly. There's a whitewash to my vision, like someone's turned up the brightness of the sun to near blinding.

Craig straightens up from the embankment. "Alis—"

His voice bobs as he lunges toward me, gripping my upper arms as a wave of dizziness overcomes me. He manages to keep me from falling over, but I'm still sinking because my legs are water and my head is swimming. Craig comes down with me, maneuvering me to sit against the embankment. He's crouched in front of me, his furrowed brow being eaten by white fuzz.

"Is it your head or your throat or—?"

"No, I'm—sorry, I'm just hot," I say breathlessly, leaning my head back against the brick and closing my eyes.

"When did you eat last?"

I roll my head against the wall in a head shake because I don't remember.

"Okay, I'm gonna get you some water? Stay there. Don't move."

I open my eyes as he stands, holding his hands out for a moment as if to make sure I don't tip over. He starts jogging away, probably aimlessly. I bring my knees up and put my head on them, fighting through a wave of nausea.

It's not the first time this has happened—there have been some hot summers over the years, and I have not been in a t-shirt in a very long time—but I'm really hoping that I don't pass out because I'm sitting in the middle of a sidewalk and that would be embarrassing. Through the ringing in my ears, I can hear shoes scuffing and voices peaking and fading as shadows cross over me. I try to think about cold water and glaciers and winter, but I'm not sure that's helping so much as making me realize how thirsty I am.

Craig returns, his shadow falling over me. He taps lightly on my hand. "Here."

I bring my head up, my brain floating and my heartbeat fluttering nauseatingly. He twists open a plastic water bottle and hands it to me, squinting at my face. I only get a quarter through before he puts a hand on my hand. "Slow or you're gonna puke."

I lower it reluctantly, gasping. A man in a fedora sends us a nasty glare as he skirts around us where we're taking up the whole sidewalk. I glare right back up at him so I don't have to look at Craig.

"Here," Craig says again. He's holding up another bottle, glistening with condensation. "I'll hold it on your neck."

I'm so hot that I don't even argue. I lean my forehead on my knees again and flinch when the cold touches my skin, but then it seeps into me and feels so good that I sigh.

"Alis, are you sure it's nothing to do with your throat? I know I've been joking around, but Lachlan said—"

"It's not. I'm fine."

"Maybe we should go back."

"Craig, it's—" I hesitate, but I get the feeling he's not going to stop fussing over my stupid throat, and I know I have to give him more. "It's happened before, so I know what it feels like. It's just the heat."

He's quiet for a moment. "Okay, but I also think you need to eat."

I pull my head back up, and he slips the water bottle off my neck. I take the sandwich out of my hoodie pocket and hold it up to him. "I think I squished it."

He smiles at me. "It's going to taste just as good. Trust me, it's *good.*"

I drink more of the water first, looking beyond his shoulder to the Museo across the street, which doesn't help the fact that his eyes are still latched on to my face. I know when I feel better, the embarrassment I'm going to feel about this is going to be painful. But for now, I feel surprisingly calm, and I think it's his utter *lack* of embarrassment about sitting in the middle of the sidewalk with me that's doing it.

I start unwrapping the sandwich on my thighs, and my hands are shaking so obviously that Craig splays his own hands out toward them and says, "You see? That's low blood sugar right there."

"Okay, Dr. Miltenberg," I say, and take a bite of the sandwich.

We sit there for another ten minutes, fielding more glares and a grumpy woman who shouts in Italian at us, until I finish half of the sandwich and drink the rest of the water. It is *really* good, and I do start to feel better, but I think my stomach is the size of a walnut because I can't do any more than that.

After Craig reluctantly eats the rest of it, he offers to help me stand, and I shoot him a glare powerful enough to make him raise his hands and step back. I get up myself, carefully, because if I swoon into his arms, then I'm really going to throw myself into the Arno.

"Let's go find some shade somewhere," Craig says. "Or, better yet, we find you a lake that you can walk into with all your clothes on."

I smirk at him as I straighten up. I am eternally relieved that he hasn't asked the one question I dread anyone ever asking me: *Why don't you just take your sweater off?* As we walk, though, I think about that relief. I hold it in me, frowning at it, because there's something not right with it.

Then it collapses into a prickling sense of unease instead, and that does feel right.

Because *why* hasn't he asked me that?

26

"You're very fast when you walk," Craig says breathlessly, plopping down next to me. We've found a nice spot on a hill at Boboli Gardens, with views of the Fountain of Neptune and the sandy-stoned Palazzo Pitti peeking through the hedges beyond it. The slope is high enough that I can see over the palace and the cobbled rooftops of Florence to the hazy blue mountains obscuring the horizon.

"I think you're just slow, actually," I say. My feet are pulsing in my boots, so I start unlacing them.

"I like to take my *time* when I'm on vacation." He rests his elbows on his knees and looks over his shoulder at me. "How are you feeling?"

I pull off one of my boots. "Like a fucking drama queen."

Craig looks thoughtfully at me for a moment before arranging himself cross-legged in front of me. "For the record, I've had heat exhaustion three times, and I puked two of those times. The third time was at Canada's Wonderland, and my mom had to lie me down on a bench and fan me with a map. That was just last year, by the way."

I swear it used to be a lot easier to glare at him, but now I can feel myself smiling again at the image he's just instilled in my mind. I can't wrap my head around how he's able to just tell me things like this, like it's the easiest thing in the world. I think it's one of my favourite things about him.

We smile at each other for a few seconds, in which it feels like anything can happen. Then I see his gaze drop to my throat, and his face falls before his eyes dart to the base of the tree behind me. "I'm just glad it wasn't anything worse."

I pull my other boot off and roll my eyes. "Craig, I'm *fine*. I don't have brain damage."

He shakes his head at the tree and speaks softly, almost to himself. "Your parents must be flipping out."

I freeze up. Then I immediately try to unfreeze and put all my energy into keeping my face neutral.

I expected he would bring them up eventually, especially since he talks about his mom so much, but he's caught me off guard.

I remember when this first started happening when I was younger. One of my teachers said *Your parents must be very happy with your report card,* and I spent the rest of the week wondering why she would think that. Later, for reasons I can't remember, one of them said *Your parents must be very proud of you,* and I went home and watched them, wondering if they were proud, but I just didn't know what that looked like.

Eventually, as I watched more TV and read more books and paid closer attention to other families, I started to understand why those teachers said those things to me and realized that I was looking for things in my parents that weren't there. They didn't like me like other parents liked their kids. But I already felt like a pariah because I liked playing with girls more than boys, and I didn't like sports like my dad did, and I much preferred the girls' sections of the department stores. This was just one other thing that made me feel abnormal.

So I made it my mission to keep it a secret, to just nod and smile at whoever insinuated anything about my relationship with my parents. But then I met Jordan and spent more time at her house. I started to see what it was like to live with people who liked you, and that made my parents less and less tolerable. There was one night when my mom screamed at me for what felt like hours until my ears started to buzz, and because I had grown to trust Jordan and because I prayed she would tell me I could move in with her, I told her. I told her about this sense I had that every day of their lives, my parents were regretting their decision to have me more and more.

But she was the whole world to her parents, and even when they had that messy divorce, they rearranged their lives to make sure she was happy. I know because I watched it happen, and it made me feel like I was bleeding inside. So when I told her, she said, "I'm sure that's not true." I couldn't blame her because I had seen how everyone assumed things about my parents, how there was this default behaviour that people expected of them, so I think she really *was* sure that it wasn't true.

But I don't need to hear that from Craig.

"What did they say about it?" he asks. He's squinting at me as he picks at the grass beside his knee. At least I must be doing a very good job at keeping my discomfort off my face, because I know he loves to ask me about what my face is doing.

I consider lying, but I'm really not a good liar, and when I ask myself what normal parents would say if someone tried to strangle their child, I come up empty. So I decide on: "I'm not telling them."

Craig stops picking at the grass. "Don't you think you should?"

"Did you tell *your* parents about your seizure?"

"Uh, yes, I did."

Right. Of course he did. Why would I say that?

I decide to lie back in the grass, hoping that will be enough of an indication that I don't want to have this conversation. I catch a glimpse of the leafy canopy above me before I flop an arm over my face, listening to the birds calling back and forth to one another.

Then Craig says, evenly, "Are they assholes to you?"

I've made him swear again. I pinch the bridge of my nose. "They're fine."

"So what are they going to say when you go home with finger marks on your neck?"

"Craig, can we leave this?"

"No, because—" he lets out a frustrated noise that

makes me drop my hand. He squints out toward the fountain before turning to me with this helpless look in his eyes I haven't seen before. "Because I feel like I know nothing about you. I feel like everything I learn about you is just stuff that I happen to notice or that I hear from somebody else, and *that* stuff is mostly just crap. It's like you can't stand to talk about yourself, and I just really wish you would."

"Why?"

His eyebrows raise, and he gives me this broken laugh. "Really?"

"*Yes*, really." My temper flares, and I shoot up onto my elbows. "Why?"

"Because I *like* you," he says, his fist tightening in the grass. His eyebrows curl up and inward, and his voice is barely there as he adds, "A lot."

My heart has started hammering against my ribs. I watch his eyes grow rounder the longer the silence stretches.

Now I know I have nothing to lose, because if he's screwing with me, I'm done with him. So I swallow against my fluttering nerves and say, "Prove it."

His face slackens. The flush of his cheeks has spread to his ears, and I can see his chest rising and falling.

Then his mouth tightens into a hard line of determination. He plants his hands on either side of him and pulls himself up on his knees. My heart leaps as he closes the distance between us, catching my lips with his.

It's nothing like last night when I crushed my mouth against his, and he moved hungrily and breathlessly against me. This one is delicate and pressing, with an edge of desperation that has his nose squashing into mine. Instead of that striking heat in my stomach, there's a slow, spreading warmth, and my chest feels like it's unfolding.

Too soon, he breaks off, and his breath tickles my lips as he says, "Happy?"

"No," I whisper back.

His hand comes up to cradle the side of my head, his fingers hot at the base of my skull. His lips press back in, and it's almost too gentle. But then they start moving, sliding my lips apart, and I wrap my hand in the front of his t-shirt to keep from floating away. There's nothing but the pulse of blood in my head and his thumb brushing over the shell of my ear.

When he pulls away, he keeps his nose on mine, and we breathe together for a moment. I feel so lightheaded I think I might start disintegrating.

"Please," he says, stroking his thumb over my ear again. I know what he's asking of me, and as much as I don't want this moment to end, I know if I wait any longer my thoughts will catch up, and I won't be able to tell him. And for some reason, I want to tell him.

"It would annoy them," I say. "If I told them."

He looks down, taking hold of my hand where it's still clutching his shirt. I look at the fan of his eyelashes on his cheeks and the dusting of freckles over his nose as he asks, "Why do you think that?"

"They don't want to deal with me. They never have."

"But if..." His hand comes off my head as he pulls back

to look at me. "Someone hurt you. They wouldn't care about that?"

I can already feel myself coming back to earth, my body growing heavy as I adjust to the gravity. His eyebrows are pulled together, his eyes darting over my face, and I know he's just confused. He's not *sure it isn't true*. He's not sure about anything.

I unfurl my fingers from his shirt, letting his hand drop away from mine. I watch my hands as I slide them down over my thighs, trying to channel that wave I felt with Dakota in the cathedral and praying the thing in my stomach stays still.

"My dad would think I probably did something to deserve it. If he knew it was Theo, especially. He golfs with his dad, and he's always telling me I should be friends with Theo, you know, like maybe that would stop me going around wearing nail polish. And my mom would... she has this thing where if it's not about her, it's not a big deal. And if it's not a big deal, and you make a big deal—or even just a *deal*—out of it, she's going to lose her shit. So I don't get them involved anymore, and they don't ask."

The leaves of the tree above us rustle as a breeze blows through, and I feel it cooling the burn on my neck where his fingertips used to be. I watch as an ant crawls up and over my leg, nearly disappearing against the black fabric. Only when Craig's silence stretches on for too long do I chance a glance at him.

His lips are pressed together, and his eyes are almost contemplative. "Are they the bear trap?"

I feel a jolt of surprise that he remembers that. My

cheeks heat, and I shake my head at my legs. "That was just me being drunk—"

"Alis."

I look at him from under my lashes. His face is very serious, and it strikes a little bit of fear into me because he's turning out to be really hard to bullshit. Or maybe I'm just not trying very hard to bullshit him.

I sigh. "They've given me three choices for my life."

"What are the choices?"

"Law like my mom, engineering like my dad, or medicine, because who doesn't want their kid to be a doctor?"

He grimaces. "No offence, but I can't see you doing any of that."

"Yeah, well, they won't see me doing anything else."

"Does that matter, though? If you don't want to do it, you should just tell them—"

I shake my head again. This is exactly the conversation I didn't want to have. I'm not going to try to explain to him why I can't *just tell them* because if he had any idea, he wouldn't have suggested that in the first place.

"Please don't—" I cut myself off, my voice hardening. "Craig, I didn't tell you that for you to fix it or feel bad for me or whatever. I told you because you asked, and I want you to keep kissing me."

His expression softens, and I watch his eyes flick to my lips and back up again, sending a little thrill through me. His mouth curls into a small smile. "I will. I will keep kissing you. But I need to ask you..."

He has his worried face on again, and I feel a ripple of unease as I wait for him to speak.

"Are they the reason..." he trails off, his Adam's apple bobbing. The unease rises right under my skin, making the hairs stand up on the back of my neck. I watch his mouth open, close, and open again. "Are they the reason for the... you know, the goth thing?"

I'm so relieved at this stupid question that I breathe a laugh. "It's not *goth*."

"Sorry, 'emo'? Is that the right term?"

"It's not *anything*. It's just, I don't know. I like black. It's comforting."

"Comforting?"

"It's not cold and empty," I say, thinking of my giant, echoing house. "Like when I think of a void, I think of this big white space that goes on forever, and it creeps me out. But black is like the underground, which is full of all sorts of stuff, like worms and moles and shit. I like that."

My face is about three hundred degrees right now, and it has less to do with me talking about worms and more to do with the way Craig has been hanging on to my every word.

"Yeah, I don't know what you would label that," he says. "Maybe wormcore? Dirtwave."

"Shut up," I say, but I'm laughing.

I think it's time to ask him a question instead because his gaze has the full power of the sun behind it, and it's almost unbearable. I think I'm going to ask him why he wears that goddamn hat all the time, but then he unfurls himself from his position to come sit beside me, stretching his legs out next to mine.

"Not that you need a label, anyway," he continues. "I

sort of feel that way with my sexuality. I didn't have to figure out how to come out to my parents because, apparently, when I was little, I told them I was going to marry Jim Hawkins from *Treasure Planet*, but I would've been cheating on the hot green villain lady from *Kim Possible* because I was already engaged to her at the time. And that's just how it's always been, me having many spouses of many genders. And a few talking animals, but we don't need to discuss that."

He looks down his shoulder at me and seems very pleased to see the stupid smile I have on. I feel his fingers touching mine in the grass, and I look at the freckles on his perfect nose and then at his soft pink lips, and I want to kiss him again, but I think I prefer when he kisses me.

"Fine," I say.

His brow furrows. "Fine what?"

"Fine, I'll listen to the goth mixtape your pen pal sent you."

His eyes go so wide I'm afraid they're going to pop out of his head. "Wait, really? You know, you and Jade would really hit it off. I met her on Omegle when I was scrolling through penises at the tender age of thirteen, and she told me she lives in Tasmania—which, by the way, I didn't think was a real place, I thought that was something the Looney Tunes made up..."

I let him keep going for what feels like an eternity, fully beaming at the side of his face. I can't understand how I ever thought he talked too much. I think he can do the talking for both of us for the rest of my life, and I'd be okay with that.

Noor sends Craig a text saying she wants to meet back up, and her timing really could have been better because Craig did say he was going to keep kissing me. Instead, we head to a large piazza surrounded by grand, cream-coloured buildings, and Craig and I move toward the shady bit by a merry-go-round. There are kids riding ornate horses and a couple cuddling in a half-moon as they spin by, and Craig asks: "Would you ride the merry-go-round with me?"

I look flatly at him. "Hard pass."

"Probably for the best," he says. "You might get scared by all the children."

"I was not *scared* of the child—"

That's when my phone buzzes in my pocket, along with a three-tone text sound, and everything in me stops cold.

There's only one person I've assigned that sound to, and I didn't think I'd ever hear it again.

"What?" Craig asks, his smile falling as he steps closer to me.

There's a reason I didn't block her, but right now, I'm failing to remember what that reason was, or why I can't just ignore her right now. There's a beautiful boy right in front of me, and he told me he likes me, and we're in Florence on what I think maybe *is* a date, and this is not what I want to be thinking about right now.

But there it is, drowning out every other thought. I have to look at it.

"Nothing," I say to Craig, but his eyes are clouding with

concern for the second time today, and I'm wracking my brain for a way to get rid of him.

I decide on: "Gelato."

"What?"

"I think I really need some gelato right now."

He breathes a laugh, looking perplexed. "We can find some gelato."

"Okay, but can you—? I think I want to sit."

"Oh," he says lightly. "Yeah, I can do that."

"Thank you. Sorry."

Maybe I say it a little too earnestly because he looks even more suspicious now, but he only asks, "Pistachio again?"

"Mint." Jordan hates mint, and I hate her for making me send him away like an asshole, so it feels right.

"Still a weird flavour," he says, heading off. "Go sit, and please don't pass out."

I nod like I'm going to try my very best not to pass out. I feel a fresh tear of irritation and wrench my phone out of my pocket. I have this fleeting thought that maybe I imagined that sound, or maybe it came from somebody else's phone, and I'm freaking out for nothing.

Then I see it:

JORDAN

New iMessage

I stare down at it for a long time.

Theo would be back by now. She would know what happened. I mean, I assume she would know because she'd want an explanation for why he's come back early. But maybe he lied to her. Didn't he say she asked them not to mess with me? Maybe she'll be angry. Or maybe he's been chomping at the bit to tell her what I said and how it was in her honour. Maybe she's texted me a picture of them cuddling in bed right now to let me know their relationship is at an all-time high.

My heart is pounding, but Craig won't be gone long—there's a lot of gelato in this city—and I know I need to rip off the bandaid.

I tap open the message.

> Are you okay?

I have to read it over several times before I actually believe what I'm seeing. There are no texts above it because I deleted all of them the night of the party, and then she never tried again.

She did that to me, and then she just left it. And *now* she's asking me if I'm okay?

Suddenly, I can hear her voice, as clear as if someone hit play on a recording.

Fine. Is this what you want?

And I know, this time, I can't stop it coming.

27

We'd discussed that a long time ago, just before high school. If everyone we knew was stuck in a burning building and we could only rescue one, who would we choose?

I didn't hesitate when I told her it was her. Of course it was her. But when she said the same about me, I didn't believe her. Her parents may have been divorced, but she loved them, and they loved her, and I didn't expect her to let either of them die over me. I wasn't delusional.

I really didn't have anyone but her, and that was never true for her. Sometimes, in my darkest moments, I wished it was so I could know for sure that I had one person whose only person was me. She would tell me I was her burning building person, and I'd wonder what it would feel like to know that was true, that she really would pick me over anyone else.

I was an idiot for thinking those texts could have come from her, but I thought that last one was proof. I didn't think there was any scenario in which she would have told other people about that conversation and not have been embarrassed.

And I was desperate. It had been nearly a month since Jordan told me she needed a break from me, and she hadn't spoken to me at all since. Walking through the halls at school, seeing her holding hands with Theo and laughing with the Halfwits—it made me feel like I was unmoored and seconds away from drowning.

So, I had to risk it. I had to go. I ignored every instinct I had.

When I got to her house that night, the party was already in full swing—music booming, cliques of people everywhere, the place busier than I'd ever seen it. I found Jordan in the kitchen, drinking next to Maya, who was swaying on the counter.

Jordan's eyes went wide when she saw me. "What are you doing here?"

I froze, cold dread trickling through my veins. Her eyes turned wary the longer she looked at me, and I knew, then, that I had made a mistake.

Then Maya let out a snort, covering her mouth. She tipped over a bit and laughed again as she caught herself.

Something plummeted in my chest. "It was you."

"In my defence, it was Eric's idea," Maya said. "I'm just more poetic."

Jordan whirled on Maya. "Did you text him?"

Maya rolled her eyes. "Okay, don't pretend you didn't know we were going to do that when we were on your phone. Eric always does stuff like that—"

"What? Maya, you said you wanted to mess with guys on Tinder—"

They started arguing, but I couldn't listen because I felt like I was melting from humiliation at how I actually thought Jordan might have said those things to me, and I showed up here, exactly like the Halfwits wanted me to. And now they were arguing about it like I wasn't even there.

It also meant she told them about the burning building thing, and my mind was having a field day with all of the ways that might have come up, how they laughed about how desperate I was.

Over their heads, down a hallway, I saw Eric pointing a beer can in my direction as he shook Theo's shoulder, trying to get his attention.

I needed to get out. I was going to shred myself to ribbons for this.

I turned and left the kitchen, moving back through the crowded living room. Everything and everyone was cast in a purple hue from LED lights that didn't belong in this house, this house I knew better than my own. I felt like I was in a nightmare.

Jordan's voice bobbed as she caught up to me. "Okay, Alis, wait—"

She tried to grab my arm, and I shook her off. "Leave it."

"No, I didn't know they did that. I'm sorry, I—you can stay? Please stay—"

The slimy thing in my stomach shrieked, flinging acid everywhere. Now she was pitying me? Now she had the nerve to think I wanted to stay here following her around like a kicked dog?

My vision went red. I felt like my head was going to explode as I whirled on her. "Are you for real? Are you actually for real right now? I don't even know who you are anymore. Four months ago, you wouldn't have been caught dead with these people in your house, and now you're telling me I can *stay*? It's like—like, you start fucking the guy who tortured you for three years, and suddenly you own everyone around you."

There were people turning their heads toward us where we stood in the middle of the living room, appraising over the rims of their beer bottles and red solo cups. Jordan's eyes widened, her jaw tightened.

"We were—" I started, but there was this pathetic

whine in my voice that I had to swallow before trying again. "I don't get how this happened. It's like you don't even remember—"

"*Obviously,* I remember," she hissed, just loud enough to be heard over the music. Her eyes darted to the side, then back at me. "Can we go outside?"

"Why? Because I embarrass you?" I flung my arm out to the room. "Who even are these people?"

A boy on the couch with a girl on either side of him shouted: "People who were invited!"

There were snickers among those who were already listening, and those that hadn't been were now slowly tuning in. I could feel them giving us a berth, like maybe we were about to start wrestling.

Even in the purple lights, I could tell Jordan's neck was turning crimson. Her jaw was pushing out, her nostrils flaring. I could feel myself becoming grounded with anger because, finally, I had her attention again after weeks of her pretending I didn't exist. If she punched me in the face I didn't think I would be mad—at least it would be some sign of life, some acknowledgement that what we had meant something. I wouldn't feel like the crazy person who'd imagined it all.

Maya wormed her way through the crowd and came over to cling onto Jordan's arm, pouting at me. "I'm sorry we teased you."

Jordan leaned her head away from her, almost like she was disgusted, and my heart leapt with hope. But then she fixed her eyes back on me and said, "I think you should leave, Alis."

I was going to leave. I was. But now I wanted her anger. I wanted her to cry. I wanted her to feel anything toward me at all. And when I realized this, I also realized how pathetic I was for wanting it, and I hated her for making me want to grovel and beg.

So, when she started to turn away, I could feel something in me harden, and I knew I couldn't let her have the last word no matter what it cost me. "Well, fuck you, too, Jordan. Have fun with your psychotic side piece and your brain-dead bitch of a friend."

Jordan stopped. There was a chorus of laughs and *ooo*s that made me feel at once wretched and triumphant.

Maya whirled, her mouth hanging open. Suddenly, she didn't look so drunk. "Excuse me?"

Eric had pushed his way up to the front of the crowd and was gunning for me, but to my surprise, Theo put his arm out to stop him. He shook his head at Eric, but his hungry, glittering eyes never left me and Jordan.

If anyone had been pretending not to stare at us, they weren't bothering anymore. I tried steadfastly not to look at them. I had been used to being a freak show at school, but it didn't bother me because it was me and Jordan against the world. Now it was Jordan and the world against me, and I didn't feel nearly as invincible as I used to. Still, my anger and my desperation triumphed any sense of self-preservation, and I kept going.

"She agrees with me," I said to Maya, who was still glaring at me with her mouth open. I curled my fists at my sides because I could feel my hands shaking and my heart beating in my ears. "She called you a bitch of the first order."

There were some disbelieving laughs, a few murmurs. Then Jordan's hair whipped around her head like fire as she spun back to me, her eyes narrowed into slits.

"Fine. Is this what you want?" Her voice wavered, but she took a decisive step toward me. "Yes, we were friends. But you know what, Alistair? Unlike you, I've moved on because I realized I don't want to be friends with someone who is so *needy* and so *pathetic* that they have to"—her face twisted into an unrecognizable sneer and she raised her arm, making a motion like swiping a blade over her forearm once, twice—"fucking cut themselves for attention."

I remember how her jaw was still tight and angry when it snapped shut, how her arm was still floating there in that position, but her eyes changed. They went wide with horror, all the rage snuffed out of them. She'd gone pale, and I could see the chalky texture of her foundation on her skin.

I remember how my brain was glitching afterwards, like it kept going back to what she just said and trying to reframe it as something else, only to come to the same conclusion. Each time it did, it felt like a cold needle plunging into me, until I was all ice.

I remember seeing their purple-hued faces, all of them, on me. Some were a pale imitation of the wide-eyed horror on Jordan's face. Some had hands creeping up to curl over mouths. Some had eyebrows raised, poised between laughter and concern, looking around at other faces to determine which way to lean. Some had begun to sag and twist with discomfort, turning away.

I remember hearing voices but not words as I squeezed through bodies, head down, avoiding eyes. Down the driveway, onto the sidewalk, nothing but ringing in my ears. I walked until the pine tree in the next yard blocked me from view of her house and barely had time to grip the fence before throwing up.

I remember staring at my watery vomit on the pavement, and then a blur, and then being back in my room in the pitch black, praying it had all been a bad dream and knowing it wasn't.

I remember it all.

28

At some point I hurled my phone to the ground, and now I'm smashing it with my boot, over and over again. There's a succession of growling noises, and I think it might be me, but I don't do anything about it because there's this zinging sensation up my spine with every stomp, and it feels so fucking good. Only when the screen has turned to powder and the casing looks like a pile of used matchsticks on the stones do I finally stumble back, breathing heavy.

Every person within eyesight is looking at me. Some are stopped to stare in apprehension or fascination, others are looking sidelong at me as they continue strolling with their loved ones. But I don't care—my blood is singing. Who knew that you could do that? You could just smash your phone to bits whenever you want. And the world resumes, and the weight on your shoulders lifts, and the thought of your ex-best friend on the other side of the ocean staring at her unanswered text fills you with fiery satisfaction.

A little laugh bubbles out of me. I feel like there are tiny pebbles rolling through my blood, making me shake. It's like when I tried to go to the gym, and I lifted weights because it was easy at the time, but when I got home, my muscles were spasming uncontrollably because I'd never done it before. Now my body's recovering from whatever *that* was.

The bits of hair that have escaped from their tie are trembling at the corners of my vision. I look down at the pile of phone on the stones.

That's Jordan. That's that *night*. Nothing but dust now.

"Ayo, Alis!" I look toward the voice to see Drew swaggering toward me. He's carrying at least six different shopping bags. Behind him, I think I see Dakota and Noor, but they're still just figures in the sunny distance.

He frowns as he comes to a stop, putting his bags down on the ground. "Where's Mr. You're Actually Amazing?"

It takes me a second to register what he just said to me, and when I do, another laugh bursts from me—this one a high-pitched giggle that has Drew leaning away from me. Then his face lights up and he says, "Did you have wine again? That was hilarious."

"No," I say, laughing again. I put a hand over my mouth and feel rising panic thinking I'm never going to go back to normal.

"Nah, dude, you're definitely on something. Is it weed?"

It's at that moment that Craig returns with two tubs of

gelato and a water bottle under his arm. "Okay, they only had *chocolate* mint."

"Is he on something?" Drew asks him, gesturing to me. My eyes widen at him as if I can telepathically shut his mouth.

"What?" Craig laughs, but he's looking at me more intently now.

"I'm not *on* anything," I snap. I'm annoyed enough now that I don't think I'm going to laugh anymore, though I still feel like I have jumping beans embedded in my muscles.

Craig is frowning as he hands me my gelato. Then Dakota and Noor stroll up, and Dakota flashes me a smile while Noor gives me a jerk of her chin. Her arms are crossed as she looks between me and Craig with a somewhat suspicious squint.

Before I can ask her what her problem is, Craig asks, "Is that yours?"

He's pointing at the mess on the ground, his brow furrowed.

It's not like I can lie when I don't have a phone now. "Yes. It fell at a bad angle."

"It looks like it fell on *all* angles," says Drew. "How are you not crying right now?"

I scoop up a spoonful of chocolate mint and shove it in my mouth very quickly when I notice how the tiny spoon is shaking. I put it back in the tub and rub my hand down my thigh instead. The gelato is too sweet and feels like glue going down.

"Should we go get a burner or something when we

head back?" Dakota asks. "Aren't your parents gonna freak out if they can't reach you?"

"I'll use Craig's phone," I say, trying to keep the irritation out of my voice because it's Dakota, but I'm beyond done with the attention being on me.

Craig and Noor look at each other, and Noor raises her eyebrows inquisitively. Then Craig bugs his eyes out and shakes his head minutely, like he doesn't understand her question. Or maybe he doesn't like her question. Whatever it is, it makes my stomach twist with unease.

It's not like I can call them out on it, because if it's about me, then I don't think I want to know, and if it's *not* about me, then I'm just going to look like a self-centred ass.

"All right, well, let's go back," Drew says. "My arms are hurting."

He picks up his shopping bags, and we start heading out of the piazza. I pick up the remnants of my phone first (I'm not a litterer) and everyone starts chatting about the day they've had, which is good news for me because Craig doesn't get a chance to needle me about the phone. I know he wants to—he keeps glancing behind his shoulder at me as I trail behind the group, and he isn't smiling.

"Noor and I wanted to go into the basilicas, but Drew kept dragging us into stores," Dakota is saying, shooting her brother a withering look that I didn't think she could achieve.

"I told you churches creep me out," Drew says.

"You're wearing a massive cross around your neck," Noor notes.

Drew sucks his teeth, flinging the pendant. "Because it

looks sick, okay? How come these motherfuckers get to hang out *in a park,* and no one's on their case for being philistines?"

I raise my eyebrows at the back of his head. I don't think I've ever been called a motherfucker or a philistine before, which is an accomplishment on his part because I've been called a lot of things.

"Weird, I was actually just about to call you a philistine," Craig says to him.

Noor says, "No, you weren't."

Whatever telepathic conversation they had before, they don't seem to be angry at each other about it. In fact, Craig ends up giving Noor a piggyback for a few minutes, and when she hops off, his white shirt is clinging to his back with sweat. It's a welcome distraction now that I'm coming down from whatever high I got from smashing my phone. But then he reaches behind him and peels his t-shirt off his skin, tugging it a little to get the air flowing again. So I start thinking about other things, like how Craig won't be able to send me texts anymore and how I no longer have anything to plug my headphones into.

It's funny how, for a second there, I'd almost forgotten she existed. Yet the moment she popped back in my life, with three little words, she had me losing my mind again. From all the way across the ocean.

29

There was a moment during our walk back to the
hostel, after I'd stealthily dropped my soupy gelato
into a garbage bin, when I felt something brushing against
my hand. I looked down to see Craig's knuckles grazing
against it, his index finger reaching out to cross over mine.

I didn't realize he'd fallen back next to me, as I'd been
trying very hard not to separate from myself. So when it
happened, I didn't even think—I slid my fingers between
his. It was immediately sweaty, but I hung on and put all
my mental energy into the little sun of our entwined hands
as if I could give it enough weight to tether me to earth.

And it worked. We came up to the hostel, and I was
still in my body, and I remembered everything I did to get
there. I was so happy about this that I turned my face up to
smile at Craig, wishing I could thank him but not knowing
how I could possibly do that without sounding like a
lunatic.

I'm still thinking about our hands now as I sit up on

the hostel's rooftop terrace, watching Craig and Noor where they're lined up at the L-shaped buffet table in the corner. When Lachlan told us we were getting caterers, I expected she meant a few sandwich platters, but the table is packed full of chafing dishes containing a whole range of Italian delicacies that made Craig light up like a Christmas tree when he got up here.

I got myself some gnocchi with butter and grabbed a table of five under the pavilion. It's cooler now, and I've showered off the sweat I've been swimming in all day, so I feel significantly more human. I think I might even feel *happy*, and maybe it's a temporary side effect of having a boy hold my hand in public for ten minutes straight, but it's enough to drown out thoughts of Jordan and my pulverized phone.

Dakota and Drew take their seats in front of me without even asking, as if that's just the way of things now. When Craig and Noor come back, I notice Noor has changed into a white crop top and low-slung jeans.

"I didn't know you had abs," I say to her.

She puts her plate of tiramisu down at the end of the table and glances down at herself like she didn't know it either. "Ballet."

My eyebrows jump. "*Ballet*?"

"Ballet since I was three but mostly hip-hop now."

I know I'm staring open-mouthed at her like a freak, and I don't even really know why. She's a person. She has hobbies. But the thought of her, with her wolf cut and her deadpan face, in a *tutu*?

She's like one of those little Russian dolls, except each

nested doll grows more colourful and more detailed than the next. I want to sit and talk with her forever until I get to the very last one.

Craig comes round the table with a paper plate so loaded, he has to fold it to keep everything from tumbling off the side. "How come you said to me *Of course you skate-board* but you're looking at her like she just did a magic trick?"

"Because you're"—I wave my hand vaguely at him— "but she's…"

"Deep and mysterious?" Craig offers.

"Yeah," I say. "Yes. Exactly."

"That's fair," Craig says, taking his seat next to me. "But I'll have you know, there's a lot of cool stuff you guys don't know about me."

"I know everything about you," Noor says, just as I say, "Like what?"

"Loads of stuff," he says, then fails to elaborate. I grin at him, and Drew snorts while he shovels spaghetti into his mouth down the table.

I've managed to get through half the gnocchi on my plate when Lachlan stands, tapping a glass as Bilodeau turns down the music. The chatter quiets, and her voice booms over us. "So, I know we've got a couple of days left on the trip, and final exams coming up—"

There are groans abound. She holds up a hand, bowing her head. "Yeah, yeah, no exam talk in Europe. But I just wanted to say a few things now that we're all here."

She dives into this impassioned speech about high school, about graduation, about how we've all done a lot of hard work to get where we are. My mind starts to drift as I'm reminded of just *how much* hard work I had to do to get where I am and how much more work I have ahead of me. I put down my fork as my stomach sours.

As she starts talking about friendship and cherished memories, I look around at my classmates squinting at her against the fracturing sunlight. Nobody's talking or laughing or on their phones.

I try to pull my attention back to Lachlan.

"...but if there's one thing I can promise you," she's saying, "it's that whoever said these four years are the best years of your life were wrong. Trust me when I say that there are many, many better years ahead, for all of you. It's been a pleasure being a small part of your journeys, and I wish you all the best of luck after graduation. Cheers, guys."

She lifts her glass, and everyone else raises their own glasses and starts whooping and cheering, and I think she's blushing as she sits back down.

When the music and the chatter pick up again, Dakota turns back around in her seat, smiling as she wipes the tears glistening on her cheeks. Drew's looking down at his plate like he's bummed out, so Dakota puts an arm around his shoulders and starts shaking him.

"*Stop*," he groans.

"You can cry, baby brother."

"I'm *older* than you," he says, but he lets her keep her arm around him.

I look at Craig, following his gaze to where Noor's leaning back in her seat with her arms crossed. My entire body freezes up when I see that her lips are tugged down at the corners and her eyes are watering.

"Aw, no," Craig says softly, pushing back from the table. He gets up, holding his arms out to her. I expect her to tell him to shove off, but she stands and snakes her arms around him, burying her face in his shoulder. Her hands are clasping each other, white-knuckled, over the small of his back, and Craig has his cheek pressed against the top of her head while he rubs her shoulders.

I look around at everyone else, and there are similar displays happening all around me—people hugging, people grabbing at each other, people laughing at their crying friends even though they're crying themselves.

I feel a pang of discomfort, spreading steadily into anxiety. Lachlan's speech did nothing for me; it felt somewhat foreign, like she wasn't really talking to me. But these people are mourning high school like it's actually something they're going to miss.

And they're crying about it, openly, like it's nothing.

Craig and Noor break apart, and when Craig cups her face in his hand and wipes a tear off with his thumb, I have to turn my gaze away. I look down at my plate, wondering how I was ever hungry. In my peripheral, I notice Dakota tipping in her chair to try and get in my line of vision, and she flashes me a smile when I meet her eyes. "You okay?"

"What?" I ask, my skin prickling. I have to stop myself from reaching up to check my face for wetness, as if this crying disease has somehow reached me without my knowledge. "Yes. Fine."

Craig comes back around, and I glance at Noor as she

settles back in her chair. There's this moment when I'm waiting for her to apologize or be embarrassed, but she just dips forward and starts in on her tiramisu again.

Craig sits back down, and my pulse starts galloping. He stretches his arm across the back of my chair, and when I feel the heat of him there and the weight of his eyes on the side of my face, a spike of panic tears through me. I don't want him to open his mouth.

I shoot up from my chair. Noor pauses with her fork in the air, and the Mitchells both raise their eyebrows at me. I scramble for what to say. "Washroom. Sorry."

I leave the table and head for the other end of the terrace, toward the hostel doors. I'm feeling jittery as all hell and not having any idea why. The more I try to understand it, the more the thing in my stomach starts to squirm; the more it starts to squirm, the more the urge builds like a dark cloud at the back of my head. I feel like a line of dominos collapsing.

I push into the hall, but I don't reach the end of it before the door I just came through clicks open again.

"*Hey*," comes a grating voice. "I need to talk to you."

Fuck my whole entire life. I consider ignoring her, but since I'm already angry, I spin around. "What?"

Maya is coming down the hall toward me, her flat-ironed hair flying behind her. She's wearing her makeup again, but she still doesn't look entirely like herself. Maybe it's just seeing her without the rest of the Halfwits that's weird to me.

She comes to a stop, putting a hand on her hip. "Jordan

called me to ask about you. She said you didn't answer her text."

"My phone's broken."

Maya rolls her eyes. "Okay. I actually don't like you, which I know you know, but I do care about Jordan whether or not you want to believe that. And she, for some reason, still cares about you. She just wanted to know if you were okay. Which, I didn't think Theo would ever do anything like that, and you should know I wasn't in on it."

"Good for you. You can let Jordan know her boyfriend's handprints are healing just fine. Is that it?"

"Oh my *God*," she groans, rolling her head on her neck. "You are seriously so petty."

"Petty?" I can't help the laugh that bubbles out of me. "Maybe you should stay out of shit you don't know anything about."

She bugs her eyes out at me. "Uh, I do know something about it. I was standing right there."

I go cold with dread. Conversation over.

"Bye, Maya," I say, turning to go.

"I just don't get why you're so pressed about it still. Most people don't even believe it," she says, raising her voice. I hear that door click open again and spin back around, my blood spiking. I see a slice of Noor coming into the hall as Maya continues, "And the others either don't care, or just feel sorry for you! Isn't that basically what you wanted—"

One of my hands latches onto her shoulder and the other shoots out to cover her mouth, smothering her. It only lasts a second before she's wrenching back, sputtering, her eyes blazing with rage and shock.

"What the fuck?" she spits, swiping an arm viciously over her mouth as she stumbles back from me. "Don't touch me!"

I put my hands up. I didn't mean to. I didn't. But Noor is coming down the hall, her face pinched with confusion, and I couldn't let her hear whatever she was going to say. Maya turns to leave, swiping her hand over her mouth again.

"Your *friend*? Is a fucking nut job," she growls at Noor as she goes.

Noor glares at her back, then meets my eyes.

"I didn't mean to—"

"Alis, it's fine, she's..." She waves an arm dismissively at where Maya disappeared, her eyes flicking across my face. "What's happening right now?"

"Nothing." My palms prick with sweat, and I curse myself internally for the way my voice is shaking. "It was... about the fire."

Noor looks at me for a long moment. Then she wipes a hand down her face, sighing. "Okay. There's something we need to talk about—"

The door clicks open again, and I see the bright yellow of Craig's hat before he slips into the hall, spreading his arms in question. "Why'd she just fly out of here like a bat out of... why do you look sick?"

God, my face. My backstabbing fucking face. I'm starting to think he was a liar when he told me how deep and mysterious I was since, apparently, everyone can read me like a book.

The squirming thing is throwing a fit inside of me, and I really, really need to go before I start spewing acid all over the floor.

"You're going to talk," Noor says over her shoulder. "Now."

Craig stops dead, his face paling. He glances at me for the briefest second before widening his eyes at Noor. "What?"

"Yes. We're asking now."

"*What* are you asking?" I grit out, my heart pounding so hard I feel like I'm going to faint.

Noor's mouth opens, but Craig puts his hand on her arm. "Wait."

He comes up to me, his lips pursed like he's trying not to vomit. All of that beautiful flush in his cheeks is gone. He takes my hands and looks down at them between us, running his thumbs over my fingers. When he raises his eyes to mine, I'm too paralyzed to do anything but listen.

"We know what they're saying," Craig says. "And I need to ask you if it's true. That you... that you're hurting yourself."

The world lurches around me.

This is it. This is the worst-case scenario.

He could've told me he never wanted to see me again, and I wouldn't feel like I do now, like that crumbling foundation I've been standing on has finally given way, and I am in free fall.

I snatch my hands back from him, and my voice is

hollow in my ears. "You're not supposed to know about that."

Only when I see the way his eyes go round and his lips part do I realize what I just said is a confession. The humiliation I feel from the look on his face is almost worse than the party, worse than anything I've ever felt before.

"I didn't... I thought it was just another rumour," he says quietly. "But then when we—in Rome, when you pulled away, I thought that maybe..."

My mind is racing a mile a minute because this doesn't make any sense. He's not supposed to know. And if he knows, then why would he...?

A shiver runs down my spine, and everything in me stops cold.

All at once, I understand. And I don't know how I ever saw it any other way.

I stagger back from him, my knees feeling like water beneath me. I almost don't want to ask, but I have to know for sure. "Since when?"

Craig frowns. "What?"

"Since when did you know?"

"Since Paris."

"Since *when* in Paris?"

He swallows, and his face slips into an expression that looks very much like fear. "At the fondue place. Eric said... but why does it matter? I'm asking—"

"That was the first night in Paris. And then you spoke to me for the first time the next day, on the Eiffel Tower. Why? Why did you do that, Craig?"

"Because I—"

"Because you felt bad for me? Because you thought you were going to save me? You thought you were going to make me all better like you did with your mom?"

His face goes slack. "That is *not* what that was."

"So, it was a coincidence," I say, and feel a hysterical satisfaction at how ridiculous it sounds. "You just accidentally spoke to me for the first time in four years the day after you found out I was a head case. Maybe—*oh*. Did it get you off, then? Is that why I'm suddenly so attractive to you?"

"*Alis*," Noor says, and the mix of surprise and anger in her voice is the most emotion I've ever heard from her.

I look between them, and they're both staring at me like I've just morphed into the Hulk, which isn't that remote a possibility. I realize I haven't spent a second of this conversation trying to deny what they know, and I don't care. I'm under a red sheet, everything dulled but for the ringing in my ears and the urge to destroy everything.

Craig opens his mouth. Closes it. Puts his hand on the back of his neck, squeezes. His eyes are glinting like maybe he's crying, and that only makes me angrier.

"Okay," he croaks. He clears his throat and looks at me, his eyebrows raised in mollification. "If you need an explanation for that—"

I cut him off with a slice of my hand. "I don't need your explanation, Craig. I need you to stay the fuck away from me. Seriously, I cannot express to you how much I don't want to see or speak to you again, ever. Either of you."

I don't wait for my words to hit true. I turn and leave as quickly as I can, because the thing in my stomach feels like it's trying to kill me, and I can't endure it a second longer.

30

I haven't cut myself in a while since I discovered a better way. A less messy, more subtle way. Part of it was because ever since that night, whenever I held a razor to my skin, I would have this little voice in my head calling me an attention whore, and it would ruin the ritual for me. The cutting would become a reaction to that voice instead of a balm on whatever had me cutting in the first place.

In some ways, the burning is even more effective. It's so brightly intense but lasts only a few seconds before turning almost numb. The cuts leave these long, stinging impressions that I don't always appreciate, and cleaning them sometimes takes long enough that the regret catches up before I'm done.

But now, I want to bleed. I want the cleansing feeling of the acid being drawn out from under my skin. I want to see the damage as it's happening.

I've got the folding knife I bought, and I'm thinking about how perfect it is that the communal washroom has these self-contained shower stalls with locking doors, as if the universe is begging me to do it. I lock myself in and sit on the floor between the toilet and the raised shower tiles. I pull my sweater off, then roll up the sleeve of my shirt.

I decide to use one of the straight replacement blades, like I'm used to, instead of the knife. I'm trembling so hard I can barely hold it. I'm not usually this much of a mess beforehand—usually, the ritual calms me; the anticipation of pain brings a cold sense of determination. But now my head is screaming with all these moments between me and Craig, now suddenly so insidious.

The way he was on my ass about my eating, buying me food and cold water bottles and feeding me pain pills and pushing and pushing about my parents and trying to worm his way closer so he could be there the moment this pitiful excuse for a human being started writhing around at his feet begging for help, begging to be saved by him. By perfect, faultless Craig, who was going to cure the world with laughter. Who was going to cure me of my fucked up little habit.

How could I not have seen it? He'd been in my orbit five days a week, every week, for four years. And then, suddenly, he decides to ask me to light the cigarette that he barely dragged at and sits with me on the train, and tells me he cares about me so he can fuck with my head enough to get me to kiss him—

I growl between my gritted teeth and push the razor in.

My vision goes white, and I cut.

I think about how this used to be mine, and only mine, and no one ever knew any better. I think about how the one person I ever had the courage to tell went and told everyone else. I think about how I was so worried he would find out and abandon me, I never considered it was the reason he was around me in the first place.

How exciting it must have been to discover the pyro was also a cutter. I was the perfect pity project, gift-wrapped, his to reveal one layer at a time.

Isn't that basically what you wanted?

I laugh bitterly, blood welling. If only Maya was right. If only Jordan was right. If only I did it for attention.

The pain is bright and blinding, and it's not enough. I cut into myself again and grind my teeth until my jaw creaks, breathing quick, hard breaths through my nose.

I feel like my heart is shredding itself. I feel like there's going to be nothing left inside of me when this is done. Maybe nothing left on the outside either because I'm making another cut without even deciding to do it.

There's this keening noise filling the stall, and it can't be coming from me. But when I put my hand over my mouth, it's muffled, so I know it is.

That's when the knocking starts. I keep my hand over my mouth, listening.

It's distant, several shower stalls down. Knock, knock, knock. A muffled voice.

Then footsteps. Another knock, closer this time. The metal squeal of a handle turning.

I let my head drop back against the tile wall and squeeze my eyes shut.

Go away, I think.

Knock, knock, knock.

Goawaygoawaygoaway—

I drop my hand from my mouth. I dig the blade in.

"Go away," I growl through my teeth and slash.

And then I gasp, dropping the blade. It tinkles on the tile.

I don't know how I know. It hurts like hell but doesn't feel much different than the rest. Yet I feel myself pale, an icy prickling under my skin.

There are three knocks on the door. "Hello? Is this occupied?"

It's Noor's voice. It's Noor, on the other side of the door. She tries the handle, and it thunks against the lock.

I'm staring at my arm, held in such a way that the blood is spilling into a pool in the crook of my elbow. Among the chorus of nerves already singing up and down my forearm, I'm not really feeling it, but the skin is split too wide, the blood coming too fast.

I feel a cold spike of alarm, and it springs me into action. I drag myself over to the ledge by the toilet and swipe the extra roll of toilet paper. I start unravelling it, wrapping it round and round my arm.

I hear Noor say, "I don't hear the shower."

There are four flat-handed bangs on the door this time. Then comes Craig's voice: "Alis, are you in there?"

I drop the toilet paper, and as it bounces off me and onto the floor, I can see the patchy spot of red on it from where it hit my lap. It rolls through more blood on the floor, and *fuck*, fuck me, I've made a mess—

I squeeze the toilet paper against my arm as hard as I

can, holding it to me like a broken wing as I fold the rest of my body over it. I close my eyes.

When I open my eyes, it'll have stopped. The paper will be white. There's no way I messed up this badly.

Slowly, I uncurl. I hold my arm out before me. I open my eyes.

The toilet paper is soaked through. I watch it growing darker and thinner by the second.

The world slides out from under me, and I tip to the side, feeling the pinch of the discarded blade under my palm. My ears start to ring.

I've killed myself.

I'm going to die on the floor of this grubby hostel shower in Italy. Some cleaner is going to find my body, and Lachlan is going to have to identify me and ship me back in a box to my parents, who will be so relieved.

I expect to feel numbness, acceptance. That's how I always imagined I would feel if it ever happened. When that doesn't come, I wait for that peaceful feeling that came over me when Theo was choking the life out of me.

But instead, I feel something ice cold grip my heart, and one thought, over and over:

I don't want to die.

Suddenly, nothing else matters but that.

My vision tunnels. I feel strong enough to lift a house despite the amount of blood that's left my body. I scramble up to my feet, my boot squeaking wetly over the floor. I make it to the door and twist the lock. I don't have a care in the world about who might be on the other side, only a singular, frantic hope that there's anyone at all.

31

I wrench the door open with my good arm, the ruined one pressed against my chest.

My knees nearly buckle with relief as I see them. For a split second, Craig is leaning against a sink, wringing his hat in his hands, and Noor is pacing with a phone pressed to her ear.

Then their eyes meet mine.

All the colour drains from Craig's face as he straightens up from the sink. Noor stops her pacing, her widening eyes darting to my arm, then to the mess of the stall behind me.

"Wait—wait—forget about that," she says into the phone. "Come now. Bring it, yes. Come right now."

I hold my arm out in front of me. "There's too much."

Noor puts her phone in her back pocket and stretches her arms out toward me as if I might fall on my face. "Okay, Alis. Go back in there and sit down. Can you get some—" She looks over her shoulder at Craig. "Can you get some towels?"

Craig appears to be in a state of paralysis, holding onto the sink behind him. His lips are chalk-white, his eyes locked on my blood-drenched arm. When I look down at it now, I feel almost relieved. This can't belong to me. I don't feel it.

As I watch, a little river of blood in the crook of my elbow starts dripping onto the blue tile floor.

Noor snaps her fingers in Craig's direction. "*Craig.* Go get some towels."

He looks green now. When his gaze flicks back to Noor, it seems to snap him out of it, and he rocks in place for a second before bolting from the room. Then he's gone, and I'm hit by a wave of dizziness that has me falling into the stall door, my hand slipping over the handle.

Noor darts forward and wraps herself around my good arm. She steers me into the stall.

"Sit," she commands, dragging me down to the floor with her. I scoot myself back into the spot where I'd been before, and Noor settles on her knees, looking around at the mess I've made. I'm thinking about how I'll have to buy her new jeans after this.

Noor stares at the blade on the floor, then the folding knife in its case. She licks her lips, which are a strange colour, and glances up at me. "I had to send him away in case he fainted."

I nod, and it feels like the air around my head is thick, slowing down the movement.

She starts peeling the toilet paper off my arm, but it's practically dissolving off of it. I must be in shock or something because when it's gone, and she's looking at the rest of my arm, at all of the other cuts and burns—the old ones, and the four new ones—I don't even care. Not one bit.

"Um," she says shakily. Her brow is sweating, and I see her fingers tremble when she grabs for the roll of toilet paper I'd discarded.

"Was Lachlan on the phone?" I ask.

She starts wrapping the roll around my arm like I was doing before. "Yes, she's coming. She's taking her... sweet time."

She seems a bit out of breath. She cuts off the toilet paper, wraps both her hands around my arm and squeezes. I feel a bit of pressure but no pain. Then she bows her head over it and closes her eyes like she's praying.

I have to actively search for my lips in order to speak. "Are you okay?"

"Shh," she says, shaking her head. Her face is grey and pinched, and her hair is trembling. She doesn't even look like her anymore.

When the stall door opens, Lachlan is there, holding a white plastic briefcase. Time is moving in that slow, glitching way so it seems like she's blipping from one place to the next until suddenly, she's kneeling next to Noor. The briefcase has a green cross on the front, and it's so green, I feel like I'm falling into it, like it's the only colour in the world.

I hear, like through a radio, Lachlan say: "Noor, leave it now. Go outside."

I try to focus on Noor because there is some screaming

part of me deep beneath it all that feels like it's never going to see her again. Then I regret it because she's such a strange, sickly colour, and when she gets up, she goes so quickly despite the slowing of time. It's like she teleports, and then it's just the stall door banging where she disappeared.

Lachlan is at the sink suddenly. "Do you feel like you're going to fall asleep?"

I'm trying very hard to shake my head. It feels impossible, but it must happen because she says, "Good. Don't."

She flicks water off her hands and is back kneeling next to me. I'm having so much trouble deciphering the look on her face as she starts unwrapping the bloody toilet paper around my arm, so I watch her ear instead. She says something about flexing rusty muscles, and the ear moves a little as she speaks.

It is taking everything in me to concentrate on what she's saying, and I can feel that familiar fear and frustration trying to smash its way back to the front of my mind.

"...other ones are probably okay, but this one needs stitches. I'm going to pack it up before we go, okay? You're gonna be..."

Stitches. Stitches. The word sounds so weird, and it's all I'm thinking about as I sink deeper and deeper into wherever that place is that I go.

Stitches.

Stitches.

Stitches.

I'm sitting on a table, looking at the darker splotches on my dark jeans. I feel a light tugging on my arm and see a blonde woman's head bowed over it as she threads a needle through my skin. There are already many threads in place, crisscrossing over the gash, while the other three other cuts have already been bandaged.

The rest of the scars are thrown into sharp relief under the lamplight. The longer I look at it, the less it looks like an arm and the more it just looks like this pale, mangled thing being autopsied. I decide to look around the rest of the room—a very small room with cream walls and a computer desk and Lachlan sitting on a chair, bent over her phone between her legs.

I close my eyes, trying to remember. There are snapshots of things—the orange walls in the hostel, a rumbling feeling, people rushing around a bright space, a red-faced baby—but that's it. Lachlan must have accompanied a zombie here.

I feel a different sensation on my arm and look to see the doctor putting a bandage over the sutures. Then she rolls away on her chair toward the desk, and Lachlan pulls her head up. "Finito?"

The doctor nods once. "Finito."

She pulls out a little bag of bandages and raises her eyebrows as she shakes it at the pair of us. "Ventiquattro ore."

Lachlan nods. "Grazie."

The doctor raises a hand at her in acknowledgement. Then she gets up and nods at me as she goes, her face practically bored, like she didn't just stitch up the most horrible arm in the world. I say *grazie* to her back as she leaves the room, white coat spreading behind her like a cape. Then I tug my sleeve over my arm, wishing I could never look at it again.

"Are you back with us, then?" Lachlan asks, standing from her chair with a sigh. Her face is drawn, and even the flap of hair on the unshaved side of her head looks tired.

My voice comes out whispery. "How long...?"

"Two hours, give or take."

I feel, then, such a crushing guilt, I think I might crumble under the weight of it. I put my face in my hands.

"It's okay, kiddo," Lachlan says. "Makes sense you wouldn't want to be around for that."

I move the heels of my hands up to my forehead and look down at my boots. "Did I say anything?"

"In the cab, I asked you how you were feeling, and you told me you felt like you were in a dream."

The memory comes back to me like a flashbulb going off. Sitting in the backseat, Lachlan's face flashing orange from the passing streetlights, the rumbling of the car beneath me. Then, trying to speak with great difficulty, like towing each word through molasses. She asked me if she could hold my hand, and I must have said yes because she put it in her lap and covered it with her other hand. I remember feeling it in the way you might feel your numb arm after you've slept on it weird.

I wonder, if someone were to relay the whole night to me in detail, if then the memories would come back to me. Maybe they're only buried somewhere beneath the surface.

Still, I think I'm okay leaving this buried. I don't want to remember the walk through the hostel or to know how many people saw my mangled arm in the hospital waiting room.

There is one thing I do have to know, though. I lift my head. "Are Noor and Craig okay?"

I remember the way Noor nearly ran out of the stall as if she couldn't get away fast enough, and I have this burning image behind my eyes of Craig, paper-white and gripping the sink. I think the leech in my stomach has multiplied.

"Well, Craig's texts have finally slowed down. I was about to put him on mute," she says, smiling. I can't bring myself to smile back. "I think you scared them pretty good."

"I'm so..." I start, but I don't even know what I am. Sorry doesn't cut it. I feel sick to my bones for what I've done.

She shakes her head. "Let's go back now, eh? You look like you're about to fall over."

I nod and slide off the table. I do stumble to the side a bit because my legs feel foreign. She grabs my upper arm for support, letting go as soon as I'm steady. "Good?"

"Yes," I whisper. I don't know why I'm having such a hard time speaking at normal volume. I don't even feel the pain in my throat even though Noor's pills have long worn off. I don't feel the stitches or the cuts, either. I wonder if I've stopped feeling pain like a normal person.

Lachlan pays the receptionist. I have no idea how that works or how much that costs, but she wouldn't let me use my credit card, and she told me not to worry. So I stay quiet and let her walk me outside as she calls for a cab. We wait out in the dark, silently. We watch an ambulance pull into the hospital with its lights flashing, and I wonder if the people in the back of it are having a worse night than I am.

We get into the cab, and the impossible happens: I fall asleep. I wake up to the stuffy quiet of a stopped car and Lachlan patting my good arm, telling me we're here now. I didn't think I would ever sleep again, never mind fall asleep instantly in the back of a cab.

She gets out of the car and goes around it, opening my door for me. Then the extent of my exhaustion is hard to ignore. Maybe it's from blood loss, or maybe it's from whatever I was doing for the two hours when I wasn't in my body, or maybe it's from the unprecedented viciousness with which I was slashing myself in that stall, but I look at the steps leading up to the hostel's front doors, and I don't think I can do it. My muscles feel like they've atrophied to nothing, and my eyelids are the heaviest things in the world.

She bends so she can see me under the roof of the car, then holds out a hand. "Almost there, kiddo. Then you can sleep."

I don't want to keep her waiting, so I take her hand and let her pull me out. She, too, has these very warm hands, and now I'm thinking about Craig's hands, and there's a pain in my heart that I didn't think was possible.

I let go of her as soon as I'm standing and consider collapsing there on the pavement, but I know she's not going to let me sleep there, so I start dragging my feet up the steps, through the door. Lachlan goes to the receptionist's desk and starts murmuring to the woman behind it, who keeps glancing nervously at me. I have the vaguest recollection of seeing her when I was in the dream state and wonder if maybe she's the one that had to clean up my mess. I put her on the list of people I've probably traumatized tonight.

The clock on the wall above her head says it's almost midnight. When I turn my head, I notice the door to the lounge is propped open, and through it, I see this dilapidated pleather couch that seems to glow invitingly. I leave them talking about rooms and keys and start floating toward it.

The couch has this bubbling, circular mark on the bottom cushion as if someone placed a hot pan on it and melted the pleather. I flop down on it and sling an arm over my eyes, thinking about how fitting that is.

32

I'm looking at someone's khakis, a shelf full of board games, and a black-screened TV. I'm hearing my name and feeling a light pressure on my shoulder. Only when I notice how my arm feels like it's been shredded and put back together again does it all come rushing back to me.

I roll my head up to see Bilodeau straightening up from where he was shaking my shoulder, and I have half a mind to ask him to smother me with a pillow.

"Bon matin," he says. Then in English, "They're going to start coming down for breakfast soon if you want to go upstairs."

That's enough to get me to sit up.

"How are you feeling?" he asks. I feel sad that he's not speaking in French to me, like he thinks I've lost my mind and can't understand the language anymore.

There's a crick in my neck from sleeping on the couch, and I start rolling it out, grimacing. The bruises around my throat are tender and aching. "Fine."

I start getting these horror movie flashbacks of blood everywhere, and my heart leaps as I look down at myself. If I wasn't wearing black, I don't think the hostel would've allowed this. Probably not good for business, having a blood-soaked teenager sleeping in your lounge.

Bilodeau holds out a keycard to me. "Mrs. Lachlan moved you into her room. Everything's in there for you."

Right. I take the keycard from him and get up to start my walk of shame toward my teacher's room. I wonder how long he's been down here, and if he and Lachlan were taking shifts watching me to make sure I didn't go and kill myself. At this point, I'm thinking a worm squirming on a fishing hook has more dignity than me.

When I reach the door to the stairwell, a cold stone of dread drops into my stomach.

What if I run into one of them on the way up there? What if they try to talk to me?

In my mind's eye, I see Noor, looking like she was praying over my arm, and Craig, sickly green and paralyzed.

"Do you need help finding your room?"

I look toward the guy at the front desk who'd spoken. He's smiling at me in that nervous way you might smile at your weird neighbour, which makes me realize I've been standing frozen for far too long. "Oh, no. I'm good."

I start moving. Luckily, it's early enough that I manage to avoid any run-ins with my classmates. When Lachlan answers the door, her hair is wet, and she smells nice. Her face, though, is pinched from lack of sleep and probably a world of stress.

"Hiya," she says, holding the door open for me. "Feeling okay?"

"Yes," I say, shuffling inside.

Lachlan watches me move to the furthest of the two twin beds. There are dust motes floating in the white light streaming from the window, and I send them scattering when I sit.

"So feeling like crap, then," she says.

I don't have the energy to deny it. "Yes."

My backpack and the sweater I was wearing yesterday are both on the floor next to my feet. I pull on the sweater, and the extra layer makes me feel a little bit less exposed. Lachlan moves to sit on the edge of the other bed, the springs creaking underneath her. I look at her knees a couple feet away and brace myself for the interrogation.

"Did I ever tell you why I became a teacher?"

I glance up at her, frowning. She clasps her hands between her legs, waiting for an answer, so I shake my head.

"At first I didn't really understand it because I always hated school. Growing up fat and gay in the nineties will do that to you."

I feel my eyes widen. I wasn't expecting that kind of honesty, and she smiles at me like she knows it. "In school, I was bullied badly for these things that I couldn't control, and instead of being reassured at home, it was only affirmed to me that I should be ashamed of myself. So here I had two horrible places I was forced to go to each day, with no refuge from either. But when I got to college, that really changed things for me. I had these very cool professors who were always honest and real in ways that I never thought adults could be. They were just *people*, you know, and they treated *me* like a person.

"But for the first nineteen years of my life, I didn't feel like I was worth anything, and that left a lasting impact. I still felt like an alien everywhere I went, and I continued to do self-destructive things, especially when life was going well for me. It was like I wanted to sabotage that before it came back to bite me, you know? If I hadn't met the very persistent, patient, wonderful pain-in-the-ass people that I met in college, who pushed me to get help, I don't think I would be here right now."

She lets that hang between us, and I swallow the tight feeling in my throat.

"So, as I grew older," she continues, "and I heard other people's stories and continued to learn things about myself, I really started to see how much that lack of care in my childhood coloured my life. I started to wonder how different I would have been if I had those cool teachers in elementary or in high school, and I realized I wanted to be that person for other people. I wanted to be the adult I never had."

I feel this uneasy mix of guilt and gratitude, like I don't deserve what she's told me, but I'm really glad she did. I also have no idea what to say in return, but I don't get the chance; she puts her hands on her knees and says, "So I'm wondering, knowing that I used to be in a similar place to where you are, if that might help you talk to me a little."

I feel a wave of nausea. "I don't know what you want me to say."

"Could you tell me why, maybe? Why you did what you did last night?"

I think it's only my gratitude for the way she started this conversation that I'm able to speak. "I have something... it feels like a leech in my stomach, and it burns when it moves? And it's so... it's awful, and I think it's trying to kill me."

I realize when I say it that it's nonsensical, and it doesn't even answer her question. I wait for her to give me that look that Jordan always did, like I'm a crazy person.

"That's why you hurt yourself?" she asks. "Because it helps with that?"

I stare at her for a moment longer, but her face remains the same—calm, patient. It makes me feel at once pleasantly surprised and wary. "Yes."

"I felt it in my stomach, too, actually."

My eyes widen. "The squirming thing?"

"The shame," she says. "The shame was all I knew. It was like I didn't know how to be any other way except ashamed of myself because everything seemed to be telling me to feel that way, and I had no one to tell me otherwise at a time in my life when my brain was still growing, still gathering information about myself and the world. That started living in me, too; controlling my life, leading me down very dark roads."

"Did you... how did you...?"

"I'll tell you one of the first things I learned that help me. I used to think the same thing as you, that there was this evil thing inside of me. But I learned that it's not evil; it's my body trying to protect me."

I frown at her. I want desperately to believe everything she says, but that can't possibly be right. "I can't... like, I can't *eat* when it's around. What, does it want me to starve to death? How is that protecting me?"

She narrows her eyes thoughtfully. "Well, it helps to remember that we're really nothing more than glorified apes, you know. Apes with brains that were built for surviving, and that's it. So, think about the evolutionary purpose of fight or flight. When you're in that state, your body shuts down all the other parts of you that aren't a priority to your survival in that moment. Your heart starts pumping fast and hard to help you get ready to act. Your mind starts racing so you don't get caught unaware. Your body thinks you're in danger—you don't have time to stop for a snack, right? So, you stop feeling hungry, you start feeling nauseous."

"But I'm not in any danger."

"Even if you're not in any physical danger, your body can think you are. You're like a sponge, going through life, absorbing all of these little moments. No matter how insignificant that moment may seem to you at the time, your body is going to remember how you felt during it. It's going to start learning what kinds of things make you feel at your most vulnerable, and it's going to start doing its best to steer you away from those things."

She purses her lips, and I watch her tuck the hair behind her ear just for it to fall back in her face again. "But the problem is, eventually, your body may just start acting on old patterns instead of reality. It's going to look at a tree shaped like a monster and think it's a monster, even if it's only a tree. Then, if it succeeds in steering you away from the tree, maybe you're going to miss out on all the fruits that are hanging off it. Do you see what I mean? Your body's going to think it knows what's best for you, even when it doesn't.

"So, when I started seeing it that way—you know, with compassion, knowing that it's only trying to protect me—it helped me control it. It helped me tell it, you know: thank you, body, but *I'm* the one in charge. *I'm* going to make these decisions for me."

I massage the heel of my hand into my forehead, feeling a headache blooming. She makes it sound so simple, and somehow that makes me feel even more help-less. "I don't feel like I'm ever going to be in control. I can't stay *in* my body half the time. It kicks me out. I can't remember *two fucking hours* of my life yesterday."

"That makes sense too, though, doesn't it? That if you're in this exhausting fight or flight mode all the time, your mind would eventually just"—she makes a motion like she's pulling something out of her ear—"separate itself from everything?"

"Has it happened to you?" I challenge.

"Well, everyone dissociates sometimes," she says. "I once went out to dinner with my wife after a very hard week, and I didn't remember a word of what she said to me once we got home. But if it's happening to you often, to that extent, then I think it's something you need to get some help with."

My stomach sours. "Because it's not normal."

"No, I'm—" She closes her eyes, shaking her head, and

for a second, I think she's just going to give up. But she meets my eyes again, and her voice is calm and soft. "I'm telling you this because it *is* normal. The things you're feeling and the reactions you're having are very normal. I understand why you do what you do, Alis. Everyone needs a way to deal with emotions that feel too big, and sometimes, we're not given the tools to do it in a healthy way. A safe way."

I shake my head. "I've never messed up like that. And I wasn't trying to kill myself."

"I know you weren't, kiddo, but you could have. And the rest of it... the amount of times... you have to understand why I'm worried about you, right?"

I wrap my bad arm around the burning in my stomach, the cuts stinging and pulling. I'm watching my knee, wondering when it started bouncing like that, when Lachlan asks, "Have you ever told anyone about this?"

I snap my head up. "No. I'm not—it's not like I'm doing it for attention. I didn't want anyone to know."

Lachlan's brow furrows. "Well, even if you did, wanting someone to know you're in pain isn't something to be ashamed—"

"I *don't*. I didn't. I just do it because nothing else helps."

As I say it, I'm acutely aware of how much it didn't help last night; how all I felt was pain and anger, then fear, then exhaustion, then the squirming thing trying to tear me apart. I feel suddenly terrified that I've crossed some kind of line, that *nothing* is going to work anymore.

"Okay," Lachlan says, and half of me wishes she were

yelling at me instead of using that light voice, like she's pacifying a rabid dog. "What else have you tried?"

I want to tell her I've tried music, noise, to drown it out. But I play it loud enough to rattle my eardrums. I play it loud enough that I have to clench my fists in my lap to keep from tearing off the headphones, and I know she's not asking me to tell her all the different kinds of pain I've tried. I wrack my brain for any kind of half-baked answer to fill this unbearable silence and come up with nothing.

Lachlan clasps her hands between her knees. "Alis, it would mean a lot to me if you would let me help you. I know some very good people back home who see people like you all the time—"

My stomach bottoms out, and I shake my head vehemently. "I'm not going to some psych ward."

"I'm talking about someone to talk to. Someone who can help you figure out another way to cope."

I don't realize I've wrapped my hand around my arm, squeezing the cuts, until she reaches across the space to latch onto my hand, her voice full of soft pleading. "*Stop.*"

I look at her, at her sad eyes boring into mine.

No one's ever told me to stop.

Suddenly, there's a shard of glass in my throat when I swallow, and my stomach shoots through with panic at what that might mean. When I blink, there's a hot, heavy feeling to it, and my vision cracks like a window.

Startled, I swipe at my cheek. There's wet glistening on the side of my hand.

Why are you crying?

I spring up from the bed, backing out of the aisle

between them. Through the smudge of my vision, I see Lachlan with her arm outstretched toward me. "It's o*kay*, Alis."

It's not okay. Why am I crying? I haven't cried in ten years, and now I'm crying? Because she needs to deal with *that* right now?

I wipe the tears viciously away with my balled-up sleeves. I squeeze my eyes shut and rub them until I can see properly again.

Lachlan gets up, and I step back from her. "I don't want to talk about this anymore."

Her shoulders sag hopelessly. "What kind of assurance do I have that you're not going to do it again the moment you leave this room?"

I cross my arms, because the more I squeeze the cuts, the more the shard in my throat softens away. "So, what, you're holding me hostage?"

"Honestly, I don't know." She looks to the window, running a hand through her hair. "I don't know what to do."

My chest tightens. I didn't expect her to say that or to look so dejected as she did. She literally saved my life last night, and then she told me all that personal shit, and here I am, being an asshole.

I drop my arms, and my voice is barely above a whisper. "I'm sorry."

"You don't have to—" she cuts off, huffing a very sad laugh. I let her come up to me and place her hands on my shoulders. "Kiddo, there's nothing to be sorry for. I just really want to do right by you, you know?"

I nod, but I can still feel that pain in my throat, so I say, "Can I go change now?"

"I need you to promise me two things first. Can you look at me?"

My heart trips into a gallop as I do it, because I know I'm probably going to have to lie to her face.

"I got you a phone," she says. "If you feel like you're going to hurt yourself again, you're going to text me first. I don't care where we are or what time it is or how guilty you feel about it."

Even if I wanted to—which, after last night, I think maybe I do—I know for a fact that when I feel the urge, I'm not going to have that much control. Still, she's looking at me with this air of preparedness, like she's willing to go to battle the moment I open my mouth to say no, so I say, "Okay."

Her eyebrows raise. "Are you actually going to, or are you just saying that to shut me up?"

"No, I... I will try." It's the most honest thing I can say.

"Okay. Second thing: please don't push your friends away, Alis."

The shard is back in my throat. "I don't think I'm going to have to."

"No? Do you *know* how many texts I got last night? Craig was—"

I step out of her grip, squeezing my eyes shut as my stomach fills with acid. "Please don't tell me that."

"If you're going to push them away because you think you're doing them a favour, then trust me: you're not. That's all I'm saying."

I really, really need her to stop talking. I'm telepathically begging her.

"Will you think about what I said?" she asks. "About maybe seeing someone back home?"

"Yes," I say, and I don't even know if I mean it, but she finally nods. She holds up a finger and goes over to her giant purple backpack, digging through it. Then she hands me a complete dinosaur of a flip phone that I don't even think I'm going to know how to use.

"You are bringing this *everywhere* you go, and you're going to answer immediately if I call you. And if you're not down in the lobby at exactly nine a.m. for the coach, I'm going to make a scene when I come looking for you."

"Fine," I say, and I think it's a testament to how much I like her that I manage not to roll my eyes.

PART V

VENICE

33

Lachlan's ensuite bathroom looks nothing like the stall from last night, which I'm grateful for. I really would like a shower to melt the stiffness out of my body, but I can't get my bandages wet, and I'm really not in the mood to look at my arm, so I do an awkward sponge bath in the sink instead. I try not to focus on the pinkness of the water that goes down the drain.

I put on my baggiest sweater and a pair of black sweatpants. The sweater hides most of the now bluish-purple bruises on my throat, but I don't feel anything when I look at them. At least they weren't put there by me.

I do, however, look away from the mirror as soon as I'm able because I look like a fucking ghost. I suppose having a mental breakdown, almost bleeding out, and then sleeping on a stiff couch will do that to you.

When I turn off the taps, I stare at my hands trembling in the sink. The last time I felt this anxious was just before I stupidly walked into that party. I should've listened to the way I was feeling then. If I had, if I didn't go in there, then no one would know, and Craig would've never talked to me in Paris. I wouldn't have stitches in my arm. I wouldn't have subjected so many people to the horror of that shower stall last night. I wouldn't be a burden on anyone but me.

I would still be invisible, friendless, and alone.

Yet, as I think about that version of my life, I don't feel any longing for it. That isn't what I want either. I don't want to go back to being feared and hated and never laughing and never drawing on anyone's shoe and never kissing anyone. I know I don't want to go back to that just as well as I knew I didn't want to die last night.

But it doesn't matter what I want now. I had to open that door, but I knew it would mean losing them. I'm not even sure I hadn't already lost them, after what I said to them. Noor is too nice to let me bleed to death, but from the way she sprinted from the stall, I think I can count on her never looking at me again.

And Craig, well. He must be wondering why he ever wanted to try and fix me in the first place. He sent all those texts to Lachlan to make sure he didn't end up killing me instead because that probably wouldn't have made him feel very helpful.

I don't understand the ache in my chest when I think about him. Now that I know he's known this whole time, the idea that he ever liked me is the most preposterous thing in the world. Why would he try to get close to me after finding that out if not to make a pity project out of me?

I should hate him.

I'm gripping the sink and trying really, really hard to hate him. But I'm just thinking about the way he kissed me really softly under the tree and feeling like someone's scraping out my insides with a melon baller.

I swallow hard against that horrible pain that keeps coming back into my throat, then splash some cold water on my face until it softens away.

I get to the lobby at nine as Lachlan asked, finding only a handful of my classmates standing around. I look at them warily to see if somehow they know about what happened, but they're all minding their own business. Still, I tell Lachlan that I'm going to go to the lounge because the thought of sitting in the lobby waiting for Craig and Noor to come down those stairs is excruciating. I sit in an armchair, listening to Lachlan bark "Late!" at everyone who comes downstairs.

She comes to get me at boarding time, waving her Rainbow Tablet at me in the door.

I shuffle up to her. "Sit with me on the bus."

"Don't be ridiculous."

"Please."

She presses her lips together. "Fine, but you'll have to explain to Mr. Bilodeau why I can't show him how to play *Candy Crush* like I promised."

When we go outside, everyone is already loaded onto the bus, and I'm trailing my teacher around like a hungry stray. Yesterday, I may have found that humiliating, but today, I think I would actually start crawling if it meant I never needed to face Craig and Noor again.

When I get on the bus, I keep my hair in my face and avert my gaze from everyone on it. Lachlan slides into the first empty seat, and I slide in after her. My heart pounds at the thought of someone calling my name, but no one does, and I'm embarrassed for thinking they would.

When I pull my headphones out of my bag, it takes me a second to remember I don't have my phone anymore.

"Shit," I whisper, leaning my head back against the seat.

Lachlan looks at the headphones in my lap. She wrestles her phone out of her back pocket, opens Spotify, and hands it to me. "Don't use my data."

"Is there good music on here?"

"Depends how much of a snob you are."

As the coach starts moving, I look through the forty songs she has downloaded on her phone. I know about half of them and like about five of them. There is some Paramore on here, but that just reminds me of Jordan. If it wasn't for her, I'd have my own goddamn music to listen to right now.

For the greater part of the three hours it takes to drive to Venice, I listen to all of Lachlan's music except for Paramore. It's at a normal volume for most of the ride unless I start getting the urge to turn around and see where Craig and Noor are sitting, at which point I grit my teeth and turn it all the way up.

When we're twenty minutes out, I pull the headphones off and give her the phone back. "Not all of it is bad."

She snorts at me. "Your opinion is noted."

The coach lets us off in a parking lot a little ways away from our hostel. Lachlan and I are first off the bus, and I manage to not look at anyone's face while the rest of my classmates unload.

It's an obnoxiously sunny day in Venice. Seabirds laugh overhead as I trail behind Lachlan's big purple backpack. We walk along the sparkling Grand Canal with about a billion other tourists, and I inhale the smell of brine and fish and try to remind myself how far removed I am from home, but I suppose that hardly matters anymore. Anywhere I go, *I'm* still going to be there, fucking everything up.

We arrive at what appears to be a very large house refurbished into a very small hostel. The hallways are cramped, the stairs can only take people single-file, and there are bugs flying in and out of every open window. My room is on the top floor, and by the time I reach it, I'm breathing heavy and swimming in sweat. I also think I made a mistake because Dakota is dragging her bag into my room.

"Oh, hey," she pants when she sees me, holding the door open for me with her back.

At the confused look on my face, Drew says from inside the room: "Yeah, Noor and Craig are in here, too. Weird that they suddenly trust us not to have sex with each other. Or hetero sex, at least."

"Filter, Drew," Dakota moans. Meanwhile, my blood has turned to ice.

Dakota gives me a strained smile, still holding the door. "Take your time."

I have no choice but to mumble an apology and make my way into the room. Dakota lets the door shut, and the sound is like a prison cell closing, and my heart is in my throat.

The room has two twin beds with their headboards against one wall, a bunk bed against the other, and a loft bed on the wall next to the door. There's a desk underneath it with a Bible sat neatly in the centre, and Noor is up on the bed above it. She's using her phone screen as a mirror as she rubs sunscreen on her nose.

Dakota sprawls on the bottom bunk, and Drew is already tossing his bag on the bed above her. So, of course, the only bed left is the twin right next to Craig. I'm watching him walk over to the closest one and feel a pang in my chest when I see he's wearing that same green shirt he had on at the Eiffel Tower, rolled up to the elbows.

"Can I just say? This is wonderful," Dakota says from her bed. "I actually like everyone in this room."

"Ditto," Drew says.

Craig sits down on the edge of his bed, props his forearm on his knee and then wipes his hand down his face. It comes to rest over his mouth, and I'm standing frozen with my pulse crashing in my neck as his eyes slide up to mine.

The neutral expression on his face collapses in an instant. His forehead crumples, his hand curls into a fist over his mouth, and when he closes his eyes, a tear squeezes out of one so fast it seems impossible.

"Craig?" Dakota says, sitting up. Her voice snaps me out of my paralysis, and when her head turns to me, I immediately drop my bag and leave because I won't be able to bear the accusation on her face.

I'm about to go rip into Lachlan for this roommate bullshit she's pulled, but I only get to the top of the stairs before the door squeals open again behind me.

"I can't do this." Craig's voice is so wretched that it makes me stop in my tracks. "I'm going to lose my mind if we do it like this."

I physically can't ignore him when he sounds like that, so I turn around and focus all my energy on keeping my face blank. His brow is still furrowed, his lips pressed together. He's clutching his ribs like he has a side cramp, and I think I actually prefer the ashen, haunted look from last night over this.

"You can't just push me out like it was nothing," he says raggedly. "Even if you think it was nothing or that I was... I need you to let me explain."

My heart is wrenching so badly at the look of him that part of me just wants to forget everything and run to him and hang on forever. But I keep coming back to the timing of the day he spoke to me, like tonguing an empty tooth socket. I can't reconcile it. And I can't stand knowing that he put his hands under my shirt when he *knew* I'd be an ugly mess.

The thing in my stomach is yowling and writhing and begging me to run.

I hear Lachlan's words ringing through my mind: *It's*

going to look at a tree shaped like a monster and think it's a monster, even if it's only a tree.

I close my eyes so I don't have to look at him at all—tree or monster.

He told me he wanted to explain. The explanation could be horrendous. It could be everything I don't want to know and don't want to hear.

But if it is, then really, how much worse off can I become?

And if it isn't?

If it isn't.

I put my hand over the thing in my stomach.

I'm the one in charge, I think. *I'm going to make these decisions for me.*

I open my eyes. "Can we go for a walk?"

34

There are men in candy-striped shirts and straw hats selling gondola rides everywhere I look as we make our way down the canal. Craig trails behind me like a scolded child the entire time, possibly because I'm walking too fast for him. I don't slow down.

Part of me thinks it's a bad idea to trap myself on the water with him with no escape, but judging by the number of people swarming this tiny city, a boat seems like the only place where we'll actually be able to be alone (minus the gondolier, but hopefully his English is limited enough that he won't understand how disturbing my life is.)

Plus, I'm not leaving this city until I've been in a fucking gondola.

I choose a gondolier at a less busy spot near one of the stone bridges arching over the canal. His black scythe of a boat bobs in the water behind him, empty, and I wordlessly hand him the wad of cash I took out from the ATM before making my way down the dock. Maybe a bit rude, but I'm sure Craig is giving him a polite smile to smooth things over behind me.

I sit on the love seat that looks like it's meant for cuddling. Craig, rightfully, does not sit next to me but in the red upholstered seat on the other end of the boat.

As we start moving, I watch him looking out at the ancient buildings rising out of the water, their brick walls patchy with stripped plaster, their arched windows and wrought iron balconies like something out of a Shakespeare play.

"Talk," I say.

When he turns his face to me, his mouth is pulling at the corners, and his eyes dart none-too-subtly from my face to my arm. Then he bows his head, pressing the heel of his hand into his forehead. "Every time I look at you, it's like I'm seeing a nightmare."

I pretend like my heart isn't shredding and keep my voice even. "Is that it?"

"No." He inhales deeply and lifts his head. "I'm going to keep looking at you until it stops."

He does, and it looks as painful for him as it is for me. Eventually, the muscle stops jumping in his jaw, and he lets out a long breath. "Okay."

I grip the seat under my thighs. "Why did you talk to me on the Eiffel Tower?"

He takes his hat off, runs a hand through his hair, then puts it right back on. "Do you remember first day of eleventh grade?"

I glare at him. "No."

"Well, I do, because up until that point, I only ever

had…" He cocks his head, squinting beyond my shoulder. "Okay, a lot of crushes, but never anyone I actually knew. And I say up until that point because when you walked into Miss Richard's class after growing your hair out and going, like, full throttle into the whole not-goth thing, I was crazy for you."

I ignore the way my stomach swoops. "You're full of shit."

"Ask Noor. She might vomit, but she'll tell you I didn't shut up about you."

"Then why didn't you ever say a word to me?"

"Because you *scared* me, Alis. You were scary. And not in the burn-your-house-down kind of way, but in the I-am-way-cooler-than-you-and-I-don't-care-about-your-opinion kind of way. Not to mention you were like *attached* to Jordan, who was even scarier. I was very comfortable with pining from afar."

I narrow my eyes. Did he even go to the same school as me? He's telling me he looked at *me* and thought, hey, there's a person who doesn't care what other people think about him! Were they pumping fumes out of the vents? It would explain a lot.

"It still doesn't answer my question," I say. "Why Paris?"

He rubs his hands down his thighs. "I told Noor, before the trip, that because we're graduating in a month, I was just gonna do it. I was gonna talk to you. I was gonna do it when I saw that Kristen was trying to swap with someone at the fondue place. I asked Noor if she thought I should, but Eric was sitting next to me, and he heard and thought he'd try to… you know, warn me off."

I feel a wave of nausea. "And?"

He's quiet for a moment, staring at the red carpet as the water plunks against the side of the boat. When he finally turns his face up to me, it's as anguished as it was back at the hostel. "I wasn't lying when I said I didn't believe it at first. But I did... I considered that, if it was true, then maybe you could use a friend? But I didn't—it wasn't the *reason*. I didn't even think about it until that night in Rome, when you stopped me and I saw the look on your face and... I'm sorry, Alis, but I told Noor what happened because I didn't know what to do. I had a feeling, and I wanted her to tell me I was wrong, but she didn't. So we agreed that I couldn't keep pretending I didn't know, and I kept looking for a way to bring it up—"

"It wasn't your *business*," I say, my voice shaking. "It's not anybody's fucking business."

He furrows his brow, looking almost angry now. "Is that actually what you think? Like this is fine, and everyone should just ignore it?"

"I didn't mean to drag you and Noor into it. Or Lachlan, even, but I thought—I thought I made a mistake, and I had to open the door."

"You think I'm mad at you for opening the door? Are you mad at me for having a seizure at the beach?"

"What?" I scoff. "That's not the same thing."

He shrugs. "Tell me how it's not."

"You can't control it."

"So you can control what you're doing? Why don't you stop, then?"

The thing in my stomach twists, and my vision pulses.

"I'm not this helpless crazy person, Craig, no matter how much you wish I was."

He doesn't even flinch. He just looks at me, his mouth twisting, before his eyes drop to my feet. "Alis, are you just trying to push me away because you don't want me around anymore? Because I seriously can't understand how you could think I'm enjoying this. But I would get it if... like, I know I can talk a lot, and I get on people's nerves sometimes, and I know I don't exactly have a six-pack or any... you know, *experience*. Part of the reason I never talked to you was because I thought I didn't have a chance in hell, but then you kissed me, and I thought maybe..."

"Don't be fucking ridiculous," I say.

His eyes slide back up to mine, and his throat bobs. "I actually don't think I'm being ridiculous at all, and I wish you would just tell me the truth."

"You are literally perfect. *You* are perfect. That's the truth, and it doesn't make any sense that you would want to be around me after last night. I'm not what you said, Craig. I'm not whatever person you thought you had a crush on, I promise you that."

"No, you're really not." He says it flatly, with this finality that's like a knife to my heart. But then he continues, "To be honest, I don't think I would've gotten along with that person because I'm pretty sure he wasn't human. But you are, and you still scare the crap out of me because I've never in my life felt for someone the way I feel about you."

His voice goes rough at the end. I lift my head to see that his eyes are glittering with tears, but his jaw is set, and his face is utterly determined, like he's trying to convince me.

And I believe him. I think I really believe him, and it scares the hell out of me, too, because I don't think he knows who he has feelings for. He doesn't know that the last person I let get close to me was in tears by the end of it, telling me she needed a break from me. He doesn't know that when he was holding my hand yesterday, it was the only thing keeping me in my body. He doesn't know the extent of my parents' hatred for me, and if he did, he would know there's something wrong with me. There must be something deeply wrong with me for them to hate me so much.

There's a sharpness in my throat when I swallow, and I know it has nothing to do with the bruises. I feel that icy panic I'd felt back in Lachlan's room, and something pulls my eyes to the bridge arching over the canal in the distance.

That's where I see her.

My mother: straight-backed, thin-lipped, her hands white-knuckled over the balustrade, staring right at me.

Then I blink, and she's gone, replaced by a stranger. And I don't think she was ever there to begin with.

We pass through the shadow of the bridge and come back into sunlight, the boat rocking gently beneath us, and I feel like my insides have been put through a meat grinder.

When did the thing in my stomach grow claws? When did I start *hallucinating*?

I bring my eyes back to his eyes, Craig's eyes that hold

all the light in the world even when they're sad. I feel something like the wave I felt under the fresco with Dakota, except this one is white-hot and frothing and feels like it wants to drown me.

"I think I'm insane," I say, my voice raw. "I think I'm really insane, and when you finally figure that out, you're gonna leave."

Craig looks at me for a long moment, his face unreadable. He puts his hands on the seat beneath him, glancing at the gondolier over my shoulder. He's checking that he didn't overhear. He's checking to see if we can pull over, if he can jump overboard. His eyes come back to me, he opens his mouth—

"Can I come over there?"

I don't answer. I must not have heard him right.

"I'm gonna come over there," he says. Then he gets up halfway, holding his arms out when the boat wobbles precariously. He smiles sheepishly at the gondolier as he moves across it, then squishes himself next to me on the love seat.

He leans back to look at my face, his eyebrows rising.

"I think you're really hurting, and you're not telling anyone," he says. "And I'm pretty sure that would drive anyone insane."

I don't understand him.

I think I wanted so badly for it to be true that he never really liked me because that was easy. That made sense. This doesn't make any sense at all, and I don't know if it will ever stop feeling too good to be true. Every second I spend with him, I'll be waiting for the other shoe to drop.

But I also *want* to spend every second with him. I love everything about him. I love the way he's never embarrassed by anything. I love how he can make anyone laugh and the look in his eyes when he does, like it's the only thing he needs to breathe. I love that he says everything in earnest as if it's the last thing he's ever going to say. I love that he kisses me so gently, like he doesn't want to break me. I love how every time he's near me, it feels like he's anchoring me to earth.

I love that he's still here, and I'm so tired of fighting that. I'm even more tired than when I fell asleep in that cab last night and could barely move, and I think that's why I resign myself to just telling him the truth.

"I don't understand you at all," I whisper.

"That's fine," he says. "I just want you to believe me."

"I'm trying."

"Okay." His eyes wander to somewhere by my ear, and he brings up a hooked finger and brushes his knuckle, featherlight, over my cheek. There's an eruption of tingling in the back of my skull that runs all the way down my spine, pooling in my fingertips.

I'm pretty sure no one has ever touched me like that.

He drops his hand back into his lap, swallowing visibly. The flush in his cheeks has spread to his ears. His lips part like he's going to say something else, but I beat him to it.

"I'm sorry," I say. "For yesterday. For everything."

His lips purse, and he dips his head. "I didn't know if you were trying to kill yourself."

"I wasn't."

"I know that now, but I didn't yesterday. And that's the

thing, like... I think I need you to let me in, Alis. Even just a little bit."

My heart thumps hard against my ribs. I focus my eyes on his hands—his hand that brushed my face—and force the words out. "Last night was an accident. I'm usually more careful because I'm not trying to... to maim myself or something. I just need to make it more painful than everything else."

Craig is quiet for a moment. When I chance a glance up at him, he's scratching at his forehead just under his hat, looking like he's steeling himself for something. "I, um... I was reading about self-harm last night, and I think maybe I understand that a bit more now. I kind of thought of this thing my mom said about how she used to faint at the sight of needles? Then she went into labour with my brother, and she was begging for the epidural, which was the biggest needle she'd ever seen. She preferred to have that plunged into her spine than go through the contractions because that pain was easier."

The thought of him researching that last night makes me want to sink through the bottom of the boat. But how can I blame him for it when I did exactly the same thing on the train after his seizure while he was sleeping so heavily? When I needed, desperately, to know that he was okay?

My palms are suddenly covered in sweat, and I run my hands up and down my thighs. "I guess. Yes."

"Did I say something wrong?" he asks.

I breathe a laugh, my hair sliding over my face as I grip

my knees. "You have to get how uncomfortable this is for me, right?"

"I know, but I guess I'm trying to tell you that it doesn't need to be. But I also know that's not really how it works," he says. Then he sighs, dragging his hat off his head. "God, I'm sorry."

He leans forward, running both his hands up through his hair. "Seriously, before I met you, I didn't think I was so, like...*naive* about everything."

"I don't think you're naive," I say. "You just... you see the best of people. And the world."

He drops his hands and sits back, giving me this pained little smile. "I'm pretty sure that's the same thing."

"It's not. It's one of my favourite things about you."

His eyes go round with surprise, like back in Rome when I told him I liked his jokes. Maybe I need to tell him how much I like him more often.

But then his lips slide up slowly, and he puts his hat back on and says, "Only one of them?"

I roll my eyes, turning my face to the water. "Your cockiness is my least favourite thing about you."

He laughs, and his hand comes over mine. I let him thread our fingers together as I look out on Venice. We've come out into a much wider stretch of water, and up ahead, I can see the Rialto Bridge spreading over the Grand Canal like a pair of angel's wings. Angry-looking clouds shroud the sky behind it, and our boat rocks more forcefully as a strong breeze stirs the water.

"You know, I'm fine if you're really not okay sometimes," Craig says softly. "But I can't just not know one way or the other."

"You always know."

"What?"

My cheeks heat. "You always know what I'm feeling. It drives me up the fucking wall, but you do."

"I mean, you have a very obvious face," he says. I give him my most unimpressed look, but he just squeezes my hand. "But I don't want to have to guess."

"I don't know how to talk about shit like you do. My dad is emotionally constipated, and my mom's two emotional states are passive aggressive or plain aggressive, so we didn't really have sharing circle."

"You just did it," he says. I furrow my brow, and he elaborates. "You just talked about sh—stuff."

"Well, that's my quota, then."

"Okay, but one more question."

I sigh. "What?"

He puts his hand on the side of my head and brings his face an inch from mine. "Do you still hate me, or can I kiss you?"

He must feel the way my skin is buzzing under his hand. "I never hated you."

He grins, and I can still feel it on his lips when he kisses me.

35

The rain starts not long after Craig and I get off the gondola, and we don't get back to the hostel in time to escape it. By the time I shut myself into our room's ensuite washroom, my arm is itching like a bitch under my wet layers of clothes, and as I peel the bandages off, I find I'm having a hard time looking at it. This isn't something I've ever had trouble with before, but I can't remember the last time I've had so many fresh cuts at once. I *never* had stitches in one of them, even though a few of the old ones have healed so badly, I think they probably should have.

I spend so long sitting on the toilet preparing myself to redress it that Craig sends me a text to my borrowed dinosaur phone asking if I'm okay. And I realize that's how it's going to be if we do this. Him worrying about me every time I go to the washroom.

I send him as short a reply as I can—I have to hit the 9 four times to type a *y*—before steeling myself and getting to work.

At some point, I'm just holding my arm in the sink, watching rivulets of water run over my ruined skin and circle the drain, when I have this growing, insidious thought that my life has become a video game, and I'm merely an avatar. I flex my fingers and wonder at the mechanics of them. Did they always look like that? Was everything always so bright and squishy and solid and wet?

I go through the motions—literally. I don't make any conscious decisions. I'm aware of time moving slow as molasses around me and this uneasy feeling like as soon as I leave this washroom my whole life is going to go blip. Game over.

It's one of the weirder dream states—or dissociations, I guess—that I've had. I mean, all of them are weird, but this one had an existential element to it that I didn't like at all. I'm very glad when I come back, looking at my sleeve. I have to pull it up to make sure I actually did change the bandage, and it looks fresh, and it feels okay.

Then Craig texts me to tell me that he, Noor, and Drew are in the lounge, and they're about to play cards, and dread sinks its cold claws into me.

I can't just go down there and play cards with Noor like nothing happened. But I can't... how the hell am I supposed to apologize for last night? I remember how serene I felt when she unwrapped the toilet paper and saw the arm that I didn't think anyone would ever see. I don't know how I managed to separate so thoroughly from myself then—it seems impossible now, as I feel close to vomiting at the thought of looking her in the eye again.

My thumbs hover over the keyboard, and I notice the state of my nail polish. Every single fingernail has a chip in it, and I'm wondering how I let it get this bad. I never let it get this bad.

I don't think I can go back downstairs until I fix this, especially if I'm meant to play cards. Especially if I'm meant to face Noor.

When I come out of the washroom, I notice Dakota lying on her bottom bunk with one knee propped up on the other. There's a smiley face on her shirt that matches the yellow barrettes in her hair. She looks up at me over what looks to be a shiny new book about the history of Venice, flashing me a dimpled smile. "Hey."

"Hey," I say, frowning. "Are you sick?"

"No, just a very drained introvert. I needed to recharge."

I point at the door. "I can go."

"No, no! You're fine. Stay if you want."

I feel sort of weird interrupting her, but as I look down at my nails again, it's too hard to ignore. So I pad over to my bed, wincing when the springs squeal as I sit on it. Dakota sniffs quietly and goes back to her book.

Once I finally finish texting Craig that I'm with Dakota, I lean over the bed—more squealing, more cringing—and dig through my bag for the bottle of black nail polish. I pull open the drawer of the bedside table because I'm about ninety percent certain there's going to be another Bible in there.

I'm correct. That's two Bibles. I wonder if there's going to be more Bibles by the time we leave.

I place the Bible on the bed, unscrew the cap, and splay my fingers out on the embossed cover. But as I move to swipe the brush over my index finger, I notice the way my hand is shaking.

I stare at the little tremors wracking it. It's worse than the fucking turbulence.

Do I shake after dissociating? I haven't noticed. I'll add that to the list of shit my body does without my permission.

I try to work through it, but I mess up almost immediately. I cluck my tongue in spite of myself, and Dakota's head turns.

"Need help?" she asks. I'm about to tell her it's fine, but she's already tossing the book she was reading and hopping to her feet, her eyes twinkling excitedly. "I love doing it for other people. It's like meditation to me."

I raise my eyebrows a little at her eagerness. "Um, yeah, if you want."

I tuck my back against the wall as she comes onto my bed, sliding down on her stomach in front of me. "Wait, do you have remover? We should take this off and do it again."

I get out the little bottle of nail polish remover, and she rolls off the bed to get a box of tissues from the desk before repositioning herself. Then she pats the Bible.

I hesitate, my heart speeding up a little. "You really don't have to."

She wrinkles her nose. "I mean, I really want to, but I won't if you don't want me to."

"No, I do. If you want to."

She grins at me, and I smile a little because I, too, can hear how stupid this conversation is.

I put my hand down for her, and she takes the remover and gets to work.

Dakota apparently doesn't talk at all when she does nails, and the only sound apart from our breathing is the gentle plinking of rain off the fire escape outside the window. I watch as she tilts my fingers very carefully, very slowly, her thumb gently pressing into the back of my hand as she does it. When she brushes, there's this little frown of concentration on her face, like this is the most important task she's ever undertaken, and my stomach is so full of warm fluttering, it feels like I'm going to take flight.

I'm listening to the rain and our breathing, feeling like we're the only two people in the world, when Dakota makes a mistake on my pinkie. She tuts quietly and carefully uses her own nail to scrape away some stray paint, and the warm fluttering spreads into an ache—a deep, fierce ache in my chest that hurts like hell.

I didn't think anyone could care this much.

I didn't think they could care this much about my pinkie finger.

"There," she says. She gives the back of my hand a little pat. "Next hand."

She looks up at me, smiling for just a second before it flickers and dies. "You okay?"

I can only assume my face is doing things again. I bow my head and rub my fist over my forehead like I can erase whatever it is. "Yes. Sorry."

I give her my other hand, clearing my throat and looking out the window. I can still feel her looking at me in my peripheral, and my skin prickles with anxiety.

Then she says, "My mom used to do my nails. Every night, a different colour. She died five years ago."

My heart plummets as I turn my gaze back on her. "Jesus. I'm really sorry."

She shrugs. "She was sick for a long time, so we were as prepared as we could be when it happened. But I like to do the things that she liked doing to feel closer to her. Like, I'll go walking the routes that she used to walk, and I'll keep filling up our bird feeders even though birds kind of scare me, and I'll rough up Drew's hair, and I'll do nails. Feels like, for a second, she's standing right beside me."

I watch as she finishes up my other pinkie finger just as carefully as she did the first one. "You're very good at it. The nails."

She beams up at me. Then she twists the cap back on the bottle, and I can't help but feel a little bit of mourning when she takes her gentle hands off mine. "You know she was part of the reason why I never once thought you started that fire."

I just stare at her because I have no idea what she could mean by that.

She pulls herself up on her knees. "In ninth grade, I was waiting outside for Drew after school, and I saw you crossing the bus loop. You stopped walking suddenly and bent to pick something up, then you turned around and came back to school toward that big grassy patch near there? You put it down by the tree, then you left again.

Afterwards, I was really curious, so I went to look, and it was this fuzzy orange caterpillar."

I don't remember this at all, and I don't know why it's making my cheeks heat. Dakota's dimples deepen as she continues, "My mom used to do that all the time. She'd always be saving things from the middle of the sidewalk and the parking lots. She couldn't go fishing with my dad because she didn't want to watch him piercing the worms on the hooks. So I never forgot that you did that even four years later, and when I heard people saying you were burning down houses and killing cats, I knew you weren't the kind of person who would do that. Maybe that's kind of childish, but..."

She trails off, shrugging. I feel flustered but also so touched that my heart has started aching again. I clear my throat. "I—um. Thank you. That actually means a lot to me."

"I'm really sorry we weren't friends sooner," she says, her face falling a little. "I thought maybe we could've been, and I don't know why I didn't try."

"Because Jordan and I were closed-off assholes who spent all of our time judging people from afar."

I had no idea that was going to come out of my mouth, but as soon as it does, I know it's the truth. We didn't let anybody in—if anything, we actively pushed them out. We slotted them into little categories and stuck all those categories under a larger one: Other.

"I didn't think you were assholes," Dakota says. She cocks her head and smiles sheepishly. "Maybe a bit scary, though."

This reminds me of what Craig said on the gondola, and my lips quirk. "Craig was more scared of me than you were."

"That's because he *likes* you."

Ah. So apparently everyone knew that but me.

That's another example of how thoroughly Jordan and I managed to cut ourselves off from the world—we hated everyone so much, the possibility that anyone could take any interest in us became an impossibility. If Craig Miltenberg had told me he liked me when I was still orbiting Jordan like she was the sun, I would've thought he was messing with me and ditched him in a much ruder way than I had on the Eiffel Tower.

The truth is that, when I was eight years old, I gave myself fully to the first person who ever showed me kindness, and I never made room for anyone else. That's no one else's fault but mine. And though I don't think I'll ever understand why she chose the people she did, I think I am finally starting to understand the real reason why Jordan wanted to be free of me.

36

I leave Dakota to her recharging after thanking her for doing my nails with what, judging by the look on her face, was a disproportionate amount of earnestness. But I couldn't help it—I don't think I'm ever going to forget the gentleness with which she did that, or what she told me, or how safe she made me feel for those few minutes. It gave me the boost I needed to go down and finally clear the air with Noor.

But as I'm making my way down the last set of stairs, I hear a whimper. I look over the banister to see Maya curled up on the end of a sofa in the lobby, pressing her phone facedown into her thigh as she quietly cries.

I pause, the stair creaking under my foot. Her eyes dart up to me before she quickly looks away, raising her chin and forcing her face into an expression of neutrality that really doesn't work with the shiny tear tracks on her cheeks.

I'm starting to wonder how hard I hit my head against

those lockers when Theo attacked me because, in that moment, I actually feel bad for Maya Papadakis.

I start moving again, trying to remind myself of all of the diabolical shit she's pulled on me these last few years, namely the text she sent that led to the most horrible night of my life.

But when I get to the bottom of the stairs, instead of bitterness, all I feel is guilt for ignoring the crying girl. I roll my eyes at myself and turn to her, crossing my arms.

"Are you okay," I ask, my voice flatter than I intended it to be.

"Go away," she says thickly.

Wonderful! I fulfilled my moral duties, and now I can leave. I turn to do just that when she adds, "This is *your* fault, you know."

I swear, the universe is testing me. I take a deep breath, flexing my hands at my sides as I turn back to her. "So I guess Jordan is the one that made you cry? Because apparently everything she does is my fault."

"Everything's about *her* now," she hisses, chucking her phone to the other end of the couch with a bitter twist to her mouth. "Ever since that stupid party, she's become a total maniac. First, she was insanely angry at all of us for telling people you started the fire, and then when she got over that three minutes later, she started thinking the fire was karma or something for what she did to you. So now, she's having some kind of spiritual crisis and dragging Theo into it. She hogged him literally this whole trip, and then he goes and gets sent home because she drove him crazy with her whining, and none of this would be happening if *you* didn't make it impossible for her to apologize to you."

I expected the squirming thing to show up a long time ago. In fact, I'm shocked I'm still standing here humouring this when I'm sure I should have bolted at the word *party*. But if there's acid splashing in my stomach, I can't feel it beyond the beginnings of the other thing—that earthquake that overtook me when I smashed my phone in Florence. I can feel it beginning to swirl up in me now; my pulse speeding up, the pressure building in my head.

I take another step into the lobby. "First of all, can I just say? You sound like a great friend. Really one of a kind. I can see why she hangs out with you."

Maya opens her mouth, but I speak louder to drown her out. "Second of all, she didn't look me in the fucking eye *once* after that night, so whatever apology she's trying to give me? She's not trying very hard."

Maya scrunches up her face, her legs coming down off the couch. "She sent you like fifty texts afterwards that you ignored!"

"Oh, did she? I wonder why I wasn't in the mood to read her texts that night? I'm sure she couldn't even fathom why I wouldn't respond. Good thing she tried again—"

"Do you hear yourself? *This* is what I mean. You're impossible. Like, I get that she embarrassed you, but to act like—"

She may as well have just smacked me in the face. "*Embarrassed* me?"

My teeth are aching like they're begging me to literally bite her head off. The earthquake is in full force now, making my muscles shake, making me want to scream until my vocal cords tear.

Embarrassed me. Yes, that's what she did. That's what that was. Fucking embarrassing, that's all. And now Jordan has people believing that *I'm* the problem, that *I'm* the reason she never even looked in my direction since that night.

I take another step, stabbing a finger toward my own face. "It's not *my* responsibility to ease *her* guilt."

"That's literally not what I—"

"No, she's a coward, okay? She's a coward, and you're insane."

"No, *you're* insane! You both are." I'm already turning away from her, shooting her the finger over my shoulder so she has to yell the rest at my back. "I don't know why she ever left your side because you guys are *made* for each other!"

I burst through the lounge doors at the end of the hall, relishing the new shape of this anger. It feels less like what I'm used to and more like a much bigger, darker cousin of what I felt when we were playing Catan and Lachlan cut off my road with hers or when the boys in gym all those years ago would team up against me and would never play by the rules. It's an infuriating sense of injustice, almost refreshing in its purity. I want it to keep filling me up until I explode.

Inside the lounge, I find most of my classmates and some other backpackers scattered over chairs and couches, playing board games on the floor or eating at round tables. There's music playing—something vaguely depressing despite everyone's apparent good mood—and it could be louder. It could be much louder. I feel like a live wire as I make a beeline toward Craig, Noor, and Drew where they're playing cards by a rain-streaked window.

I pull up a chair at their table, letting the chrome legs screech over the floor, then plop down on it and enjoy more screeching as I scoot myself in.

They all stare at me over their cards.

"Man, you really light up a room," Drew says.

Noor is sitting next to him, and only when I meet her eyes does the squirming thing finally come alive. That anger I've been feeling begins to twist itself down more familiar avenues, veering away from Jordan and barrelling toward me.

How can I call Jordan a coward when here I am, tearing my eyes away from Noor to stare at the table because I can't even begin to apologize for what I made her do?

And isn't it true that I deleted all of Jordan's texts that night? Isn't it true that I did everything in my power to keep people away from me after that, becoming the most awful version of myself?

You're impossible.

The urge hits me so hard, I'm nearly blinded by it.

I *am* the problem. I'm always the problem.

"Hey, you want some wine?"

I look to Drew. He's pulling a crumpled water bottle out from under the table, red liquid sloshing around the bottom half.

This. This will work. Just like in Rome when it felt like

nothing bad could happen to me. It's going to cleanse Maya's words right out of my head and push the grimy feeling from my blood.

I take the bottle from him and manage to get one sip in before everyone's eyes shoot up to somewhere above my head. I can feel the figure looming behind me just before I see a pair of fingers reach down and pinch the bottle like a claw crane, pulling it up and out of my hand.

I spin around to see Mr. Bilodeau standing there, levelling the table with disapproving old man eyes.

"No," I say, gripping the back of my chair. "I need that. Jesus Christ—I'm eighteen, we're in Italy, it's legal. Can I just have some fucking fun, please?"

"*Hey*," Bilodeau warns. He shakes the bottle at the table as if showing a dog the shoe that it destroyed. "No more of this."

Then he walks away. My fingers tighten around the chair as I watch him disappear through the lounge door, presumably to dump my saving grace down a toilet.

"Shit," I whisper, closing my eyes. The blood is throbbing in my head, and that godforsaken shard is back in my throat.

Why would he put it in a *clear* water bottle? Like that doesn't defeat the point of *putting* it in a water bottle?

I am painfully aware that I need to calm down; that I've just crashed their card game and they're all looking at me, waiting for me to calm down. But the more I tell myself to calm down, the more I hate myself for how difficult it is, and the less calm I feel.

"Alis," Craig says, and I don't even need to look at him

—I can feel that concerned look on his face, and I can guess exactly what he's thinking. He's never going to know fucking peace now.

So needy. So pathetic.

The squirming thing is writhing and burning, and I can't do it anymore.

The urge has me practically salivating as I get up, chair legs screeching and heads turning all around to watch me go.

I push through the lounge doors and feel a shape in motion just behind me, following me out into the hall. I must look like I want to punch something because Lachlan demands, "Where are you going?"

"None of your business."

"Alis, I'm going to follow you for the rest of the day if I have to," she says, tailing me to the base of the stairs.

"Then I'll file a restraining order," I fire back, hearing how stupid it sounds as I say it. I make it halfway up the first set of stairs when the lounge door whips open again.

Craig stumbles into the hall, head swivelling around and limbs carrying him too far forward, so he has to double back when he sees me. "I have an idea!"

It's such an absurd thing for him to yell right now that I actually do stop. Lachlan does, too, gripping the banister two steps beneath me.

"I was thinking about how it's probably really cold and wet and uncomfortable outside right now," he says breathlessly. He adjusts his hat and raises his eyebrows hopefully. "You wanna go for a walk?"

I stop in the empty alley outside the hostel, feeling the rain come down. My fists clench at my sides, and I bow my head, letting the drops hit the back of my neck.

The first few are cold enough to shock. They take my breath and sharpen my focus, so all I'm doing is bracing myself for the next one to hit bare skin. It's coming down hard enough that soon my neck is slick, and I raise my face up to the sky instead, closing my eyes.

I run my hands up over the wetness on my face and push it back into my hair, trying not to think about the urge still clawing at me.

"What's going on with you?"

I open my eyes and find Craig just in front of me, backdropped by cracked yellow plaster. He has his shoulders near his ears and a wince on his face as the rain assaults him, and there's not even a hint of accusation in his voice —just that soft insistence. I can't stand it.

"Go back inside," I tell him.

He shakes his head, water droplets flinging from his fringe. "Tell me what happened."

I turn my face back to the sky. "Nothing. This feels better."

Now, finally, some irritation seeps into his voice. "Feels better than *what*?"

"Than thinking about *fucking Jordan*!"

Craig is silent as the rain pounds down on the cobblestones. When I look at him again, his shoulders are more relaxed now that he's drenched through. He blinks drops from his eyelashes as he asks me, "What did she do?"

"You already know what she did."

He frowns. "Was she the one that told people about…?"

So I guess Eric left out the details of how that actually got out. How kind of him.

I close my eyes. God, if only she'd started a rumour. If only she said it behind her hand, and it circled around the school in whispers and stares. Maybe it never would've even reached me, and I could have been blissfully ignorant to what they knew. Instead, it was this spectacle, this brutal humiliation and betrayal that even now, even after I remembered it so vividly yesterday and thought I'd broken through to the other side, it still won't leave me. It's this hot, heavy tar in my veins, sloshing around when I move.

I don't want to be friends with someone who is so needy and so pathetic that they have to cut themselves for attention.

"She said that to you?" Craig asks.

I know I've said it out loud because of the churning nausea in my stomach, but it doesn't make it any less jarring when he responds to me.

"She said that to *everyone*," I say, the words tearing painfully on the way out. "Everyone at her stupid party. And then she just—she left it. Like it was nothing. I can't understand how...?"

My voice cracks, and I open my eyes because I need to know. I need to see in his face if this thing has the right to be splitting me apart like this, or if Maya is right and I've been the petty asshole this whole time.

"I'd been doing it since I was eleven," I tell him. "I told her when I was fourteen. It took her three seconds to tell the whole world something it took me *three years* to tell one person. And after I showed her—I *showed* her the extent of it, she says it was just... for attention? Like I wasn't fucking *dying* inside?"

I could feel how wrecked my voice was getting halfway through, but now it chokes off, and I fold over with my hands on my knees. My heart feels like it's peeling itself into ribbons. The whole world is tilting, tipping me back into that dark room I shut myself in that weekend, trying not to puke as I thought about going back to school, as I thought about my only escape from it.

But when I was in that room, there was no hand sliding over my back. There was no one pulling me up. There was no one holding the side of my face and turning it to them, looking at me with this shattered expression reflecting exactly what I'm feeling. I see it for only a second before he's pulling me into his chest, my arms sandwiched between us. There's a feeling like a hot balloon engulfing against my ribs.

And then he wraps his arms around me, and it bursts.

The first sob that tears out of me is wet and horrible, even muted by the rain. His arm tightens around my shoulders, the other cradles my head against his soaking chest as the rest comes. Everything that had been teetering precariously inside me is collapsing like a landslide, and Craig holds me as if I'm going to shake apart if he doesn't.

The last time I cried, properly, was on that day my mother grabbed my wrist so hard and showed me what a powerful distraction pain could be. It's as if I'd been wrapped in these microscopic chains, one lassoed around me every day since, and I hadn't noticed until now as they're all breaking apart. Each sob is wrenching and painful, and I can barely breathe, but they send my blood pumping more freely and my muscles moving in ways they hadn't been able to before.

Craig doesn't quiet me; he doesn't tell me to stop. The longer it goes on, the more I understand that this is bigger than Jordan, bigger than what she did. This is coming from that sadness that's been underlying everything since I was a kid, a sadness that I thought was bottomless but now seems to be overflowing out of me. I have to wonder if it's ever going to stop.

I don't know how long it takes, but it does. I focus on the weight of Craig's mouth on the top of my head, on the feel of his humming chest under my cheek and the hush of the rain in my ears, and eventually, it all slows. All the tension has left me, and I'm like a rag doll just breathing in his arms, my bones half as heavy as they used to be.

His hand falls away from my wet hair and onto my wet back instead, his thumb rubbing like a windshield wiper between my shoulder blades. He lifts his face up from my head, and I'm immediately missing the warmth of his lips.

"Feel better?" he asks softly above the rain. I'm thanking the universe for that rain, disguising the mess I probably made of his shirt.

"You have no idea," I say sleepily against him. I feel almost drunk with relief.

I stay there for a bit longer until I feel a little shiver run through him and remember that he's probably not very comfortable. I pull away from him, wiping my sleeve under my nose and fighting against the embarrassment bubbling up in me.

"I'm going to stay out here for a minute," I say. "But you can go inside."

His hands are curled into fists—one pressing against his sternum, the other at his side. The flush on his cheeks is blazing in the cold, but his mouth is pulled down at the corners, and there's a sadness to his eyes I've never seen before.

His mouth opens, but he says nothing for a moment. Then, "I'm really sorry she did that to you."

I expect to feel the thing start squirming, but his words are only sinking deep into my heart, warm as an ember. I think about what Lachlan said, about how no one ever told her she was worth anything. It feels, somehow, like he's telling me I am.

My pulse kicks up a frenzy as I look at him, thinking about how his chest was warm even in the cold, how his body was humming and alive under my cheek and felt like the safest thing in the world. I'm remembering the feel of his mouth crushing into the top of my head like he was trying to kiss down to my brain. I'm watching how he's standing there, dripping rainwater, for me.

There's a rocketing heat from my belly to my chest, and I dart forward, my hands coming up to his neck. He catches me around the waist as I pull him down, latching onto his lips. His fingers tighten in my sweater, his palms warming through me, and he starts dragging me toward him as he walks backward.

He breaks off when his back hits the wall, and I'm wondering if maybe the whole crying thing was a turn off for him. But then his eyes dart hungrily back to my lips, and he pulls me up against him, my hands slipping from his neck to his collarbones. I stare at his pink lips and the dark smattering of his freckles and think about how he's almost perfect, except—

When he kisses me again, I creep my hand up to his head and pluck his soaked hat off, which makes him breathe a laugh through his nose and pull away again.

"I hate it," I say.

He grins, his breath ghosting over my mouth. "My head is lonely now."

I drop the hat at my feet and slide my hands through the wet hair above his ears. Then I pull on it so his breath hitches nicely as I kiss him again.

When he comes back up for air he says, "I had a dream that was almost just like this once."

My whole body erupts with fluttering. "Almost?"

He nods, and his hands tighten on my waist again as he spins us around so my back is pressed up against the wall.

My stomach fills with lava as he looms over me. His hands release my waist to entangle in my hands instead, bringing them up against the wall on either side of me. Then his gaze roams to my neck, and he pauses.

His eyes flick back up to mine. "I forgot about the bruises."

"Fuck the bruises," I growl, and I'm going to murder Theo if he doesn't—

But he does. He nuzzles his face into my neck, and his teeth hook onto my earlobe. My vision bursts with stars as his lips close around it.

My jaw goes slack, and I tip my head back against the wall, bearing my neck further. I have the most glorious view of his arm where it's holding my hand up against the wall. I watch the rainwater skating down over every ridge, thinking about licking it off.

When he releases my ear, his breath is like steam against my neck. This time, I close my eyes so I can feel everything in vivid detail, the way he kisses behind my jaw and slides his lips down to my pulse. When his teeth scrape against my skin, my blood spikes, and I gasp. It feels like the back of my head is swarmed with bees, every single thought overtaken by buzzing.

When he reaches the bruises, his lips ghost over them, dropping light, hot kisses on every inch of my skin. I shudder, squeezing his hands until I think it must hurt.

Part of me wants more, but most of me is filling with warmth, knowing he would never hurt me. So I just stay there at his mercy and let him keep kissing me however he likes to do it in his dreams.

Eventually, Craig and I come out of the rain, drenched to our bones. We seem to silently agree that we're not going back into the lounge, and make our way upstairs instead. I'm dismayed to see that he grabbed his hat off the ground before coming inside. I look at it hanging from his fingers like roadkill and decide that it is the one thing I would actually love to set on fire.

Dakota is gone when we get to the room. My wet clothes are clinging uncomfortably to me for the second time that day, so I grab my bag and start heading toward the ensuite. Craig sits on the side of his bed, watching me.

"Alis, can I ask you something? About Jordan?"

I stop. I notice I feel surprisingly calm at this question and turn around to face him. "Sure."

"Did you guys ever talk again? After?"

"No."

"Okay. Um..." A bit of water leaks from his hat to the carpet as he wrings it absently between his knees. "It just sounds like you were friends for a really a long time, and for it to end like that... I just think maybe that's part of the reason why it's eating you up so bad? And I think you should talk to her. For closure and because I really think she owes you an apology."

There are about fifty different arguments bubbling up inside of me all at once, and I open my mouth to let one of them fly, uncertain about which one it's going to be. As I look at his face, though, I see he's wincing a little, like he's expecting me to do exactly what I was about to do. And I realize I don't want that. I don't want him to think that he can't tell me what he thinks, that he can't give me advice without me shutting him down. If I'm like that, eventually, he's going to stop telling me things altogether, and I can't even handle the thought of that.

So I say, "I'll think about it."

"Okay," he says, and he tries to smile, but the tips of his hair are shivering and a violent shudder rolls through him instead. "I'm going to take my shirt off now because I'm cold."

"Okay," I say. I'm also cold, but I've forgotten about that.

Then a key jiggles in the door, and Drew comes in, and I do like Drew, but in that moment his presence is very much unwelcome.

He jerks his chin at the pair of us. "Hey, Craigslist."

I frown at him. Craig lets out a high-pitched giggle and squeaks out, "What did you say?"

"Craigslist," Drew says lightly. "That's your unit name. Saving myself some time."

Craig grins at me. "Brilliant."

Then all of a sudden he's standing up and taking his shirt off like he promised. He has a happy trail leading under the elastic of his briefs that's making me very, very happy. I watch him go around the other side of the bed, and I'm admiring the slope of his love handles and the way his shoulder muscles move deliciously as he digs through his bag.

"Where's Noor, by the way?" Craig asks.

That effectively pushes every nice thought out of my head at once.

"She's coming, I think," says Drew. "She was talking with Ben about the physics of time travel, and I was like, *yeah, nah*. So I dipped."

Craig pulls a t-shirt over his head. I'm suddenly very cold again.

Drew plops down on Dakota's bed. "Why the hell did you guys go out in the rain anyway?"

"We didn't go far," Craig says, looking at me in a way that makes all the blood rush to my face. I bite my lip to hide my smile before shoving into the washroom.

As I lock the door behind me, I realize that I have to deal with my arm again, and all sexy thoughts evaporate once more. I pull off my sopping sweater and peel off the bandage, grimacing as I drop it in the garbage bin.

But as I'm re-dressing it, I start doing something different.

I will never tell anyone, ever—but I pretend I'm Dakota. I imagine that concentrated frown on her face and the gentle way she held my fingers, and I try to do the same as I clean my arm, touching the scars and the cuts as carefully as she would. I put on the bandage slowly, gently pressing the edges over the stitches. I'm a bit queasy, but I manage to stay in my body the whole time.

When I'm finished, I feel tired in that full, fuzzy way, like drifting in and out of sleep in the back of a car. I almost want to skip tonight's dinner and just collapse on my bed for the night.

But because the universe likes to play sick jokes, the first person I see when I come out of the washroom is Noor Amini, sitting on the end of my bed. She's changed into a satiny olive tank top and navy paper bag pants, and I notice she's wearing perfectly winged eyeliner as she gives me a once-over like she's checking for blood.

There's no one else in the room to save me. I think she's kicked everyone out. My heart starts hammering as I meet her eyes.

"I was avoiding you," she says. "But I'm not going to do that anymore."

My blood spikes, and I'm filled with a strange sense of relief. I could've sworn I was the one avoiding *her*.

I let my backpack slide off, dropping it next to my leg. "I'm so sorry."

Her fingers tighten on her knees. "I would've been fine yesterday if you didn't ask me if I was okay. People ask me if I'm okay, and then it makes me realize I'm not okay."

"But are you—I mean, were you—"

"Okay? No. I had a panic attack. But that was probably the longest I've ever held one off. And at least Craig bounced back from whatever catatonic state he was in so he could help me breathe."

A fist tightens around my heart. "I'm really sorry."

"I don't have a thing with blood, you know." Her mouth twitches downward, and her voice wavers almost imperceptibly as she says, "I just couldn't believe you did that to yourself."

My head fills with the image of her head bowed above my bloody arm. My mouth is so dry, it takes a second for me to swallow. "I promise that will never happen again."

Something flickers in her dark eyes, and she shoots up from the bed. "What do you mean by 'that'? Do you mean you won't cut yourself again, or you won't ask us for help? Or maybe you just won't do it in a public shower? Is that the 'that' you're talking about?"

The bite in her voice is unprecedented, and her words needle into me. When I blink, I feel a fat, hot tear skip down my face.

Wonderful. Now that I've opened the floodgates, it looks like I'm going to have to make up for ten dry years real fucking quick.

Her shoulders drop, and her voice softens. "Alis, I *saw* you. I know it's not as simple as 'it's never going to happen again.' I just want you to not bullshit me, and I think me and Craig both deserve that."

I saw you. She's talking about my arm, about the rest of it.

I swallow against a wave of nausea and nod. "Okay. It might happen again, but I'm going to try harder to—to not."

Noor's eyes scan my face for a moment. "I believe that. Thank you."

I still don't feel like I've said everything I have to say, but everything I think about saying doesn't feel like enough. I open my mouth for a long time with no words coming out before I swipe my hand over my cheek and say, "Thank you for coming to look for me. Last night."

"Craig was worried, and he wanted me to tell him he was being stupid," she says, wrapping her arms around herself. "I said to him, 'No, Craig, you're not being stupid—you should be worried.' But I'm hoping one day you'll start liking yourself as much as we do, and we won't have to worry about you anymore."

Her words sink into me and leave me aching. I can feel my chin wobbling, and I take a deep breath and try to hold it together because I have the sense that she will not be as forgiving as Craig if I snot all over her nice shirt.

She takes a step toward me. "We can distract you. If you feel like you need to do that."

"Yes, I... Craig distracted me very well," I say, which sounds so ridiculous when I'm crying that I start to laugh. Her deadpan face looking at me laughing makes me laugh harder, and I put an arm over my mouth and try to stop because the laughing is making me cry more.

"You're really a mess," she says, but she's giving me that rare little smile. It sobers me enough that I'm able to stop. I close my eyes and hold my fingers over them for a second, breathing deeply like she taught me.

"If you really need a hug, I can make an exception," she says.

I shake my head. "That's okay. I had one today already."

When she doesn't say anything, I drop my hands to look at her. Her brow is still a bit pinched, and her eyes are less flat than usual.

"I forgive you, by the way," she says. "But I wasn't really that mad."

I laugh wetly. She doesn't hug me, but she does give me an awkward shoulder pat, which feels like a win.

As much as it feels good to be forgiven, I find those aren't the words I'm clinging to afterwards. I'm lingering on what she said before, when she told me she hoped she didn't have to worry about me one day.

One day.

As if there is a future for me in which I'm not alone.

39

That night, I have what I think would qualify as a sleepover.

I had sleepovers with Jordan sometimes, but it's been a long time since I had one of those really unhinged sleepovers where no one could sleep because *everything* was funny. Everything. Most funny of all was the silence that descended when we were all ready to go to sleep, and someone would crack up and send everybody else giggling again. At one point, Drew threw a pillow at me because we'd been doing so well, and I ruined it again, but then Craig threw a pillow back at him in my defence.

And now, it's a little past two in the morning, and finally, they're sleeping. All of them, I think, judging by their stillness and their soft, even breathing.

I'm all too aware now that it's the last night of the trip, and I have this tight, mournful feeling in my chest. I've been lying here for an hour, staring at the fissured stucco ceiling and thinking about worlds colliding.

Whenever I think of the world back home, I'm thinking about Jordan. It's like her presence in it, the weight of our history together, and the overbearing hurt of what she did that night overshadow everything else. I think that's why I'm having such a hard time imagining Craig and Noor and the Mitchells in all of those spaces that Jordan and I used to occupy. I start to wonder how much easier it would be to believe that I could keep them if I could purge the memory of her and make that world I'm coming back to something fresh and new, where I could be anyone and have anything.

I think about that, about the feeling of coming clean.

And then I'm struck by an idea that feels like it could change everything.

I watch Craig for a few minutes to make sure he's really asleep because I know where his mind's going to go if he sees me creeping out of the room in the middle of the night. His arm is flung out into the space between my bed and his, and his head is turned away from me. I watch his chest rising and falling, and maybe I'm smiling a little.

Then I peel my covers back and try to get out of the bed as quietly as I can with those ancient springs moaning beneath my weight. I keep my eyes on Craig as I grab my boots, but I already know he's a deep sleeper, judging by how hard I had to slap his face to wake him up in Rome.

Noor flips over in the loft bed, and I freeze. But she just lets out an uncharacteristically cute sound and lies still again.

I pad out of the room, wincing again at the creaky door before shutting it softly behind me. I lace up my boots in the dimly lit hallway, which smells even weirder and older at night, then make my way down to the lobby.

The hostel is deserted except for a young moustachioed guy sitting at the front desk, bobbing his head to an old song coming out of what looks like a crank radio. He takes his feet off the desk when he sees me and tries not to look like he's bored out of his mind.

I ask him if he has paper and a pen, and he gives me a stack of printer paper, which is excessive—surely, I don't have that much to say.

But when I sit at a table in the lounge and pull a piece of paper off the top of the stack, I hesitate for only a moment before the words start pouring out of me.

The things I write to her are sometimes vicious, and excruciating, and unfair, like our fights always were. Other times, they're startlingly vulnerable, like they've come from depths of me that I didn't know existed. I find myself oscillating, dizzyingly, between my love for her and my hatred. I write about how much it meant to me that she called me cool, that she never once made fun of me for what I wore or the way I talked or the things I liked. I write about how she made me feel like I was crazy. I write about how I don't think that I would still be here if she hadn't invited me to her house a few weeks after we met and if she hadn't kept letting me in after that. I write about that night, how she tore my fucking heart out with what she did, and I'm not sure I can ever forgive her for it.

The more I write, the more I understand I don't actually hate her at all. I write about my love for her and how it always made me feel like I was on fire, and as good as it felt sometimes to feel so much, it was also breaking me down further and further every day until I was nothing but nerves. I tell her that I know now that that isn't what love is supposed to feel like. I tell her that I understand what I was doing to her—putting so much pressure on her to be everything for me because she was all I had—and how I should have let her go a long time ago.

When I'm finished, it's nearly four in the morning, my hand is cramping like a bitch, and I'm very glad that the man at the front desk gave me so much paper. There are tears drying on my face, and I can't breathe through my nose. I feel like I've just drained an abscess that I didn't know had been blistering and chafing on my soul for years.

I knew pretty quickly into writing it that I wouldn't give her the letter. That had been the plan initially, but I wouldn't give her this letter if my life depended on it—not only because it's raw and exposing, but because it would hurt her more than it would help her. And I know now that I don't want to hurt her.

On the one hand, I know Craig is right—I don't want to leave our friendship where it is. I don't want what Maya and Theo said to be true, that she's sitting around in the wake of the fire, spiralling and hurting herself.

On the other hand, if there's anything that writing the letter showed me, it's that talking to Jordan often leads to fighting or questioning my sanity or both, and I don't want that either. I'm done with that.

I sit there for another ten minutes, staring at the papers strewn all over the table, covered in my chicken scratch.

Then I stack up the pages and fold them before heading out into the alleyway where Craig kissed me over and over, and then out to the promenade where I find a bench in front of the canal, still wet from the rain.

It would be almost midnight for Jordan, but she's a night owl, so she'll probably be awake. I hope she is because I don't know if I'll have the guts to do this come daylight.

I dial her number—I don't think I'll ever forget it—in my dinosaur flip-phone. My heart pounds heavily in my ears as I wait through one, two, three rings.

"Hello?"

I wait a second, silent. I need to make sure it's her voice and I didn't mishear.

She says again, warily, "Hello?"

I feel the wave come up, and I speak. "It's Alis. Don't say anything. I just want to say that I forgive you, and you can forgive yourself. I mean that. I'm okay now, and I want you to be okay, too. So thank you for everything. And I really am sorry about Elton John. He was a good cat. But please don't call me back, Jordan. Just... be free now, okay? Bye."

I hang up the phone. The shard is back in my throat, and I expected I might not be able to get through what I said without breaking down. As a breeze blows through, I clutch the phone in my hand and wait for it to happen. I watch the amber reflections of the streetlamps ripple and smear on the water. I listen to the anchored rowboats plunking over gentle waves and breathe the briny maritime smell of Venice, and it's like a balm on the sharpness in my throat and the ache in my chest.

The tears never come. Instead, it feels like in Paris under the pink sky, and at the fountain with its rippling coins, and in that reverent quiet of the cathedral—for just a few moments, all the pain goes away, and everything in my head goes quiet.

40

I don't think I moved an inch last night because I'm so stiff when I wake up that I actually wince when I pull myself up. I blink blearily around the sunlit room, but everyone's bed is just an empty mess of sheets.

I paw around for the phone on the table next to me, noticing the ink smeared on the side of my hand. The screen reads ten a.m., and I have a text from Craig asking if I'm awake.

I send a *y*, and after about twenty seconds, he slips into the room. I'm pleasantly surprised to see that the hat is still gone despite it probably being dry by now, and his hair is an organized mess.

"What were you doing, just standing outside the door?" I ask.

He creeps into the room as if I'm still asleep, making his yikes face at me. "I forgot to take my pills, but I didn't want to wake you up."

"What pills?" I ask before realizing how weird and invasive that is. "Never mind."

"Epilepsy pills," he says anyway, plopping down on the side of his bed. I watch him drag his bag between his knees and dig around in it, swiping his hand up into his hair like he's not used to it.

"Isn't that more important than my sleep?"

"Depends how angry you are when you're woken up before you're ready." He pulls out an orange bottle, shakes a capsule out in his hand, and looks at me while he dry swallows it. I can see his eyes scanning over my face, my bruised throat, and back to my face. I feel a flush rising up my neck, but I don't look away.

The pill bottle rattles as he puts it away. Then he lifts from the bed and, given his height, simply turns around and plops onto mine without even moving his feet. He bounces a little next to my knee, filling the room with screeching springs.

"Please stop," I say.

"I was testing to see how noisy this bed is, just in case."

I tip my face forward into my hands so he doesn't see the heat in it, and he laughs, which just makes it burn hotter.

"No *way* I can make Alis Woodson blush," he says.

I whip my head up. "I'm not *blushing*. I think I'm just allergic to how fucking cheesy you are. Part of me thought you were about to bring me breakfast in bed when you came in here."

"Ah, but you don't like breakfast," he says, patting my knee. "So that would've been an empty gesture."

I don't know why my throat feels a bit thick at this. Just the fact that he knows this about me, I guess. And the fact that he's not wearing his hat after I told him that I didn't like it, and that he's still here after everything he's learned about me and everything I've put him through.

"Damn, I really don't wanna leave," Craig says, his smile falling.

The lump evaporates from my throat, and my blood runs cold.

Given how thoroughly it was consuming me last night, I don't know how it slipped my mind this morning that this is the last day. Our last day in Venice, our last day in Europe.

I'll be sleeping in that house again tonight. That lifeless, soul-sucking house with its grave-like silence and erratic poltergeist.

I could wake up tomorrow, and all of this could have been a dream.

It's a good thing Craig is looking out at the glittering fire escape and not at me, so I have time to school my expression into something other than spine-chilling dread.

"I think we should stay here and go island hopping until we find a fishing cabin to hole up in forever," he says, looking back at me.

I try to smile at him. "You're going to fish for us?"

"Yeah, that's what I do with my dad when I visit him in Vancouver. We entered a fishing derby once when I was like five, and he cried when I got second-place trophy for fattest fish. I've got a natural gift."

I purse my lips. "Wow. You're a fish whisperer."

"I *am* a fish whisperer. You'll see. I'll bring you to Algonquin, and we'll rent a boat." His eyes widen, and his fingers tighten on his knees. "I mean, if you want to."

"Yes, I want to."

I want to more than he knows. I want to go there right now, direct flight. But even if this goes on, and I go to his house for Friday night dinner, and we take a trip to Algonquin, none of that changes the fact that I've still got another three months of going back to that house night after night before I go to whatever school I decide to sell my soul to. I have a life sentence ahead of me.

Craig grabs my fingers where they've been pressing at the bruises on my throat. I barely noticed the dull ache of them. Now, as he gently pulls my hand back down, the thing starts squirming again.

"Sorry," I whisper, scratching at my forehead.

"What are you thinking about?" he asks softly.

I'd been wanting to tell him about what I did last night anyway, so I decide to use this segue to my advantage, forcing away thoughts of the future and trying to focus on that moment last night when I'd felt so at peace.

"I want to show you something." I untangle my hand from his and lean over the bed, pulling out the stack of papers I'd shoved into my bag. I've been told many times before that my handwriting is illegible, so I'm not really worried when I drop the creased papers between us, writing side up.

He looks down at it, then up at me under his lashes. "You've written a very long doctor's note."

I roll my eyes. "I wrote Jordan a letter."

His eyebrows raise. "You wrote Jordan a *manifesto*."

"Okay, *anyway*," I say, and a grin breaks out over his face that has me fighting my own smile. "I'm not giving it to her."

His face sobers. "Why not?"

My palms start to sweat, and I busy myself with stacking the papers back up and putting them down next to my leg instead. Then I swallow against the dryness in my throat and fix my eyes on his shoulder. "Yesterday, when I was talking with Noor, I apologized to her for... for Florence. And she told me she forgave me. And when she did, I realized it didn't really do anything for me. The forgiveness. And it got me thinking about how you said that Jordan owes me an apology.

"I was so... resentful, I guess, that she never apologized to me that I didn't realize I never wanted her to. If she did, that meant I'd have to admit that I could never forgive her, and I felt wrong for that. Like, I felt selfish and childish for feeling so bitter over something that probably wasn't that bad. That's what I kept saying, that it wasn't that bad, and she looked so guilty for it afterwards, and I didn't have a right to feel..."

My voice goes froggy, and I clear my throat, pushing on despite the tight feeling in my chest. "But in the alley, you said to me that you were sorry that happened, like it... you know, like it mattered, and I wasn't crazy for being messed up over it. There were so many people at that party, and no one ever came up to me and tried to tell me that it was wrong, except for Dakota. There was this—this contradiction between that and what I was feeling, and it was like it was ripping my brain apart."

My heart is beating hard and heavy, and I look down at Craig's hand where it's resting on the bed, wanting to hold it but not knowing how. "So I think I didn't really want her apology, I just needed... I needed someone to tell me that she owed it to me. Which you did. So thank you."

All of my nerves are tingling in the silence that follows. Craig rearranges himself so he's sitting cross-legged in front of me, then takes my hands in his, and I finally look up at his face.

He raises his eyebrows, and his eyes have this earnestness to them that reminds me a bit of Lachlan. "You aren't crazy. That was... I mean, it was awful. Anyone would've told you the same thing if they weren't so wrapped up in themselves, you know? But Alis, I'm just... I'm wondering about closure. Like if you never talk to her again—"

"I did. I called her last night."

His eyes brighten. "What did she say?"

"Well, I didn't actually let her talk? I just said what I needed to say, and I told her I forgive her because I think that's what she needed to hear. But the letter... it's not about her. Like, obviously, it's *about* her, but I just mean it's not her closure. It's mine."

His eyes are so warm as he looks at me, it feels impossible. Then his gaze shifts to the scribbled pages next to my thigh and his voice turns almost wistful. "She is really lucky, I think, that you had that much to say about her."

I stare at him with my brow furrowing deeper by the

second because that expression *can't* be what it looks like. But that's so clearly what it is that even I can't deny it.

He glances back at me, his face growing wary. "What?"

"Are you jealous right now?"

He wrinkles his nose at me, but his ears are turning red. "No. You're silly."

My lips are sliding upward. "Were you jealous of Jordan?"

"Nope."

"Then why is your face—"

He cuts me off with a groan, throwing his head back. "Okay, fine. *Please* can you write a manifesto about me?"

He's almost pouting at me, and I try to wrangle my face into something very serious even as my stomach erupts with butterflies. "If you piss me off enough, I probably will."

This clears the silly expression from his face, and his eyes drop to my lips. I feel a thrill that turns my stomach hot as his eyes slide back up to mine, darker than they were before.

We go in for the kiss at the same time, so it's a little violent and off-centre, but we adjust quickly. He starts pressing me back down onto the bed until there's a crunch as I land on the mess of papers.

Craig breaks off, his hands planted on either side of me. "You know what you should do with that letter?"

"What?"

"You should burn it."

I grin at him. Then I rake my fingers into that beautiful

curling hair at the back of his neck, pulling him back to me.

41

That morning, at the thought of going home, a kernel of dread was lodged at the back of my mind, and it kept swelling and swelling as the day went on. I think I managed to keep myself together pretty well, sitting at breakfast with Craig, Noor, and the Mitchells and taking one last stroll by the canals. At least, Craig didn't once ask me if something was wrong.

But now, I'm sitting in a dimly lit cafe at the airport with Craig and Noor, and Craig looks at his watch and says, "We should go back to the gate in, like, twenty?"

And that's when the dread cracks open like an egg and leaks down my spine.

"Oh, fuck," I whisper. It's the last thing I say before my next inhale hits that brick wall stacked up against my lungs.

It's exactly as it was in Rome in Noor's room—the inability to breathe, the intense fear that I'm about to die—

except, this time, Noor lets me grip her hand across the table, grinding her bones to dust, and Craig has his hand on my back and is turned in the booth in such a way that I think he means to shield me from the view of the dozen other people in the cafe.

But as my breathing returns to normal, Craig's efforts have done nothing to stop the crushing humiliation that comes down on me, knowing I've just been gasping and flailing—and, I now realize from the wetness on my face, crying—in the too-quiet cafe. I untangle my hand from Noor's and put my elbows on the table, dropping my forehead into my hands. Then I remember my hair is up, so I tug it down and let it fall into my face and wish people would please, *please* hurry up and start talking again to fill the brutal silence.

Craig's hand is rubbing circles on my back, but if anything, that just makes the squirming worse because now *he's* seen that. I want nothing more than to run to the bathroom and hide, but the thought of how many eyes would be on me as I did that keeps me frozen in place.

A few conversations have picked up again, and I hear Noor say, "I had one backstage at a dance recital in front of my whole team and my teacher once."

"Mm," Craig says sympathetically. "I had a bladder malfunction during a seizure in seventh-grade gym class. That was fun."

Okay, that's probably worse. And maybe I'm a horrible person, but it feels like a balm on that keen sting of mortification, and I'm able to lift my head once I feel the tears have dried under my palms.

Noor is looking impassively at me, picking at her thumb on the table, and I'm glad to see I didn't break her hand. Craig's hand drops away from my back, but he keeps himself turned in the booth with his elbow on the table. He smiles softly at me, but his eyes are strained.

I look back at the table. "Thank you."

"What's going on?" Noor asks.

I sit back in the booth. Now that the dread has burst, I feel raw and deflated, and I just want to curl up and sleep in a hole. "Nothing. I don't know where that came from."

"I'll remind you that you said no more bullshit."

"Technically, I didn't say that," I murmur, looking at her under my lashes. She stares right back at me, her eyes getting narrower by the second.

I sigh. I can't win a staring contest with her. "I have to decide on a school. When we get back."

"But you don't want to go to school," Noor finishes.

I cross my arms, shrugging.

Craig asks, "What would you do? If you could do anything."

I haven't thought about it because I always knew it was hopeless, and it bordered on torture to think otherwise. As he asks me, though, my mind conjures an image of the woman with the fire engine hair back in Paris, the masterpieces on the walls above her head.

"It doesn't matter," I say.

"How does it not matter? It's your *life*."

"My life is controlled by my parents. They're paying for everything, and they only pay for things if it makes them look good. I've never been allowed a job because time working a job is time that could be spent studying, so I don't have a single penny except the credit card that *they* gave me, and if I do one thing to embarrass them or piss them off, I'm cut off. I'm out on my ass."

"They wouldn't seriously throw you out—"

"Yes, they would."

"But if you told them—"

"No, it's not an *option*," I snap, straightening in my seat. That angry, frothing wave is back, and the words are being pushed out of me before my brain can even catch up to what I'm saying. "I've had a surveillance camera in my bedroom since I was five. They're barely home, so they watch me to make sure I'm still studying because they may not give a shit about being parents, but the Woodsons are sure as hell not going to have an idiot for a kid. I could stay home alone for days and eat fucking Lucky Charms for breakfast, lunch, and dinner, but if my grades started slipping? If they started slipping, they would lord over me everything I have, telling me it's all because of them, and how hard they worked and how ignorant it would be of me not to work just as hard. And if they're not lording it, they're taking it away. Oh, you can't concentrate on your math homework because you're fucking starving? That's too bad, Alistair—shouldn't have gotten a B+ in fifth-grade geometry!"

This last part is punctuated by me smacking my knee into the underside of the table. Noor flinches, and Craig's hand shoots out to steady his coffee cup. The satisfaction of the pain is swallowed immediately by guilt and, afterwards, a flush of embarrassment for my outburst.

I put my hand on my forehead. "Sorry."

"Alis—"

I cut Craig off. "No, I'm just—I'm telling you there is not a single threat they haven't followed through on. I'm an investment to them. If I told them no? If I told them, what, that I wanna go to *art school*? That's their investment falling through. That's me being a shameful, ungrateful failure of a child, and they can't have that. So they *would* throw me out. They'd throw me out naked in dead winter, and they wouldn't even fucking blink."

I let out a helpless laugh. I can't *believe* that all came out of my mouth, but more shocking is how still that thing in my stomach is now that it has. I don't even care how insane they find it all, I just want them to believe me. I really, really just need them to believe me.

"Jesus," Craig breathes. I look at him where he's still gripping his coffee cup and notice the flush is gone from his cheeks and his eyes are round and distressed.

I feel my heart fall, my stomach curdle. I shouldn't have hit the table. "Sorry."

"No, not—I meant your *parents*."

Across from me, Noor is clutching her ribs, her face a weaker imitation of Craig's. "Alis, that's not normal. You know that, right?"

She's raising her eyebrows like she's trying to convince me, but she doesn't have to. The relief that flushes through me is so powerful, it tilts the world around me.

"Yes, they're—" I let out another laugh, this one breathy, alleviated. "They're fucking certifiable."

Craig and Noor look at each other in that way that

means they're speaking telepathically. Then Craig asks, "Do you want to leave them?"

I think about how I'd been praying Jordan would offer to let me live with her practically since I met her. "I would've been gone a long time ago if I could have."

"There are other options," Noor says. "You don't need their money. There's financial aid and scholarships, like what I'm doing. But you don't even need to go to school. If you wanted to... I mean, the nursing home has live-in jobs. I could talk to my dad. And there are apprenticeships and trades. There's also WWOOFING, and—"

"And I have a spare room," Craig says.

My blood spikes, and I whip my head toward him. I wait for him to laugh, to wink, to nudge me with his elbow, but there's not even a hint of a smile on his face. I didn't think he could pull off deadpan jokes, but there's no way what he just said *isn't* a joke.

My face must be doing something because Craig's ears have gone red, and he swallows visibly. "I'm just—I'm just saying that if you tell them, and it doesn't go well, you could crash in my brother's room while you figure things out. Or Noor's couch. We're not going to let you live on the *street*, is all I'm saying."

I look at Noor, expecting her to balk at Craig offering up her couch to me, but she just nods.

"You..." I breathe, not even knowing where to start. "Your mom's not going to want some random in your brother's room."

He shakes his head. "No, you don't know my mom.

She's the neediest extrovert to ever live. If she could house all of my friends and her friends and their friends and have big Jewish dinner parties twenty-four seven, she would."

"'All your friends' as in me," Noor notes.

"And my skateboard friend Dave, but I think he's a pothead now, so maybe not."

They exchange smirks, like this is all normal and not completely absurd. I could be an axe murderer or an *actual* arsonist, and how would he know? Worse, I could be a terrible housemate, and then he'd have to find some way to kick me out without hurting my feelings. Or, more likely, he's just trying to be nice, and he's overestimating his mom's willingness to take in someone who's had to make two trips to the hospital in one week. I'll show up on his doorstep with nowhere to go, and he'll have to turn me away, and I'll be completely screwed.

Even if this were a real possibility, if I could ever bring myself to squat at one of their houses, I don't know that I'll be able to muster up the courage to leave my parents, knowing that I'll have nothing but my few belongings on the other side. I can be trapped and secure, or I can be free and unmoored. But what scares me the most is how that choice no longer feels like the no-brainer it was a week ago.

Craig's hand has found its way over mine where it's gripping the edge of the table, and I can barely swallow around the lump in my throat.

"I don't know if I can do that," I say.

I can hear how thin and wobbly my voice is, and Craig's lips purse sympathetically. Noor isn't much better to look at—I didn't know her eyes could even get that sad. But it feels less like they're feeling sorry for me and more like a collective sadness, like we're all sitting on a sinking boat together, and the thing in my stomach stays quiet.

"We're just telling you that you're not trapped, okay?" Craig says. "You don't have to do what they say. And we'll be there, whatever happens. We'll figure it out."

I look to where Noor is nodding her agreement. There's a landslide in my chest at the sight of the two of them, and I'm just marvelling at how this happened to me. I find myself thinking about all of those pink sky moments, about that common thread between them. I don't think it's that they made me feel numb, or insignificant, or overwhelmed with awe; it was just those quieting thoughts, like the universe was turning down the volume so I could listen as it told me that everything would be okay. And right now, even though I've got no idea what *okay* is going to look like, I'm still listening.

"And seriously, don't worry about my mom," Craig adds, leaning back in his seat. "She's been willing to, like, go to *battle* for you since I told her you brushed sand off me after my seizure."

"Jesus Christ," I say, letting my hair fall over my face as it burns up.

Craig chuckles. I feel his hand come down on the back of my head and smooth my hair down, and that makes me cry *so* quickly, it's unbelievable. At least it's not an ugly cry and just this sniffling, leaky thing that I think I'm doing a good job of hiding up until Noor says, "Maybe you should hug him, Craig."

"Maybe *you* should hug him, Noor," he says, but he wraps his arm around me and pulls me in anyway.

EPILOGUE
ALGONQUIN PARK

"I thought you didn't like sugar," Noor says, because I have a massive wad of marshmallow in my mouth, and I think I might be moaning a little. But unlike Craig, I have manners, so I wait until I swallow before I speak.

"I don't," I say. "That just tasted burnt."

"Maybe we should get Noor to cook for you from now on then," Craig says, and Noor gives him the finger from where she's drowning in an Adirondack chair across from us.

The bonfire had a rough start, given it rained all last night and our logs were wet, but it's going strong now, and Craig's right—it's the best smell in the world. I'm running a stick through the flames and using the charred end to draw things in the dirt like a ten-year-old.

"By the way," Noor says, sucking marshmallow off her fingers, "my dad says Alis is an old people magnet."

I stop drawing, frowning at her. "He actually said that?"

"Not in those exact words. But they really like you there, and he's wondering if you're going to stick around."

Shakir got me this housekeeping job at the nursing home where I help out with changing bed sheets, cleaning the bathrooms, tidying up after meals, and hanging out with old people like I used to when I volunteered. It's live-in, so I've got my own room there with meals included, and while that also means I don't make very much money, it's not a bad job. It keeps me afloat, which is more than I ever imagined for myself in a world without my parents.

"I mean, yeah," I say, digging my stick back into the dirt. "At least until I figure out what the fuck I'm doing with my life."

I know we graduated only two months ago, but I still have this unshakeable sense of urgency about my future, like the longer I go without a plan, the more likely it is that I'm never going to have one, especially now that Craig and Noor and the Mitchells are all just a couple weeks away from starting school—or in Drew's case, his apprenticeship. I've been meaning to ask him about that, to figure out if something like that might be an option for me, but I never got around to it. To be honest, I've been avoiding even broaching the subject.

Sometimes, I see that tattoo artist in Paris on the backs of my eyelids before I go to sleep, and I indulge, for a little bit, in those fantasies where maybe I'll get to do that one day. But then I'll hear my parents' voices in my head telling me what a stupid, impractical flight of fancy that is. I keep wondering how long I have to stay away from them before they stop intruding on my thoughts like a bad radio station.

Craig taps me on the arm with the back of his hand, and I look to see him raising his eyebrows at me with half a roasted hot dog in his hand. He got rid of his ratty old hat, but when he told me that it was a comfort item for him, I caved and told him he should buy another one. At least the one he wears now is a mossy green, so it pairs nicely with his tawny freckles and burnished red hair. He looks like he belongs to the woods surrounding us.

I shrug at the hot dog, and he hesitates, looking to Noor. "Is it off-limits for me to feed this to him right now?"

"I feel like you absolutely don't have to do that," Noor says.

"Is it off-limits?"

"I'll close my eyes."

I open my mouth and let Craig put the hot dog in it, and then I laugh through my mouthful at the grimace on Noor's face. I guess she forgot to close her eyes.

When we got back from our trip, I still had a splinter of doubt in my mind that this thing I had with them was going to last beyond the little European bubble we'd built for ourselves. But while things were a little weird to get used to in our final month of school—like migrating from my lunch ledge to sit with them at a cafeteria table, or letting Craig hold my hand in the hallway—it turned out I didn't really have anything to worry about. They stuck with me.

Even when shit really hit the fan, they stuck with me.

The conversation with my parents went pretty much

how I'd expected, until it didn't. I told them I wasn't interested in the programs they picked out for me; they told me they wouldn't pay for anything else. They seemed to think that after cutting me off with a curt "end of discussion," I'd just hang my head and cut my losses.

But the thing was, I'd spent weeks working up to that conversation, expecting their anger, expecting a fight, and when I was met only with my mom's derisive smile and my dad barely sparing me a glance over his book from where he sat in his armchair, my patience shattered.

"I'm telling you I'm not fucking going," I snapped. "It's not a discussion."

I could see my dad's head lift in my peripheral, but I kept my eyes on my mom. She'd been buttering a piece of bread, but she stopped then, slapping her knife onto the counter.

"No?" she said, raking a hand back through her hair as she turned to me. "Where are you going then? Because I'll tell you what: if you're going to choose to be a loser, you won't be staying here. You think you can just lounge around—"

"No one's *lounging.* I haven't *lounged* a day in my life."

She rolled her eyes. "Oh, give me a break."

"I don't even know what I was doing any of this for," I said, struggling against the lump of anger and frustration that was forming in my throat. "You only ever cared about the things I was doing wrong."

"What, were you expecting a gold star? A parade? Because that's not how it works in the real world, Alistair.

Believe it or not, no one's going to give a shit about you out there."

"Well, maybe that's how it should work for, I don't know, a five-year-old? An eight-year-old? An eighteen-year-old who's been killing himself for straight As his whole fucking life for his checked-out dad and narcissistic—"

Her eyes went livid just a second before the blow. My head whipped to the side with a sharp crack as she back-handed me, and I stumbled into the kitchen island, fire blazing over my face.

Through the pain of it, I heard my dad say her name. It wasn't exactly a warning in his voice, but there was enough of an emotion in it that I lifted my head to look at him through the hair sticking to my lips. He had one hand on his knee and his book face-down on the armrest like he was bracing to get up. I saw how his eyes had gone a bit wider, his face a bit paler. He was looking at me like he was actually seeing me.

This is it, I thought. My heart felt like it was suspended.

But time stretched on too long, and eventually, none of us were holding our breath anymore, and I realized that was the extent of what he was going to do. And when I understood that, there was this strange sense of calm that overtook me. Everything went quiet inside as if I'd been turned to stone.

I blinked, my eyes still watering from the sting on my face. I straightened up, letting my hand slip from the island.

"I'm done," I said. The words were quiet, but there was

something like wonder dawning in my voice as I realized that I meant it with every fibre of my being. "I'm so done with this shit."

I wasn't even speaking to them anymore; I was speaking only to myself.

When I turned away from her, the hairs on the back of my neck stood at attention, like my body was prepared for her to come after me, but I didn't run.

"You are not welcome here anymore," she called to my back, and I swear I heard a waver in her voice. "Do you understand? You're not getting *anything* from us."

I didn't respond. I went upstairs, and I wasn't dissociating exactly, but I was on autopilot as I started packing my stuff. I wasn't thinking about where I was going or what would happen when I got there; I just knew I was going.

I hadn't expected the number of calls I got from her after I'd gone. At one point, I was afraid she would somehow track me down and come knocking at Craig's door looking for me. Even now, I wonder sometimes if she'd been bluffing—if I hadn't left of my own accord, would she have let me stay after all?

But if having friends has taught me anything, it's that there's a difference between someone wanting you around and wanting you in line, and I'm not at all confused about which of those was true for my parents.

It turned out leaving them was easier than I thought it would be, but *having left* was a lot harder. I no longer felt that all-encompassing dread, because I didn't have to go to school, and because the thing my parents taught me to be most afraid of had finally come to pass, and I survived it.

Was surviving it. I was no longer trapped. But because I'd been trapped my whole life, it was like my mind was trying to find some way to compensate for that.

For the first couple weeks, while Noor and her dad arranged the live-in job for me, I stayed in Craig's brother Daniel's room. The first thing I noticed was that there was a lock on the *inside* knob of the bedroom door, which was the weirdest thing in the world to me. I figured Miranda probably had a key to it, but still—no camera and a lock on the door.

I should've been exhilarated, and yet all I felt was guilt.

The guilt was a constant. I felt guilty for having that much privacy. I felt guilty for eating their food, for using the bathroom. I felt guilty when the floorboards would creak under my weight. I felt guilty for moving, for breathing, for taking up space. I felt like an intruder, and no matter how kind Craig and Miranda were to me, no matter how many times they assured me that I wasn't a burden, I was still counting down the days until I could leave.

In a way, that guilt kind of saved me, because if the lock on Daniel's door made me feel guilty, using it to make sure everyone stayed out while I burned myself made me feel a million times worse. It felt like a betrayal, and I knew I needed to find some way to stop. I *wanted* to stop.

I agreed to let Lachlan get me in touch with a counsellor, Erin, at a local mental health centre. I was nearly sick with anxiety before my intake phone call, but Erin was so relaxed and casual about the whole thing that I felt stupid for being so scared in the first place. By the time I was settled at the nursing home, I was also having in-person sessions with them twice a week, and I finally told them about my urges. There was still that voice in my head screaming at me to shut up, that they were going to think I was suicidal and lock me up for my own good, but they didn't do that. They didn't even tell me I had to stop.

"For most people, self-harm isn't something you can quit cold turkey," they told me. "But we can slowly scale it back, one baby step at a time. Sometimes, we'll take one baby step forward and two big steps back, and that's okay, too. It's not going to happen all at once."

The elastic I wear around my wrist now is a baby step. I snap it against my skin when I start feeling the urge. There are a lot of things they told me to try, like holding hot sauce in my mouth, gripping ice in my hands, and squeezing a stress ball until my wrist aches. Sometimes these things are enough, and sometimes they're not. I try not to get too angry at myself when I resort back to the lighter, thinking about what Lachlan said about self-compassion and what Erin said about treating myself how I would treat a child.

"Because that's who's hurting, you know," they said. "Little Alis is still in there, and he just wants to be loved by you."

It's fucking hard. I didn't think being nice to myself would be the hardest thing I'd ever try to do, but it feels like a miracle when I manage to do it over the other, much louder voice in my head that tries to tear me down in the most vicious ways it can. I'm starting to see what a bizarre thing that is to carry around in my head, and sometimes, just acknowledging that is enough to make it quiet down.

Erin is also trying to help me with the dissociation, teaching me how to ground myself in reality when I can feel myself detaching. She helped me muster up the courage to tell Noor about my episodes, and Noor encouraged me to tell Craig, and neither of them thought I was crazy. It's something I really need to start wrapping my head around, that people's reactions to things are almost never what I expect them to be.

So that's what I'm trying to remind myself of now as our bonfire starts to die and the sky fills with stars above us, because there's something I've got to tell Craig tonight, and none of the imagined outcomes swirling around in my head are bringing me any comfort.

I spend a lot of time at Craig's house—it's much more tolerable now that I'm not actually *living* there, mooching off their groceries—and we end up having "accidental" sleepovers more often than not. Once, I heard Miranda flush the toilet down the hall from Craig's bedroom, and I looked up at him from where my head was on his chest and asked, "Do you think she cares that we're doing this?"

"Nah," he said, flashing me a grin in the dark. "I think she'd rather become someone's Bubbe sooner rather than later."

I opened my mouth to say *I think you've forgotten how babies are made*, then thought better of it when I realized I would be shining a glaring beacon on the fact that we still haven't had sex. Like proper sex. Namely, because everything we do, we do with me fully clothed, and we both know why this is, and neither of us has mentioned it. Three months in and it's like a rubber band stretched taut between us, and I know it's about to break. I've seen Craig open his mouth to bring it up so many times that I'm surprised he hasn't exploded.

But I can't let that happen because if he brings it up, I know I'm going to freak out on him. I have to do it myself.

I have to do it tonight.

When Noor gets up from the bonfire, I know it's almost time, and my mouth goes dry.

She throws her stick into the fire and looks seriously at the both of us, flames dancing in her eyes. "Fifteen minutes."

"Fifteen minutes what?" Craig asks.

"It usually takes about fifteen minutes for me to fall asleep, so I ask that you wait fifteen minutes after I enter my tent before you start audibly fooling around."

"So only inaudible fooling around in the meantime, got it," Craig says with a nod.

Sometimes I wonder if Craig's told Noor about our weird one-sided sex life. Probably not, because then she wouldn't be making assumptions that we have raucous sex in tents.

I am fiercely avoiding Craig's eyes when Noor disappears into her tent, but because of his freakish inability to feel uncomfortable about anything, he just gets up from his chair and reaches his arms up to stretch his back, letting out an overtly sexual moan as he does it.

"I will kill both of you," Noor says loudly from her tent.

Craig grins at me, and I do my best to smile back. Then he tells me he's going to put out the fire and hide the food from the bears, so I head to the tent, feeling seconds away from throwing up. I turn on the lanterns, settling down cross-legged among the blankets and sleeping bags, then switch out my sweater for one of Craig's so I can stick my nose in it and remind myself how much I love him.

Too soon, he comes into the tent, smelling overwhelmingly of bonfire smoke.

"Oh my *God*," he says. He turns to aggressively zip up the tent flap before falling on his knees in front of me, taking my face in his hands. "You are *glowing*."

He's so fucking cheesy. The cheesiness is something I really had to get used to, and it only gets worse the more time we spend together. Though I do secretly love that it's always directed at me.

"You realize you only say that to me when I'm wearing your clothes," I say, holding my arms out to show him the sweater pooling over my hands.

"Do I? I don't think that's true." He gives me a peck on the lips before pulling back, his eyes darting across my face. I know it's coming before he even says it. "Why's your face like that?"

My heart is pounding in my ears, and it takes me three tries to get the words out. "I want to tell you I'm ready. To... you know, to do it properly."

He stares at me. His throat moves as he swallows. "So, this is kind of confusing for me because this is the greatest news of my life, but also, I cannot in good conscience have sex with you when you look that miserable about it."

I feel a prickle of irritation. "Can you just ignore my fucking face for once?"

"No, Alis." He shakes his head, sitting back on his

heels. "I don't want you to feel pressured into it, like, even a little bit."

"I know it has to happen and... I want it to happen." I realize I'm not sounding very convincing, even though it is true. I wish more than anything that I never ruined my skin and this wasn't so hard, because I really am horny. All the time.

"Okay, can I propose something?" Craig folds himself into a cross-legged position in front of me, his knees pressing into mine. "You show me now, while we're not... you know, in the middle of it. Then maybe you'll feel more comfortable when it happens and actually enjoy yourself."

The world tilts. "Now?"

"Yes." He strokes my face with his knuckle, and it never fails to make the back of my skull explode. "As much as you want, as quick as you want."

I'm trying really hard not to cry, because suddenly, I know I'm going to do it. I know because my heart is throwing itself against my ribcage, and I can see the flyaways on the sides of my vision start to tremble.

"I promise you're fine," he whispers, rubbing his hand over my leg. "Deep breath."

I do as he says, trying to ignore the voice in my head telling me this is the end, that he's going to leave me. He has shown me, time and time again, that I can trust him. Everything else is a story I'm making up in my head.

A tree shaped like a monster.

I pull up my sleeves and hold out my arms to him. I watch him look down at them. I look at the perfect slope of his nose, those beautiful copper eyelashes. I am at once eternally grateful and endlessly frustrated that his face isn't as obvious as mine.

Then he takes his own deep breath and brings his head up, and I see that he's crying.

My heart launches into my throat, and I snatch my arms back, shaking the sleeves back down.

"No, I'm not—" Craig starts, his eyes widening. He swipes at them. "I'm not crying because of—"

"Then why?" I demand. My arms are cradled against my chest, and my words are painful around the lump in my throat. "I know they're repulsive and ugly, and we don't have to—"

"*No*," he says firmly. "No. I'm sorry, but there's nothing ugly about you."

God, I want to run. I want to bolt from this fucking tent. I'm trying desperately to believe him, to not give in to that shrieking thing in my stomach. I've been doing so well, and I swear it's been shrinking, but this is my worst nightmare.

Craig sniffs, swiping his palms over his cheeks again. "Alis, like, all those are to me... I can just see that you've been trying really hard to be okay even when you had every right not to be. And I just hope you know you can let yourself be not okay sometimes? But mostly, I'm just so proud of you right now. I'm seriously so proud of you, for everything. For standing up to your parents, for the counselling, for *this*. And you know I'm an easy crier; we've discussed this, I get it from my dad—"

The relief and the gratitude I feel is so violent, it knocks down everything inside me until I'm collapsing forward into his chest, wrapping my arms around his stomach. He holds me while I cry like he's done so many times before because my heart feels close to bursting at his words—

I'm seriously so proud of you, for everything

—and for once, I just let it be. I let it burst.

It's still a wonder to me that he stays and that his staying doesn't feel like something I have to hold on to with all my strength. He's someone I can fall on when I'm too heavy to stand up on my own, and he's okay with it, and somehow, I've really come to believe that.

That night, we don't do anything except hold each other. Judging by the state of me after showing him just my forearms, I think we'll probably do it in complete darkness when it happens. I think we'll be in the dark for a long time. But the thing is, the prospect of a *long time* doesn't fill me with dread like it used to. Now, when I close my eyes and try to imagine my future, that blank space in the centre of my brain takes on shapes and faces—still nebulous, still uncertain, but *there,* against an impossibly pink sky. So even if it takes a long time, if it takes a billion baby steps and a lot of fucking waves, I have that nebulous future, and I have *them,* and all together, it feels a lot like hope.

ACKNOWLEDGMENTS

So this is an Acknowledgments section, which means the book is in your hands, and this actually happened, and I can't take it back. That's a little terrifying, but also *dang*!!! Who did that? *I* did that. Taking a moment to acknowledge me for doing that thing I hate: being *vulnerable* (barf).

Baby Lex would be very surprised by this book. She'd say, "I thought you were going to write dark academia books about magic and werewolves! Something with a John Williams soundtrack!" And to that I say: never say never. But this was the first story I ever wrote that came, truly, from my soul. I began writing this for me, and then somewhere down the line it became something for everyone who has ever resonated with Alis' struggles and felt alien, ashamed, or alone in those struggles. If that's you, then know that I see you, and I hope you will always be able to come back to this story when you need to feel understood, and when you need a reminder that it won't always be so hard.

Now on to the list of people I need to thank, starting with my very first editor, Chris Barcellona, who parted the clouds so the sun could shine through. Not only did you help me trim down a beast of a first draft, but you built me up when I thought for sure I was going to get torn down, and that was invaluable in getting me here. I so appreciate your vision and kindness.

To my copy editor, Nevvie Gane: thank you for your eagle eyes and for appreciating Alis' love of tattoos. I know nothing of tattoos, so that was validating.

To my beta and sensitivity readers: Jamie, Oskar, Margo, Lewis, Quinn, and Bim. You all gave me a piece of advice that made this book better. Thanks for your keen reader's intuition and your encouraging words. And a special thanks to Katie Griffin, who took a chance on a stranger and sensitivity read this for mental health stuff. You are a very generous soul.

This messy book is smashed between the most beautiful covers I could have ever imagined, courtesy of Nicolae Negură, who is a wizard with an ink pot. Thank you, Nicolae, for making these characters come to life in such vivid colour.

Emily, my flatmate-turned-best-friend: I may not have survived writing this without you. Literally, I would've forgotten to eat and drink and my eyeballs would've fallen out of my skull, still sizzling from the blue light of my computer screen. Thank you for getting me to look up once in a while, and for bringing me the world's best hot chocolates. Your warmth and thoughtfulness astound me every day.

Brenda, your infectious energy is one-of-a-kind; thank you for your enthusiasm and belief in me, and for adding some Jewish light to my life.

Darlene, I am forever grateful for your support and I

am so lucky to have you in my life. Thank you for cheering me on even from all the way across the ocean.

To my siblings (lol imagine I didn't include them here, they'd be so mad):

Linds, the fact that you read this, and did it so fast, and told me it was making your hellish ride to Montreal go a little bit quicker—all of that meant the world to me, not just because I love you, but because you've got great taste. Thanks for being so supportive and for always indulging my "I need your opinion" texts.

Jaclyn, you are my biggest cheerleader. You've never wavered in your faith in me, even at my most stubborn, and I appreciate your wisdom more than you know. Thank you for pulling my head out of my ass time and time again and for always helping to put things into perspective.

Dad! I told you I'd get here. I may not be raking in millions, but I'm here, and you never doubted I would be. I hope this makes you cry like my second-place prize for fattest fish did. Thank you for passing on your creative genes to me, and for pushing me toward my dreams.

This may be hard to believe, but I actually love my mom even more than Craig loves his mom. Mom, I'm sorry I gave Alis such a hard time, but the fact that you cared so deeply for him is a good indication of what kind of parent and what kind of person you are. Thank you for always being there, even if that means listening to me lament about the same thing over and over again. You never fail to make me feel better, and I treasure every millisecond I spend with you.

He will never read this, but for posterity: thank you to

my dog, my baby boy, Norman, for making me get outside and touch some grass, and for always bringing me a little bit of joy even on the bad days.

Finally, the chalet with the bunker club in Switzerland was inspired by Balmers Hostel in Interlaken. That place was sick. I would also be remiss not to thank that one guy on my group tour of Europe in 2018 who asked, completely seriously, "Wait, can I do Easier Kulm?" before reluctantly climbing up Harder Kulm. That will now live in this book rent-free forever.

I hope I didn't forget anyone, but if I did, here's my promise that I'll write another book, and I'll get you next time.

Until then,

Lex

RESOURCES

If you or someone you know struggles with self-harm, here are some resources that can help:

- Crisis Text Line: crisistextline.org
——United States: Text HOME to 741741
—— Canada: Text CONNECT to 686868
—— United Kingdom: Text SHOUT to 85258
——Ireland: Text HOME to 50808
- To find a helpline in your country, visit findahelpline.com/
- To Write Love On Her Arms: twloha.com/find-help/
- Self-injury & Recovery Resources (SIRR): selfinjury.bctr.cornell.edu/resources.html
- The Mighty's Guide to Understanding Self-Harm: themighty.com/topic/self-harm/what-is-self-harm
- Kids Help Phone (Canada): kidshelpphone.ca
- Self-Injury Outreach and Support: sioutreach.org
- Calm Harm is an app to help manage the urge to self-harm: calmharm.co.uk
- This list is continually updated at www.lexcarlow.com

ABOUT THE AUTHOR

Lex Carlow is a Canadian-born, Scotland-based author of young adult fiction. She holds a degree in psychology from Toronto Metropolitan University and has a passion for mental health and the messiness of the human experience. When she's not trying to write a book, you'll find her at a concert, exploring beaches with her dog, or buying copious amounts of tea. You can visit Lex on her website at www.lexcarlow.com or on the socials under @carlow.lex.

If you liked this book, please consider leaving a review. Reviews are the lifeblood of indie publishing and really help get indie books into the hands of readers. You can scan the QR code below to visit *Earth to Alis* on your retailer or book review site(s) of choice. Thank you so much for your support!